Love and Terror

DOROTHY WEIL

authorHOUSE®

AuthorHouse™ LLC
1663 Liberty Drive
Bloomington, IN 47403
www.authorhouse.com
Phone: 1-800-839-8640

Published by AuthorHouse 12/20/2013

ISBN: 978-1-4918-2696-6 (sc)
ISBN: 978-1-4918-2695-9 (hc)
ISBN: 978-1-4918-2694-2 (e)

Library of Congress Control Number: 2013918470

To my wonderful family and friends

And in memory of Janice Forberg whose
art graces the cover of this book

The person, gentleman or lady, who has not pleasure in a good novel, must be intolerably stupid
—Jane Austen

American history is longer, larger, more various, more beautiful, and more terrible than anything anyone has ever said about it
—James Baldwin

Part 1

SUDDEN DEATH

1

Judith

At the Romanos' swimming party for the history faculty, after too many margaritas, she jumped into the pool topless. Down under the surface, she cooled off, refreshed by the water beneath her breasts. She sobered up enough to hear laughter coming from the poolside. Oh God! This was Cincinnati! Her husband was head of the department! She wondered how to get out of the water without further exposure. She swam a few lengths as several of the men cheered; finally she was saved by her hostess who placed a large towel by the edge of the pool.

She was one of the first generation of women to have the pill and women's lib. They were supposed to change the world. But here she was, brilliant, successful Dr. Judith Howard, at loose ends and having an old-fashioned identity crisis, while her sister Moira, who had gotten into drugs, drink, and sleazy men, had a good job and a nice condo in DC. Cliffside College where Judith had taught English for a decade had closed; couldn't compete with the expanding grasp of the universities with their big name architects, their "attractive" grounds and luxurious student suites. Her body had turned on her. Sudden clammy sweats kept her awake at night, and drenched her clothes. She had wedged an ice bag into her evening purse at one of the university's grand balls.

If Eric went ahead with his aim to head the university and God forbid succeeded, her life would be an endless round of cocktail parties, teas, dinners, football, sucking up to donors—all the things she hated. Why was he interested in the job? That didn't sound like her old Eric.

Anger had taken over their home like an uninvited relative, an invalid aunt demanding attention and service. Where had she come from? Whose family was she?

Their sex life veered from a wild lovemaking to lying as far apart on the bed as possible, like figures on a sarcophagus.

At Christmas Judith received a letter from her eleven year old niece, Moira's daughter:

> "Dear Aunt Judy, thanks for the cool sweater. I hope you're having a wonderful Christmas like when I visited you. Your home was so beautiful and you were like a beautiful princess. I wished I could live with you. Love, Zelda."

Judith was trying to convince Eric to go with her to a marriage counselor at the time. His typical expression of emotion was cool irony, and she needed something he couldn't or wouldn't give: the part withheld that flew the skies in his small plane. He said "People don't change." He was so willing to let things slide, to accept things as they were.

"Then why did we march against the Viet Nam war, and get tear-gassed for it, and protest against going into Iraq?" she said. "Why are we working so hard to defeat Bush? You think you can change the whole world, but not one individual." While he studied the history of the world, he had little interest in hers, or his own.

Nothing changed, and Judith could not go on pulling rebellious stunts. She decided to take a job in DC at one of the universities she'd applied to; it was only a a one-semester "lectureship" teaching Jane Austen's novels, but it was a prestigious offer.

"You can get a new job here," Eric argued.

Like she hadn't looked.

Maybe he didn't know how rare positions in English studies were; maybe he hadn't noticed women in their fifties were being cut from jobs, not being hired for them. Judith's colleague, a fellow Ph.D, was answering the phone at a local community center.

Judith was lost in her old Tudor house, the rooms echoing with dreams and memories. She had worked hard for her degree—(she remembered once writing a paper with a bottle of wine in one hand and a pen in the other). She didn't want to think about William . . . Or her mother.

Maybe some time apart would be good for her and Eric.

What would she have done if he had said, "Please don't go. I need you"?

He said, "You have to do what you have to do."

When they quarreled, he held out his hands—not to embrace her, but as though to tamp down a fire.

When she came to DC for her job, Moira asked her how she could be sure Eric wouldn't get involved with another woman.

"How can he be sure I won't find another man?" she quipped.

Eric once admitted that the women in his classes, young and leggy and adoring, were tempting, and one tucked her panties into his jacket hanging on his office coat tree. But he wasn't stupid enough to mess around with students. A member of City Council arrived at Judith's door one afternoon: would she help him with a paper he was trying to write? A neighbor tried to talk her into bed. There were others, but they were too dumb.

Judith looked in Moira's cheval mirror. Her eyes, which she considered her best feature, were large, with thick brows. People said they looked as though they were painted on. Eric had always liked her eyes. Her body was firm, courtesy of yoga, which Eric made fun of, and bicycling which he shared. It was hour-glassy, not the popular pipe-stem thin.

Moira assessed Judith's reflection, and said, "You're pretty cocky. But hey, if tits and ass are really what it's all about, you should be the most popular girl in town. Your hair, though: a stork could nest in it."

Settled in now, Judith looks out the window of her office at the university in DC. It's a beautiful September day. The students are playing Frisbee on the well-manicured green. She glances at a poster on her wall: "Art is the education of the feelings." Her mantra.

In her own life, the only place she ever heard the truth was in fiction. She thought the sexiest line in literature was Mr. Darcy's "What think you of books?"

She wants her students to read, read, read—great works of imagination.

Her students have changed over the years, become celebrity worshipers, shoppers, and lovers of violence. Narcissists glued to their Ipods and BlackBerrys, and God knows what future gadgets, shrinking the human heart into something small and dried up.

It can be repaired, she thinks. It can.

That is why, even at the somewhat late age she completed her Ph.D, she chose the craziest and least marketable degree.

And has taken a temporary post.

Where she and Eric are going, she has no idea. They've gotten together several times over the months she has been gone from home. They talked, but just carried on with the status quo. Sparred a round, then gone back to their corners.

Maybe it would all work out.

It had been an instantaneous, complete, falling in love: two Chicago *wunderkind.*

She just needed to get back up on her feet—get her pride back.

Judith's cell rings. Eric. She is so surprised.

"I was just thinking of you," she says.

He tells her he is going to the hospital to get a long-postponed knee replacement.

"Why didn't you call me before? Do you need me to come out?"

They were polite, did the decent thing. Most of the time.

"No need," he says. "It's routine. David is picking me up in a bit. It's no big deal."

"Well, it is," she says. "I feel terrible."

She wonders if that could be the point of his not telling her—make her feel guilty? Eric had never been a dirty fighter. But of course, she thinks, our motives are often hidden from our more acceptable selves, out of sight like paintings turned to the wall.

She wishes him well. Should she go home even though he said not to? His surgery *is* routine. Everybody she knows has had a hip or a knee replaced. Still . . . .

"Don't worry," Eric says. "David will call later."

Judith has difficulty settling down. If Eric did not want her to come out, why didn't he wait until after the surgery to call her? It would be good to see him no matter what. When not with him, she always cools off.

She loves the guy!

She misses his body, his sense of humor, his confidence, his independence.

Last year, driving home from the Romanos' swimming party, she thought he would be furious.

"I'm sorry for making a fool of myself, and embarrassing you," she said. "I'm sure I shocked everybody."

"Oh fuck 'em," Eric said. "They got a free show."

His shortcomings were never about freedom of expression.

2

David

Why did his father say not to call his mother? Was it Natalie? What's going on?

First his mother goes off to DC to teach, then his father starts with this girl. David thinks this kind of stuff is more for people his and Lydia's age, who God knows are having their problems . . . .

He steers his BMW past the great bronze "Genius of Water" monument on Fountain Square. It is still in place in spite of many changes to the downtown; "the Lady" at the top still holds out her arms flowing with water, as she always has since he was a kid, since before his grandparents were born. It's vaguely reassuring. He passes Music Hall, a great monster of a place where his grandfather is on the symphony board.

David thinks about the case he is in the middle of. He has subpoenaed the other side's emails, but they demanded a few days to produce them. He knows what the delay is all about: associates scrambling to erase their porn.

David needs like hell to win this case. He isn't a big money magnet for his law firm. He hates searching out and buttering up potential clients, and he detests golf. So he hopes becoming a top litigator will pave his way to making partner.

7

His ultimate ambition is to be a lawyer like Joseph Welch or Clarence Darrow, fighting political bullies and ignorance. If his father were a lawyer instead of a history professor, he would be going after giant corporations and defending civil rights cases. David will be like his heroes. Eventually. For now he must concentrate on money and paying off his and Lydia's debts. Though together they pull down over two hundred grand a year at their firms, they are up to their necks in debt.

He soon reaches the university area where he grew up. A friend called the neighborhood "Brigadoon" because he thought it looked as though time had passed it by while it slept.

"What era did it fall asleep in?" David asked.

"The fifties."

David's father was born here, and David had lived here most of his life. Their old Tudor house is within walking distance of the strip of stores, the too-tiny public library, the movie theater (being revived as an art theater after a period of smelling like pee and endless showings of *The Texas Chainsaw Massacre*), the apartment building with sagging wooden porches, the ethnic clothing shops, the Cincinnati Chili parlor.

The only big changes since David was a kid are the closing of the hardware store and the appearance of four Indian restaurants.

Except for the lights of the movie theater, the area is grayish, a little dowdy, very different from the mall where he and Lydia drive for shopping—which has everything from two humongous supermarkets to the Gap, Old Navy, several pricey restaurants, Whole Foods—Whole Paycheck David calls it.

As he nears his old home he happily breathes in the smell of Indian spices and chili. Huge old trees line the thoroughfare to the residential area, streets where ordinary places like his parents' sit side by side with twenty-room houses and even a few actual castles built by the old-time beer barons, his grandparents' former home among them. He and William had a blast there as kids, running around the bell tower playing medieval knights.

As David pulls into the driveway of the Tudor, a shower of walnuts rain down on his car from the monstrous volunteer tree his father has vowed to cut down since David was in high school. The dark brown front door is open and his father steps into the outer hall. He looks at his watch, then turns and picks up a fuzzy black and white suitcase David remembers from his childhood. The Howards don't embrace change easily.

Nevertheless, David notices his father is dressed in a pricey-looking leather jacket, flannel trousers and an open collar shirt. A contrast to his casual outfits of T-shirts and white socks with black shoes. Maybe the new look is courtesy of Natalie—who's close to William's age for God's sake.

His father is looking at his watch.

David says, "We've got plenty of time."

"No problem."

David looks at the house while his father gets into the car. He and William had enjoyed a happy childhood in this old Tudor mess. He prefers it to his "McMansion," which William calls the place that he and Lydia live in—to Lydia's annoyance. It is in a subdivision where all the neighbors are young and white, have wine cellars, and get married in St. Tropez.

In the car, David slips *Hard Rain* into the deck, something both and he and his father can enjoy.

The drive to the hospital is not far, but near the university the traffic thickens, and David pulls into a lane with a car on his right that he didn't see. He jerks the car back into his own lane.

"Jesus Christ," his father says.

"We're OK."

David thinks, maybe he's taking this operation harder than he's let on. It is David's mother who habitually gasps and presses an

9

imaginary brake in traffic. His Dad would be silent. When David and William were kids, any complaint their father had about them would wait until they were at home and then the misdemeanor would be organized and delivered in the clear reasonable tone of one of his history lectures.

William once said, "Would you just hit me?"

Is his father doing this operation for Natalie? He had been limping for quite awhile in pain and David's mother had suggested replacement many times, but he'd resisted, tried shots and practiced denial.

The hospital takes up six or eight blocks on one of the city's seven hills, in a neighborhood of once elegant homes, now offices or apartments with fire escapes. The entrance door opens automatically and an eerie voice says, "Welcome to Good Shepard Hospital. This is a non-smoking facility. Please observe the no-smoking rule."

After the usual form-signing and card-displaying, proofs of insurance and identity, David and his father are taken to a small room where a nurse weighs the patient and takes his medical history. He sheepishly admits to having smoked for some thirty years.

Then a tall, rather too jovial doctor comes in and talks about anesthesia.

David's father signs the necessary papers and the nurse pitches a backless blue gown on the table and leaves the room. David looks over the McCullough book he has brought, while his father undresses and puts on the gown. They wait.

"What's that you're reading?"

David hands his father the book.

"I'd like to look it over. Soon as I can read."

"I'll leave it in the room. I think you'll be groggy the rest of today. I was from my colonoscopy."

"Aren't you young for one of those?"

"They have to pay off the machines."

David's father chuckles. "Right you are."

The nurse comes in and gives him a shot.

They sit. David looks at his father, perched on the examining table. He is well-built and strong, full of energy. He has always looked good. With his slim build, thick brown hair, noble nose, large blue eyes, he could easily pass for less than his fifty-some years. One of David's young women colleagues who had studied American History with his father said he was really hot.

David is not unhappy that people think he resembles his father.

He wonders again about the rift or whatever between him and his mother. No one had predicted it and the Howards do not mind one another's business. Is it mid-life crisis? It is appearing in his parents' generation in one form or another it seems. Lots of divorces. Affairs. Sudden purchases of sports cars.

David's father drums his fingers on his thighs.

"What in the hell are we waiting for?" he says.

"You know hospitals."

He pulls his gown around him.

"This plastic seat is damned cold."

In the backless blue gown, David's father looks for the first time ever, a little vulnerable, and a feeing of tenderness comes over David—for this paragon, this giant figure in his and William's life: the professor with a wall full of awards, a shelf of books with his name on them, head of his department with a shot at being the next president of the university.

His voice is growing slurred.

David gets up and looks into the hall.

"You don't have to stay," his father says.

"I'm fine." David had hoped his impatience to get back to work hadn't shown.

They wait some more. His father's eyes are closing.

Pretty soon an orderly comes in, a man in blue scrubs. David's father is very groggy now and David kisses him on the cheek.

"Break a leg, Pop," he says, "or rather—I guess you kind of did that already."

David's father waves weakly and the orderly rolls him onto a gurney. David walks alongside it as they guide it down what seems like endless hallways and into and out of elevators. At the door to the operating area, the orderly indicates that David has gone as far as he may and directs him to a waiting room.

David tries to get comfortable in an arm chair. He looks at his watch. They are about on schedule. He reads the lead stories in *Time.* More American troops killed, more Iraqis dead. The world is a god damned mess: a stupid unprovoked war going on, horrible torture at the Abu Ghraib prison camp. He can barely look at the photos of the naked men abused and humiliated. By Americans.

The whole Howard clan had protested when Bush announced the war downtown at Union Terminal. Why had they, ordinary citizens, known the whole thing was phony when the *Times* and the rest of the media fell for it? Gone to sleep, gone along.

David's father had helped plan the march.

David thumbs through the magazine to the features, and skims an article on "tweens." Apparently this is a hot market, hyping the right labels and diets for girls not yet teenagers. Well, who is he to talk? He and Lydia had made sure Phoebe had the right stroller, the right crib, etc. Still, he doesn't want Phoebe, at seven, to become a "tween." He had named her after Holden Caulfield's bright little sister in *The Catcher in the Rye.*

David thinks about going to the lobby for something to eat, but the only food place there is Wendy's. He and Lydia avoid junk food, especially for Phoebe, but for themselves as well: *e coli, avian flu, carcinogens.*

David wonders how his father's surgery is going.

Where is William? He said he would be over to wish his father well and stay with him after the operation. William, his baby brother, the talented one, the prodigal. Everybody's darling.

Interrupting David's thoughts, a nurse comes into the room, looks around and comes over to him. His father's surgery was successful, she says, and he is being moved to a private room.

Relieved—the Howard luck is holding up—David follows the nurse down several long corridors.

He finds his father in a small room with sunlight shining at the window. He sits in a chair with a blanket over his knees.

David sits in a chair opposite him, with a nurse standing by.

"How's it goin'?" he says.

His father smiles weakly.

"Legs feel a little numb."

"Want some water, Mr. Howard?" the nurse says.

"I—"

David notices him begin to shake. The nurse slams the water pitcher on its tray and races to David's father. She takes his wrist, rushes to the wall and presses a button.

David sits frozen, staring into his father's eyes. There is no life in them.

"What's happening?" David says.

The nurse is shouting, "Mr. Howard! Mr. Howard!"

3

Judith

She goes to the lunch room and drinks a cup of coffee and reads the *Post*. She looks through the ads for a longer-term rental. She must get out of the expensive monthly place she is in.

A student, a boy she has spent hours coaching in the importance of clear, accurate language, plops down opposite her and asks for ideas for his Rhetoric paper. She suggests George Orwell. "Think about the weaselly words our government is using to divert us from what is going on in Iraq—like 'collateral damage' to mean civilian deaths."

"George Orwell?" he says.

When Judith returns to her office, she checks her voice mail. David. He says Eric has gotten his surgery. Please call. He sounds upset. Oh my God, she thinks. She tries to call David, but gets no answer.

Judith takes a stack of student essays from her briefcase. She rifles through them. It is hard to think of anything else with David's words reverberating in her mind. Could something be wrong?

Judith looks out the window. The sun is still shining on the perfect grass. The students are gone, back in class. Eric has always been so healthy, she thinks. In January he went hiking in the Rockies with colleagues. Besides flying his own plane; he plays tennis every week indoors or out. He is the strongest person she knows.

Judith calls her home number in Cincinnati and gets the recorded message. Eric hasn't changed the wording. It is still "Eric and Judith here. We will call you right back."

She tries William's cell, but of course he never remembers to turn it on.

4

William

He started his day at the scuffed wooden bar of the Bookshelf Coffee Shop and Bar, having his regular cup of coffee and raisin bagel. He enjoyed the cozy atmosphere created by the shelves of old paperbacks and art books, the smell of hazelnut and the hiss of the cappuccino machine. He felt pretty satisfied from last night's romp with Angie (he liked the way her hair kinked when she undid her long braid and it spread on the pillow like light brown waves).

He studied the art on the walls: charcoals of a small child on crutches in front of a bombed out building, an Iraqi man carrying a wounded girl. The work of yet another earnest artist preaching to the choir.

William knew all the regulars getting their morning caffeine fix.

"How'd it go last night?" he asked Hattie.

"Not bad." Hattie glanced over at the darkened nook where she performed with a Blue Grass foursome several nights a week, singing and playing the guitar. She dunked her scone into her café au lait.

"Anymore, kids want hip-hop," she said. Her Tennessee accent was twangy as her guitar. "Or New Grass."

16

Jimmy, the barista, noticed William's cup was low. He put aside his *Vampirella* comic and poised the coffee pot over the cup. He was jumpy as a Chihuahua. His hair was the color of white gold.

William checked his watch: he was supposed to meet David at the hospital, but the group of kids he read to at the Lookout Literacy Center was meeting unexpectedly due to a teacher in-service day. He would have to be late. William gulped down his coffee, refused the offer of more.

"See you all later."

The others at the bar waved: Hattie, Mel, whose bakery was the best in town, Velma and her partner Ariel, filmmakers working on a documentary about the neighborhood riots.

Walking to The Lookout, William chose his route carefully; the secret of living in Cincinnati's "Over the Rhine," so-named for its German background, was knowing which corners and streets to avoid. Like Constitution where the gangs were in charge. He passed St. Mary's church, one of the oldest in the city. The stained-glass windows were covered by plywood boards.

Other places were still boarded up from the riots, mixed in with open businesses. The people, furious at the police for shooting a young black man, had not touched the art store that had been in its location forever, or Smitty's Men and Boys Shop, displaying red slacks, silky shirts and wide-brimmed hats in windows glittering with blinking lights. William never saw Smitty's clothes actually worn; the street people wore black hoodies and baggy slacks. He figured Smitty's outfits must be reserved for dances or funerals, or the club the police were always threatening to close down.

At Washington Park William saw his friend Reverend Allen, who must be in his eighties by now, leading a small group of sign-carriers demanding "U.S. Out of Iraq." William waved, gave the thumbs up sign. Reverend Al was back on the streets having just gotten out of jail for climbing a fence at the White House to protest the Iraq war and the imminent re-election of Bush (if you considered his first term election). Over the years he had been arrested some twenty times for trespassing and not paying his taxes because they financed war. He'd lived through at least three, and had usually gotten out of jail by going on hunger strikes like Gandhi.

For his pains he was poor and had been kicked out of his Presbyterian church. To William he was a hero, someone who lived his beliefs. William tried to learn from him, even considered joining his small group of religionists, but he could not swallow the whale.

William grew up a Unitarian and was reading now about Buddhism—

Shit, he didn't know what he believed now.

William walked through the park: two blocks of trees and grass, stone picnic tables and a bandstand. Men were setting up their chess boards under the trees. White teenagers with Mohawks, and black kids with their pants so low slung they could hardly walk, hung around in separate groups. There was litter all over, in the bushes, on the lawn, on the fence by the school.

A young guy in ragged jeans and a grimy T-shirt was sitting cross-legged on the grass, holding up a cardboard sign: "Out of work porn star."

William flipped him a dollar.

He said hi to Denny, a wacko street person who made his own fur scarves, inevitably after a spate of neighborhood cats went missing.

Looming over the park and all this was Music Hall, a four-block red brick monster where the symphony played. William's grandfather, John Howard, was on the board, and he and William's grandmother went every Saturday night (probably not missing a concert in the almost sixty years they had been married).

Opposite the great doors and huge stained glass windows, Gloria, a plump, sixtyish woman, sat on a park bench beneath her blankets and mounds of plastic bags. She refused to live in the shelter—"they steal your stuff"—and when annoyed with Cincinnati's rules on panhandling, used the City Hall steps for her private bathroom. William exchanged good mornings with her, then walked down a block to the storefront that housed The Lookout.

Volunteering here was supposed to help keep him off coke. William's grandfather, who gave money to run it, had set William up with the group when the family decided he was in need of something constructive to do. Rather than being yanked out of Over the Rhine where he had made his connections, he was forced to become part of it and see up close the results of the drug trade.

William had to admit he was lucky to get busted so early in the game, and to have a good sponsor—Tim, a middle-aged white guy with dreads, a one-time hard-core addict with whom William went around preaching the clean and sober gospel. He could make coke vivid as Satan, addiction terrifying as *Revelations*. Although William did not yearn much for his old habit, Tim never let him get overly confident.

"You've tasted the forbidden fruit, my friend. You're OK now, but one setback, and you're begging for a smoke, selling your soul for a line. You'd sell Angie. You're still on the edge of the pit where the whores of Babylon are takin' numbers for your ass. You've got a future. Lots going for you. Don't squander it. Think Gloria, once a beautiful intelligent woman, over there peeing on the steps of the very venue of law and order."

William listened, but he felt strong. Things were going pretty well for him. Angie made a difference; they ran into each other

19

in a mosh pit (literally). He couldn't believe now they'd gone in for that stuff. He was writing again. He felt useful reading to and providing a safe place for kids with no one at home and no place to go when school was out.

William could hear them, children from six to twelve, all the way from the street, arguing and fighting in the Lookout store front.

He went inside to a chorus of "Here comes Captain Corduroy!"

"Knock it off. Everybody sit down. I gotta be someplace," William said.

"Blow me!" somebody yelled.

There were ten kids in the group, most of them pugnacious; several, William thought, probably with ADHD. They couldn't read, write, or sit still for long. They were not the cleanest kids in the world either. As a volunteer visiting nurse, Angie came once a week to check them over: tongue depressor in the mouths, a look at scalps for head lice. She gave them tooth brushes and toothpaste, and papered the walls with posters reminding them to wash their hands before eating and to change their underwear daily. Apparently they paid no attention. Angie had bought them all T-shirts and underpants with her own money, but the stuff just disappeared.

Half his kids had parents on meth or the local novelty OxCon.

Much scraping of chairs and exchanged punches, and the kids were more or less in order. William opened his book, and began reading *Charlotte's Web*. He had decided that if the kids were ever to be literate, simply learning to love stories might help. They quieted down somewhat as he read.

When the session ended, he noticed that one of the boys, Casey, looked sick. He would have to take him to the clinic, an old school building on Elm, where Angie worked at her paying job.

20

In the waiting room William and Casey had to sit a long time. At last, Angie appeared dressed in her professional white smock, her long hair neatly pulled back in a braid. She looked the boy over, said he was running a fever and his ears were inflamed inside. William gave Angie the mother's cell phone and home numbers.

"I need to get to the hospital," he said. "You know my father's being operated on and I wanted to be there—well, I'm late—but I'll be there when he comes out of surgery."

Angie put Casey on one of several cots they had, and William told her he'd look in on him later.

"You OK?" William said.

"I'm OK, William."

The boy seemed happy to be lying down on a clean bed.

On the bus to the hospital, William read the reports from Iraq, then turned to the movie section of the *Times* he had bought for his father. He read the review of the movie starring that luscious actress. He'd be reviewing it for *Street Voices*, the give away paper sold by the Drop-In Center for alcoholics—which he considered the city's best. His father would be back in his room by now and want to read the latest news and do the crossword puzzle.

5

David

He is pushed into the hallway by a team of technicians and doctors rushing into his father's room, crowding around his father with some sort of emergency equipment.

"What's happened, what's going on?" David yells at the nurse.

"We'll see."

Is his father dead? What should he do?

The nurse comes out of his father's room, running along with the medical team toward the elevator, his father on a gurney. David tries to go to him, but a woman in a suit approaches him, takes him by the arm and yanks him away.

"Is he dead?" David says.

The woman steers him to a waiting room.

"Try to calm down," she says. "We're doing everything we can." She disappears.

David paces the room, his legs like broken stilts.

He calls his mother. Voice mail.

As he waits for news, he thinks there must be something he can do. Should do.

Death? It has no meaning for him. His great-grandparents died, but they were supposed to. They were old.

People are coming and going. David jumps every time someone enters the room. An official-looking woman comes to him and says his father is in Intensive Care. He experienced "fatal arrhythmia." What does that mean? Fatal? Time just stops.

His phone vibrates against his chest. His mother.

6

Judith

She goes into the women's rest room and sits on a toilet, stunned like a bird flying into a window. She stares at the hook hanging on the door. He must not die. He *must not.* She must get home as fast as she can. What to do first? She has to get a plane ticket. But can't just leave. She must explain to the head of her department what has happened. Let her office mate know. She can't just disappear. Check her classroom. Pack. No not pack. Talk to the super at her building. How long would she be gone? She has to think.

She tries to cry, but just stares at the toilet stall door.

Finally she stands, unsteadily, and goes to the sink, pats her face with a wet paper towel. It has that smell of wet brown paper, nasty, gluey.

Judith goes back to her office, picks up her purse and walks quickly to the nearby street where she can get a cab.

"Where you want to go?" the driver asks.

A child's rhyme runs through her head.

Lady Bug, Lady Bug. Fly away home. Your house is on fire. Your children are gone.

7

$\mathcal{D}$avid

$\mathcal{D}$avid never cries. But he feels like crying now. He calls Lydia and leaves a message. He tries William; his phone is not turned on. Anyway, what would he tell them?

What else can he do? He tries his grandparents' number. No answer.

He calls Lydia. Voice mail again.

He calls his firm, tells the receptionist he will not be back that afternoon.

He calls the dog-walker and tells her to be sure and take Lenny out.

Eventually, a nurse comes and tells David to follow her.

"He's alive?" he says.

"He's very ill."

They go into a dim chamber through an automatic door marked ICU, and toward a small alcove.

To get to his father's bed, David has to push through six or eight anxious people blocking the entrance. A solemn-looking man steps forward and holds out his hand. David thinks he is a doctor.

"I'm the hospital chaplain," he says.

David almost pushes him out of the way. His father is not fond of clergymen. Even his own Unitarian minister gets on his nerves.

David reaches his father's bedside. He is like a mummy swathed in white sheets, his arms tied to the bed with gauze. His eyes are closed. His face is white. He looks dead. There is a tube in his father's throat and wires all over his arms and neck. Jagged lines on several monitors go up and down.

"Dad?" David says.

No answer.

David has never seen anyone so still. Eyes closed tightly as though in death, lips stretched by the throat tube, hands and legs stiff.

David grabs for the next person in a doctor's coat.

The man turns and takes David's hand. He introduces himself as Mr. Howard's cardiologist, Doctor Sanders. Mid-forties, an open, pleasant face.

"Is he in a coma?" David asks. All the observers but Dr. Sanders have left now, and he stands behind David like a ghostly presence in the darkened room, still but for the burbling machines.

"No, he's not in a coma. He's in there," Dr. Sanders says.

"Will he be all right?"

"We don't know the extent of the damage."

"Dad," David says again. He takes his father's hand. The back has a needle in it attached to an IV machine.

Dr. Sanders explains the meaning of the constantly shifting numbers on the several monitors: one is the heart beat, another the blood pressure.

He is so *still*. So far away, lost in some dark place.

"Pop," David whispers. "I'm here. Can you hear me?"

No response. Of course his father can't talk with the tube in his throat. His eyes remain closed.

"His body has had a terrible shock," Dr. Sanders says.

"There was nothing wrong with his heart, was there?"

"He had some blockage, but his heart was compensating."

The doctor disappears from the small room.

David looks out the window just beyond the bed. He can see the spires of St. George's church near the university. Should this guy have let his father go ahead with the knee operation?

Fear covers David's body like rime. He has never seen his father sick. Never more than a cold. If he died . . . . nothing . . . . where his father had been . . . .

He holds his father's hand and whispers his love.

Soon William comes into the room.

David puts his arms around his brother and the two cling together for a moment, staring at their father, swaddled, white, unmoving.

"I can't believe this," William says. "He wasn't where he was supposed to be and they said he was up here and was very sick." He whispers to David, "He looks so awful."

"Yes."

William bends over the bed and says, "Dad, can you hear me?"

No response. Only the swishing of liquids in the tubes and the whirring machines. Outside the space, the bustle of the nurses and aides scuttling from one cubicle to the next, an occasional doctor swooping by to check a patient.

David looks at his brother: his own features are mirrored, but younger, darker in complexion, chin stubble, out of fashion plastic glasses, pony tail.

"Are you OK?" he asks.

"Yeah. I guess. Oh, Christ." William puts his head in his hands.

A nurse comes in and checks the monitors.

"We can't do the angiogram today; that would tell us more about the heart," she says.

"Didn't he have one before the surgery?" David says. As far as he knew it had been all right.

"That was before the event."

"Jesus," William says. "A heart attack?"

"It was more an electrical thing." The nurse tries to explain, but her words seem to come from far away and the brothers' eyes are on the monitors.

"There's no clot on the lung," she says. "I don't know exactly how long he was without oxygen."

"So he might be brain damaged," William says.

"We hope not. With sudden death—we don't know."

David opens his cell phone to try Lydia again.

"You can't use cell phones in here," the nurse says.

"Oh right."

David snaps his phone shut.

She leaves the cubicle. He and William stare at each other.

"Sudden death?" William says.

"I was sitting just a few feet from him. He was . . . . gone."

"We better call Mom."

"She's on her way."

8

Judith

Judith picks up the wine glass Moira has just refilled. Looks around her sister's living room. The ceilings in the historic building are high, with crown molding. Her sister is older, worn-looking, but with the same painted-on eyes as Judith's.

"How high are your ceilings?" Judith says.

"'Bout twelve feet."

"I like 'em. This is a great building."

"If only I could afford it . . . ."

Moira pours more wine.

"I feel guilty," Judith says.

"Not your fault."

"It was supposed to be routine . . . . and he called . . . ."

"Of course, but take it easy . . . ."

"I wasn't there . . . ."

Moira refills Judith's glass and her own, and says, "I always thought it would be that stupid plane."

"I wouldn't go up in it."

Judith rummages in her purse. What is she looking for? "I just can't believe this—"

"Slow down now."

"What am I doing?" Judith says. "I have to get home."

"David and the others will do the right thing."

"Need to do something about my classes, my apartment, a flight . . . ."

"Losing your job won't help Eric. Talk to the boss person at the university. Get somebody to take your classes."

"Yes, you're right. It's . . . ."

How long would she be gone? Maybe a day, maybe a week. Maybe just hours. Maybe not at all.

"David said . . . his heart stopped."

Judith pours herself another glass of wine. She is so sleepy she can barely hold her head up.

The apartment door opens; they hear it down the long hallway.

In a second or two, Zelda, bending under a heavy book bag, comes in the room. She is twelve, but already has ample breasts which are quite evident under her light T-shirt.

"Aunt Judy! What are you doing here?"

She comes over and kisses Judith. Her long hair brushes Judith's neck.

"Eric is real sick, in the hospital," Moira says. "Heart thing."

"Holy Shit!"

Zelda pats Judith on the back.

"The Prince? Sick? I hope it's not too serious."

"Zelda, go make some tea, sweetie."

As the girl leaves the room, Moira whispers to Judith, "Did you ever see such boobs on a kid that age? It's all the hormones in the food."

They hear the tea kettle bang on the stove, cups rattle.

Judith leans back in her chair, her head on the pillow.

Zelda pops back into the living room.

"I always call him The Prince 'cause he was born in a castle. And he's damned cute for such an old guy."

Once upon a time, Judith would have laughed.

"I have to get a cab," she says. "Right now."

"Number six on the phone index," Moira says. Judith shakes off her fatigue, gathers together her books and purse and calls a taxi.

Her head spinning, fighting sleep and panic, she tells Moira and Zelda goodbye.

At her own apartment, Judith calls the head of her department, who asks her to come into her office first thing in the morning. Judith calls Delta. Recorded crap.

She digs a suitcase out of her closet and lays it on the glass table in the sterile living space of her rental. She takes out a notebook and tries to list the things she must do. She lies on the bed, her computer showing information on flights to Cincinnati.

She hugs her pillow. He can't die. He can't die. He can't die.

9

David

The waiting room is cheerless, brown leather chairs and couches, picked over magazines, a coffee vending machine. Several worried-looking people doze or sit talking.

Lydia calls. David tries to keep his voice steady as he tries to explain what happened. His father and grandfather would get the facts and maintain calm, and that's what he is determined to do. But his voice is quivering.

"Can you take over at home the rest of the day?" he says.

"Of course," Lydia says. "I'm so so sorry. This is so— unbelievable. So awful."

"I don't know when I'll be home."

"What shall I tell Phoebe?"

"God, I don't know. Just Grampy Eric is sick. She knows he's in the hospital. Maybe nothing for now."

"Right."

David snaps his phone shut.

"We better call John and Betsy," William says. "I wouldn't be so surprised if it were one of them, but not Dad."

"Yeah."

"Oh, would Dad want us to call Natalie?"

"Probably not."

"Does Mom know about her?"

"I don't think so."

"You get to tell her," William says.

"Thanks."

David looks out the window. His stomach is growling. He tries to get some coffee out of the vending machine, but not even a drizzle comes out.

He opens his cell to call his grandparents. Can John and Betsy take this kind of blow? They are in good health. They are world travelers. They actually still ski. His grandfather goes to his law office every day. But they are close to eighty and David's father is their only son.

Betsy answers.

"This is hard," David says. He explains what has happened, as vaguely as he can.

"Oh my God. How bad is he?"

David envisions his father, her son, lying next door, totally dependent on machines, so white, so near death.

"We're not really sure."

"We'll come right over."

"He's—asleep now," he lies. "Maybe tomorrow would be better."

"I don't know what to say."

"I don't either," David says. "This hit us from behind. He had just come out of the knee operation."

"How did that go?"

"Fine they said."

"Is he comfortable? Can we bring him anything?"

David pictures his father still as death, shut down. Betsy probably imagines her son propped against pillows, spooning up broth.

"My brother had that heart attack, remember? He was home in a week."

She sounds so hopeful, like Phoebe when her hamster had clearly died.

"He's just taking a little nap," she'd said.

"I don't think Dad's up for visitors," David tells his grandmother.

"We're not visitors. We'll be there soon," Betsy says.

"They're coming over," David tells William.

"What do we do now? Seems like all of a sudden we're the parents. An Over-Achieving Super-Dad, and an Under-Achieving Writer."

"Already fried and it looks like we're just getting started."

"We can't leave him," William says. "Dr. Jack says hospitals are the most dangerous places in the world."

David fiddles with his cell phone; William chews at his fingernails, which are bitten to the quick.

Their grandparents come into the room hurriedly: John, a tall, white-haired man, dressed in a suit and tie; Betsy, a slim older woman, wearing a cashmere sweater set and tailored slacks. They hug David and William.

"When can we see him?" Betsy asks.

"We'll go in now," David says. "He looks pretty awful."

"I've talked to the director of the hospital, he's a friend of mine," John says. "Eric must have a heart bypass as soon as possible."

"Doctor says he has a charmed life," David says. "To be alive."

"I like that, a charmed life," Betsy says.

"If you think they made the right call in the first place."

"We should sue the bastards who did this," William says.

John and David, the two lawyers, exchange glances.

"We'll see," John says.

The family go into the ICU and stand around David's father as if he were lying in state. Betsy bends over him and whispers in his ear.

"Does it help to talk to him?" John asks David.

"The nurse said it might be frustrating to try to respond when he can't because of the throat tube."

"Does he understand?" Betsy says.

"We don't know."

"We don't want to tire him. We'll come back tomorrow," John says.

"I'll stay with him tonight," William says.

When his grandparents leave, David says,"I'm going to get some coffee."

His heart is jumping around in his chest: *systole, diastole, systole, diastole.* "Mr. Howard! Mr. Howard!"

10

William

Don't die. Don't die, William whispers to his father. They are alone now. The only sounds in the ICU cubicle are of soft shoes coming and going. The only light is from the machines keeping his father alive. It's eerie. Like being inside an aquarium.

He rests his head on the rail of the bed. Occasionally his father's breathing is so shallow, William puts his hand on his chest, to be sure he is alive. He does not look like a man strong enough to face another major surgery.

He does not belong here. The center of the fortunate, successful Howards.

Hunger gnaws William's guts. He has had no lunch, and when the nurse comes in and asks him to step out while they do a transfusion, he slips out of the room to get a quick bite in the cafeteria. He finds himself piling his tray with bacon, eggs, fried potatoes, fried apples, gravy, biscuits and butter, jam, two boxes of milk, coffee, a large order of fried onion rings. He eats ravenously. The other people in the room seem to be gobbling too. Their plates are piled high. The large room is noisy, the air full of anxiety. Trays bang on the dirty dish conveyor, go into the maw of the kitchen.

Until his drug years and work at the Lookout, William was a stranger in this world, the world of pain and people living on the edge— He lived most of his life in one house, a house filled with paintings and flowers and everywhere books, books, books. It was warm in the winter, cool in the summer. It was a secure place, with a yard for him and David to play in, on a safe cul de sac arched over with sheltering trees. He and David walked to the neighborhood school. Their mother always had dinner on the table, plenty of snacks in the fridge. They belonged to a swimming and tennis club, took family trips, had decent allowances. They all watched "Soap" together.

The only real loss he could remember happened when he was very little and his family first came to Cincinnati and their cat Mehitabel went missing. But they got a new cat, and endless guinea pigs and fish and whatever they wanted. Life had seemed so simple: baseball, tennis, trips to the library, Saturday afternoons at the smelly movie.

Betsy and John were always there in the background in the castle which they bought in the fifties for practically nothing, a derelict Betsy spent a lifetime restoring. Though political liberals, his grandparents were old-style Cincinnatians, cautious, resistant to change. In his one lecture to his grandsons about money (it was generally a taboo subject, somewhat bad taste), John let them know that he actually had never bought anything he couldn't write a check for.

Their high standards never wavered. Betsy got the best people in renovation to return her castle to its original glory. Every inch of painted ceiling was restored, every leaded glass window cleaned of years' old grime. She set the table for Thanksgiving and Christmas with the precision of an English butler. She would not use boxed orange juice, or frozen food. She would not accept a thank you note by email. He and David found that out the hard way—at Christmas. Her life work was preserving the distinguished buildings in the city.

And his parents: people thought they were made for each other even though they were so different. They communicated between themselves with mysterious phrases like "that's *real coffee*," which must mean something; it cracked them up. They finished each other's sentences. They used phrases like *terminus ad quem* and *terminus a quo* in everyday conversation. Their fights were mostly ironic exchanges, sometimes barbs, but wrapped in humor. They were unique, yet grown together. "Like the lichen and the liverwort," his mother said. William once said they should have their own talk show, and they wouldn't even need any guests. His mother accused his father of thinking history was only who conquered whom, that he should know more about what artists and common people and women were thinking as well as Bismarck and Hitler. He said she should know what the Albigensian Heresy was all about and understand the Treaty of Worms.

He wanted her to fly in the small plane he loved, but she said it looked like a Volkswagen with wings, and stayed on the ground. She wanted him to go snorkeling.

There were times when his parents would limit their conversation to things like newspaper delivery and garbage day. Tension would occasionally hang in the air like smog, but William had never seen them come right out and fight.

He thought their living separately was agreed on, and wouldn't last. But something had gone wrong. One of the Romano boys told him his mother had dived topless into their pool. William didn't believe it.

The thought made him queasy.

His *mother*?

And then there is Natalie.

William is glad Betsy and John are nearby. They were there when he needed help. He admires their basic good will, their decency, their refusal to adopt the trendy. With his father lost somewhere between life and death, he is especially grateful for their unflappable personalities, their united front.

11

Betsy

Betsy pulls off a shoe and throws it at John's head, winging him on the shoulder.

He has come into the bedroom where she is lying down and says, "Betsy, are you all right? Would you like to go out for a nice dinner?"

"I hate the word nice," she says. "Go away."

She is trapped, groveling before death.

For the first time in her life she knows terror.

She is helpless, furious.

She hears John leave the room and go to the kitchen.

She cries, horrible sobs hurting her ribs.

Eric is the person she loves best in the world. Her son. The father of her grandchildren. So handsome. So smart. A serious man whose occasional smile lights everything around him. How they had cared for him, protected him, from childhood until he left home. His body was made strong by healthy food and good care. He always had space to run and play, to swim and ride and climb. He had been surrounded by books and art and a beautiful home. A castle.

She and John built him a trust fund. His teeth were treated with fluorides.

At the hospital Betsy had thought, this can't be my son. This mummy lying in a hospital bed. It was horrible: a tube in his throat, and tubes and wires all over him and the frightening monitors clicking incessantly: white sheets, white face. Eric's hand was already purple from needle stabs.

She looked to John, standing a little way back. He asked technical questions about the numbers on the blood pressure monitor.

He studied the monitor and shook his head.

Betsy kissed her son's cheek. No response. The cheek was cold.

"We love you," Betsy whispered into his ear. "We love you so much, and we're all here to do whatever it takes. You'll be back with us. I know."

This is unbearable, she thought.

Betsy and John drove home from the hospital in silence. They were quiet as the elevator ascended the twenty floors to their condominium, where they had moved after selling the castle. They silently entered their aerie overlooking the river, guarded by the resident manager scanning the TVs in the foyer. Their dog Ginger, blind, toothless, incontinent, small and limp, lying in the kitchen in her little bed.

Outside their big windows was the endless sky, giving the feeling that you could step out into the air. Huge hawks glided gracefully above the river. Today they looked threatening.

John glanced over the mail, pitched most of it into a waste can, and then gathered up his keys and briefcase. "I'll be at the office till about six," he said. "I'll take Ginger out when I get home." He kissed Betsy on the cheek, went into the hall and pushed the button for the elevator. "Better call Adrian," he said.

Betsy went into the bedroom and crawled onto her bed. How could John just carry on with his son lying so still and sick? Take everything so calmly. Rush back to the office from the hospital after dropping her at home. Go on with his routine, while she felt her life might end.

She made herself call her daughter. Another answering machine. Betsy hates the damn things. She left a message. Would Adrian come out? She was probably in the wilderness with a bunch of convicts or spoiled high school kids she is teaching to survive in the mountains.

"My son. My son." Her son should not go before her. It was so wrong. The worst thing that can happen: burying a child.

Eric's birth was hard. But such joy. He seemed to come from some enchanted place, to know things unknown. Betsy had never thought babies were cute until she held her son in her arms.

She remembers him coming home from kindergarten, dejected as though something terrible had happened. She finally pried the problem out of him: "I c-can't skip." Betsy laughed and took him by the hand, then hopped him around the room until they were skipping and his face lit up with pride.

He made her a necklace of dried macaroni and placed it around her neck.

"I love you better," he said.

"Than what?"

"Daddy and Adrian."

She is so proud of his achievements—being a distinguished professor, a writer, maybe president of the university, a peace maker.

Betsy wonders what Judith will do. She should have been here for her husband. Betsy does not know what had gone on between her and Eric—but she has been married to the man for thirty-some years. Why so much tension? Eric was a sweet man.

When he decided against attending law school to go into history, her maid Effie said, "I told you my Eric wouldn't be no lawyer. My Eric would never put nobody in jail."

Betsy has never seen her son even raise his voice at Judith. She is fond of Judith, but she has plenty of faults: she is so intense and competitive. Demanding. Eric drove the boys to school and even washed dishes, though he was so busy at the university. Judith could look more attractive. She wore her clothes a size too big. And that hair. Piled on her head and held in place with pins from a UNESCO catalog, it looked like a pile of knitting. She was a so-so housekeeper and a bit of a nag. What was their sex life like? She was right, of course, that Eric didn't take care of his health.

Why did he have to smoke, the nitwit? Betsy agrees with Judith on that one. Smoking could have affected the heart. Or was it the anesthetic as William thought? Eric's doctor told him his heart was strong enough for the surgery.

How serious is this Natalie thing? Eric and Judith's living apart. What about all the times she herself either thought about or *did* leave John? Going off to their Michigan cottage, or to "visit her sister." But those were short breaks, not long enough to tempt a husband to find someone else. She was the one who—well that was seconds compared to her and John's years together.

How could Eric's heart have failed? He was always so strong and full of life. A force. He is her favorite, she has to admit that. Adrian is, well, not what she had dreamed of in a daughter.

She tries Adrian's number again. No go.

Betsy feels herself sinking. This isn't them. This sickness. There was only John's one surgery—gall bladder—so routine. Her hysterectomy. They are fortunate and privileged, but also they have worked at staying healthy and in good spirits, trying to outwit time. These last few years have been a hide and seek game with life. They were "It."

She will *not* be like John's parents! His mother spent her last years in a wheel chair, demanding and bitter. His father was living in a nursing home, his brain cells slowly washing away like sand.

After fifty, yes, a certain sadness crept in. But Betsy fought off sadness, kept busy and thanked heaven for having good health, and refused to complain about the minor aches and pains. She hates the giving up she sees around her—whining and complaining about age. If you don't like wrinkles and sags, fix 'em: that's what she did (a nip or two around the eyes and neck). She eats lightly and exercises: "Curves" now, in the past yoga, Jazzercise, aerobics, Pilates. She is always shocked and annoyed when some busybody offers her a chair or help with her groceries.

Now she knows fear.

This is when John comes in and offers dinner and Betsy pitches her shoe at him.

12

Judith

If her own house proves too big and empty, she might go to Betsy and John's. She is especially fond of John with his quiet supportive ways. What a lovely man. He is so devoted to Betsy and treats her like a queen. The whole family knows she has never pumped a gallon of gas in her life. She always had plenty of help to run her castle; every day for thirty years Effie had put on the coffee and brought her breakfast in bed (now John does).

Judith and Betsy get along all right, though Judith could see her mother-in-law biting her lips when she came into her house. Her eyes examined the rooms, mentally re-arranging the furniture. When the boys were toddlers, she retrieved their spitty pacifiers from the floor with a frown, and washed them.

David lives too far from the hospital, and Judith and Lydia are not chummy. Judith feels Lydia is the one driving David into debt. And she treats the child like a fragile vase: no crib when she was a baby (head could catch between rails, bumpers could smother). She worries about stroller construction, the water, the air, pet dander, peanuts. Phoebe's schedule is so tight, Judith barely saw her except when the child was performing and an audience was needed. Judith's own kids had been free to run all over the neighborhood, climb trees, make mud pies, and she and Moira were never supervised: their mother spent her days playing bridge on one or another country club veranda. Their father was remote, absorbed by business, a darker Eric.

David, Lydia and Phoebe are waiting for Judith at the baggage area in Cincinnati. A beautiful family: David tall and smiling, with Eric's thick brown hair, noble nose and generous mouth, Lydia slim and stylish, and Phoebe, grasping her "Pup in a Pouch," her face shining. Judith flies into David's arms. Oh, how comforting it is to be in the strong arms of her son and to feel Phoebe's arms around her waist. She throws her arms open for Lydia and they hug. She bends down and kisses her granddaughter. She has grown!

"Oh, it's so good to see you. You look more grown up than ever."

"How was the flight?" Lydia asks.

They talk all around the big topic on all their minds.

"Phoebe and I will scoot on home," Lydia says. "She has a harp lesson this afternoon."

She and Phoebe wave and go off to the parking area.

"Let's go straight to the hospital," Judith says to David. "Is there any change?"

"I'm afraid not. The nurses tried to take his breathing tube out this morning, but they couldn't do it."

Judith and David put her bag in his car, and they drive over the river to Cincinnati.

Judith cringes at the sight of the hospital: it's a Frankenstein's monster of a building. Grafted onto the original brick colonial and clock tower are several steel and glass additions, and a post-modern wing lurching to one side, its walls seeming to swell.

David hands his car keys to the young guys at the valet parking service. The doors of the hospital open wide and the eerie recorded voice announces, "Welcome to Good Shepard Hospital. This is a non-smoking facility. Please observe the no smoking rule."

David guides Judith past the gift shop, the front desk, the Wendy's, the super-sized photos of prominent doctors. He points out the portrait of Dr. Sanders smiling down on them like an inscrutable and omnipotent god.

Once inside the cardiac unit, they walk down a long hallway with patients' rooms on both sides and three nurses' stations.

Judith feels herself weaken at the door of the ICU. What will she find? She pauses.

"Wow."

David takes her arm and they go into the dim chamber.

William is standing beside the bed. Judith hugs him, then goes to Eric.

Her arms go numb. The white, rigid, swaddled figure in the bed is not her husband. She turns away.

At William's grasp on her arm, she turns back. This mummy still does not seem like her husband. She makes herself bend over the still body. She whispers that she hopes he can hear her, that she loves him.

David explains the meaning of the numbers on the several monitors.

"Blood pressure's high," he says.

Judith and David hover in the room for a while, and then he suggests taking Judith home so she can rest.

"They'll try the throat tube again soon, and then we'll know more, hopefully," William says.

Judith looks over her younger son. He seems jittery. But she is grateful he is here. She hugs him again, then leaves him in the dim room with his father.

In David's car, Judith slumps in her seat, devastated. Nothing could have prepared her for the look of her husband. Lifeless, hollow. A body with no mind. The mind far away if not destroyed.

"Mom," David says. "You all right?"

"Hmm? My God."

David pats her hand. She welcomes the touch.

She feels so guilty and remorseful that she had not been here when Eric went into the hospital. Had he been trying to spare her? Or wanting her to come home?

Judith and David drive to their old Tudor. The familiar trees of the main street are orange and red, beginning to drop a scattering of brown leaves. They pass the shops, the movie, the fire station. Judith smells the spicy Indian food of the restaurants. The chilli. Eric loved both. Would she ever see him again adding hot sauce and chutney, and diving into his favorite dishes?

On the front path of the house, a few walnuts hit the stones. There is a spider web across the big brown front door, which creaks when they open it.

"Welcome to Transylvania," David says.

Judith tries to laugh. "Nice." She sweeps the web away with her purse.

She follows her son as he lugs her bags up the stairs and deposits them in the hall.

"You know you're very welcome to come and stay with us," David says.

"I know, thanks. But this will be easier; you're so far out."

Judith notices David recoil. None of the Howards approve of his move to the suburbs. They like the mix of people in the city, and being close to the places of its history and culture.

"I get downtown in twenty minutes," David says.

Judith regrets her "so far out." She stands on her tiptoes and kisses David on the cheek.

"It can't be easy seeing your father this way."

"Not for you either."

"No."

David wanders onto the patio. He appears to be checking out the garden and the woods, but Judith knows he is giving her time to gather her strength, to face the house and the emptiness of it.

Judith sits on the bench in the front hall. After being away, it is like coming to the house for the first time. Close to thirty years ago. She and Eric looked the place over, and after complaining to the real estate agent about the ancient heating—a Rube Goldberg contraption, two furnaces, one working and an old clunker from World War II—the single bathroom, the wallpaper hanging loose in places like shedding skin, Eric simply said, "We'll take it."

When the agent left, she said, "Aren't there two of us here?"

"Hmm?"

"Do you get to decide things by yourself?"

"Do you want the place or not?"

"It's fine," she said. "But—"

Eric's peremptory "we'll take it" without any discussion with her, was one of the many resentments she held onto. There were others that—like bodies that stayed buried and then escaped from their graves on Halloween—came back when she was angry.

Judith walks around the downstairs. There are books in every room. On shelves, on tables, on chairs. The living and dining rooms look much the same as when she left. On the walls are Rothko and Stanzek reproductions, and some Japanese Ukioyi prints Betsy had given them. A copy of the Robert Indiana LOVE poster hangs in the back hall.

Judith loved to paint when she had time, and several of her watercolors of the children playing in the garden are on the sun porch walls. The room is full of magazines, the television set, more shelves of books. Here she read *The Lord of the Rings* to the boys, snow piling up around the windows sealing them in, cozy as the cats Frodo and Pippin and Mehitabel the second.

Photos cover the credenza: the family smiling in front of pensiones in Paris and Madrid, on trails in Zion and Yellowstone. Though travel was arranged around Eric's conferences and research, she loved the trips they took; Eric would stop at every historical marker and explain the battles fought nearby. They drove down the Natchez Trace to Memphis and Vicksburg, to William Faulkner's home and Graceland—and a stop at a famous restaurant where everything was fried, even the pickles. There they were at Christmases and family birthdays.

Did Eric have a premonition that something might go wrong? Were there clues?

Judith wanders down the hall and steps into his study. He had so many projects. Was he overworked? Inside his messy den, layers of papers and books, like geological strata, hold records of civilizations created, dynasties destroyed, battles for land, the mess and mayhem of history. On the shelves are rows of professional journals featuring Eric's articles along with his books: *Japanese Americans in World War Two, Revisiting Pearl Harbor, Viet Nam and American Hegemony*— all of which had caused academic warfare. More distance between him and his father, which began over Viet Nam.

He had been working on a new book, a review of the events leading up to the current war. He had hoped to go to Iraq. And he continued, year after year, on a survey of historical theory, from religious determinism to the sociological; he was even reconsidering the Great Man theory, studying the larger than life figures who sometimes step forth from the ongoing flow to bring radical change. Like the story of the world itself, Eric's survey had no end in sight. Judith called it his Mr. Casaubon book.

"Oh that's cruel," Eric had said.

The smell from Eric's cigarettes still hangs over the room. A gray smell. There are a few burned ends in an ashtray on his desk. Judith dumps them into the waste basket.

She looks at her husband's lumpy chair from which he studied the past. Delving into the endless purges and pogroms, massacres and genocides, he tended to be more optimistic than she about the world. Did the horrors of the past make the present seem better, imply hope for the future?

"It may be a cliché, but those who do not study history are doomed to repeat it," Eric said regularly.

"And so are those who do," Judith said.

Judith calls Moira, gets a recorded message, tries to tell her sister about Eric, but can't get the words out. Leaves a message asking for a return call. She calls her principal: she cannot say when she will return to DC.

The family's one remaining cat, a third Mehitabel, jumps on the desk where she usually sat while Eric worked. She rubs her head against Judith's hip and bawls her out for being missing so long. Seems to be asking where Eric has disappeared to. Judith rubs her back and carries her into the living room. She buries her face in Mehitabel's fur. It is soon damp.

Through the porch windows Judith can see David pacing the garden.

She picks up the mail that is piled on the dining room table. Familiar return addresses. Cards. One is an out-sized post card with a hand-drawn red heart and the message "Good Fucking Luck. And *Lots* of Love" printed in red. Judith is examining it when David comes into the room.

"I'm glad you're here," he says.

She kisses him on the cheek. She holds up the card and says, "Who the hell is Natalie?"

Part 2

WHEN REASON SLEEPS

13

Judith

Judith goes up to her and Eric's bedroom and tears open the bedding; she smells the sheets, the pillows. They smell of sweat: Eric's. She knows the odor well. She goes to the closet: no women's clothes, just a line of Eric's shirts and slacks thrown over hangers carelessly. He was always in a hurry.

To be so easily, so quickly, replaced!

She goes into the bathroom and opens the medicine cabinet. A box of tampons! But examining it, she recognizes her own brand. She pitches the box into the waste can. Eric's aftershave, aspirin, the usual things, a familiar rusty spot on the lower metal shelf.

No wonder he told her not to come home for his surgery. He hated confrontations.

She will leave. Right away.

Leave him to Heaven. And his god-damned girl friend.

She goes to the computer in Eric's study. It takes a while to boot up. She types in Delta, reservations. The light on the telephone is blinking and she presses the button: calls of condolence and "can I do anything?" go on and on. Natalie is among them. Her voice is high pitched, sounds young.

Judith's face burns. When did Eric take up with this woman? Was he seeing her all along? Before she left? What?

Judith puts her head in her hands. It is pulsing like the red light on the phone. She slams the receiver back into its charger. She tears Natalie's card into pieces and throws them into the waste can.

She feels dirty. Ridiculous. Everyone would know about this at the university. All their friends. Anger and humiliation tear her apart.

She is so tired. She goes to the second floor to the bedroom and lies down on her and Eric's bed.

The light is fading at the window. The familiar sounds of the place surround her: the moan of doves, the walnuts thudding on the lawn, the far off hum of the expressway. She falls asleep and dreams Eric has driven his car into the river. She has escaped, while he is trapped. Still dreaming, she thinks, this is only a dream, then thinks, panicking, it is real, and she rushes back to the river where Eric is floating in the water. He'd been there too long to live. But when she turns him over and attempts CPR, he responds.

She goes back downstairs, turns off the computer, where the airline is offering her resort bargains.

Just don't think, she tells herself.

Forget Eric's cheating. Try to be the girl who got herself to college on scholarship, paid for her books by working in the dormitory dining room. Worked for peace. Raised a lovely family. That need her now.

She goes to the garage to check her car, to see if it is running. Her ancient Audi (a hand-me-down from Betsy) is in its usual place in the garage next to Eric's Jetta. She hopes it will start. Had Eric run it occasionally as he said he would?

Eric's disregard for cars, clothes, appearances, all the things most Americans seem to prize, was one of his more lovable traits. His mind was on the big events of history, the problems of the world. A hole in one of his own socks was relegated to the importance it actually occupied in the universe.

Judith trudges back upstairs to the kitchen. She should eat. The fridge is hoary, contains nothing but a few TV dinners. The peace lilies at the windows droop. She gives them some water.

What is Eric's affair with this woman all about? Is it love? Sex? Sabotage?

Did she fail him?

She goes to the hospital and sits beside his bed. He has not moved, this thin, sick, still, white stranger.

14

Judith

Eighteen. Brown hair to his shoulders, a well-formed nose, a thin muscular body. The star of their World History class at Chicago. He seemed to pop up everywhere: at the campus theater watching *The Rocky Horror Picture Show,* throwing a football on the midway, rosy-cheeked, black-haired, smiling, a cigarette dangling from his lips.

After class one day, he sat down next to her in the cafeteria where she was having coffee. Their professor had praised Judith's paper on Thucydides, and Eric said pretty girls weren't usually so smart. She lectured him on sexism, and fell at his feet like a bird.

She thought he might be wanting to get together, but he was recruiting her for an anti-Viet Nam protest.

Hanging out at Ernie's, an old beer and burger joint near campus, with ancient "Schlitz" signs and checked table cloths, everyone furious, they joined in, shouting about Viet Nam. Eric began driving around campus and Hyde Park in a pickup, yelling into a bull horn, encouraging students to join the anti-war movement. Judith ran through the classrooms of the university and scrawled peace symbols and meeting times on the blackboards. Their group threatened to napalm a dog on campus to show the horror of what was happening to Viet Nam children. The outrage from the neighborhood was furious. But was it worse to scald a dog than a child?

They got a puppy from the pound.

And gave it to a little boy in the park.

August. Judith and Eric and their cohorts joined forces with other groups demanding a peace plank and an anti-war nominee from the Democratic convention.

Judith painted posters and made signs to carry to rallies. She hated the war. With her whole body. Her whole mind. The young men sent off to die. For what? An old man's pride. To prove the U.S. could never lose.

Everybody was fucking away like mad. Another change enraging the entrenched war hawks. But Eric hadn't made a move toward Judith. Was he interested in her as more than a fellow rebel? One night, she went to his apartment and jumped into bed with him. He threw his arms around her, surprised and eager. Their two young bodies were perfect. Lovely. They had not been apart since.

"Why didn't you jump on *my* bed?" Judith asked.

"I was going to. But I was afraid you might slug me."

One afternoon as they were resting from making love, they heard the sound of one of their friends coming down the hall.

When he came in, Judith was sitting on Eric's bed, her clothes back on, but her legs partly bare in her cut-off jeans.

The friend was full of news about the plans for protest. He sat beside Judith on the bed, looked her over. He took a marker from his pocket and scrawled a heart on her ankle.

"What are you *doing*?" she said.

"Trying to see if I can mar perfection."

A week later Judith found herself and Eric a shabby room and kitchenette and they moved into it during the Thanksgiving break.

Judith's dorm director tried to talk her out of going: she was too young. Her mother said, you girls are crazy giving it away. But nothing could have stopped her.

She liked Eric's body, his hair, his eyes, but his appearance wasn't the main attraction. Eric was the first male intelligent enough for her. She didn't want some good-looking nitwit. She packed her books and her few pairs of jeans and T-shirts and left.

She was like a proud housewife presiding over the chipped Formica table and mismatched wooden chairs she and Eric salvaged from curbside stuff set out for the garbage truck. She loved having her own little kitchen with its two plates, two forks, two knives, and small stack of pans.

Sleeping with Eric at night, Judith would reach out for him, and feel happy with her arms around his slim body. Sitting together in bed one evening, she braided their long hair together into a single plait.

Judith loved to lie under the covers in the morning, enjoying the slant of light coming in the window, while their cat Mehitabel, a slim Siamese stray, padded imperiously over their backs. But Eric was ready to go when his alarm rang.

She teased Eric about his banker's habits. For all his rebelliousness, his dissatisfaction with "the establishment," his hippie hair and clothes, he kept a schedule like a businessman's: up at seven, shower, dress, off to the library to study as though it were a job.

Judith liked to sit on the bathroom hamper while Eric shaved. She shuddered as he raised his chin and shaved his neck. It looked so vulnerable, and occasionally he drew a spot of blood. She could see his penis through the slit in his shorts, resting in a nest of black hair. She had never seen a grown-up penis before, only pictures or little knobs on statues. She reached in and held it for a moment, like a baby bird.

She loved these moments of intimacy, the closeness, the fragrance of Eric's aftershave which he dabbed on and that lingered behind his ears.

Sitting by their bright window, cutting out bits of colored paper for their Christmas tree, Judith felt a euphoria she never experienced in quite the same way again. She watched the snow begin, a few individual flakes hesitantly moving this way and that, as though trying to decide where to land. Then their numbers swelled, and filled the view, blowing hard, and soon the sky was opaque. The streets were blanketed white. She wished they could be snowed in.

Her peace melted away as the white snow became gray ice, frozen in piles like small glaciers, sending rivulets of icy water into the gutters. Judith and Eric caught ugly colds that dragged them down for several weeks. Judith felt desolate when Eric announced he was going to New York to join a march protesting the war. He was still coughing as he crowded onto a bus with other students. She wished she could go along to be with Eric, but she was still too sick. He left her a stack of pamphlets to address.

Judith watched the march on television, trying to spot Eric among the thousands of people. When he came home, they were both well, full of energy, made tender love, carried signs and joined the protesters sitting in on the campus.

Hospital sounds: beeps, soft footsteps as nurses check their silent patients mingle with fading young lovers' words, and long ago chants.

"You could play Ophelia," he had said. He tucked straw flowers and marigolds in her hair.

"Hey, hey, LBJ: how many kids did you kill today?"

Judith kisses Eric's cold forehead. "What happened?" she says. "Wake up. Please wake up."

15

David

David drives home that night, his head about to burst, replaying the scene of his mother discovering Natalie's card. He feels like a rat for letting her find out that way, though tattling was rotten too. She was as mad as he had ever seen her, but said she didn't blame him and William for not telling her. It wasn't their job. He stuttered that it had all happened so fast, the scheduled surgery, the heart failure. They had hoped Natalie would not be around much longer. His mother wanted him to leave, he could tell, so he took off.

He speeds along Columbia Parkway above the river and out to the area of "Maple Ridges" and "Garden Places," subdivisions of huge houses like his own.

The floodlights around the doors, windows, and garages are bright, lighting the small lots like night baseball fields, though there is little crime in the area. After all, that is one reason so many of the people here had moved out of the city where burglaries and shootings are reported every day, more each year.

David pulls into the garage, punches in the numbers on the alarm system. He is greeted by Lenny, a poodle-sheepdog mix. Big, sweet, dumb—thus the name—the mutt puts his paws on

David's shoulders and licks his face. David takes him for a short run in the woods behind the house.

"You stay out of trouble today?" he says to Lenny. There is a pattern of chewing up Lydia's expensive shoes and he is only tolerated by her because he is so gentle with Phoebe, who adores him.

David stops in the kitchen at the refrigerator and sticks a finger into some sort of casserole Lydia had probably picked up at "What's for Dinner?" He scoops up a few bites.

He goes up the grand staircase. He has to step over workmen's gear cluttering the hall. Though their master bath is bigger than David's childhood bedroom, Lydia is enlarging their dressing rooms and installing new fixtures. David has tried to slow her down, but she is determined.

He goes into their bedroom; his wife is propped on pillows, reading. She looks beautiful, blond hair spread around her face. She opens her arms when he sits on the bed to take off his shoes.

"David, how is your father?"

He flings himself onto the bed beside her, and lays his head on her breast. He describes his father, all wrapped in white, in a ghostly world. The battle they face to get him breathing on his own, then strong enough to undergo another major surgery, while the injured heart is in danger of giving out again. Lydia strokes his head. She is quiet a moment, absorbing David's news, then says, "David, you have to be prepared if your father would not make it."

"I know."

He gets off the bed with a groan. "I'm going to go check on Phoebe," he says. He walks down the hall to his daughter's room. She sleeps in a canopy bed fit for a princess.

She looks so fragile, hair blond as her mother's but wispy, her arms clutching her stuffed dog, Sadie. His little girl is like Sleeping Beauty, ringed around by palace guards who try to keep her safe.

Nothing bad has touched her yet, though malevolent fairies have tried to penetrate the sacred hedge.

Once, fixing Phoebe's lunch, he felt something strange in a slice of bread and pulled out a needle with black thread in it.

There are too many wackos out there, he thinks: rapists, pedophiles, gun nuts—and softer insidious forces—advertisers targeting her, stealing her time and her childhood; TV tempting her to mindlessness, gadgets coming between her and the world of nature.

Now a real evil crone has entered her castle with a sharp needle: sickness and maybe death. David walks over to the bed to kiss her lightly.

Phoebe pops up at his approach.

"I'm not asleep," she says.

"Why not?"

"No reason. Is Grampy Eric OK? Can I go see him tomorrow?" Her voice is light, sweet.

David sits on the edge of the bed. "Not tomorrow, soon."

"What's a heart attack?"

"Where did you hear that?"

"Momma talking on the phone."

"Well, it's when someone's heartbeat is a little—"

"Sick?"

"Yes." David smooths the hair back on Phoebe's forehead. His daughter deserves a carefree childhood. She is entitled to her innocence.

"Daddy," Phoebe says. "I want to ask you something."

David goes cold.

"Yes, sweetheart?" He quickly tries thinking of euphemisms, gentle phrases.

"Can I have a yogurt?"

Relief. Reprieve.

"Sure thing."

David gets up from the bed and starts toward the door.

"The kind with the little penguins on the box," Phoebe says. "With blueberries."

David goes down the wide stairway to the kitchen. The shadow of the chandelier creeps before him, covering his path like the dark shape that had fallen over his bright life.

He gets Phoebe's yogurt and sits by her until she finishes it, then tucks her in. Her skin is so soft, so new.

He goes back to his and Lydia's bedroom, undresses and gets into bed beside his wife.

He is so stiff it hurts. Lydia has been working so hard lately, she often doesn't have the energy for sex. David is tired too, but the tireder he feels, the readier he is. Lydia murmurs, "early day tomorrow."

David kisses her all over and buries his head between her thighs.

"I just gotta," he says. He opens her vulva with his tongue. The inside is like a fresh oyster, succulent and briny. Soon they are making love as though they are creating life. Maybe they are. They want another child. To be a family. More than ever.

He goes to the hospital the next day. No change. And the next and the next.

16

Judith

Judith goes to the kitchen and looks in the fridge. She has eaten almost nothing since she got home. It is filled with cheeses, fruit, chops, wine. Betsy of course. This is what she would do. John would carry the packages.

Judith nibbles at some cheese. She isn't really hungry. She goes outside into the garden. The sun and shade lay on the grass and flowers in complicated patterns from the big trees. Cardinals squabble with the jays raiding their nests. The flower beds are overgrown.

She has looked over the house for any signs of Natalie, but has found nothing. Only another card in the mail, "LOL," with the red marker—like the signs of deer in the garden—nibbled impatiens and begonias.

The garden is strange to her now. She feels dismissed. Unwanted, like the kid her mother thought was a tumor, a useless lump, and seemed to think the story did not hurt. Judith has been called brilliant, beautiful, original, brave and bold, but those words bounce off her. At bad times her mother's words live inside, like ugly potatoes sprouting feelers from their eyes.

The phone rings and she rushes into the house. What? What could be happening?

David. The ICU nurse is trying again to wean Eric from the throat tube.

Judith calls William.

She bathes, heads back to the hospital.

She drives her Audi to Over the Rhine to pick up William. His neighborhood looks seedier than ever. The front door of his building has a window that looks unsafe; the shade is grimy as those roller towels they used to see in gas station restrooms. The ones she forbid David and William to touch.

Why is he living like this?

There is a note on the door: "Have to take care of a kid till his Mom gets home. I'll come on the bus. Chow. William." *Chow?* What the heck? Oh, *Ciao*. Judith has to laugh. William never could spell.

The hospital waiting room is full of people chattering, rustling magazines, getting up and down from chairs; the sound of coins trickling into the snack machine, candy bars dropping with a thump.

David greets her and they sit and wait.

Judith goes over to the coffee machine, but like the others gets nothing but a brackish dribble.

By the time William arrives, the dinner carts are coming down the hall; the three can hear doors opening, metal trays clattering as they land on plastic tables.

Eventually a nurse comes in from ICU. They hope she has good news for them. They've had so many disappointments. She is walking with a confident air. She comes over to them and says they can come visit their patient. He has been weaned from the throat tube, and is breathing on his own at last.

"Hallelujah!" William says. He and David exchange high fives with each other and Judith. They all walk quickly into Intensive Care.

The churchly air of suspense in the ICU subdues them, and they approach Eric cautiously. After so long, how will he be? Will he be able to talk to them? Judith leans over the bed, examines his gaunt face. It is still impassive. He moves slightly. He lifts an arm. The corpse is coming to life. He opens his eyes a crack. He works his lips stiffly. Judith stands back while David pats him on the shoulder. Eric coughs hard, then again, and coughs up a large string of thick clear stuff. The nurse suctions it out.

He is trying to say something. Finally, he gets his voice up to a volume they can hear.

"Fuck! Fuck! Fuck!"

Everyone pulls back a touch, but then laugh.

"Go, Pop," William says.

"How do you feel?" David asks.

"Get Mom."

"She's right here."

Eric turns to Judith and stares as though trying to figure out who she is.

"Where's my wallet?" he asks. "My watch? Did you take them home?"

Whoa, Judith thinks. Now he seems to think she has been here all along. Had he had a stroke when his heart stopped, suffered some brain damage? Has he forgotten that she is teaching in DC, that he has a new girl?

"What can we do for you?" David says.

Eric tries to pull the suction cups of his heart monitor off his chest. "I'm going now. Take these things off me."

William says, "Dad, *N-O*. They have to keep tabs on your heart." The nurse replaces the cups, and says, "I'll get the doctor." She leaves the family alone.

Judith and her sons look at one another. What is this?

"I have to stand up," Eric says.

"You can't do that, Pop."

"I have to pee."

David explains about the catheter and plastic bags attached to the bed. Eric looks puzzled.

"Where are we?" he says.

"Dad, you're in a hospital. You had a serious setback. You're going to be OK now. They just took your throat tube out and you're breathing on your own."

"Why is everything outside that window so still?"

"That's St. George's church and Calhoun Street, over by the university."

"No it's not. It's too still."

"Now look, Dad—see the cars moving along the street?"

Dr. Sanders comes in, looks his patient over, checks the monitors.

"You probably should step out now," he says to the family. "He needs another transfusion."

Judith bends down and kisses her husband on the cheek. He looks so pitiful. He doesn't smell like himself; he usually wears a fragrant aftershave she likes. Now he smells medicinal, like alcohol and chemicals.

"Don't let her out of your sight," Eric says to David and William. "She will disappear."

He quiets down and closes his eyes, babbling something indecipherable, like a badly tuned radio, playing two stations at once.

When Dr. Sanders joins the three outside Eric's cubicle, they tell him how strangely Eric is acting.

"ICU psychosis," Dr. Sanders says. "It goes. When one is available, we'll move him to a less noisy cubicle at the end of the corridor. He'll do better there."

"I hope so. God," William says.

"He's been through a terrible ordeal. He's very sick. And intensive care units are confusing: people coming and going constantly, lights on and off."

"How long does this go on?"

"Sometimes a day or two. It all depends—"

Dr. Sanders disappears. He does that so unobtrusively, Judith thinks. Like magic. This place is eerie. No wonder Eric is confused. She and her sons go back to the waiting area.

"I'm going to take off," David says. "I want to be with Phoebe and Lydia. They're pretty upset."

"Of course."

"I'll stay with him tonight till he falls asleep," Judith says.

"Are you sure you should?"

"I want to."

"Mom, be sure and turn your cell on when you drive around here," David says. He frowns at William. "And you too. There was another shooting in your neighborhood last night."

"There's one every night. I know who the bad motherfuckers are and I keep my distance."

David hugs Judith and William. "This is good," he says. "That Dad can breathe on his own."

"Of course," Judith says. David leaves and she sits quietly with her younger son for a moment. Tears run down her cheeks. William puts his arms around her.

She hangs onto him for a moment.

"There's a Greek place near here," he says. "I'm going to run over there and pick up something to eat."

Judith watches him go. William: her wild one. When he was a kid, he was so super-active, so competitive, David had looked at him running around shirtless, and said, "If William were in *The Lord of the Flies,* he'd be one of the hunters."

Soon Judith sees William coming down the hall bearing bags of food, and they sit in the dim hall and eat pickled mushrooms and grape leaves.

"David told me what happened—about her card," William says.

"Oh yeah. Nice little welcome home."

"We're cowards."

"Well—"

"Could you rat on your father?"

"I don't care to meet her."

"David has told everyone that we want family only for now."

"Apparently your father hadn't noticed I'd left." Judith wishes she hadn't said that, it sounded bitter (which it was) and she swore she'd never call Eric 'your father' to her children. ("The kids" as she still calls them).

"He asked for you," William says.

"Yeah, while out of his mind."

They eat quietly for a moment.

"We're home free," William says. "We are."

The nurse comes into the room and gives Eric an injection.

"He will settle down now," she says.

Judith thinks "don't let her out of your sight" sounded like love.

17

Judith

Alone with Eric, she caresses his arm, but he pushes her hand away.

"You just want money. All of you—"

She has never before heard Eric complain about money, much less accuse his family of greed.

"Why isn't David here?"

"He *was*."

"Tell him to get his ass over here."

"I can't use the cell phone in here."

"Where are we?"

"We're in a hospital. You had a heart problem. You're going to be OK now. They just took your throat tube out and you're breathing on your own."

"Why don't you kill me? This is torture."

Judith wonders if she should have been so sure about staying the night with Eric.

She's helpless here.

After several hours of abuse, the cardiologist, Dr. Sanders, comes into the cubicle.

"How are you, Mr. Howard?" he asks. Like the other doctors, he speaks as though the patient is deaf and stands as far from him as possible (do they think heart disease is catching?).

"Fine. Get me out of here."

"Pretty soon. We want you to go into a private room soon as possible so you can get some real sleep. Would you like a little something to eat?"

"No."

"Vital signs are not bad," Dr. Sanders says.

"They go up and down so much," Judith says.

The doctor approaches the bed.

"Mr. Howard, you *must* stop smoking!"

What a funny time for a lecture, Judith thinks, when the patient is out of it, and probably not up for making rational decisions. Further, why hadn't his internist gotten on his case thirty or forty years ago? She and Betsy had. Judith had thrown cigarettes in the toilet, cut them up with scissors, and shown Eric pictures of people with emphysema, but he was sneaky and skilled at tuning you out if he didn't want to hear you.

Dr. Sanders slips away.

The abuse goes on and on. Judith is spared only while Eric is taken off for yet another CAT scan. He comes back, still angry and convinced the scene outside the windows is a picture.

"They're going to move us to a quieter spot after while."

"No. They will get rid of me."

"Now, now."

Judith looks at her watch. She's been standing by Eric's bed for hours, most of the time being told she is torturing him.

"If I go get something to eat will you be OK?" she asks.

Eric shakes his head.

"Stay. I don't want to get lost."

73

Oh God, Judith whispers to herself. She is getting desperate, wants to call for relief, but doesn't want to leave her husband. She rests her head on the metal railing of the hospital bed.

If only the damned beeper would stop going off and scaring her.

She looks into the aisle for someone who can see what is wrong, but there is an emergency and everyone is scurrying around on other business.

Eric is still mumbling.

"Don't leave. If we are separated they will get rid of us."

When he is not talking this way he is trying to escape from the bed and tearing at his restraints.

This out of control person can't be her husband, the most rational person Judith knows, usually amiable except for the few times he lost his temper during the boys' teen-aged years or the memorable moments when his impatience caused more than an exasperated glance at his watch or a string of swear words. He dealt with William and David's childhood misdemeanors with lectures that William could mimic perfectly, usually beginning, "Now you may not understand why such and such is not acceptable, but . . . ." and so on and so on.

The kids' friends were amazed to see them kiss their father, talk back to him, tease him.

This paranoid in a washed-out gown is Eric's opposite. Eric's thoughts were always clear as water.

Hospital aides come and go: a man from respiration with a mask for Eric to breathe into; a nurse who pricks his finger for a blood sample; people checking the monitors, on and on.

As promised, a nurse and orderlies come and move his bed and equipment to a quieter cubicle.

"I don't want this hospital. You're moving me to a new room. Why can't I go to a different hospital?"

"Eric please."

"This one is moving."

The new space is smaller than the other, with a similar view. Judith had planned to go home and rest after the move, but she can't find a calm moment when she feels she can leave. As the scene outside becomes completely dark, Eric is in China, he is on a boat, people are plotting to kill them. Men outside the window are going to start shooting any minute.

"Keep your head down," he warns Judith.

The room *is* threatening, she thinks; so much stuff hanging on the walls look like torture implements, weirdly reflecting the movement in the room; there is an extra stand for IVs, with deadly-looking hooks pointing toward the ceiling.

When their regular nurse comes in, Eric draws her to him, and Judith's hopes rise at the rational tone he speaks in for the first time that day.

"If it would not be too much trouble . . ." he whispers. Though exaggeratedly formal, this is more her husband. "If it would not be against your professional vows"—he points at the hooks—"would you help me go over there—so I can hang myself—"

Judith's heart turns to water. Does Eric truly want to kill himself?

The nurse takes Eric's pulse and leaves the room.

Eric keeps talking about suicide. Oh God, is he really suicidal? She has never been this scared.

The nurse returns with a hypodermic and approaches her patient.

"I think I better stay with him tonight," Judith says. She points to a recliner by the window. "I could crash in that chair there."

The nurse doesn't say no, so Judith stays while she gives Eric more sedative. Judith takes her shoes off and lies back in the chair, looking at the confusing lights outside and the ever-moving shadows in the corridor. As Eric gradually mumbles and tosses his way into dozing, she actually falls asleep even though the chair is incredibly uncomfortable and pops into the upright position every time she moves.

In the middle of the night, she is awakened by the lights going on and a tall blond nurse, a new one, rushing into the room. Eric's bed is covered with blood and blood is spraying all over the bed and walls. Judith leaps to her feet.

"What's happened?"

The nurse tries to stop the blood spurting out of Eric's side. Two male aides come in and tear off the bright red bedclothes while the nurse tries to get an IV into a vein. The blood keeps spewing.

Judith thinks her husband is bleeding to death.

"How bad is this?" she asks.

"He's losing a lot of blood . . . . he pulled his PICC line out," the nurse says. "We just have to get him set with a way to get his meds and IVs."

Judith watches anxiously as the team remakes the bed and sponge the blood off their patient. They turn him over and pull him on a pad to a comfortable position, like movers sliding heavy furniture over a floor. When he is cleaned up and sedated, silent and passive, Judith returns to her chair, feeling guilty for having fallen asleep. She wrestles with the uncooperative chair.

What if Eric lives but has blood in his brain, has had a stroke? Without that brain that guided him, ruled him, that was so admired by everyone who knew him: that wouldn't be her husband.

As he settles down, he reaches for her hand and presses it to his chest.

When the morning sun lights the room, Judith hears the cheery voice of Dr. Hale, Eric's primary physician, a handsome man about her husband's age, wearing a bright yellow shirt and brilliant red tie. He fills the doorway, smiling. He glances at his patient and says, "looking good." Then he adds, "Did you have an out of body experience?"

Judith sees him out. Does the man have no sense? He disappears, like the Cheshire Cat, leaving behind his scary smile.

The place is becoming ever more unreal.

A small man comes in, carrying a basket. He looks like Mrs. Tiggy Winkle.

"I'm Brendan," he says. "Mr. John Howard hired me to help out. I can take occasional weekdays and some nights." He goes to Eric and touches his shoulder. "Good morning, Mr. Howard." He is alert as a squirrel. He reaches into his basket and takes out a small quilt along with thread, needles, and patches.

With the new helper on duty, Judith goes into the waiting room and collapses into a chair. She calls David.

"I'll be there soon. I've gotten a dozen messages. Natalie's called a couple of times. Jerry Romano from the department. But I headed them off," David says.

"Good," Judith says. "Believe me, we're in no condition for visitors." She describes the Walpurgisnacht.

"Go on home. Maybe we've been a little too up about Dad's progress."

Judith drives home to the Tudor. The hospital neighborhood is not a safe looking one; David was right about that. She is light-headed and spacey, scared.

18

William

His Dad is in a private room now. There are chairs for visitors, a pull-out bed and a small bathroom. There is less window than in the ICU, just a slit like something in a dungeon.

Opposite the bed is a marker board and next to that a large clock. A nurse and aide come in. The aide writes the day's date on the marker board, along with her own name Joni and the nurse's name, Olga. The nurse takes his father's temperature and they leave. Later, a young woman comes in and wipes the names Joni and Olga from the marker board and writes her own name Viola and the name of the night nurse, Sheri. An African American woman, very slim and tall, comes in and sweeps the room with a wide broom. "I'm Lakesia," she says. When she has done her job, she silently leaves.

When the room quiets down and his father sleeps, William regards the man who had seemed so invincible, now deathly white, maybe dying or damaged. William regrets the bad times he's given him: his adventure on coke, dropping out of college. He is the only Howard who doesn't have some sort of advanced degree and a goal in life. Every other Howard was the "smartest kid in the class" at their various schools. His grandfather graduated from Harvard where he was the editor of the *Law Review*. His grandmother edited a book on Cincinnati architecture. His mother is a college professor. His big brother David is covering himself with glory at his law firm. William's dad had been on his way to the presidency of the university . . . .

"Your dad is the most intelligent guy I've ever known": people were always saying stuff like that. One of the city councilmen who hung around Over the Rhine, especially near election day, did a double take when he realized that William was the son of Eric Howard.

William's shabby jeans, T-shirt, and pony tail must have tagged him a member of the neighborhood element that represented the poor long-time residents against the developers and gentrifiers. Which he was.

"Much smarter than I'll ever be. Brilliant," the man went on.

Sometimes William got tired of his father's brilliance—it was too much to live up to.

William's head pounds: Guilty! Guilty! Because of the stress he caused the family. He was fifteen. Sitting in Betsy's garden, the water in her fountain plashing, the trees perfectly pruned, the rows of flowers neat as children dressed for church (Betsy could not tolerate a dead bloom or a single dried branch on a bush), William felt bored. He decided his family was too predictable, too comfortable, even smug.

They lived on a little island of privilege, while the rest of the world struggled for a footing.

The Discreet Charm of the Bourgeoisie, he thought. He bought a Che Guevara T-shirt.

He was going to East Hills Academy then. He had gotten jumped at his district high school for calling a bully a Neanderthal.

The guy knocked him to the floor, yelling, "I'm no fag, you fag," and kicked him while he was down. William's parents quickly popped him into private school, and it was there he met his friendly coke pusher, a preppy from a wealthy family, who took him to Over the Rhine for connections.

He took to blow like ice cream. Doing coke was so much more fun than sniffing glue. While high he could write some really cool shit; the girls loved him. He played the piano better—kicked up his heels and for a while had a high old time (pow!).

God, how great a small line or a little catnip would go now. Keep him cool. Help him deal with the idea of never being with the father he knew. He must call Tim for support soon. He needs one of his sponsor's hell-fire sermons.

Would he make it up to his father if he survived—go to law school or med school or into education? In high school he had been every teacher's dream. During his brief stint in college, he turned out papers his professors handed around to the class for the other students to learn from. His current publications: a couple of poems in an obscure journal and an article or two about Over the Rhine in *Street Voices*—not exactly Pulitzer Prize stuff. But hey—

Whatever, he shouldn't be thinking of himself. Get over yourself, he thinks.

Dr. Mittendorf, the orthopedist who operated on his father's knee comes in—a bland looking man with sandy hair and eyebrows. He pulls the sheet away from his patient's legs and unwraps the bandage on the right knee. The knee is swollen to twice its size, purple with blood and bound together by ugly stitches.

"Looks good," he says.

To William it looks like a rotten cantaloupe.

The doctor announces that his therapist Patty will be in soon to work the knee. And with that he is gone.

Patty, a cheery young woman with a high voice (William soon finds they are all cheery and have high voices), appears carrying a machine about the length of a leg to exercise the knee. She places it on the bed and William helps her strap his father's leg onto it, with much difficulty from an inert limb and a struggling patient. Patty puts ice bags over the knee, and plugs the machine into the wall socket under the bed. It begins to move the leg like a piston.

"What is this?" his father demands.

"It's to exercise your leg," William says. "Remember you had your bad knee replaced."

"Well, take it off."

"We don't want that knee getting stiff," Patty says. "Now just try it for me."

When she leaves, William pulls a chair alongside the bed while his father complains that the machine hurts.

The man is like a beetle on his back, a clunky box around his neck monitoring his heart, needles in his arms, a heart ticking away like a time bomb, a catheter up the man pipe, the sutured leg on a torture rack.

After an hour, Patty comes back and removes the exercise machine.

"I have to get up," his father says. "I have to pee."

When his father is not fussing over his ability to pee, he is groping about beneath his gown. We men sure are obsessed by our junk, William thinks.

His mother comes into the room.

"Doctors say he needs sleep and rest. And he's not eating anything."

81

William's father is trying to lie on his side but the bulky heart monitor prevents it. His mother tries to adjust it to make him more comfortable.

He continues to struggle.

"Stop. You're going to pull out your IV."

He grabs her wrists. He is surprisingly strong.

"You can't force me to stay here. I'm not your prisoner."

William's mother tries to pull away.

"I'll break your god-damned arm! You have no say over me."

William pushes between his parents, and loosens his father's grip. "You're in a hospital, Pop. You're very sick. You can't get all excited like this."

William's father quiets down a bit, kicks his sheet off and squirms.

William whispers to his mother, "He's like Jekyll and Hyde. The nurse gave him a sedative before. He ought to be winding down a little."

"Don't whisper about me," his father says. "I know what you're planning."

William holds up his hands in a peaceful gesture.

"To get you well is our only plan."

His father lies back down. In a few minutes he is dozing. "He bit the nurse who gave him a shot," William says. "Well, she claimed he bit her. Actually I think he was just gritting his teeth, and her arm got in the way—kind of."

"How long should this paranoia go on?"

"They're getting concerned. He called the nurse a bitch."

William's mother looks worried.

She sits with William for several hours

The slit of a window darkens like a slash down the wall.

"You go home now, I'll stay," William says.

His father keeps up his insane talk. Some machine beeps continuously; a nurse comes in and "fixes" it, only to have it start up again. And again. William feels worse and worse for whatever part he might have played in his father's becoming ill. He is dying for sleep. As things finally quiet down, and all the lights are off, the various aides come and go, dark shapes moving in and out of the room like burglars, then with dawn, becoming pale and changing into quiet stagehands.

Leaving his father after his long watch, William is so tired, the twisting turning hallways of the hospital morph into threatening angles and curves.

He hits the outside air with relief, but still feels unreal walking the blocks to his bus stop. In the nearly empty bus, he watches the streets go by—dark shapes of men on every corner trading money for drugs.

William slumps in his seat, his head resting on the grimy window. Was that his old dealer on that last corner? He looks back as the bus passes by. He feels an urge to get off and go back, but pushes it away.

He dozes off for a few moments, and is nudged by one of the neighborhood regulars.

"Your stop, man."

"Thanks."

William still feels light-headed walking the few blocks to his apartment.

David and Lydia often ask him if he isn't afraid in his neighborhood at night, afraid of being mugged. He isn't. And tonight, he thinks, compared to the time he just put in, mugging would feel good.

19

Judith

Judith listens to the sounds of the midnight hospital: a dropped pan, the squeak of a shoe in the hall. While Eric sleeps, she turns back again to the beginning of her and Eric's life together. Like turning the pages in a book to an earlier chapter. Had she read it right? Missed something?

"Are you gonna burn your draft card?"

"No. I'm not a conscientious objector."

They were in their small apartment in Chicago.

Judith admired Eric's stand, but felt scared.

"Will you get drafted?"

"My number's about up—as it were."

Judith must have betrayed her horror, for Eric laughed and said, "My only regret is that I have a life to give for my country."

"But—"

"My father was a god-damned hero in World War Two."

The voices at Ernie's got louder. The crowd had to do something. Force the Democrats to end the war. Then Martin Luther King was shot down in Memphis. Judith and Eric were stunned, sickened.

What was happening to their country? There was looting and burning and people killed nearby; Mayor Richard Daley's angry Boxer-dog face all over the newspapers and TV, urging the cops to "shoot to kill" any rioters.

"Daley is getting desperate," Eric said.

He was on the phone with his father every day or so. His father would be a delegate at the convention, staying at the Hilton with the others, right across Michigan Boulevard from the park where Eric and Judith would be protesting the war and the likely candidate they called "Hubert the Whore."

"Hubert Humphrey is a bag of wind. A sell-out," Eric yelled as Judith listened. "No way!"

Judith could only hear one end of their argument, but Eric was angry.

"I *will* be careful," he said. "You be careful. Not to continue this pointless mess."

Eric listened a moment.

"We're gonna be peaceful; we're getting permits."

"Won't your father kill you?" Judith asked when Eric hung up.

"Not if he believes in his own principles."

Eric was busy all summer working with MOBE (Mobilization to End the War, something something).

More death. They couldn't believe it: Bobby Kennedy shot and killed.

Everywhere in town were signs of things out of control. When Judith and Eric stopped in Ernie's one day, a group of Chicago policemen were at a nearby table, in uniform, drinking beer. They weren't wearing badges but still carrying guns. They took in Judith and Eric's jeans and head bands and long hair with contempt.

The whole city was like a pair of boxers warming up.

Then Czechoslovakia. Soviet tanks down the main streets, flattening everything in their way.

All the energy of Eric and Judith and their friends was aimed at August. Mobilizing, planning. Gathering converts. When the delegates arrived for the convention in "Czechago," as the students called the city now, the place was set for battle. Judith and Eric marched downtown with a crowd: the MOBE group, the Yippies, the SDS. Among thousands, linking arms in a righteous cause; it was a better high than any drug. Judith and Eric were angry, ecstatic, strong, their cheeks fresh as apples.

Judith could see the police lined up along Michigan, a solid line of blue, of shields and guns, helmets, gas masks. Her dream fascists. Her legs shook and she looked back toward campus, but she marched into the crowd in the park, like a soldier following the recruit in front of him, trying not to think. A man dressed as Uncle Sam strode around on stilts; kids in sneakers and jeans and dashikis draped themselves in American flags. From all sides came voices raised in anger, rage, and joy. People were snake dancing, singing. The sounds of hard rock pounded in Judith's head.

TV cameras were everywhere, poised for violence. It was expected, maybe longed for. Someone pitched a garbage can through the big glass lobby window of the Hilton where Eric's father was staying. Eric flinched, looked up at the windows of the hotel as though searching for his father's face.

The night of the convention, Judith and Eric waited and waited with the protesters. The air was full of threat, everyone listening, waiting. The city's nerves taut. Guns aimed at the park.

Around ten o'clock, voices called out. "Humphrey's in. The peace plank is out!" spread through the crowd. Everybody was yelling, and began stampeding the bridges to the city to rush the convention hall. One of the young men lowered the American flag.

The police came at them like dogs released, swinging clubs and grabbing hair, spewing tear gas. People were battling back with sticks and rocks. Police wagons came screaming in and kids were dragged and prodded into them. Blood everywhere. Curses and yells. Judith and Eric were knocked down, breathed grass and feet and dust.

Two policemen grabbed Eric and pushed him toward a wagon. He fought back, cursing and kicking. His shirt was torn. His head was bleeding. He shouted "get away" to Judith. She pulled hard on the policeman's jacket, but he pushed her off and they threw Eric into the wagon and closed the door on him. Judith watched it pull away with a horrible whine. Where were they taking him? She was lost. Pushing and shoving people all around. Screaming, yelling, shouting, crying. Where was the jail? She screamed for help. But there was no one to help. She must get back to the apartment, see if she could reach anyone to find Eric. She was swallowed up by a crowd barging across the one open bridge to the city and was carried along by stampeding bodies. She could hear the sounds of sirens, voices, bull horns behind her as she ran to the IC station.

On the rackety IC car, exhausted, smelly, panicked, Judith slumped in her seat. The other passengers glared at the her and muttered, "hippie." She gave them a peace sign when she got off. She trudged through the dark streets of the neighborhood, depressed, dirty, her hands cut, her eyes stinging from tear gas, her skinned knees burning.

She walked up the steps to the apartment wearily, sat down in the chair by the window and looked out at the yard, yellow in the flickering street light. What was happening to Eric? She looked up the number of the police and called the city precinct, but the line was busy. It was busy all night as she watched and waited. Was he being beaten? Anyone who could help would be in jail also or at the protest site. She watched for Eric until the light began to come up in the morning.

Her back was aching and fear overwhelming her when finally she saw a dusty, ragged figure get out of a taxi and climb the cement steps of their building. Judith ran down to Eric. He pushed her away.

"Where were you? What did they do to you?" she asked.

"Jail. I'm OK."

There was dried blood and dirt on his head and neck.

"I didn't know what to do," Judith said.

"Of course not."

"How did you get out?"

"My father," he said, disgusted.

He flung himself on the bed.

"God Damn it!" he said. He wiped his face on a pillow.

Judith went to the bathroom and got a pan of water and a wash cloth. She bathed the cuts on Eric's head, and cleaned his hands.

"There's a whole jail full of people down there. I should be with them."

"I'll get you something to eat."

Judith fixed Eric a plate of scrambled eggs. When she returned to him, he was calming down. He pushed the eggs away. He looked terribly tired.

She rubbed his sore shoulders. She licked his face like a mother cat.

Later that night they made love, angrily, then sweetly, and all the following week.

Eric begins thrashing around in his hospital bed. Judith rubs his arms, but he stays restless.

"Would you like for me to lie down with you?" Judith says.

Eric doesn't object so she lowers the bed rail and crawls in beside him. The bed is very narrow, but it feels good to cuddle him in her arms. He begins to relax.

Judith whispers, "Eric, do you remember us?"

20

John

He was eighteen when the notice came. He went down town to the draft board to be inducted. It never occurred to him to do anything else. Everybody was going. They were an army of righteous Americans fighting to defeat the Nazis and the Japanese. The war was the turning point of his life. The greenest of the green, he had never kissed a girl or shot a gun or lived among other men. Never known the kind of guys he went to basic training with: big guys from the hills who charged into bayonet practice happily, while John didn't like stabbing even the practice dummy. Then there he was, being sent overseas in a crowded ship, he and the others in slings like insects, one on top of the other, little room to breathe; then riding to the front in a train car, a "forty and eight," which held forty men or eight cattle, digging a fox hole and hoping to survive the bombs landing all around him. Seeing comrades explode like bags of blood, dragging his buddy to safety. He had a silver star.

He came home a man. He was proud of his service. But after the bombs exploding in his ears, the dying, mutilated buddies, the dirt and sickness, the blood, he wanted peace.

The years after the war were the best. He found his beautiful Betsy at Finley Market where she worked at her family's cheese stall; she was like a Magic Lily, which grows straight up and leafless from among humbler plants—actually she was surrounded by broccoli, and cabbages and turnip greens. On their honeymoon in Europe, they walked the streets of Paris and Rome, proud Americans, heroes striding along the streets; good-looking, healthy, rich.

They were young, strong, with a great future.

At home, they settled down. John went to law school. Betsy produced a healthy daughter and a son. They were a typical American family. Dinner on the table at six. Car pools to scouts and lessons. Baseball in the back yard. Vacations camping. Kids doing well in school and college.

When Eric was a boy, he and John were tennis partners, Little League winners. They rigged up a zip line from a tree in front of the castle to the second floor balcony, and Eric and Adrian would go whizzing through the air on it. Eric regularly beat John and Adrian at pool in the basement. What happened to that wonderful boy? All of a sudden he became so serious, skipped the family games, stopped getting haircuts and grew his hair below his shoulders. It looked sissified to John, who wore his hair in a short military cut from army days (a trustworthy manly cut like Glenn Ford's). John didn't know what to make of the hair, and his music and his sudden bad language (John had never said fuck in his life).

Then there they were on opposite sides of Michigan Avenue in Chicago. Eric with the rag tag crowd in Grant Park, himself in the Hilton planning to cast his vote for Hubert Humphrey. John's memories are all but faded. Odd details stand out. Someone put a sign on the men's lavatory hot-air dryer: "Press here for a speech by Hubert Humphrey."

He had to laugh: Humphrey *was* a bit of a windbag, and John was disappointed by the fact that he had not yet come out against the war, but he had called the delegates and assured them that he would as soon as he was nominated (how impressed John had been by a call from the vice-president of the country!). Eric's sobriquet, "Hubert the Whore," hurt (because there was a little bit of truth in it)—but John still thought Humphrey a decent man, just hanging on tight to President Johnson's coattails, to secure the nomination. That was politics.

At the convention hall, John was pushed and shoved among the crush of yelling factions—Daley sitting high up in the stands surrounded by his minions like a tin-horn dictator, cursing and shaking his fist at the peace representatives.

In the midst of all this, John was worrying about Eric out in the streets; TV news and stories were going around the hall about tear gas and police clubbing the protesting kids.

He was frantic when a young man in an HHH hat came to the delegation and told him Eric had been arrested. John left the convention and cabbed to the police station. Was Eric hurt? His head bashed open? John rushed through the questions at the police desk, pulling rank as a lawyer and delegate. He was led to the cell where Eric was piled in with a crowd of kids. He was ragged and beat and dirty. Relief and shame flooded John's body. His son, in jail. Behind bars. No Howard had ever been in jail.

Eric was so angry. As they sat waiting for his release, he said, "Your man's no better than Nixon."

"You'll see." John put Eric in a cab and the boy didn't look back. John returned to the convention.

Back in the crowd, John found himself joining the chant "No more war, no more war"—

He had not told Eric about that—not for any reason—just that time and life moved on. He felt guilty later that he had supported the war as long as he had. Eric was right about it, and John had hung on to his opinions because marches and mobs were not what he grew up with, and from loyalty to his own political connections. He had learned from his son.

Had he ever told him so? Had he shown Eric what he said to the local newspaper about the convention: "Mayor Daley has done for Chicago what Lee Harvey Oswald has done for Dallas." He was rather proud of it. Eric would have appreciated it. But again—

They had never crossed the street dividing them: Michigan Avenue.

He and Eric never talked about those days. The rift faded somewhat in time but never went away. John was still annoyed—no, damn it, mad—at the way Eric wrote about *his* time in his books. Questioning the good war and America's part in it: revision based on no experience of war, no knowledge of what it was like when John was young: calling the atomic bombs dropped on Japan racist, questioning Pearl Harbor. John resented having his war stolen, his history changed, his story revised, his life rewritten. Eric had not seen men killed or walked through the streets of London watching the people clear the rubble brick by brick—

John had sat on a broken wall among dust and bombed out houses, buried corpses, fallen houses and churches and stores. He found a pair of false teeth in the crumbled mortar. Where was the person it belonged to? One of the front teeth was hanging loose, and he, oddly, pointlessly, tried to work it back into place.

When he came home from his war, he didn't sit on his ass. Like his son, he had ideals. His own fire. His pride. He had worked to change the ward system in the city and helped get rid of old-time party bosses. Long before the civil rights movement, he had worked to get black people into the local amusement park, and theaters and restaurants and clubs (and gotten a black eye to prove it). He worked to elect the first black mayor of the city. He marched in Selma.

Well, he supposes, *Today's Young Turk is tomorrow's Old Fart.*

When John and Betsy visit Eric's hospital room, they are pushed aside by one attendant after another: a man checks respiration with a plastic mask, another gives breathing exercises with a yellow ball in a tube, a young woman brings in the leg machine with its constant thirst for ice. Eric is given blood and insulin tests (needles in the arm and stomach). The various personnel repeatedly ask Eric where he is and what his name is, his birthday.

Dr. Sanders comes in bringing the heart surgeon. John's friend, the hospital medical director, has recommended this man, Dr. Graham, as the best. He is tall, has white hair, and is dressed in a white lab coat. He is followed by an equally tall, thin, female acolyte. They shout good morning to Eric (most everyone on the staff shouts), look him over, with Dr. Sanders standing by.

"We need to schedule Mr. Howard for a bypass as soon as possible," Dr. Graham says, "there's a leaky valve along with the two blocked arteries. But first we need to clear up the kidneys. The blood pressure and insulin are high."

John and Betsy exchange looks of fear.

Kidneys? This is a new one on John. His friend had said Eric could recover if his kidneys and lungs held out. Further, he wonders if it is wise to discuss the surgery in Eric's hearing while he is so weak and vulnerable. Should he be worrying about the future right now, when his job is to reclaim his sanity and gain some weight for the strength to go through a second difficult and dangerous operation?

Dr. Sanders says, "We must get past this confusion too. I hear he was terribly agitated again. We want his mentation sound."

"Right," Dr. Graham says. The acolyte takes notes.

They talk to John and Betsy and into pagers at the same time. Dr. Graham looks at his watch and they hurry away.

"He's like the White Rabbit in *Alice*," Betsy says. "His *mentation?* What kind of word is that? *Mentation!*"

"How bad is his mind?" John asks.

Dr. Sanders frowns. "This kind of thing is usually temporary, but it can be more serious."

He murmurs into his pager, and leaves.

Betsy looks rocky to John. He wants her out of this sick room.

"Maybe you could go to one of those malls and get Eric a robe," he says. "I'll stay with him."

Betsy demurs, but at John's insistence, leaves. She is the queen, but when he uses a certain tone of voice, she gives in.

Eric waves goodbye to her, saying he will see her at dinner, and babbling something about having a scotch together in a bar.

When John and Eric are alone, Eric says, "Dad, will you do me a favor?"

"Of course."

"See if you can find my car keys. I need to go over to the office and do some work today."

"Son, can we postpone that until you feel better?"

"I'd rather not—but If you say so. I guess I'm the prisoner here." Eric closes his eyes.

A moment or two later he announces that he must go to the bathroom. His legs are so weak it takes John and a nurse's aide to guide him to the toilet. The aide doesn't return when John pushes the buzzer for her, so he wipes and washes his son as though he were a baby.

Back in bed, Eric drifts off to sleep.

John thinks: this is so wrong. In the natural order of things, if one of them were to be near death, it should be the father. Here he is back to cleaning his son who can't make it to a bathroom on his own. Like a baby. John recalls getting up in the middle of the nights when Eric was first born. Betsy slept like a stone and it was often his job to give Eric his bottle and change his diaper. His tiny red penis was wrinkled like an unfledged baby chick. He was such a cute little fellow. When he was older he would stand in his crib and Betsy would sing "Goodnight Sweetheart" to him.

I suppose I haven't been a close father, John thinks. Not one to have personal talks with my son; Betsy did all that.

John is glad that now he and Eric are at least on the same side politically, both members of the city's reform party, and together in this dark year, outraged by the lies, the spying, the torture, the greed, the country turning into a place of super-wealthy and hopeless poor. Above all, the pointless war that is all about oil and American hegemony, maybe even a son's desire to prove his father wrong.

21

Judith

She first met John and Betsy at the castle. She and Eric had come to Cincinnati to let them know about their plans to get married. The battle between Eric and his father in Chicago had left both offended. Eric refused to work for Humphrey, and his father accused him and his fellow "peaceniks" of accomplishing the doubtful goal of electing Nixon.

Betsy and John were part of the hated "over thirty" generation that could not be trusted. They were materialistic, authoritarian, elitist, part of the system, up tight. Their lifestyle was pretentious.

Judith was angry at her father also. He was anti-black, anti-women, anti-gay.

She didn't know any good parents.

Eric had told Judith that his parents lived in a castle and his mother reigned there like a queen. But she had thought he was exaggerating. She had seen some palatial homes in Chicago and Cleveland, most now museums or funeral parlors, but never a real castle on a suburban street right next to Colonials, Tudors, and modern ranch houses. The Howard castle had a bell tower, Gothic windows, stained glass. As she and Eric walked up the flagstone path to the front door, Judith felt in her purse and fingered a joint for luck. She expected a uniformed footman to open the door, but it was opened by Eric's mother.

She was slim, somewhere in her forties Judith judged, with beautiful translucent skin. Her hair was teased a la Jackie Kennedy into a dark halo around her well-sculpted face. She was wearing stockings, heels, and a gray and pink St. John's knit. Oh boy, Judith thought.

"I'm Betsy," she said. She held out her hand to Judith and kissed Eric on the cheek.

"Eric, your hair," she said.

Eric felt his long locks. "What's wrong with it?"

"Nothing I guess." She appraised Judith, who in spite of her contempt for fashion, felt suddenly dowdy in her earth shoes and ankle-length cotton dress.

Walls went up. Judith couldn't think of a thing to say, and Eric was no help.

Betsy led them into a small sitting room off the great hall and an enormous formal living room. "Sit," she said. They sat in antique velvet chairs and it seemed no one could think of anything to say.

"So how is Castle Howard going?" Eric finally asked.

"Pretty well," Betsy said. "I'm working on the second floor bedrooms. I've uncovered some beautiful woodwork. Dear Ralph is researching it before I do anything drastic."

"Dear Ralph is Mom's fag friend," Eric said.

He looked around the room.

"You could house a dozen poor families in here."

"I don't want a dozen poor families in here," Betsy said.

Eric scowled. His social conscience was not being taken seriously.

"Did you ever hear the term limousine liberals?" he said.

"Yes, they're people who have become affluent themselves, but have not lost their concern for others nor their principles."

Wow, Judith thought. She could see where Eric got his sharp tongue—

Eric looked annoyed. Judith could not see how they could make a wedding announcement at the moment. It was hopeless. Too much tension in the air. Eric's parents would never like her. Now she just wanted to shock Betsy, so she pulled out the joint she had been saving for after this was all over.

"Do you like pot?" she said.

Betsy gave her a long appraising look.

"Why not really, dear," Betsy said, "I think I'll stick to my martinis. But you go right ahead."

Judith was so taken aback she popped the marijuana back into her purse.

"Now that I think of it, it is about time for cocktails," Betsy said. "Let's go to the kitchen and mix up a batch. Eric, your father will be along soon."

Judith and Eric followed Betsy into a cavernous kitchen, something like the ones in English costume movies. She took frosted stem glasses out of the freezer and a bottle of gin from the refrigerator. She studiously mixed a batch of martinis in a Steuben glass pitcher and poured herself a drink.

"Judith?" she said.

Judith nodded. Why not? Things couldn't get any worse.

Eric, still scowling, said he would wait for his father.

Judith's drink came in a crystal stem glass with a plump olive in it. It smelled like perfume. Judith took a tentative sip. She had never drunk a martini before. It was really cold. It tasted like perfume might. It seemed to flow right into her veins.

Eric looked as though he could use a little of Betsy's bar tending. He paced the kitchen, struck a pan among a row hanging from a rack above the island, starting a series of tinny sounds. Betsy led the way into the sitting room. Betsy and Judith sat down with their drinks, while Eric walked to the window, pushing aside the heavy drapery and peering out.

"Here comes Dad," he said. He tensed up further. The three heard a car pull into the port cochere, then the side door open and the sound of a person hanging up his coat and dropping his briefcase on a table.

John appeared at the doorway, paused and took in the scene. He was tall, slim, with Eric's noble nose, but a more hesitant expression. He looked Eric over appraisingly, concentrating on his son's hair. His hello was abrupt. Judith thought he might be deciding whether to shake Eric's hand or embrace him. He did neither, but took a seat next to Betsy.

The election of Nixon was a continuing sore point between him and Eric. It was almost as though the man himself were sitting right there in the room in one of Betsy's velvet chairs.

"Dad, this is Judith," Eric said.

"Happy to meet you."

"Do you want a drink?" Betsy asked.

"Why not?"

Betsy stood.

"Eric?"

"Just a beer. I'll get it."

"I'll have a beer too," John said.

"You always have a martini after work," Betsy said.

"Always is a long time."

For a sharp woman, Judith thought, Betsy seemed to miss the fact that John might be trying to find some small common ground with his son.

John laughed. Judith was relieved.

"One beer, one martini," he told Eric, and Eric went to the kitchen.

Judith saw John look her over surreptitiously. Her shapeless gown suddenly seemed more pretentious than the St. John knit. She wished she'd worn something a little nicer.

"Where are you from, Judith?"

"A little of everywhere. I lived in Louisville—and Cleveland— oh a long time ago, for a short time."

John spoke slowly as though picking his way along a path full of word boulders. Judith decided that he was shy.

Eric's parents were so different from hers, she thought. Her father was the dominant one, kept her mother, who spent her days playing cards and sipping wine, in her place. Here it looked as though Mother called the shots.

Eric returned with a martini in a juice glass and a can of beer.

"There are steins and cocktail glasses in the pantry," Betsy said.

"This is fine." Eric handed his father the martini and took a long swig from his beer.

"We haven't seen you for awhile, Eric," John said.

"Well. We thought we should tell you our plans in person."

"I hope you're not thinking of dropping out of school. Everyone's kids are dropping out, or changing universities or something."

"No. Judith and I are getting married, this summer."

Both parents took a moment to digest this statement.

"You're pretty young," John said.

Betsy took a longer time to react.

"It's fine with us. But why would you want to get married?" she said. "You've been living together, I gather happily, for quite awhile, right?"

Judith was shocked; she liked to think of herself as unshockable, but Betsy's attitude was so unexpected. Her own mother was so disapproving, fought with Moira over her sexual activities. Her father (when Moira told him what Judith was doing) actually called Eric her "paramour." Her mother never mentioned Eric's name until Judith told her they were going to be married.

Everyone was scrambling for terms to designate a live-in partner; there had been no vocabulary for what was becoming a trend. 'Roommate' was too silly; 'significant other' was making the rounds.

"Will you want a big wedding?" Betsy asked.

"God no," Eric said.

"Where are your parents living now?" John asked Judith.

"Pittsburgh."

"We might get married here," Eric said.

"Here?" Betsy asked. "Here at home or in Cincinnati?"

Eric sort of gulped. "Cincinnati. In a park."

"That would be lovely. But it will surely rain or be too hot. We can have it in the great hall, or the garden if it's nice. I better get the bedrooms finished and the gilding on the pier glass repaired, and—"

"We don't want any fuss, Mother," Eric said. "Just something simple. You don't have to do anything. We—don't even know exactly when or anything . . . . I mean, it's just—we're just thinking about it."

"I see."

The rest of the interview went as awkwardly as the initial meeting. Eric announced that he and Judith had to leave to meet a friend, blocking his mother from taking over and making further plans. John looked dazed.

"I guess congratulations are in order," he said.

At the door, Betsy also seemed puzzled and unsure. John put his arm around her shoulder. Judith had never seen a tender gesture like that between her parents.

Betsy flashed Eric and Judith the peace sign. They hadn't told her and John about the baby.

22

Betsy

At first Eric and Adrian had loved the castle. It was empty, dark, spooky, with electric bulbs hanging on wires from the ceilings. A family with a half dozen children, a pack of wolfhounds, and no money had been living there for years, but finally the bills destroyed their day dreams.

Eric and Adrian slid down the long banisters, climbed out on the turrets with the pigeons, camped all over the place in sleeping bags and frightened their friends with tales of hauntings, stagings of which they arranged for friends sleeping over.

But as they grew older, her kids were embarrassed by the pretentiousness of their home, growing more so as Betsy began to renovate and restore its original opulence.

Eric was absorbed in his stamp collection, his books on history, baseball and tennis. Adrian liked to cook, camp, and take care of animals; she had dogs and cats, guinea pigs, white rats. Betsy gave up trying to change her children, and tolerated their interests as long as the less domestic animals stayed in Adrian's room and the kids' stereos were played on the third floor. The dogs were allowed the run of the house (though not on the furniture); after all, Betsy and John always had their own—ever shrinking in size from a St. Bernard to little Ginger, a tiny long-haired Dachshund. She probably ought to be put to sleep, Betsy thought; she was totally blind, incontinent, and too weak to walk, but John claimed she was basically healthy and lifted her gently from her bed and carried her, like a little soaked rag, to the lawn supposedly to empty her bladder.

Betsy told herself she and John were lucky to be tolerated by Eric and Adrian. They were growing up in an era of lost children—The bombs and riots, kids teargassed, jailed, that girl shot by the National Guard, young people "dropping out," turning against their families, some dead on drugs.

To mold one's children to one's desire was an unproductive struggle—to see inside their heads, to know their dreams—impossible.

Betsy gave up her notion of beautiful weddings for her children. Adrian worked on and off as a "wilderness guide," and was living with another woman in the California mountains, where she bathed in a tin tub and at sundown could hear the roaring of mountain lions—And anyway, if she married, she wouldn't be the bride of Betsy's dreams; she ate like Betsy's German relatives and had the figure to show for it.

At least Eric had agreed that if the weather turned out miserable, he and Judith would shift their ceremony from the park they had picked out to the castle.

"But no fuss," he decreed.

"You must have flowers," Betsy said.

"They throw away perfectly good ones at the florist's."

"Really they do," Judith assured her, and Betsy found herself accompanying her son and future daughter-in-law to the dark, littered alley behind the nearby florist, plucking good blooms from among the wilted and dead.

"What about food?" Betsy asked. "I have a good caterer."

"We can cook it," Judith said. "And people will bring things."

She and Eric dragged Betsy to the market to buy vegetables. The young people loved it: the men yelling from one stall to another; the hall with its ceiling of hams and turkeys hanging above the butchers' counters; the twisted, braided, and foot-long breads.

"Oh, this is great," Judith said.

"Mom used to work here," Eric said.

"No way."

"That stall called 'CHEEZ' used to be Keysey's, and her family ran it."

Betsy caught Judith's look: she was expecting a more elegant background.

Eric sang to the tune of *Molly Malone*: "She *was* a cheese monger/ Sure and it is no wonder/ For her father and mother were cheese mongers too."

Betsy laughed. Eric was fond of reminding her of her modest origins. She didn't resent it. He could do no wrong.

The day of the wedding, the heavens blackened and poured rain. Even the park shelter was flooded and Eric had to agree to being married in a castle.

The place looked as though the gypsies (or Rom, Betsy had been warned) had set up camp: the guests wore tie-dyed skirts and shawls, even the bride (she had fallen in love with Betsy's white wedding dress, but couldn't get the side zipper to close over her growing belly). Her lack of a bra was evident when she moved. The discarded flowers were in glasses and jars all over the place and people arrived with dishes covered in foil. Eric would not allow Effie to serve; she came as a guest along with her daughter, a pretty teenager with corn rows. The vows were written by the bride and groom, the obey rule omitted and replaced by generous escape clauses. The ceremony was presided over by Reverend Allen, who had recently been defrocked by the Presbytery. He wore a checked polyester suit that looked as if it had come from the Free Store.

Adrian, who had come home for the event (tracking mud onto the carpets and leaving drink rings on priceless furniture), wore a gray dress with her slip hanging about six inches below the hem in back. She wasn't wearing a bra either. Betsy had gone to Saks to find something to wear, something "mother of the groomish," beige silk or a Pucci sheath, but nothing she was shown seemed right. She finally settled on a cotton skirt made in Jamaica and an expensive appliquéd T-shirt. Her regular clerk grimaced.

"But Mrs. Howard, it's not you."

"I know," Betsy said, "but neither is this wedding."

Eric had invited all Betsy's relatives who were still alive, along with the more conservative, well-dressed Howard clan. He wanted to connect with his roots. Judith's father and mother came. He asked questions about how much it cost to run the castle. Judith's mother seemed not quite there. The sister, Moira, was drying out at some clinic.

The music was provided by William's friends: steel drums, flutes, recorders, harmonicas.

Actually, as the evening went on and everyone got good and drunk and whirled around to polkas for the Keyseys and rock for the young people, Betsy threw herself into the dancing crowd, doing her best to follow their gyrations. She tried to get John to join in the feverish whirl, but he stood to the side, wryly observing the events. Betsy danced with Adrian and several of Eric's friends. When the rain let up, Eric and some of the other young men raced outdoors to shoot baskets. Betsy was horrified as Judith hitched up her skirts and, along with Adrian, chased after them, and the evening continued until very late with a wild basketball game, David in utero.

Why had they not known how happy they were? Betsy wonders. When she looked back, her whole life seemed beautiful, even the times of stress were sweet and valuable, things to recite and savor like beloved poems. To think she had gotten angry when Eric had driven across the street to mail a letter when he first learned to drive; it was funny. That she had been perturbed by Judith's messy hair and her forgetting to put up draperies in the den, neglecting to sterilize the baby bottles, her fussiness about Adrian's weight. Her quarrels with John. He hadn't supported her ambition to be an architect. They didn't share their interests: she had her book, *The History of Rookwood.* He had his, their financial records.

Betsy takes her turn wearily to sit with Eric at the hospital. She reads to him: *Gulliver,* a childhood favorite. Her poor boy is like Gulliver among the Lilliputians, far from home, tied down and helpless.

Betsy studies the marker board in Eric's room. It has become a palimpsest of dates and names: Rick over Toni; Shari over Beth; Amanda over Steve; there is Amy and Janet and Debbie, Viola, Chuck. And there is always Lakesia, who comes and goes with her wide broom. She sweeps and leaves. Sweeps and leaves. She is like a recurring character in an Absurdist play. Who is she? Is she hope? Is she death?

So much depends on Eric living. He must make peace with his father. If he could see his devotion and care . . . But though the doctors keep saying Eric's paranoia is temporary, and give it a nice name, it isn't better at all. He mumbles a lot of nonsense and tears at his IV cord and monitor.

23

David

The paranoia hangs on. The injured heart is like a ticking bomb. They all know surgery is not going to happen as soon as the surgeon would like.

Jerry Romano, his father's best friend in the history department, calls. May he come and visit? David puts him off. It doesn't need to get around the department that his father is out of his mind. There's nothing more petty than academic politics. Everyone has such sharp vocabularies, such nice manners, and such clever ways of doing one in.

Jerry is a loyal colleague, an ally in the fairly constant academic skirmishes in the department. Still, a chance remark, even well-intentioned, is better avoided.

David's father had already, before he became ill, had his hands full with claims of sexual harassment on the part of junior faculty, tenure issues, ideological feuds, demanding parents, and troubled students.

For an impatient man, he was known as a peace maker. He had come into the field at a time when Western Civilization was being attacked on all sides. Women, African-Americans, gays and transvestites, native Americans, all wanted *their* stories told.

David's father could see their point. Of course, they wanted their point of view studied and to have control of it. "Diversity" became the watchword. But he had to fight off the more extreme feminists who wanted to purge the canon of "dead white males" (like Shakespeare? like Mill?), and one cross-gender professor who was just plain crazy (he tried to borrow a dress from Judith).

David's father admitted to the family that the various gender and ethnic groups sometimes fit their stereotypes uncomfortably for maintaining political correctness: the women frequently cried when they came into his office with problems, and his first black faculty member was always late for meetings ("Nigger Time," he claimed, defying disapproval of his lateness as well as the n-word). Jerry Romano, a big man with dark hair, the kind who had to shave twice a day, was ebullient and warm as a stage Italian.

After a decade of ethnic piling on, the winds shifted and no one wanted to use the word "diversity." "I can sneak it in," Jerry said, "but just not let on I'm doing it."

Deconstructionism, Post-Modernism, the trends followed one after another—and David's father worried that the facts were slipping away under the constant movements. Currently it was all about how to study history, the history of history—what is history? And who should write it? What were their motives? A discipline had become a battle ground; maybe it always was.

David's father had been dealing with several women who accused a colleague of displaying porn on his computer which they were forced to look at when they went into his office. A white teacher was suing over tenure, claiming prejudice, even though he lost the vote on his case unanimously. Twice.

As he enters his father's hospital room, David finds the usual chaos: the things necessary to the patient's well-being and comfort—his tissues, his urinal, his call button, his phone, his water, his breather—have a way of floating about the room out of reach. David locates them all and sets them in order on the bed table.

Vicky/Dan/Iris/Olga/Tim/Ginny/Linda/Larry/Debbie/Beth are mostly helpful but too busy to always follow the instructions laid down by the doctors. Communication seems nonexistent.

David hands his father the plastic tube he must use to exercise his lungs. The ball rises half way. Frank, one of the many respiratory technicians, pops in and puts a plastic mask over his mouth; a nurse administers a shot in the stomach.

"Insulin's low," she says.

What else can go wrong?

When the nurse leaves, David asks the usual: do you want TV, to be read to? Something to eat? Dr. Graham, in one of his hasty visits, has said let up on the hospital food regime—give the patient anything he asks for, to help him gain weight. David's father has requested hamburgers and French fries, his favorite meal, and David is planning a feast of junk food while his mother fusses, "we don't want to blow another artery."

"Mom, hush," William said. "You're like Lucy in *Peanuts*."

David wonders if his father's condition is inherited, or caused by his heavy smoking, or exacerbated by stress. William's detour into dope was no help. Or his mother's leaving. And recently his father had led a battle of the AAUP against the university, all the while keeping a restless faculty and hovering parents calm.

The mother of one of his students was making harassing phone calls protesting her daughter's final grade, and came to his father's office. When she could not get him to change the grade, she showed up at the house. David got a restraining order against her, but she continued her harassment, circulating vicious rumors on the Internet.

"I feel sorry for the girl," his father said. "She's so confused. In so much trouble. Her final essay was obviously off a computer. It won't help the girl to let her cheat."

David was touched by his father's concern for the student, and not himself. This episode wouldn't do his father's chances to head the university any good. Though the faculty was behind him, the board wasn't fond of him. Too radical. Too outspoken.

Some day, David thought, he would be like his father, holding out against low standards, the easy way that seemed to prevail everywhere. His father had always worked to change the world, not just go along. David vows to do more pro bono work for low-income people. Be a bigger man.

David figures his mother is not aware of what his father has been through with his crazy stalker. The woman came along after his mother left. Did Natalie know? Was she any help? Maybe. And maybe they had all underestimated how much such pressures affected his father's health.

While David ponders his father's life, the unit's therapist, a young preternaturally cheery girl named Kim, comes in and helps his father into the big chair. She measures the flexibility of the knee with calipers and forces it to bend. David can see his father wants to yell in pain.

"Did you ever work in Buchenwald?" he says.

"Hmm. I don't think so. What's Buchenwald?"

David's father looks distressed.

"You don't know what Buchenwald is?"

"Not really."

David's father gives Kim a succinct, thorough lecture on the subject of concentration camps. David is amazed that, even while so out of it, he can pull ideas right out of his brain, like a bear reaching into deep waters and coming up with a live fish. Maybe there's hope for his mental state.

As he talks, Kim's eyes get bigger and bigger.

"I've heard of Anne Frank," she says.

After she leaves, David's father complains about her ignorance of Buchenwald.

"She knew who Anne Frank was . . . ." David says.

"But does she know of Elie Wiesel and that Anne died in Belsen?"

David thinks: he is recovering from his psychosis. They can go ahead with the surgery.

Then: "So where should we go for dinner?" his father says.

Oh no.

David explains, as if to Phoebe at two: "Now, Dad, look down. You are on a heart monitor. In a hospital bed. You were just telling Kim about Anne Frank."

His father smiles.

"Fuck Anne Frank," he says. "Let's get the hell out of here."

24

Judith

A psychiatrist, a grave, dark-haired man, Dr. Gall, comes into Eric's room to test his "mentation" (Betsy's hated word again). While Judith watches, he sits by Eric's bed and asks questions like a stern schoolmaster: Who is the President of the United States? What month is it? Eric is told to count backward by sevens (he does better than Judith thinks she could do at her best). He has to repeat lists of things: table, chair, apple, dish, cat, bottle, in the correct order. Eric, always the brightest student in his class, seems eager to pass the man's test. Judith moves her lips, silently trying to help him along.

It is the first test he ever fails. He looks disappointed in himself, as though he knows he has not passed.

"He's not ready for rehab," Dr. Gall says. "If he does not become lucid soon we will have to transfer him to the psychiatric ward."

No, Judith thinks. Images of violent or zombie-like patients flash into her mind. The place would frighten Eric, might turn him truly mad. She doesn't like this doctor. His eyes are not kind.

"This mental state could be permanent," he says.

Terrifying words, pronounced coldly, in the tone of a punishing judge.

Dr. Gall prescribes another sedative, and says Eric should have a CAT Scan.

"He just had a CAT Scan," Judith says. She wonders if the doctors ever read one another's entries in the phone-book sized record in the hall.

"He needs rest and sleep."

The psychiatrist gets up from his chair. He has not once touched Eric.

Judith follows him into the hall.

"Do we have to talk so brutally in front of the patient?" she asks.

"The facts are brutal," he says, and takes off.

Judith goes back into the room. Eric looks dejected. He sits up in bed, his eyes unfocused.

Lakesia comes in with her wide mop and moves about, cleaning the room. She takes a look at the patient.

"He's over medicated," she says.

Later David and William arrive in the room together. Judith tells them of the psychiatric evaluation.

"Dad's not crazy," William says.

"No. And I don't want him going to a scary new place."

"The more they sedate him the wilder he gets," William says.

"All these sedatives do seem to be having the opposite effect on him," Judith tells them. "Lakesia says he's over medicated."

"Mom, Lakesia's the cleaning woman," David says.

"Yes, but I think she may be right."

"She is right. He's like on a drug high," William says. "I've seen plenty of this. He's trying to come down, but then they pump him up again."

"He's got to sleep."

When the psychiatrist's "new" sedative comes in a little paper cup, after William and David have gone, Judith asks what it is. It is exactly what he has been taking all along.

Judith is furious. Frightened. Eric may never come back. She has lost hold of his hand and he is slipping away from her. They will never say what needs to be said, do what needs to be done. No one knows the answers. Not Eric. Not the doctors. Not her. The air around Eric is swarming with Goya monsters, demons snatching people up by their hair with their talons, witches flying into and out of his head.

Part 3

QUEEN OF HEARTS

25

Judith

Nothing disgusts her, nothing is too much for her while she is in Eric's hospital room. But when she leaves the narrow world of Eric and his body she often feels spacey trudging through the long, confusing hallways of the hospital, across the hot, sometimes rainy parking lot to her car. The endless stretch of concrete is always crowded with cars, so each time she comes to the hospital, she has to park in a different row or ramp, and scribble a diagram in a small notebook of where she is located. Sometimes Brendan has to walk her to her car.

Coming back to the house one afternoon, Judith feels so depleted she stops in the driveway for a moment before she walks to the front door. Once inside, she pitches her purse on the hall bench and flops down on the living room couch. When had she last had a bath, washed her hair?

She is almost asleep when the doorbell rings. She is tempted to ignore it, but her car is in the driveway. There is no escape.

She opens the door to a young woman standing on the pathway. There is no doubt in her mind who she is.

"Judith?" the woman says.

"Natalie?"

"I just came over to—well—" Natalie says.

The two women check each other out: faces, figures, hair. Natalie is pretty, slim, and has shiny brown hair, cut to sharp points like Lydia's. She is wearing shorts and flip-flops, her perfectly pedicured toenails painted red-pink. Her tank-top shows ample cleavage and a tiny red heart tattooed on her right breast.

"How is Eric?" Natalie says. "I can't get much from the hospital."

Judith is too stunned to answer.

"May I come in?" Natalie says. "Just for a minute?"

Where *are* my manners, Judith thinks. "Of course." She opens the door wide. Offers Natalie a seat by the fireplace. Natalie seems poised, about William's age, but with a smooth self-confidence.

"I think it's time you let up on the family-only arrangement," she says. "Eric will be wondering why I haven't come to visit."

"He's not in any condition for visits right now," Judith says. By strangers, she is tempted to add, along with "your lover is about to be put in the psych ward."

"There's really no hospital policy about my coming."

Judith grants Natalie has honored the family's decision.

"I might be of some help to him."

"Really, we will let you know . . . ."

"I called to see how the knee went and they said fine."

"It hasn't helped preparing him for heart surgery. You know his heart stopped."

"Heart attacks aren't fatal."

"His heart stopped. It was not—"

"You probably all feel angry at me and Eric," Natalie says.

Yes indeed, Judith thinks.

"But I can't stay away forever. Eric may be distressed by my not showing up."

To Judith, it sounds strange to hear Natalie use Eric's name; Natalie's Eric is someone different from her Eric. As Lydia's David is someone different from Judith's.

A walnut thuds onto the lawn near the open door.

"I'll give you my card," Natalie says. She digs in her purse. Her shirt shows more cleavage (even when Judith was young, you didn't show your breasts the way young women do now. She is beginning to feel like Betsy must have when she appeared bra-less in her shapeless hippie outfits).

Natalie is deeply tanned (has she never heard of melanoma? But Eric wouldn't hold this against her—he himself ignored all health rules).

Natalie finds her card and hands it to Judith.

"Natalie Bender." Her firm is Allied Communications.

"I sell software to computer companies. I used to be a secretary at the university, but I got bored of it and moved on."

Natalie reminds Judith of Lydia: apparently sure of her rights, her ability to move on when something does not please her. That there would be firm ground under her feet.

She hates her.

"I'm on my way back to the hospital now," Judith says. "I had better go. My sons need relief."

"I will call in a day or two and I can come over then."

Judith doesn't argue. She can't hold Natalie off forever.

Judith sees her to the door. As Natalie gets in her car, she calls over her shoulder. "I'm taking flying lessons!"

When she returns to the hospital that night, Judith finds William and David in Eric's room. they look worried.

"He's still talking crazy," William says. "He called the nurse a bitch."

Judith tells her sons about meeting Natalie.

"She's very insistent about visiting."

"Fine," William says. "Let's give her the night shift."

They have to laugh at the picture of Natalie stuck with Mr. Hyde, the terror of the cardiac unit.

"She's not smart enough for Dad. She won't last," William says.

"She's got that bratty kid named MacKenzie," David adds.

"She's pretty and young," Judith says. "She's taking flying lessons."

"She writes 'you're' for 'your' and dots her i's with little circles," David says.

"A capital crime," William says. "Like smiley faces."

Judith is touched by their loyalty. She makes up the pullout bed, and when her sons leave, crawls onto it exhausted.

Brendan comes in at eight in the morning.

"You look *tired*," he says. His soft voice is full of genuine concern. Judith had put in another night of abuse and raving until she is so weary she is shaking.

"I am."

Brendan begins gathering Eric's stuff for the move to a new room with a larger window that will permit the patient to better tell night from day. Judith wonders if this is the time for a move, with Eric so confused, but the room seems an improvement on the old. She and Brendan pack the breathing tubes, the urinals, the shaving gear that Eric has demanded but not yet used, the flowers from the history department, the books and magazines people have brought, the photos of Phoebe's soccer team that they have pinned to the cork board on the wall. There is a card from Natalie saying, "Get fucking well. Bitch."

Judith is stretched out on the couch of the new room when David and William come back. Brendan is trying to interest Eric in the baseball game on TV. She and her sons go into the social room next door. There is a long table and a kitchenette with a fridge full of ice cream, puddings, milk, fruit, and leftovers in plastic containers. Judith fills Styrofoam cups with ice and pours from a 24 ounce bottle of coke. William finds a large bag of potato chips and they proceed to gobble.

All of a sudden William begins to laugh.

"Dad starts out in his pedantic professorial voice, totally rational, 'you're absolutely right, William. I'm in no condition to leave here until I am well.' Then he goes, 'Now will you bring the car around and we'll all go have a scotch?'"

"I know," David giggles. "He said to me, 'you're perfectly right. I accept the fact that I can not just get up and leave here and I will cooperate, of course'—rational as hell. Then two minutes later he says, 'how about we all go out for dinner at Hartzen's?'"

"He's definitely on a drug high," William says.

Judith is giggling along with David. She almost chokes on a potato chip.

"How crazy is all this?"

William spews coke onto the table and mops it up.

All three are laughing hysterically now.

"Nurse Ratched had fits because he said bullshit."

"She has to know he's not himself."

Judith is laughing so hard she begins to cry.

"Maybe there's a Good Dad and a Bad Dad," David says. They think this over.

"But which is the real one?"

"Neither," William says. "He's just high as a kite. He has to crash."

"Lakesia is right," Judith says. "He's over medicated. That last sedative is exactly what he had before and it got him crazy all over again."

"They're creating a witch's brew!"

"I talked to Tim about it and he's sure Dad's high," William says.

"Who's Tim?" Judith asks.

"My sponsor."

"Wonderful—now we're getting our diagnosis from a drug addict," David says.

"He's clean now."

"Right."

William shoots him a look.

"We need to talk to the doctor," Judith says.

"Which one? There are about six prescribing stuff," David says.

"Double, double . . ." William stirs an imaginary cauldron.

Judith corners Dr. Sanders the next day. He asks if that is what the family wants to do, to eliminate the sedatives.

Judith is surprised to be asked for a decision.

"Well, I'm not a doctor," she says, "but it seems they have the opposite effect on him."

Dr. Graham the heart surgeon agrees, and agrees that Eric should not go into a psychiatric ward. He should start getting some exercise.

I thought he needed rest and sleep, which is it? Judith thinks. But hey, they are in Wonderland: drink this, grow tall; drink that, grow small.

Eric's bones hurt. His knee aches. Judith asks for Tylenol and the nurse brings it, loudly declaring that too much of it could "give him bleeding ulcers."

He does sleep better though, and becomes somewhat more lucid. Judith will have to accept Natalie coming to visit. Natalie: who is she? A new breed.

26

Judith

*J*udith recalls the meetings, the discussions, the militancy of her generation. For her it began one spring day, when after a winter of sloppy icy streets, biting wind and gray skies, colds and croup, and cabin fever that started Judith and Eric sniping at each other, the weather finally turned sunny and warm enough for just sweaters. She was pregnant with David and took a walk while Eric studied. She paused at the little bookshop next to the drugstore, just beyond campus, and rummaged in the outside bin of used books. Her hand almost touched that of another young woman searching through the bargains.

"Peg?" she said. She was so happy to see a familiar face—Peg from her American Literature class. She had been voluble, intense, pretty, with red lipstick and dark brown straight hair. Now her hair was wild and frizzy. She wore no makeup, jeans and a loose T-shirt, no brassiere.

"Hi there," Peg said. "Looking for *The Waves*. How about you?"

"Nothing special."

"What are you doing these days?"

"Studying." She and Eric had been living in their own little cocoon, working for their degrees with a baby on the way.

"Come to our group," Peg said. "We're working for women's rights."

"I'm all for that," Judith said.

Peg pulled a small notebook and pen from her back pocket and wrote an address and phone number on a sheet of paper.

"Seven-thirty, Thursday," Peg said.

"Are you still working with the SDS?" Judith asked.

"M.C.P.'s," Peg said.

"Oh." Judith had no idea what she was talking about. Peg could see she didn't and explained, "Male Chauvinist Pigs."

"Oh."

"They didn't give us anything significant to do. We were just pamphlet counters and convenient cunts."

Judith had never heard that word said aloud before, only seen it carved on school desks or scrawled in rest-room stalls. She said she would definitely get to the meeting.

As Peg walked away, Judith read the back of her T-shirt: "Legalize Abortion."

The night of the meeting Judith informed Eric that she would be out for the evening to attend a consciousness raising meeting.

"What for?" he asked. "Are you going to burn your bras?"

"Effigies of men. Should I make some coffee before I go?"

"Not if it makes noise. I am at a crucial point here."

"So am I," Judith said. She gathered her backpack and left for the meeting.

As she walked away from their front door, she saw Eric through the window hunched over his desk.

From this vantage point, he looked like all the other young men students, working at their books in the libraries and dorms. A stranger. She and Eric knew so little about each other. Their romance had been all sex and revolution and excitement. Now it was trying to get the landlord to fix the plumbing and begging the neighbors to turn down their hi-fis so they could work.

There was so much to talk about at the meeting: health, literature, credit, personal appearance. Once the women became comfortable together, they worked for abortion and read *Women and Their Bodies*. Like the others, Judith stopped shaving her legs and armpits and pubic hair; everything should be natural, unashamedly feminine. They didn't burn their bras, but they gave them up.

One of the women asked Judith if she hadn't known about birth control, when her pregnancy began to be obvious.

"This is a child of the Revolution," Judith said.

After a few months of getting together, the women decided they should know their own insides, that dark area that until then only male gynecologists had seen. Judith felt squeamish at the idea of being touched intimately by another woman. Only she, her doctor, and Eric had ever touched her, but when an evening was set up, a speculum smuggled out of the infirmary, she went along with the others. She had gone through plenty of vaginal exams and pap tests—something she hated, not because it hurt, but because the doctor seemed so embarrassed, so careful not to see any part of her body but the opening he was treating, while the rest of her was covered with a sheet as though taboo. He comically attended to the one part, his head beneath a sheet like an old-time photographer under his canvas hood.

Judith's group marched in support of the Equal Rights Amendment, worked for women in Congress and wrote articles protesting the sexist literature coming out of the university. They agitated for rape to be taken seriously; they helped set up battered women's shelters and child care for working women, for equal pay and for changes in language. Their heroines were Betty Friedan, Gloria Steinem, Simone de Beauvoir.

They must be independent of men, must work. But Judith had always worked. As a child she babysat for spending money, and she waited tables in a diner and at her dorm. She and Moira were not raised as princesses; they were tom boys, "latch key kids," while their mother played bridge. Their fey mom was a grand master.

Their father didn't care what his wife did, so long as she acted the part of a pretty dumbbell; he bought her a fur coat and a diamond bracelet, but would not let her learn to drive.

One of the women told Judith she knew where she could get a safe abortion, but Judith said no. Abortion was against the law, and scary. Anyway, secretly, she was rather proud of herself and Eric.

Now here they are in Good Shepard hospital. The baby a man. Eric thin and white. Judith studies his sleeping face. So pale. So impassive. What is in that head of his? How will Natalie change things? If he cares for the girl, why did he call *her* in DC the day of his surgery, after telling David not to call? Maybe he was betting she would come out anyway. *Wanted* her to find out about Natalie. She had never thought Eric manipulative. But surely he guessed his original call might have her come running. Maybe he was punishing her for leaving. He had asked for her the minute he was able to talk. Why?

Why did the mayor of the city pay a prostitute with a check?

27

Judith

"Natalie is coming over," Judith says to Brendan. "You've heard us talking about her?"

Brendan nods. He and Judith are trying to get Eric into the knee-length stockings he has been ordered to wear. They fit tighter than his skin.

"Oh the hell with this," Eric says.

"Now, Mr. Howard, we don't want our feet to swell, do we?" Brendan says.

"They aren't *our* feet."

Brendan just chuckles. He is used to crabby patients.

Judith gathers her things, noticing that Eric has managed to wrinkle his sheets and spill food on his second gown. He looks gaunt and depressed, a little scary with his robe gaping open, a day-old stubble on his face. She is tempted to leave him that way. Serve him and Natalie right. But he looks so pathetic and anxious, like a young boy about to go on his first date, that Judith almost feels sorry for him.

"I guess we should clean him up," she says.

Her own pride is at stake too; she doesn't want an interloper like Natalie thinking Eric is not being cared for.

"I'll give him a shave," Brendan says. He steps hesitantly into the bathroom, which is a swamp of ugly water awaiting a plumber, and runs warm water into the sink.

He helps Eric into his chair. Eric takes twice the time a healthy person would. He is shaking.

When he is cleaned up, Judith looks her husband over. He is wearing a fresh gown and bathrobe. He smells like Old Spice and soap. She locates a comb and runs it through his hair. She tucks in the blanket on his lap.

"Keep that on," she says. "You've been flashing the nurses."

Judith and Brendan go into the hall.

"He's so lucky to have you," Brendan says.

"I hope he throws up on her," Judith says.

"You don't either."

"I'm no saint."

"Yes you are." Brendan kisses her on the cheek.

They see Natalie walking briskly toward Eric's room. She doesn't notice them. She is elegant in a pink suit, probably a Chanel knockoff, and five inch heels. She is carrying packages from the Party Source. Judith is wearing her usual soft slacks and crocs. She feels like one of the help.

Judith goes into the social room and eats ice cream from a pint box. She is exhausted. As soon as Natalie leaves, she will tell Eric good night and go home and sleep.

She is surprised, when scraping the last of the ice cream with her spoon, Natalie comes into the room.

"Do you know how many calories are in that?"

Judith shrugs, pitches the empty carton in the waste can.

"He doesn't look good," Natalie says.

"We're doing our best."

"I'd like to send my friend Jake. He's a psychic."

"You can try. Eric's not into stuff like that."

"He's changing."

"Oh?"

"I guess you think I'm too stupid for Eric."

Judith doesn't answer.

"You have to know men. They lose interest when a woman can't give them children anymore."

Judith rises from her seat. Is she going to slap the woman?

Natalie rummages in the fridge. "I am not a bad person," she says.

Judith goes back to Eric's room. Says goodnight. She's going home. She is tempted to pull his IV and monitor out. She says to Brendan, "Don't call me this evening no matter what. I don't care if he falls out of bed and breaks every god damn bone in his body. I'll be watching *The Sopranos*."

On her way home, Judith meets her friend Diane for tea at a funky place near the university. It has some of the ambiance of the Bookshelf Coffee shop: the constant hiss of the espresso machine, jars of cookies the size of saucers, the smell of sweet liquors and whipped cream, copies of the *New York Times* scattered about on the tables.

Diane has a way of cheering Judith up. She is so warm, a hugger, a belly laugher. Full of crazy stories. She has a whole room in her house devoted to her divorce proceedings: documents, deeds, bank statements, legal papers, letters, like a shrine to the god of disappointing marriages.

"Why didn't you leave him looking ratty? Scare her off?" Diane says.

Judith is thinking about herself at Natalie's age: two kids and a demanding house with two kinds of windows: those that wouldn't open and those that wouldn't close, water bugs and termites in the basement, raccoons tearing up the roof; Eric busy as always, defending his turf at the university, David in college, William going through his coke phase, herself struggling to complete her doctorate.

She sees herself in the big mirror behind Diane. She looks tired and frumpy.

She lifts an eye bag with a finger.

"I probably ought to have gotten a nip or a tuck when Betsy offered it," she says. She does not tell Diane Natalie's nasty remark about fertility, her little wise nugget about men.

"I have just the thing for you," Diane says. "My ass fat is in a Tupperware dish in my fridge. Maybe you can use it to plump up your boobs."

"Really? In the refrigerator? Why? Can you cook with it like lard?" Judith asks.

"No."

"What does it look like?"

"It's a pinkish color."

Judith has to laugh. Her mother always said women are stupid, and she's beginning to agree.

Does she look droopy?

The tea comes. Chai with milk and sugar

"But about this Natalie," Diane says. "What is she like?"

"Pretty, sure of herself, thirty something. You know the type: right out of a fashion shoot: pink suit, stilettos, boobs on display."

Diane laughs and urges Judith on. Judith is drawing on a fancy shower she had gone to for Lydia. How different it was from her women's group at Chicago. The conversation was all about the best prams, the hottest work-outs, shoes.

"She probably reads chick-lit, runs marathons, gobbles up celebrity gossip; knows designer labels like Pentecostal preachers know the gospels. She doesn't want to be called a feminist, and is like: Gloria who? Betty who? She drives an SUV, never mind the price or the carbon dioxide. Never heard of ERA. Martha Stewart is her Joan of Arc."

"I can smell her," Diane says.

They sip their tea.

"I can't wait till he gets better," Judith says. "So I can kill him."

28

Judith

When Judith gets home, she goes to the kitchen, intending to fix something to eat. But nothing she sees in the fridge—soup, leftover noodles, apple sauce—looks good. The house seems empty and gray. She thinks about what Natalie said. About giving a man children. Fertility. She does feel less vital. She dreams of empty purses, of an old woman at the top of the stairs.

She's jealous of Natalie, and all the women profiting from the work her generation did. The Natalies and Lydias with their self-absorption, their workouts, their shoe fetishes. She looks at her feet in her crocs. At Lydia's shower she tried on a pair of stilettos someone dropped in a bedroom. She felt like one of Cinderella's ugly sisters.

Jealousy, what an ugly thing. It's corrosive.

Mehitabel winds herself around Judith's feet. Judith goes out on the small back porch and Mehitabel follows, arching her back like a Halloween cat. Judith kicks the recycle bin with her foot. She picks up a wine bottle from among the cans and glass, and throws it toward the cement curb around the driveway. It hurtles through the air and lands with a loud crash. The cat flees down the steps. Glass shards fly everywhere. Judith notices her neighbor, a man about Eric's age, standing on his back steps, staring in amazement at her and recoiling from the blast of the breaking bottle.

"Oh, hi," she says. "I thought I saw a rat running across the driveway."

Judith goes back into the kitchen. She is panting. She must get out of the house. She goes upstairs and searches her face in the bathroom mirror. She is pale. She washes her face and puts on lipstick and rouge and powder. Combs her hair. Refreshed, she doesn't look so bad. She slips into a pair of sandals, jeans and a sweater. Hot pink. It's a good color on her.

She goes out to the car and drives around and around the neighborhood. She wants something. What? Finally she stops at the local bar. It's in one of the old buildings near the fire station. There are a few scarred booths, a pool table. Stools lined up at the bar. Loud music she doesn't recognize. She take a stool alongside an elderly woman in a ratty fur coat and a man in a T-shirt and jeans.

The bartender, a young guy with a pony tail, asks for her order.

"Bourbon on the rocks," she says.

She looks out the grimy window. People passing like shadows. The liquor feels good.

She asks for a bag of the potato chips arranged on a wire holder.

The old woman gets off her stool and leaves. Judith has seen her before, on the street. She has dyed blond hair and walks with a cane. Hanging in there.

"She's a piece of work," the man on the adjacent stool says. "Comes in here every day."

How would he know? Judith thinks. Unless *he* comes in every day.

Judith finishes her drink and orders another.

"You know—I think I had you for Freshman English," the man says.

Judith looks at him more closely. After her first year of teaching she could not remember her students, unless they were particularly good or really awful. "I had you" sounds suggestive.

"That was the best class I ever took," he says.

Must have been her first year or so, Judith thinks. This guy doesn't look young. He's forty something.

"The level of sophistication was beyond anything we'd run into before."

Really? Well, maybe he wasn't just making conversation. Many of her students had never been out of their own backyards until they came to college.

Judith is about to order a third drink. Hey, why not? She is hanging out while her husband and his girl friend have a little *tete à tete*.

"I'm Ken Mueller," the man says.

"Judith—"

"I know, Dr. Howard."

She offers him a potato chip and he takes one.

"You taught us about the importance of words, of style. You had so much passion. Such intensity."

Judith picks the last crumbs of her chips from the greasy bag, drains her glass.

"Drinks are cheaper upstairs," he says.

She looks at him questioningly.

"My apartment."

"Thanks, but—"

"I have no designs. I just always liked talking to you. You have an educated laugh."

He looks harmless. He's almost an acquaintance.

"OK," Judith says. "Lead on. But just one."

The next thing Judith knows, she is following her old student up a set of dark stairs. Too bad Eric can't see her follow this guy to his apartment, for what mischief she doesn't even care. The bartender lights a cigarette and puts their glasses in the sink.

Judith has lost count of what she has drunk when she is sipping a less expensive but not too rough bourbon in her old student's apartment. It isn't a bad place. The windows are large and look out on the familiar street. She can see the marquee of the movie theater and the sign of the Ambal Indian restaurant. She can smell the spices. Ken has a nice selection of books and a CD player and stacks of DVDs. Eclectic taste.

"Nice place," she says.

"I like it here. Except the sirens from the fire station and the hospitals get pretty loud."

"Now what have you been doing since college?" she asks.

"This and that. Waiter at a good restaurant but it went out of business. Tried to run my own place. Now I'm taking tech calls for a computer company."

Ken has a nice smile.

Judith wishes him luck. Wonders if the things she taught him have helped him. His books are those of a good reader. His room is cozy. The couch Judith is sitting on is soft and she feels herself wanting to go to sleep.

"So what about you? What have you been doing?"

Judith puts her head back against the pillow in the corner of the couch and almost dozes off.

"You taught us about Viet Nam," Ken says. "And the civil rights struggle and Black writers."

Is this flattery or is he being sincere?

"It was first time we encountered a woman so into politics."

Is he or is he not trying to hit on her?

He sounds so earnest.

Judith feels he is sincere. Perhaps he is not trying to seduce her. He may be merely lonely.

She relaxes. So tired. She feels bad. Maybe she's the seducer, trying to prove something with him. Punish Eric.

She hears one of her shoes fall onto the carpet.

All of a sudden—or maybe longer—she has lost track of time—Ken is sitting on the couch and is massaging her foot. The touch feels good and she doesn't push him away.

Then suddenly she sits up. Sudden great sobs explode from her. The outburst comes from nowhere, unsuspected, uncontrollable like water bursting through a dam.

"Jesus," Ken says. He holds his hands up defensively, surrendering any desire to touch her sexually. "I'm sorry. I didn't mean to—"

Judith keeps crying. Words come spewing out like the tears. "It's my husband. He's in the hospital. He died. I mean he was dead. But he's alive. And I've been there every day and he's with someone else and he's still not well. He has to go through more surgery. He could die. And I'm so tired. He was only supposed to have a minor surgery and I was in Washington and I feel so spacey sometimes. He's been acting crazy and—"

Ken puts his arms around her gently, like a father.

"Oh God," he says. "I'm so sorry."

"I didn't mean to lead you on. I'm stupid. I was just—"

"It's OK," he says. "I see. I see. Anyone would be upset."

Judith cries and cries. Her old student rocks her gently.

Her reaction to Ken's touch has shocked, surprised her. She didn't really want booze or sex, just to cry in someone's arms.

29

Judith

Judith returns to the hospital the next morning to relieve William. Eric is sleeping. She gazes around the room. Several colorful mylar balloons scrape the ceiling.

"Gosh, you look kind of down," William says.

"I guess I am," Judith says.

Judith points to the balloons. "What are those?" she says.

"Natalie."

"Oh."

"You should invite her over for dinner—" William says, "—in our cat box."

Judith has to laugh. What would she do without William? Both her sons.

David came along nine months after the convention in Chicago and Eric's arrest. William eighteen months later.

When she found she was pregnant with David, Eric said, "I guess we better get married."

She said, "That's a hell of a proposal."

"I thought you liberated women didn't go in for sentiment."

She sulked: she might be a feminist, but she had gone to the movies every week of her life.

"Do you really *want* to get married?" she asked.

"We don't want a little bastard on our hands."

Judith swung at him.

"I'm perfection, remember?"

"I can write my own dialogue."

A baby would set back her plans. But what were they? A vague idea she might join the peace corps, teach English to children: an opportunity to serve—and travel.

Maybe twenty years younger than Natalie, she delivered David in Billings Hospital on the Chicago campus. He came sliding out easily on a sled of blood and glistening tissue, big and bawling and red with all the right number of fingers and toes and a little fat penis. Judith was jubilant to have produced such a wonderful creature. She felt the whole world should celebrate, but no bells were ringing and she was alone.

No one knew where Moira was at the time: in an ashram? a commune? jail? hang gliding?

Judith's mother said she would come to help out, but she'd have to put the dog to sleep.

Eric looked more frightened than happy. The other fathers at the hospital were snapping photos of their wives and babies, while Eric gave Judith a quick kiss, counted David's various digits and parts, and took off for the library.

He was in a hurry to get his degree. He didn't like the conservatism seeping into the university. Once the school had been one of the the most liberal. Now it was dominated by Strauss and his minions in political philosophy, Friedman and his followers in economics with their draconian social policies, Allen Bloom and his crowd in Humanities, in literature Saul Bellow with his bedroom eyes, predatory smile and misogyny. Eric was eager to teach. Marches and street protests were over: the university was the new front. The place to make change. A whole army of young people were heading for academia to teach. Create a new, aware generation.

Eric's closest friend said, "It's our job to turn them left and rob them of their religion."

"I wouldn't quite put it that way," Eric said, "but we need to civilize them."

Judith fell in love at first sight with David: the little whorl of wispy hair, his rosebud mouth that sucked so happily at her breast. His fingertips were like tiny pearls.

They were a besotted twosome, rocking and feeding.

Judith nursed David, fixed meals—dinners of Ramen noodles and marked-down hamburger—changed diapers, napped, took David for walks in his buggy.

She liked the sound of the communes young people were setting up: dropping out of the commercial world, living together in the country. Stories were going around of families growing their own food, getting their milk from goats and cows, making their own clothes, sharing child care. Splitting rails. Such a life seemed so sunny and free. Her child could live in a community, in peace, breathe fresh air.

She had to admit, looking back, how naive her ideas had been.

"Me a farmer," Eric said, "chopping wood!"

"You're right," she agreed. "You'd be a quadruple amputee in a week."

Still— she would love to escape.

As David grew a little and was more responsive, Eric began to take an interest in him. He didn't mind diapering. And he hummed "Good Night Sweetheart" to him when putting him into his crib. To give Judith a little morning sleep, he would get David dressed and talk to him: "We have a lot to learn, Bro."

In spite of Eric's growing affection for his son, as she trudged along the mall, pushing David in his buggy, seeing the students hustling by with their books, Judith began to feel lonely and out of it. She had a higher grade average than Eric, and was probably, she thought, actually smarter, but they couldn't afford two in school, and she was the mother. And she wanted to be a good one. David was the first person she had ever loved more than herself, the first for whom she might forget her own needs. He was so tiny and helpless and trusting. Then William was born. She suffered a frightening depression with his birth, but she loved him passionately.

Judith stayed with the women's group and Eric completed his doctorate. He declared the family should move to Cincinnati. He found "the Ivies" were not particularly interested in Midwesterners, and had been offered a good teaching post at the university in his home town.

Besides, Cincinnati was a good place to raise children.

Judith dreaded it. She wasn't sure what she wanted from life. But she was god-damned sure what she didn't want: being stuck in some dreary house in Cincinnati.

30

Judith

udith and Eric found they were sharing "The Amityville Horror," as they dubbed the old Tudor house, with a basement full of sci-fi sized black water bugs that crept up into the living room, and raccoons that made their bathroom on an eave right outside the the master bedroom. The house was surrounded by overgrown hedges and forsythia. The flower beds were full of giant weeds and the trees were shading the lawn into a pale green. The garden smelled of rotted fruit from a gnarled old apple tree.

Judith loved it.

She loved the ancient lead figure of a boy on the crumbling brick steps to the fish pond. The garden was a sanctuary for every creature that flew, crawled or burrowed: robins, cardinals, grackles, squirrels, rabbits, lizards, snakes, chipmunks, even the occasional family of deer, a ground hog. She was thrilled when spring blooms popped up among the weeds and the apple tree blossomed.

It was a closed world, protected by the hedges like Sleeping Beauty's court. Owls hooted in the woods behind the house, and the smell of viburnum and lilacs scented the air. The world outside was muted to a hum from the expressway. She could hear the occasional tap of a woodpecker, the plop of acorns on the grass.

She nursed to life age-old rose bushes, planted a vegetable garden. She found a wasps' nest, a family of snakes; chipmunks digging away at the stone wall of the patio. She liked being among the creatures, watching the ubiquitous squirrels leaping and running to ends of the thinnest tree branches like tight-rope walkers. It was all new to her, a new Old World. The world of fairy tales and myths.

Sitting in the shade of the maples, she read Mark Twain, Jane Austen, Tolstoy, Ralph Ellison, Ibsen, George Eliot, Chekhov, Zora Neal Hurston, Melville, Dostoevsky. David would dig in the sand between the patio bricks while William napped in his play pen. As they grew older, the boys would swim with Eric in the neighbor's pool, then come to her, dripping wet, and flop onto the lawn like newly caught fish. When she hugged them they smelled of chlorine and sun screen.

Of course the idyll had to end. The magic lifted like morning mist. She must go to work. There was no question of working. Everyone worked. She and her friends would never fall into the dependence or the despair and boredom of their mothers. One of the women in her Chicago group was now with a big law firm in New York, another was a banker.

And she? The young woman her teachers declared brilliant, predicted big things from, should not be burying her talent like the man in the Bible. At seventeen she had sent away for applications to colleges with no encouragement from her parents, had gotten a full scholarship to the university. Paid for her books with money from her job in the dorm.

She had not foreseen falling smack dab in love and having a baby right away.

Now she needed to get herself a real plan. She knew only that her work would have to do with books. She changed like a fairy tale character—from a teapot, singing in the hearth, to a woman scampering along a high wire like one of the garden squirrels.

Eric hadn't the slightest interest in anything to do with the house or garden. He was amazingly ignorant of the natural world. As a boy he was never near the kitchen when meals were prepared; Judith was shocked that he did not know the difference between a plum and a pear. His mother and her gardener took care of the castle grounds. Judith once got him to try weeding the flower beds, but he pulled out all the perennials and left the poison ivy.

From the beginning, he was aiming to be head of the history department. With the help of the younger members of the faculty, he had plunged into the fight for new more inclusive courses. He had changes to make, battles to wage. He was moving up.

They had the typical arguments about who should do what. But he had the excuse of being ineffectual. And earning the money they lived on.

Everything was growing: the walnut tree, the kids, her world as she went back to the university. She drove the boys to school, to scouts, to music lessons and sports while Eric made exciting trips to Japan and Spain, on research for his books.

She was "Having it All": family, work, measles, mumps, falls from trees, bike crashes, bee stings, allergies, mold, leaky roofs, plumbers, carpenters, carpenter ants, veterinarians, doctors, dentists, dogs and cats, termites and tent caterpillars, bag worms and heart worm, poison ivy, creeping Charlie, tree borers, exhaustion, guilt.

Then everything stopped for a while.

Her mother's cancer seemed to be in a hurry to take her. She was sixty-five. Judith and Moira were numb. The family had no customs for death, no experience in grief. Judith went alone to the funeral in Pittsburgh; her children barely knew their grandparents.

Laid out in satin, her favorite material, her mother looked pretty and serene. Judith and Moira put a favorite sea shell, a white delicate angel's wing, in her hands. She had made little mirrors and picture frames from the shells she collected on the beach in Sanibel; she was happiest there, combing the beach and locating mollusks with the sharp eye of a gull. She was beautiful in a straw hat with the sun shining through it. Those were Judith and Moira's best times with her. They begged her to tell them about her life, but she never would.

Judith's father appeared at the funeral home with a neighbor, a woman about their mother's age who seemed rather proprietary.

"He's the only man I know who would take a date to his wife's funeral," Moira said. She went back to her job and her boyfriend.

Judith was left to mourn alone. She did not know how.

She would never have the chance to tell her mother how angry she was at her, or put her arms around her and forgive.

Judith saw a therapist. The woman chipped away at her defenses.

"Your mother said terribly hurtful things. Yet you tell the story as humorous, dismiss her as 'fey.' You make a joke out of everything."

"How else to survive?" Judith said.

"You let your husband off the hook, saying he's incapable of helping with the house. He's flying in the air while you cut the grass."

"He's working hard at the university."

"Do you have to be so *good?*" the therapist asked.

"Yes," Judith said. Yes. Moira got to be the bad one, and if she added any stress it might have killed her mother, killed everything around her, like honeysuckle.

"Where do you get your money?" the woman asked.

"Out of a box," Judith admitted.

The doctor shot her a look, and Judith was in even more of a hurry to start earning her way.

She was friendless until the Romanos arrived in town. Teresa, a generous-sized, beautiful brunette, stood beside her at one of the university's interminable cocktail parties. Judith whispered, "Have you given the dean the obligatory kiss on the ass?"

Teresa laughed out loud, causing everyone to stare.

Judith and she became close friends though they had little time to get together; Judith had her ailing house, her children, her work. Theresa had even more on her hands: eight children, and also an old house. But when they did have time for talk, they enjoyed each other's company.

"I was afraid to approach you at first," Theresa said, "You seemed so smart, so together, so full of aplomb and sophistication."

Oh yeah, Judith thought.

31

Judith

She was Dr. Judith Howard, professor of English at Cliffside College, on her way to becoming head of the department. As she drove to work, she looked down at her feet on the gas pedal and thought, "I am competent. I am a competent person." She had fought every battle: sexist professors, fatigue, university presses, the boredom of bibliography. Her students were a variety: kids right out of high school, nurses and mothers coming back to school for college credit. She set up new courses in African American Literature and Womens' Studies. The trend was up: she and her students were coming into their own, and her years with her Chicago women's group helped her frame her work.

Then . . . . She didn't like to think about then.

William suddenly did not request his usual dinner portion: "give me too much." He seemed to be talking too much and too fast. Judith asked him if anything was wrong, but William swore he was fine.

She believed him, until the phone call. Midnight. A policeman. William and a buddy were caught weaving in the friend's car, and the police took them to a hospital, comatose. She and Eric rushed to the hospital in the dark, Good Shepard, where Eric now lies.

Her son was laid out on the white sheets, pale, unresponsive—William who was so full of zest and humor. Judith was afraid he was dying.

In the morning light William was still unmoving. She and Eric walked the hospital grounds huddled in winter coats, the sky leaden, their hearts sick, bad parents. Neither said anything.

William was released after several days, white, withdrawn. They had pumped his stomach of the drug he had taken, finally got some food into him. He was quiet, still pale, withdrawn when they picked him up. Their joyful sweet boy suddenly mysterious and strange.

The sun was setting as they left the hospital, a sickly winter sun.

They were all silent in the car on the way home. When they came into the front hall, David came out of his room and gave William a quick hello and disappeared, pleading heavy homework. No one wanted any dinner. Judith was in limbo. She did not know what to say or do.

Eric took William's small overnight bag to his room and then left the house. He had a meeting.

William went to his room. Judith sat in the living room in front of the cold fireplace. Her whole body seemed to be collapsing.

She rocked compulsively in the rocker by the fireplace, back and forth, back and forth, losing track of time and of herself, muttering like a mental case.

The house was quiet with only the creaking of her chair. No television, no music, no voices. She had not turned the lights on and the winter sky at the windows was now gray.

William came into the room.

Back and forth, back and forth.

William didn't say anything, and Judith didn't either, and then she shot out of her rocking chair and to her feet, propelled by hours of worry.

"You stupid stupid—" Judith yelled. She stood up, picked up the hearth broom and went at William with it. She beat him around his shoulders and head. William took the beating silently. He did not try to take the broom from her.

David heard her screaming and came running. Judith sat down in the rocker, ashamed, still muttering "how could he?" "Why?" rhythmically, hysterically.

"He" was William; "He" was Eric for leaving them alone in misery, embarrassed, afraid, angry.

David called Eric at his meeting.

"You better come home, Dad."

Eric did arrive, but too late. She had hurt her son. She would never forgive herself.

Dr. Judith Howard.

She pitched her dissertation, *Mary Shelley's Monster* (Ohio University Press, 1990) into the basement of the Tudor House where it resides along with journals full of her articles.

The scene with her son still plays in her hours of falling asleep. Her hitting him. The look on William's face.

She had never told anyone of her actions. She was not able to admit her loss of control, her remorse. Especially to the Howards. Could not show herself human, weak. Not even to Moira or Theresa.

32

Betsy

She contrasts Judith and Natalie, who is pinning a photo of a beach scene on the bulletin board in Eric's hospital room: bright umbrellas and golden sand.

Natalie is probably fifteen or so years younger than Judith. She is sexy, slimmer than Judith—and weight is something Betsy thinks her daughter in law better work on. She isn't fat, but has put about fifteen pounds on a delicate frame. She looks better with the hair cut. Now if she had some decent clothes. How has she failed Eric?

It never occurs to Betsy that Eric might have failed Judith.

She tries to pick up on what brought her son and Natalie together. He and Judith have a bond that can never be dissolved. Judith is what Eric needs now: the familiar, the mother. She must see him through the dangerous surgery facing him. But what about after he gets well? If he survives. There are attractions that can't be denied.

Betsy goes next door to the hospitality room to give the couple some privacy. She makes a pot of tea. Someone has left the radio on; the music is strange to her. Loud and harsh. William would know what it is. She turns the dial to the classical music station.

Der Rosenkavalier. The exquisite presentation of the silver rose to the young Sophie . . . .

Betsy first heard it when she was young, so long ago, and she and her friends were supers in the operas that needed extras in the crowd scenes, going on stage in *Boheme* and *Carmen*, dressed as gypsies and peasants. It was one of her escapes from the boredom of her family life. Keysey's Cheese.

She dreamed Cinderella dreams, read endless versions of the story, from fairy tales to Daphne du Maurier and Jane Austen. The heroine always landed a strong handsome man with a good-sized estate or a prince with a castle.

Her relatives were all husky, hefty Germans, as plain as potatoes. They were content with three solid meals a day and an occasional trip to the ballpark to root for the Cincinnati Reds. They recognized Betsy as someone special, someone prettier and brighter than they.

Her role as the special one, the princess, did not excuse her from working along with the others in the family cheese stall at Finley Market: Keysey's Cheese. Every Saturday. She hated everything about it. The cement floors were wet, and the damp soaked through her shoes. In winter the two-block-long, closed-in hall was steamy and smelled of wet wool as the customers, bundled in overcoats, crowded the narrow aisle. In summer it was hot, with only a few doors open to the sweltering humid street.

She stood behind a huge glass case full of heavy rounds and odds and ends of rank-smelling cheeses, all with little cardboard tabs stuck in them indicating the name and price. The loud voices of customers yelled their orders over the din in the market hall: "Gimme a pound of Swiss," "Let me taste that Roquefort," while Betsy rummaged in the jumble of soft and hard hunks to find the right thing. The smell was of sweaty socks.

Opposite "Keysey's Cheese" was a butcher counter with strings of phallic-shaped sausages hanging from hooks, slabs of ribs and bloody steaks piled in the glass case, flies stuck above on fly paper. Slap! A rib roast was pitched onto the chopping block. Pong! The butcher flipped it onto his scale. He wiped his hands on his bloody apron like a torturer, an executioner.

He and Betsy's uncles yelled back and forth, always leering with the same delight when the butcher held up a particularly large wiener and suggested its resemblance to his own member. "Hee-haw."

When her high school friends came shopping with their parents, Betsy wanted to slink down and hide behind the counter so they wouldn't see her.

At the end of her shift, Betsy would try and try to wipe the cheese smell from her hands, but it held on for hours. She would walk down the long corridor, a customer now, past the bins of dill pickles and bright yellow pickled cauliflower, green peppers stuffed with sauerkraut, more meat and goetta, more cheeses (Keysey's was the most popular), cases of cheap candy, chocolate drops her uncles called "nigger tits," stuck-together marshmallows, breads and rolls and pretzels, yellow-gray chickens and pigs' feet, always a head, ears perked up, looking angry.

Outside were the fresh fruit and vegetable stands, old kitchen chairs behind the make-shift counters and bins, in winter warmed by small electric heaters. The vendors wore mittens with the fingers cut out, like the beggars selling pencils and the crazy guy pounding his Bible and predicting the end of the world. At least outside, the colors of the peppers and oranges and melons were pretty, the smells less pungent, and at Christmas the odor of pine came from the fresh wreaths and trees stacked against buildings.

As she walked to the streetcar, an old black man was grilling ribs on an oil can and little black kids darted here and there, peddling shopping bags for a dime.

Once home and safe in her room, on the window seat, and her undisturbed dreams of a *parfit gentil knight* coming to take her from her mundane world, Betsy sketched pretty girls. She made herself a dressing table out of crates from the market, with skirts made of dotted swiss. It had a faint earthy smell, of potatoes and onion.

"She's artistic," the family claimed, not without a note of pride. But at the same time, they made sure she took her turn at cleaning the greasy roasting pans at home and pitching the rotten cheeses that could not be displayed another day at Keysey's Cheese.

Then one day her knight came along. He was handsome, a tall, shy man, wearing an army uniform, standing out from the crowd clamoring for cheese.

He had thick brown hair cut military short, a noble nose, an educated voice and smile. He looked classy.

They flirted a little, their words charged with what they both knew was coming.

After they started dating, Betsy's aunt said, "He has a rich look. I've waited on the family. It would be a good marriage for you."

Betsy frowned at her. She wasn't for sale, and was as good as anyone, including this man. Anyway, she had already made up her mind: John Howard was just the mate she was looking for: gentlemanly, cool, well-mannered—as different from the bloody-fingered, noisy butchers and loud-laughing burghers of her family as she could imagine.

Her wedding photo shows a woman wearing a form-fitting white gown, slim and translucent as a Lalique vase, her train swirling at her feet.

Betsy gave up her dream of being an architect. All her and John's friends were huddling into home life after the disruptions of the war. She scoured the house ads for a place with a "wbf"—wood-burning fireplace. Everybody was buying station wagons and producing enough kids to fill them.

By the time she raised her children and helped John get started on his career it felt too late. Anyway, neither her husband nor the university encouraged her ambitions. There were no women in the architecture department. Betsy settled for working to preserve Cincinnati's distinguished buildings, helping her friend Ralph with his research. Renovating the castle.

Women's Lib was far in the future and Betsy was treated like an ornament. The concierge at John's club asked Betsy not to sit in the lobby because she was upsetting the gentlemen. John's firm had no women lawyers until—oh when?

Now the firm's social events are full of husbands pushing strollers, and John's meetings are taken over by the women attorneys complaining about breast pumps and hormones. Imagine! Betsy thinks—annoyed—still mad at John's dismissal of her frustrated ambitions: "You're doing what the other women are." She *wasn't other women.* She was special.

The music from the hospital radio keeps Betsy in the past. She sees a slim, still-youthful woman, with two grown children. Her husband is on the board of the opera, and they attend every performance. Just being in the vast space of Music Hall with its semi circle of loge and gallery, its boxes and crystal chandeliers, its marble two-story foyer where beautifully dressed people look each other over, and gossip and chat about music and art, takes her out of the ordinary world of children and groceries and car pools, and into a place of magic, a world of the glamorous and the eccentric. She loves watching the women in their gowns: some wear the latest flowing silks; a few older women wear exotic Spanish shawls and capes obviously from the twenties and thirties—lots of dramatic

155

makeup. In the front row every night, a woman sits with two large baby dolls, cradling one in each arm. The beautiful, the odd, the old and the new, make the mix all the more exciting: the audience is part of the show.

It is a historic night. She holds her breath, along with the expectant crowd. Gino Ferrari will be on stage in minutes, arising from a puff of smoke, tempting Faust to seduce Marguerite. Tremendous applause greets his entrance. He is everything they have read about: big, handsome, electric. His first notes confirm the genius of his acting, the depth and beauty of his voice. He *is* the devil. She falls in love with him, along with whole rows of women. Ferrari is all they talk about at intermission. They feel more feminine, while the men shrink inside their dressy suits.

The next week he is *Don Giovanni*, dominating the big stage at Music Hall, his voice filling the vast space with its depth and beauty. Rumor says he lives the role of the seducer.

She meets him at a party after *Don Giovanni*. He still wears his makeup and costume, still acting the don. He sweeps off his hat and bows deeply when she praises his singing. He thanks her.

She repeats the way he says "thank you, Madam," over and over as she rides home.

At a fund-raiser, another night, he is there right beside her. Tall, handsome, electric. She is wearing her new Karl Lagerfeld knock-off, a thirties-style chiffon. She is feeling beautiful and glamorous and feels more so when he takes her hand and kisses it.

"You with the beautiful green eyes. I see you in the second row. It is too far away. I want you on stage with me."

"Me?"

"You must be a super in *Faust*. I can see you looking charming in the bodice and skirts of a peasant girl. You are a peasant girl. I can tell, never mind the chiffon dress."

She feels like a teenager again, when she and her friends swooned over Giovanni Martinelli (whom Gino resembles with his deep voice, good looks and magnetic personality).

Now she has her castle to fulfill her romantic childhood dreams, but her stronghold is under siege, not by barbarians but by the overly-civil. Her *parfit gentil knight* has turned into—a lawyer. During arguments, when Betsy is furious he makes comments like, "I withdraw that." Betsy has screamed more than once, "You can't strike things from the record in life. We're not in a courtroom."

John is dependable as the man on the Viennese clock tower; he is loving and reasonable, neat and good-smelling and kind, but his fussiness and preciseness sometimes drive her wild: he will empty a waste can with nothing in it but a strand of dental floss. At the opera, he buries his head in the program, noting the names of contributors and how much they give.

During arguments, he keeps his voice low and reasonable and even sometimes ticks off his points by the alphabet. He can never see why she needs to raise her voice simply because she is angry. Sometimes she looks back with nostalgia for the unguarded opinions, the impolite laughter, the lack of restraint of her yeoman family.

She asks the current stage manager, an amiable whirlwind named Tony, if she may, as a lark, be a super again. Of course he says yes, and she goes on stage in *Faust* dressed in a white blouse and cotton skirt.

The productions have improved since she was young, the costumes are fresh and elegant, and the volunteers are now largely adults, stock brokers, bankers, teachers, many of them gay. They all laugh and joke as they put on wigs and hats, hoop skirts and tights; they are part of the theater. She supers in *Aida* and *Carmen*, and life at Music Hall seems like a play, make-believe, and exciting.

In the wings, she watches as Gino dominates the hall, the audience enthralled by his wonderful voice and athletic physique.

When he comes off stage he is perspiring like a moving man, wrung out, not the cool "seducteur" she saw from out front. Singing, she realizes, is hard work.

"Give me your handkerchief," he says. He mops his brow with the tiny lace square she takes from her pocket. After the last act, he grabs her and kisses her behind a flat. He begs her to meet him at his hotel. She can't do that. She is married. She has children . . . .

They meet in New York. It is not safe to meet in Cincinnati. Everybody knows everybody in town. The grapevine is so efficient. Of course, that doesn't stop extramarital affairs, but for her, who does not want scandal to come anywhere near her family, New York works out better. She goes there several weekends, to help plan "sorority reunions."

In the afternoons, she walks proudly about in midtown, and window shops, enjoying her secret. She lunches alone at the Palm Court in the Plaza (women are not allowed in the Oak Room). She meets Gino at the Chelsea for martinis as the daylight fades (she sees Arthur Miller in the lobby, Jessica Tandy in the hall), or she picks Gino up in a cab after his performance when he still has a few little streaks of greasepaint behind his ears.

Was that woman really her? They were in costumes when he kissed her. He was Mephistopheles, she a country girl. So long ago. She was never sorry. She is glad she'd had the excitement of her romance with Gino. Something very different from the love she had for John and the children.

Of course the affair soon came to an end. There was her life to consider, real life, family, self, and Betsy realized she was not the only woman in Cincinnati with whom her lover had affairs. She could stand his womanizing; with his energy and looks and fame, he would not be content with a tame life. It was the line he used with all the women, as if he were reading from a libretto . . .

She suspected that John knew about the affair. But she knew that he would not want to end their marriage. She gathered that in his cool, analytical way, he assessed the situation and decided that the best course was to say nothing. It was like breast cancer, something their age group was becoming all too familiar with. You waited, and if it didn't recur within a certain number of years, you might go about your business and be all right.

The music on the radio is interrupted by an announcer's voice, bringing Betsy back from her old romance to the world of the hospital. In this sick and sterile place, she is glad she had had some fire in her life at a time when marriage and family had become routine. She understands Eric. Natalie is very seductive, and he is a manly man. Natalie does not seem to have the problems and complexity of a Judith. Eric might want someone simpler, especially with Judith off in Washington finding herself or whatever she was doing. So if Eric's choice is to be Natalie if he gets well, if they end up in the beach scene Natalie pinned to the wall, so be it. If Natalie is necessary to save her son's heart, she should be kept on.

Betsy loves Judith, but if it is to be a choice between Judith and her son, if her son needs someone different, Betsy's loyalty will be to him. That's the way it is. In love and grief there are no rights.

Part 4

KNIFE EDGE

33

William

The hospital reminds him of the House of Horrors at Coney Island where a rail car takes you through a large devouring mouth laughing raucously, then hurls you through a dark tunnel where ghosts rise out of coffins, and eerie howls of fear and pain ricochet through the blackness. So the mechanical greeting at the hospital door ushers William into a bizarre and frightening place: sepulchral halls, ghostly white-sheeted patients being rolled along the corridors, groans from open doors. William is so sick of the welcoming falsetto, he mutters "fuck you" to the recording as he enters.

Cat scans, electrocardiograms, echo chambers, sonograms, blood transfusions: it has been three weeks of constant intricate procedures, constant anxiety, wearing everyone down, necessitating long waits and patience, something William's father doesn't possess. All but the transfusions require trips to various departments in a wheelchair with a "transporter"—several of whom park his father in a cold hallway and forget about him. The knee, declared "coming along," still looks like a burst fruit.

The family discusses the heart surgery over and over: William's father can stay put and continue trying to gain strength for the ordeal of the bypass, or to go ahead with it. His blood is too thick, then it's too thin. He is able to stand and walk some and is becoming more lucid, while the bad heart with its blocked arteries and leaky valve is waiting to betray him. The possibility of pneumonia lurks in the place like an assassin. The repair of the heart would bring less fear of sudden death, but it would set back the knee and his father's strength—or maybe kill him.

"Catch 22," David says.

They go round and round, listing the pros and cons. What to do? What to do? Continue the build-up or move on? There really is no perfect choice, they all see that.

Finally William's mother says, "I don't care if they throw him out the window, let's go."

The night of the promised non-hospital food, David, and William's mother, preceded by the pungent smell of French-fried onions, arrive in his father's room bearing greasy bags.

"You've been talking about us all having dinner together," David says to his father.

"We're having your favorites," his mother says. "White Castles, onion rings and French fries!"

William's father smiles.

"And guess what I have here?" David says. He opens a bag and takes out a bottle of scotch. "Tiny bit won't hurt," he says.

William props his father up against his pillows; his mother sits at the end of his father's bed. David pours a small amount of scotch into four plastic glasses, fills them with ice and water, and offers them around.

William shakes his head no. Alcohol could start him off wanting pot, then more shit. He has called his sponsor Tim admitting to temptation, and Tim has been after him to go on some rounds with him. See the results in Gloria and the others.

William gets a ginger ale from his backpack and pours some into a plastic glass. It looks just like the scotch the others have. But lacks the enticing smell.

The sun gives the room a gold glow.

"Let's party!" David says.

The four lift their glasses.

"Here's to Pop," William says.

William's mother clicks her glass with his father's. His parents exchange a look of contentment, a look they shared sometimes at home when they were all four together. His parents smile. William can tell they feel happy in spite of the hospital beds and the tubes and IV and the stupid blue gown and therapeutic stockings, and the dangers of the scheduled surgery. They all laugh as William's mother passes around the food and they eat their burgers in two bites and pass the bags.

It's like a picnic at the edge of a cliff. But William feels oddly happy, having just himself, his brother and his parents together. No wives, no girlfriends, no children, no grandparents, just the original family, before his mother's departure, before Natalie, before his father's heart gave out, back the way it was when he and David were kids and they thought their world would always be OK.

34

David

"I want Mommy! I want Mommy!" A girl about twelve, sitting across from David in the hospital waiting room, begins screaming. She is dark haired, pretty, even with her features distorted in anguish. A woman sits beside her and tries to hush her cries, but the girl screams louder, "I want Mommy." Her voice is high-pitched, piercing. David has never seen such naked emotion. He would like to help, but there is nothing to do; several men stand by the door, he guesses they are uncles or friends, for they don't take her in their arms as a father might do. The woman is joined by another who pats the girl and whispers to her, but the girl keeps on screaming, "I want Mommy. I want Mommy!"

Her cries are so piteous, so piercing. In a few minutes, another woman comes into the room and speaks quietly to the girl. David guesses she is saying the mother has died. The girl shrieks, "No! Mommy! I want Mommy!" The woman hugs her and whispers something more. The girl squirms in her chair and pulls away. "I hate God!" she screams. The group, family or church members, David figures, continue to try to soothe her, but she cries, "I hate God! I *hate* God! I want Mommy!"

David is so distressed, he wants to do something. But what? The mother has obviously died. The child is alone, grief stricken. The people around her cannot help. They finally walk her to the door and out of the room, still sobbing and crying out, "Mommy, Mommy." David goes over to one of the men. He has been witness to the girl's terrible pain; he cannot ignore it.

"I'm so sorry," he says, "so sorry."

The man nods a thank you and leaves. The girl's cries echo in the room.

David shivers. What will happen to the child?

He sighs and takes his papers out of his briefcase. He tries to work while his father is undergoing another transfusion. His pressing case goes to court the day before his father's surgery. The lawyers are fighting with each other like a bunch of jackals with a kill. He is the lead attorney and it can't go on without him. To step away now would be to kiss goodbye the higher take for the year he's counting on to help pay off his and Lydia's debts. Meanwhile a client of his at Volunteer Lawyers for the Poor needs urgent help. Lydia is nagging him about Phoebe's birthday party which looks as though it might conflict with his court date; Phoebe is practicing for a harp recital and has extra sessions at her music class. David's calendar is a mess of scratch-outs and exclamation points and notes to himself: DON'T FORGET!

David hears the girl's screams as he is trying to fall asleep that night. Lydia is lying with her back to him, a ring of hostility surrounding her strong as the implicit "stay back" around the frantic girl. The keenness they had when they first confronted his father's grave illness has dissipated. They have had very little sex for weeks, not even a comfortable sleep with their arms around each other. Something has got to give.

Their outlook has been good with their two careers but he feels differently now: things can take a sudden turn, no one can be sure of anything.

Lydia is still straw bossing changes in the house. The mess and the sound of saws and hammers and people tromping in and out of the house makes his head hurt.

Fingers seem to be prying his brain into sections like an orange.

At the hospital he sees through the door of his father's room, a parade of men attached to IVs, shuffling down the hall. Like the living dead. He pictures himself one of them.

Lydia surprises David with a peace offering the night before Phoebe's party.

"Phoebe has an overnight and I made a reservation for us at Oscar. You need to get an evening away from the hospital and *relax.*"

David thinks not. But then thinks, maybe she's right. A relaxing drink and time for a quiet talk with Lydia would be good.

While they are dressing to go out, Lydia pokes David in the belly.

"You need to get to the gym."

Workouts are another thing, along with his family, that David has neglected. He is at the hospital every evening; he worries about his mother who has been sleeping there nights in his father's room.

He squeezes the stomach fat he's added. It isn't just from lack of exercise. Like the nurses, technicians, visitors, everyone around the center of sickness, he constantly feeds himself: burgers, bagels, French fries, onion rings, brownies, soft drinks.

Lydia drives to the restaurant in her huge SUV which David hates. He has begged her to get something smaller, more efficient, but she claims she has to have the bigger vehicle to accommodate Phoebe's friends and all their gear. It is also protection on highways.

"It isn't," David argues. "They tend to roll over and they're gas guzzlers."

He especially hates SUVs now with the war in Iraq going on. They all seem to be plastered with yellow "Support Our Troops" stickers, as though using more oil is patriotic.

In the car, he thinks of George Orwell's satires, how people are falling for the calculating non-sequiturs of the war pushers: "They hate us because we love freedom." The euphemisms are right out of *Animal Farm*: "collateral damage" for the death of women and children, "contractors" for mercenary troops.

"Oscar is the hottest new place in town," Lydia says.

Hottest usually means crowded and expensive, David thinks, but he still pictures himself and Lydia holding hands and maybe being able to cool the tensions of the last month.

She pulls into the parking lot of a busy suburban strip of eating places, boutiques, and beauty shops. She struggles to wedge her SUV next to two others equally big.

"For God's sake," David says. "I bet these blimps are carrying two people in vehicles the size of interstate trucks."

"Oh stop being fatuous," Lydia says. "I've been under pressure too, you know. Maybe I need some relief."

"You're right," David says. "I'll shut up."

They open the door of the restaurant, a black marble and stainless steel building, and a blast of noise like a suddenly blaring radio hits them: chattering voices and music bouncing from the hard walls and ceiling and floors. David can barely hear the *maitre d's* question: "M'sieur has a reservation?"

"Yes," Lydia says. She gives her name.

"It will take a few minutes while a table is being prepared. Would you care to step over to the bar while waiting?"

David and Lydia look at each other. She nods. They step over to the bar. Here the clatter of glasses and rattle of ice being shaken, the swish of the cappuccino machine and shrieks of laughter add to the din. A line-up of women perch on the bar stools, a man here and there, his darker clothes a contrast to the bright silks of the women. The women seem to David to have been cloned in a Barbie factory: most are blond with the same razor sharp straight hair about shoulder length, breasts well-displayed—perfectly round, surely plastically enhanced, about the size of grapefruits. Their "fuck me" stilettos in various colors with bondage straps are hooked onto the rails of the bar stools. David realizes that Lydia blends right in. She wears the same haircut (which he knows costs about two hundred dollars), a print blouse cut low, mini skirt and the same bunion-producing shoes.

For whom is she dressing? he wonders. He likes her best in her blue jeans and T-shirt and pigtails, the way she dresses around the house. She walks so lightly and moves so sprightly in those casual clothes instead of the self-conscious way she has to step in order to navigate stairs in her expensive sandals. She really doesn't need the heavy make-up or the hair dye.

They order drinks, a lemon drop in a frosted glass with a sugar rim for Lydia, a scotch for David.

"This place is exciting, isn't it?" Lydia says. She looks happy. This is her idea of sophistication.

David nods, tries to be enthusiastic, but the noise and crowd just make him feel morose. They look around at the drinkers, some obviously getting acquainted for the first time.

"If we weren't married, would you try to pick me up?" Lydia says.

"No," David says. "I'd be scared to death."

He remembers her at Georgetown Law: she was so cute and bright. She talked about public service law as a career, but when a lucrative opportunity came for her in Cincinnati, David, who was offered a place in a more prestigious firm in Washington, agreed to come home.

"Your table is ready, Mr. Simpson-Howard." The *maitre d'* appears with two heavy leather-bound menus. He indicates a banquette in the midst of the clatter and leads David and Lydia to it. They weave their way through the throng of waiters pouring water, customers arriving and leaving and staff asking after the happiness and comfort of the diners; they seem more solicitous and concerned than the nurses at the hospital.

Lydia slides somewhat clumsily into the center of the banquette, thrusting out her rear in her tight skirt as though spinning a hula hoop. The china is genuine, the silverware gleams, and there are three glasses at each place. The settings sparkle.

When they are settled, and the bottled-versus-tap-water issue is resolved with Carey their waiter, David orders another scotch and asks if Lydia would like another lemon drop. She nods yes.

"What's in that anyway?" David says.

"Gin. A little lemon and sugar." It's in a large martini glass like the ones on *Sex and the City.*

Another couple who look like David and Lydia's identical twins are seated at the banquette next to them.

"Why do you women wear those stupid shoes?" David asks. He gulps his scotch. "Why don't you just bind your feet?"

"They're great looking. David, don't be an old grouch."

"Promise you won't get those artificial boobs."

Lydia just stares at him.

Has she already done so? He stares at her beautifully symmetrical breasts.

Of course they are real. He would know otherwise. He knows her body—and he would have seen the bill . . .

Carey arrives at the table.

"May I take your orders?"

David nods.

Lydia picks an appetizer salad and no entrée.

David orders a pate for a starter and a steak.

Carey says, "Excellent choice!"

David thinks, *fine, the first right choice I've made all day.*

David looks over the lengthy wine list.

"Would you like white or red?" He asks Lydia.

"I don't care. I guess red to go with your steak."

"House red," David says.

"Um, we do not have a *vin ordinaire*," Carey says.

"Let me pick." Lydia selects a Cabernet.

When the waiter leaves with the order, David says, "Fifty bucks?"

"You'll like this," Lydia says. "My gourmet club has studied it."

How has David gotten so out of touch with Lydia?

"Your gourmet club?" he says.

"We have wine tastings along with cheese and things.

"Oh fine."

When had Lydia become so—so—snooty? David wonders.

"I want Phoebe to know good cheeses," Lydia says.

"That *is* crucial," David says. "Get her into a good college."

Lydia finishes her drink.

"Everything you say is sarcastic," she says.

David drains his scotch.

"I notice you ordered a single malt scotch," Lydia says. "If you're so cost-conscious . . . ."

David's pate and Lydia's salad arrive. Carey pours wine into their glasses.

Lydia eats her two shrimp and shreds of freesia and tiny lumps of goat cheese.

David offers her a cracker with pate but she shakes her head no.

"Is that all you're going to eat?" he asks.

She takes a piece of bread from its comfy little bed in a basket, and nibbles.

"You're not getting anorexic are you?" he says.

"No. I'm just not hungry. That was quite filling."

"Why on earth do you want to come to a fancy restaurant to eat a few lettuce leaves?"

She ignores him.

"Oh yes, this *is* the hottest new place in town."

Carey removes David's clean appetizer plate. David drinks a second glass of wine while he waits for his steak to arrive. He pours for Lydia.

"Thank you."

The rest of the dinner goes by in a kind of haze. At some point David sees Carey whisk his dinner plate away; Lenny couldn't have done better on the meat and sauce and potato. The wine bottle is turned upside down in the cooler and David says they will take a look at the dessert menu. He is surprised when Lydia orders a warm chocolate cake with a runny filling. He has the crème brulee. They each have a brandy.

In the parking lot, the tip calculated and added to the check for a grand total of two hundred and fifty dollars, Carey having been bid farewell like an old friend, and the *maitre d'* thanked for a lovely evening, David and Lydia grope their way to the SUV. Now they are laughing at how drunk they are.

"I'll drive," David says.

"You hate my car." Lydia's voice is loud and thick with alcohol.

"I think you're a little juiced."

"No more than you."

David rummages in his pockets for his keys, but Lydia whips hers out faster than he can locate the one to her car. She climbs into the driver's seat.

"Go slow," he says.

"I know how to drive."

"We don't want to get arrested."

Lydia pulls out of the parking lot with a lurch and is soon near the expressway, David holding onto the passenger hand grip. He belches from the rich food, wants above all to be home and safe and not getting booked in a police station. The lights along the way flash in and out of his eyes.

"Watch it," he says, grabbing for some semblance of control.

"I'm going exactly the speed limit," Lydia says.

But David's heart begins to pound furiously when they turn onto the expressway and he hears a siren and sees a police car coming behind them. Its lights are whirling and the siren sounds like the climax of some thriller with subtitles. Lydia says "Oh God" and pulls over. She puts her head down on the steering wheel.

The police cruiser speeds right by them, and passes several other cars that have pulled to the side.

"High speed chase," David says. "Somebody's broken into a Seven-Eleven." He pictures a white guy with a long list of DUI's and a real load on. It seems to happen every week or so, with somebody getting killed: a cop, the drunk, or some poor schmuck driving innocently in his own lane.

David feels guilty about his inebriation and he can tell Lydia does too. They don't say a word about it, but Lydia continues to drive very carefully.

Finally home in their big house, so empty without Phoebe, David and Lydia climb the grand stairway to their bedroom. David feels crappy: the rich food, the alcohol, the mean words—

Lydia undresses silently. David falls onto their bed in his clothes, first throwing the ten decorator pillows onto a chair. He regrets being such a jerk all evening. And now Lydia, without her makeup and her S&M shoes, looks sweet and pretty. He has been asking too much of her—to take over so many of the daily chores and put up with his anxiety and preoccupation with his father. Even in ordinary times she does too much: every day up at six-thirty, she showers and washes her hair, fixes breakfast for him and Phoebe, drives miles out of the way to the school they had picked for Phoebe; after school she chauffeurs her to her activities, works on her various boards. Evenings she pours over work she's brought home from the office. All this while looking twenty-three and scratching at the glass ceiling at her firm. She just wanted a little fun . . . .

Lydia's done all the calling and planning and work for Phoebe's birthday. She already has a table arranged in the sun room: a blue and white table cloth, blue napkins with lace edges, a centerpiece of flowers made of brightly wrapped candies, a cake platter awaiting the two hundred dollar cake she has ordered.

David goes to her and puts his arms around her. She pushes him away.

"Oh, get away," she says.

He tries to take her breasts in his hands.

Lydia marches to the bed and throws herself on it.

"I have to get up early and get the party organized."

David lies down beside her.

"I'm sorry," he says.

"Get your shoes off the bedspread. Go get undressed. Or go to hell—"

David slowly hauls himself up and stands unsteadily.

"You're so self-righteous. So god-damned pompous. And you eat like a pig."

David belches, trying to restrain the sound.

"I'll sleep in the guest room," he says.

"You do that."

David goes down the hall and flops down on one of the twin beds in the guest room. His chest feels tight and he keeps belching. He sees the butter he slathered on his bread, the steak sauce with bubbles of fat glistening in it, the potatoes swimming in cheese and cream, the crème brulee with a thin cookie like a sea fan poking up from its gooey buttery heart.

He rolls around most of the night, tugging on the sheets, trying to rest his neck on the too-plump pillow. He sleeps only an hour or so, and awakens to the sound of the little girl screaming, "I want Mommy." He leaps out of bed, but a hangover like a punch in the head sends him back onto the mattress. He regrets bitching about everything last night and spoiling Lydia's outing. He wonders how the girl's mother died. He must protect Phoebe.

35

William

"The heart-lung machine will let the surgeon stop the heart for several hours while he inserts the veins he takes out of your father's leg around the blocked arteries," Angie explained. "They'll put a large drainage tube in the upper chamber of the heart and draw the un-oxygenated blood into a reservoir. From there they pump it through an artificial lung—to get oxygen. They add a drug, otherwise contact with the plastic tubing might make the blood clot . . . ."

"Stop. Stop," William said. The thought of his father's heart's blood drained from his body, sloshing about in a plastic tube . . . . It would be as if he were dead again, part of a machine.

Man, how good a little coke would be right now, William thinks. He is in his room over the coffee shop. All he would have to do is walk to the corner. William repeats his mantra, calls Tim. This is no time to be out of touch with his sponsor. They make a date to meet and Tim asks William to go with him to a church to give a talk.

William is preparing his remarks when David calls, mad because William apparently forgot to line up a sitter for their father.

"You never listen," David says.

"No, you never listen. I told you I have to go with Tim to speak at a church."

"But you were going to call a sitter. Brendan can't come to the hospital tonight."

"I did."

"But did the service call you back?"

William has to think. He can't remember. Thought he'd taken care of the problem.

"Mom had to be there all morning when she should have gone home."

William is tempted to repeat Angie's description of the heart surgery to David. He has always been squeamish. But he has noticed lately that David has been breathing funny. He looked sweaty the last time William saw him— Having family duties: the wife, the house, the kid, the dog, William can't imagine. But why are they always so much more important than William's commitments, which the others seem to think amount to fooling around? He can't wipe away, though, feeling especially bad for letting his mother in for another hard morning when she was asking for time off to sleep; "I need to sleep till I wake up," she said, "just once." His father is invariably restless all night, then wakes at five, anxious to shave and wash, peremptory as Old King Cole calling for his pipe and his bowl.

A rivulet of sweat runs down William's back. His room air conditioner that normally kicks in with a groan, and slavers onto the sidewalk, is not working and it's hotter than hell in his room. Jimmy said he would put some Freon in it, but the bar has been busy and he hasn't gotten around to it.

"So can you get someone or go over?" David says.

"Later. I told you. First I have to do the church lecture with Tim, and we're going to visit one of our clients, Gloria. She's had a major stroke and is in a nursing home."

"Today?"

Does he have to prove to big brother that his commitments are legitimate?

David is silent. William can hear him thinking, family comes first. Don't waste your life on hopeless people.

"Aren't Betsy and John going over?" William asks.

"Betsy has a cold. She doesn't want to give it to Dad. I told you that."

"Oh. Well, I'll get there."

"And remember," David speaks as though to a deaf person: "I-Will-Be-In-Court-On-Tuesday."

The day before the heart surgery.

"*And* : We Have-A-Birthday-Party-To-Day."

"You don't have to be snotty."

"I'm just trying to get through to you."

When he turns off his phone, William lies back on his messy bed. He has forgotten to send Phoebe a birthday present or even a card. Well, she'll get too much anyway. The child has more toys than all of Peru. She's a swell kid, pretty unspoiled in spite of her parents' hovering and overindulgence. Lydia, William can live without. Men are supposed to marry their mothers, but David has married his grandmother (a compulsive home decorator). She's too plastic, too driven. Besides she reminds him of a girl in high school he had a crush on who almost laughed in his face when he asked her for a date, Mallory McGovern.

He's hot, guilty, worried. Three days until the bypass. Both of his father's legs will have incisions, along with the heart—*if* he lives through the operation. One of the aides said, "I hate those replacements; they're tricky," and she gasped when told the patient was on his way to heart surgery.

William rolls over and phones the sitter service. They have called someone to sit with his father. They are running late. He calls his father.

"Are you OK for awhile?" he says.

"I can't find the call button. Mom's gone home. When did you say they were going to operate?"

"I'll be right over," William says.

It is hot outside, typical Indian summer. William feels the sun through his jacket.

At the hospital, he stays with his father until the sitter arrives. It's Kurt, a tall white man with a German accent. He is gobbling a carryout meal, and appears to have a cold.

Doctor friends warned of pneumonia spreading in hospitals and killing more patients than their original disease.

"You have a cold?" William asks.

"Allergies," Kurt says.

Does William believe him? People are always saying they're OK when they're not.

William takes a chance. They are all over-anxious.

Or is he being the irresponsible dolt that David thinks he is?

"If he needs anything, call a nurse. OK?" he says.

"We'll be fine," Kurt says. "Mr. Howard, do you want to watch the television?"

William waits for Tim at the front door of the hospital. He can hear the truck from a block away, a clunky pick-up. Tim has shaved off his stubble and pulled back his dreadlocks with a head band. He is wearing a suit and tie, and looks clean and neat as a felon dressed for court.

The church is a suburban Protestant one, and William and Tim sit through the sermon, waiting to give their spiel. Like too many of the ministers William has come into contact with, this man hypes Salvation, promising a reward for faith. And it is an exclusive reward, only for his brand of Christians.

William's family are sort of fallen-away Unitarians, technically members of a church but—since William and David grew up— not often at Sunday services. When they first joined, it was for the children. His father detested more traditional religions: "for stealing land, enslaving people, stifling science, encouraging over- population—for the boot, the screw, and the auto da fe."

The Unitarian church was free of supernatural doctrine, and it had a history of working for peace. Besides, Ralph Waldo Emerson and Abraham Lincoln had been Unitarians.

"But do we believe in God?" William asked.

"You have the right to follow your own conscience and beliefs."

"Is there a God?" David said.

"I don't know. And neither does anyone else. It's OK to say you don't know."

At one point William thought about becoming a Hindu. He was in his drug-taking phase and looking for something exotic, turned off by the predictability of his family, the intellectualism of his religion. "We don't believe in anything," he said to his father.

"Yes, we do," his father answered. "We believe in peace. We believe in democracy and letting people think for themselves. We believe in the rule of law. I could go on . . . ."

"We believe in love," his mother said.

All right, all right, William thought. They're right. But so damn smug.

With his parents William could never work up a satisfying sense of outrage by getting an evasive answer or dismissal of his questions. Just exasperation. They had been rebels themselves, but seemed so tame, so relentlessly optimistic, believing the pendulum would swing back when things went wrong and that the modern world had forces of light that would not allow its extinction.

"If you want to pursue Hinduism, fine," his father told William. "Just be sure and study it first and be sure you are prepared for whatever sacrifices you have to make, your other beliefs, whatever . . . ."

William, as disarmed and annoyed as if his father were a dogmatic know-nothing, cracked, "Don't think I don't understand the use of reverse psychology."

William looks around the sanctuary where he awaits his and Tim's turn to speak. The stained glass windows and the quiet of the place are nice, but the minister's homily is the usual exclusionary drum beat.

Now it is time for Tim to say his piece. He ascends the podium; in his cleaned-up garments there is something of the Reverend Dimsdale about him. Something not quite right. He tells the congregation how he got hooked on drugs, lost his job, his family and friends, pimped his girl friend, lived in his car. Then he lost the car, too, and hit bottom on the street.

"It's ugly," he says. "It's ugly. And it's not just black kids and dudes like me, but your own sons and daughters. They come down town where they don't belong. Boys trading their watches and their girlfriends for a fix. Young girls forced to *suck dick* to get drugs."

William is alarmed at Tim's language before this proper-looking audience, but maybe Tim has to shock to get his message across. Still—

When Tim winds down, William takes his place; he speaks about the more technical side of drugs, and tells his story and stresses the importance of early intervention. After the service, the church members tentatively extend polite thanks for William and Tim's visit.

The two men move on to visit Gloria.

William likes Gloria. He has missed her familiar figure huddled in the park across from Music Hall. She was intelligent, funny, and good humored, when she was not panhandling or peeing on the steps of City Hall. He and Tim have tried hard to get her off meth. She came from a small town in Indiana where it was the local industry.

The nursing home is a small rambling building of no distinction tucked behind a row of houses not too far from Good Shepard Hospital. The front walk is patterned with black wads of gum. Several old people, wrapped in blankets, in wheel chairs, doze under the front awning. William and Tim go to the reception desk and ask for Gloria.

Tim said she had seemed comfortable when she got settled here, after a week or so of demanding her blankets and plastic bags. She is weaker now and does not know where she is.

The woman at the desk says, "I'm afraid Mrs. Dupree is failing."

"I'm sorry," Tim says. "Two days ago, she was—well—a little out of it, but she looked OK."

William and Tim take the elevator to the lower floor and find Gloria's room. The small figure in the bed is being watched by two women, a nurse and an assistant. She is propped against a pillow, her body covered by a white sheet. She looks very different from the woman who lived on the streets. She was never too clean, but she had bright eyes and plump cheeks, a pleasant smile. Now she looks older than Betsy. William is shocked at the change in her. He has never been this close to death, which seems to be reaching out for Gloria.

Her face has lost most of its flesh, and her lips are drawn back tightly, making her gritted teeth protrude. They look like false teeth. Her eyes are rolled back in her head, and only the whites show. Her hands are clenched. Her neck is weirdly elongated as she seems to be straining against some unseen force.

William thinks, *So this is what dying is like.*

It is far from the peaceful closing of eyes and going to sleep he's seen in the movies. It is a struggle. William puts his trembling hands in his pockets.

Tim touches his breast—he's given up smoking but not the reflex. He pats Gloria's bony hand. She does not respond.

William watches the fish in a small tank swimming through a tiny castle. Why a castle, William thinks.

In a moment, the nurse says, "Mrs. Dupree has expired." Gloria's lips are drawn over the awful teeth. Tim kisses Gloria on her forehead. William feels courage escaping him like a rope sliding through his hands. What can he hang onto?

Driving back to his apartment, William and Tim are silent. William can not erase the picture of plump feisty Gloria looking so strange, in such agony. Her blank eyes and clenched teeth, the weird elongation of her neck.

His room is airless, drab. He sits looking out his window for a long time. He tries to sleep. Tim and his obscene words to the polite, middle-class congregation keep him awake. Tim upon whom he has leaned for guidance and help.

There is no help for him. He believes in nothing.

William finds a notepad and writes. He scratches out, chews his pencil, scribbles a poem:

> Death Cat: I've seen the way
> You play with a mouse.
> You tease him with soft paw,
> Then suck him into your great maw,
> Then cough him out,
> A trembling hair-ball,
> Wet with spit and fear.
> While he lies before you stiff,
> Defenseless, squealing,
> You grin from ear to ear,

Relentless, cruel, purring,
You take him up again,
You shake him,
You pin him down,
Your heavy velvet paws upon him,
You break him.

Is death that brutal? Is there nothing more? Are we helpless? Would his father be like Gloria? Would there be no afterward, period, the end.

He runs out of his apartment, searches the streets for a dealer. He hears gun shots a few blocks away.

Death is right behind him, around every corner.

He bolts toward Reverend Allen's storefront church, knocks on the door. His body jiggling up and down.

A woman lets him in.

"Why William, are you all right?"

"Is Rev here?"

"Sure."

There are always several women helping out in this small, bare set of rooms, aiding Reverend Allen with his ministry, giving out what food they can to the homeless who stop by. William is led into the second room where Rev Al is sitting in a well-worn chair, dressed in his usual out of style clothes, reading his Bible.

The man seems translucent with his white hair, white white skin, thin arms and face, like an ivory icon.

"Why hello, William," he says. "What brings you my way?"

William can not speak immediately. He doesn't know why he is here.

"Gloria died," he says.

"I'm sorry."

"I've never seen anyone die before."

"You never get used to it."

Reverend Al is quiet, waiting for William to say what he came for.

"Do you really believe there's an afterlife?" William blurts out.

"I do," Rev Al says, "but I do not know."

"We think we can do it all on our own," William says. "I can't."

"Who is we?"

"We Howards."

"Good people," Rev says. "Good people."

William pulls the poem he wrote out of his pocket and hands it to Rev. Rev puts on his glasses and reads.

William stares at the patterns in the scarred linoleum floor.

He worries as the minister reads. What is he thinking? The words are so inimical to Rev Al's beliefs. William says them to himself.

Reverend Al is frowning. He re-reads the poem. He hands William the piece of paper.

"Death Cat," Rev says.

William awaits his verdict like a criminal.

"You are a nihilist," Rev says.

"I am, I guess" William says. "I can't believe like you do." He almost wants Rev to convert him, to give him some of his calm, his sureness and righteousness.

"An existentialist—" Rev says "—with a good heart."

"I'm so empty. So worried."

"You won't always be."

One of the women helping out pokes her head into the room.

"Time for your pills," she says.

"Oh bother."

When Rev has taken his medicine and drunk a glass of water, he offers William tea. He says, "You believe in the Golden Rule, don't you, William?"

"Yes."

"You will find your way. The right one for you. Not mine. Not your father's. I think not a traditional church."

William drinks his tea.

Someone is knocking at the door.

"Incidentally," Rev says, "it's a good poem."

William stands and pats Rev Al on the shoulder. The man seems to be lit from within.

William is still sad and confused, with no answers, but he is grateful for Reverend Al's presence, his aura. His acceptance.

"So long," William says. "Thanks for the tea."

He heads over to Washington Park. Tim is leaning against one of the trees, smoking a cigarette.

"Hey man," he says, "You OK?"

William nods.

"This was pretty heavy today, am I right?"

"Yeah," William says. Tim throws his cigarette on the grass and walks away. "Good luck to your old man tomorrow."

William sits on one of the stone benches in the park and stares at the leaves and litter.

He does not see Angie coming, and is surprised when she plops down beside him.

"Howdy."

"Hi, Angie."

She looks him over.

"Wow. You are pretty down, aren't you?" she says.

She takes his arm, and he pats hers, always glad to see her pixie face and thoughtful gray-green eyes.

"Yeah."

"Maybe we should walk a little," she says. She coaxes him to his feet.

They walk a block or two, past an empty lot seething with litter, a small garden provided by the city, past empty buildings with distinguished facades and trim, gutted or rotting inside. Signs proclaim them the property of a group seeking funds to fix them up for low-income residents, or of developers intending to turn the neighborhood into an upscale area. The war between the groups has been going on a long time. Angie and Rev Allen are working hard to keep the places for the poor, the folks who call this their home. Rev has been hit in the face once and Angie arrested at a sit-in occupying a building.

William and Angie pass a row of buildings that face the park, once derelict, suddenly sleek-looking townhouses. Angie yelps, "The yuppies are coming! The yuppies are coming!"

William tries to laugh.

They hear the hurdy-gurdy sound of the ice cream truck.

"Buy me a Popsicle," Angie says.

She and William join the line of children at the truck's window and study the pictures on the side. William buys Angie and himself Popsicles.

"Ummm, nothing better on a warm day," Angie says.

They sit in the park under a tree. Nearby men are playing chess or cards, and on the corner the drug dealers are making a sale through the window of a car: just like the ice cream man, William thinks.

"So what's got you so low?" Angie says.

William tells her of his need to be with Tim. The visit to the church and the way he felt seeing Gloria trying to hang on to her life, and how she looked.

She puts her arm around him. "My God," she says. They sit quietly for a while. Then Angie nods toward the drugmobile. "Where are the cops when we need them?"

"Arresting old ladies for not putting enough coins in the parking meters." This had happened to one of Reverend Al's followers.

William walks over to the waste container and drops in their wrappers.

"'Scuse me," he says to Angie, "I'm gonna call over at the hospital." He takes his cell phone out of his pocket.

His mother answers.

"I got rid of that Kurt," she says. "He definitely has a cold."

"He said it was an allergy . . . ."

"Well . . . . We need Brendan."

"You go home," William says. "I'll be over and stay the night. You need some decent sleep."

"I'm OK," she says. Then: "No I'm not."

"I'll get there as soon as I can."

"You sound awfully low, Will."

He tries to lighten his voice.

"How was the birthday party?" he asks.

"Lavish. Hectic. My god, did you have parties like that?"

"We never had any parties at all. Maybe a Twinkie with a candle on it."

"You did too. You always had a party," his mother says, "just not this kind of loot."

"All I got was a plastic man with anatomically correct genitals."

His mother chuckles unconvincingly. She knows his voice too well for him to fool her.

The air leaks out of their banter. They exchange love yous and hang up.

"You talk to your mother like that?" Angie says.

"Like what?"

"Genitals."

The only thing off limits for the Howards, William thinks, is outbursts of feeling. We always tell each other what we think, maybe not what we feel.

On his father's sonogram William saw his father's heart, a roiling mass of valves and tissues, the living thing. He has seen his father's real heart, but he can not know the true nature of it.

Angie tugs at William's arm. She says, "Dr. Graham is the best, William."

"I know."

They pass Music Hall. The steel drum band from the Neighborhood Center is out front on the sidewalk, banging out *Yellow Bird*. The kids, black and white, Asian and Hispanic, fat and thin, tall and short, move with the Calypso rhythm. The listeners standing by are well-dressed, mostly white suburbanites waiting for the symphony to begin inside the great hall. A few tap their feet, but they can't seem to let go. William waves at Millicent, a tiny ninety-year old black woman who plays along with the kids. The drummers are totally absorbed in the music, moving their bodies joyfully, instinctively, celebrating being alive. Some of their spirit flows into William like the good blood that must flow out of and back into his father's heart.

William takes Angie in his arms and they dance.

He would like to dance with his father.

36

David

uties and failures, at the hospital, at home, and at the office jostle in his brain: images of his father's "sudden death," the day after tomorrow's operation (he must support his mother and brother), his rotten evening with Lydia, Phoebe's birthday party (they are trying to keep her life as normal as possible).

Court tomorrow. Opposing counsel wants an answer right away about a pollution report. His colleague at another firm presses for information. His father so white, so thin. Lydia and he lying in bed as far apart as possible. Twenty little girls screaming with the opening of the birthday gifts. The ubiquitous piñata. David hates seeing children whack at an animal with a baseball bat, even a papier mache donkey. The candies and little gifts spilling down and being grabbed by over-privileged children.

David's intestines writhe around like snakes.

"You look awful."

A colleague, a man, stands in the doorway of David's office.

"Thanks," David says.

"You want lunch?"

"No time. I'll grab something later."

David's colleague disappears. David tries to refocus on his work. He keeps going on cups of coffee through the lunch hour. He has a conference call at two.

He isn't ready. He will have to come back to the office tonight after he visits the hospital. And Lydia will be stuck with all the chores again. She'll be asleep when he gets home, or pretending to be, their bed unapproachable, as off limits as a crime scene. He will make all his neglect and irritability up to her if only he can get through the trial, the surgery.

After some twenty some days of strain and worry, they are just getting to the hard part.

When five o'clock comes and the conference call has been completed along with the meeting with his legal team, David heads for the hospital. He feels a little weak, and remembers he's had no lunch. The many cups of coffee eat away at his stomach . . . .

David drives round and round in the hospital parking lot looking for a parking space. The October sun is hot coming through the windshield and gets in his eyes. This is the worst time of day to visit; all the spaces are taken and he is stuck in a line of cars. He feels sweaty. His breathing is quick and shallow.

There's a wall of smoke around the hospital entrance, a row of people puffing on cigarettes—on benches, on the side of the fountain: orderlies and nurses in white, patients in wheelchairs in their blue gowns, attached to their IVs, bandages on their throats and chests. David recognizes Frank, the man who day after day attaches oxygen tubes and ventilators, sees patients gasping for air, their lungs rotted out—puffing away.

It's crazy. The hospital is Wonderland: up is down, large is small. Sick people, medical experts, "health" workers, creating a haze, a wall of smoke. Inside, people gobbling calories, an insane round of self-destruction and clinging to life, tumors cut out, limbs cut off. He pictures a mountain of bloody arms and legs, of hearts and spleens and goiters and hernias and clogged up arteries. Where do they put them? And the waste! Styrofoam cups—the Howards use a dozen a day—boxes of tissues, rolls of paper towels, paper napkins, straws, plates, pads and plastic glasses—cotton bandages, miles and miles of tape and gauze, hypodermic needles, a fresh one for every shot. Plastic gloves in dispensers on the walls, used once and pitched into the waste can.

David goes through the front door which opens wide and he hears, "Welcome to Good Shepmerde Hospital, etc. etc. This is etc. etc. and please no etc. etc." He feels woozy walking through the long hall. The eyes of Dr. Sanders look down on him from the wall displaying the super-sized photos of well-known doctors. Past Wendy's he goes, the smell of grease and pickles, a customer line out into the hall, eaters going toward tables in the atrium, carrying food on trays. Butts on them like Manatees. More waste: the trays are cardboard, laden with cans and waxy paper cups of coke, napkins fluttering, straws rolling, tiny paper envelopes of salt and pepper, and plastic-wrapped dabs of catchup.

It all goes into Mt Rumpke, the county dump, a mountain of trash with its own roads, trucks driving up and down the hillsides, bringing in more trash. The smell as you drive past on the highway is overpowering. Birds circle the garbage like buzzards in some blasted land. Augurs of doom. Mt Rumpke's peak is the highest point in the county.

David turns back toward the gift shop. He had planned to bring his father a book of Sudoku puzzles. He heads into the shop, looking toward the counter of games novelties and balloons (more trash) (he hates his work and his life), and slams into the glass door. He expected it to open for him—like the doors of his life—

The next thing David sees is a man's face; he is wearing blue scrubs.

"You OK, man?" he asks.

David feels the marble floor beneath him, cold and hard. Behind the man's head is the ceiling tile, yellow and white, a chandelier.

"Wow—I—"

"Can you stand up if I help?"

"Sure," David says. Though he is not sure.

Has he had a heart attack, a stroke? What happened?

"You hit that glass door and fell like a dead bird." The man is black, middle-aged. "We gotta get you to the ER."

"Oh no," David says. His heart is pumping blood like an overworked fire hose.

"Let me help you up."

David lets the man take his arm and sit him up, then get him to a standing position. A second man comes along with a wheelchair and the two coax David into it.

"Are you dizzy? Any pain?" the first man asks.

Before David can answer, they are placing his feet on the foot rests and he is being whisked away to the emergency room.

He is wheeled to a desk where a woman with long curved purple nails like claws taps out his name and symptoms on a computer and his insurance and health care cards are Xeroxed. Then he is pushed to a tiny cubicle in the ER.

The room is like an igloo, and David can't stop sweating. An intern comes in and takes his pulse, a man about his own age, thin and pale. "I'm Dr. Roberts," he says. He turns David's right eyelid back and shines a light into his eye.

He can feel a bump the size of a plum on his forehead.

"Tell me what happened," Dr. Roberts says. "Your pulse is racing . . . . nasty bump you got there."

"I just didn't see that glass door at the gift shop."

"Do you have any pain? Head ache? Trouble breathing? Indigestion?"

"No indigestion." He has everything else.

"Put on that gown there, ties in front, and I'll return in a moment. We'll have to do some tests. Check your heart and lungs."

The intern disappears and David reluctantly undresses and puts on the gown. One like his father's. The intern comes back and places a stethoscope on David's chest, and then takes his blood pressure.

"Pretty high," he says.

A woman assistant comes in with an EKG machine and places a dozen cold suction cups on his chest.

"How long will all this take?" David asks.

"Better figure on several hours. We need to do a CAT scan and x-ray your lungs, blood tests."

"I don't have several hours. I'm in the middle of a case. I have to—"

"Is there someone we should call? If you go home, you'll need someone to drive you."

If?

David gives the woman William's number.

"And will you call my home for me? Just leave a message that I'll be late, OK?"

Lenny will be scratching at the door to get out, Lydia rushed and angry. His work running to midnight.

The woman leaves. He stares at the long tentacles of the EKG machine.

When she returns, the assistant looks at the print-out and says, "Your P-waves are inverted." David thinks oh my God, I *am* having a heart attack. He has been short of breath and has broken out in a sweat several times lately. He wills himself to lie very quietly. "Just lie still and don't panic," he thinks. He tries to keep his voice from sounding hysterical as he asks what inverted P-waves mean.

"Hmm?" the aide says. "Oh nothing, really, it's just a zig that usually zags." She pulls the leech-like discs off his chest with a plop-plop.

Did she have to scare him to death?

The woman takes some blood, and wheels him down the hall to a lab for his x-ray. They return him to the ER cubicle where he waits. The assistant pops in with the results of the EKG.

"Heart's OK. A little fast."

David feels surprise and relief. Not only did he not want to be sick, he would be horribly embarrassed, guilty. Breaking down when he needs to be strong.

The assistant gives David a blanket and disappears again.

Warmed a bit, David feels himself wanting to sleep. He dozes lightly.

The assistant seems to turn into William.

It is William, standing by his bed.

"I hear you went a round with a glass door," William says.

David's heart is beating more normally now. He is OK. This was just stress and stupidity. Expecting all doors to open automatically. Because they usually did. Because he has slid into his life automatically.

"I feel like an asshole."

William laughs.

"Maybe a little anal."

"I need to get home."

"I can drive you."

"How would you get home from my house?" David says.

"Not to worry."

"Can you handle a stick shift?"

"Sure. Stop being a control freak."

William kisses him on the forehead. "My calm, collected brother."

The nurse pops in and suggests that David lie still for a few more minutes, until he feels completely clear-headed.

David stares at the ceiling. The patient's view. The sound of people murmuring. Echoes of the little girl bereft and screaming.

"Will, have we done the right thing?"

"I don't see a choice. Let's get you home."

David would gladly stay here on this cot. Take the knife for his father.

37

John

Eric might die in the same hospital in which he was born. He could lose both his son and his wife. Betsy would not be able to bear their son's death.

That day long ago, when Eric was born, John looked out the window of his and Betsy's small house and saw more snow falling on the already icy streets banked by piles of dirty ice. He went to the garage and checked the car, his father's cast-off Buick, to make sure it would start.

Betsy lay on the couch reading a novel; the cover proclaimed the story of a woman who leaves her husband for a thrilling artist. John watched the news of Korea on their little TV set. Several hours before midnight Betsy started labor pains and John timed them. They were to call the doctor when they were five minutes apart, that's what Dr. Spock said. John's hands were shaking. His mother had warned that second babies were more likely to be problem births, and Betsy had some kind of complication.

The doctor said to bring Betsy over to the hospital. She got out her little overnight case, for weeks carefully packed with a clean nightgown and robe, her brush and comb, and a lipstick. Effie was called to come over and sit with Adrian.

Then the hospital was just one building with a clock tower, no out-buildings or annexes, no recorded voice welcoming visitors. John waited in the ante-room in the maternity ward, smoking and pacing the floor. He called his parents and Betsy's mother, checked with Effie to see if Adrian was all right, picked up a magazine, but couldn't concentrate.

John vowed their son would have a smoother path, a better world than he and Betsy had inherited, with parents modern in their outlook, free of old prejudices and the strict unbendable ways of the older generation. Their forbears who kept Jews and people of color out of their clubs, who would not "break bread" with a black person, whose churches and public schools were segregated. The war would change it all.

He and his son—he was hoping for a boy—would talk about these things. He would teach him baseball and tennis. And he did. So close they had been then, coming home sweaty and proud. If Eric comes out of this, John vows he will find a way to wipe away every trace of resentment between them. If that can ever be done between son and father.

That long ago day, John worried *wasn't this birth taking a long time?* Looked at his watch. Sat down. Lit a fresh cigarette. The ashtray was full. He seemed to remember Adrian had come faster. He stood up and began pacing the waiting room again, when a nurse came in.

"Mr. Howard, you have a son," the nurse said. John was led into Betsy's room. She looked groggy and a little pale, but was smiling. She held out the baby's tiny hand to John. A blue and white beaded bracelet had his name on it: "Eric Howard."

The perfect little fingers wrapped around John's. He was the father of two now. An overwhelming joy and a tremendous sense of responsibility for the lives in his hands overcame him. He would protect this boy, his *son*. No harm would come to him while John lived.

That was his pledge. But here they are again at the hour of birth and death. And once again there is nothing he can do to save his wife and son.

John pulls Betsy closer to him on the couch in their den. She is falling asleep like a kitten. He has two old girls, Betsy here in his arms, and Ginger in her tiny plaid bed.

This is usually his favorite time of day: work put aside, just the two of them and Ginger in the quiet room. Enjoying the ever-changing cloud formations beyond the great windows, the powerful white towboats pushing their long strings of barges up and down the river. The graceful glide of the big birds. This evening the scene looks sinister.

Betsy jerks in his arms, awakens as though from a bad dream. She has lost the brightness in her eyes, seems fragile since Eric became ill. Dr. Graham told John that Eric's is one of the most complicated cases he has ever dealt with.

For for the first time John thinks *he's not going to make it.*

38

Betsy

She tastes dust. She is in the waiting room of death, the dreary place no one bothers to clean, the place of shadow, unsteady floors, fear slithering around, brushing your ankles in the dark.

She sees a hag when she looks in the mirror. Eye bags, wrinkles. She seems to have aged since the day she was called and told Eric almost died. Tomorrow he is to be opened up, his heart stopped, his ribs split like one of those horrible carcasses at the meat market, his sternum wired together.

He looks so thin and weak and frightened.

Betsy frees herself from John's embrace and goes into the living room and watches the hawks swoop across the sky. Darkness begins to cover the Kentucky hills across the water. The river looks mean. Gray and cold.

John comes into the room. He looks old too.

She sees John become one of the old men walking the halls of the hospital, oddly following his son in a terrible reversal. One day he will die and leave her, her *parfit gentil knight*.

Lately he walks slowly, beginning to bend his shoulders forward.

She might lose her son and her husband.

"Would you like a drink, Betsy?" John says.

"No thanks."

He goes into the kitchen and she hears him emptying the dishwasher, his evening chore. When he is finished he comes back into the living room and turns on a lamp and opens the *Times*. The rattle of it irritates Betsy.

"Nothing ever bothers you!" she says.

John doesn't answer.

"I'm going to feed Ginger," he says.

Betsy is still in her dark place. She remembers carrying Eric, the doctor's horrible words, "incompetent womb." The fear of losing him, the endless boredom of waiting, the pains she took to keep her baby safe. Following doctor's orders to the letter: not too much alcohol, travel no more than fifty miles from home.

Betsy hears John opening the cabinet where he keeps the dog's canned food. She goes into the kitchen and sits on a stool at the island.

John gently lifts Ginger from her little green plaid bed and lays her body on a fresh towel. Her brown coat is graying. She can barely walk and her cloudy eyes cause her to bump into things when she does occasionally totter about. John carries her sopping bed pad to the laundry room and puts it in the washing machine. Then he comes back and opens a small tin of "Science Diet" and spoons a small portion into her bowl. She stands on wobbly legs and laps at the meat.

"Good girl," John says.

"You and that old mutt."

Betsy thinks: why are the old hanging on like the last stubborn oak leaves, while the young fall? Bin, John's former law partner, his mind an echo chamber. Their friend Carl, in a nursing home, unable even to swallow.

John comes over to Betsy and puts his arm around her.

"Dr. Graham is the best surgeon in his field," John says. "He strikes me as a man who doesn't want to lose even a game of tennis—*Eric is going to make it.*"

39

Judith

From her bedroom window Judith can see the top branches of the walnut tree, now nearly stripped and brittle as a skeleton. The summer sound of the cicadas and tree toads is gone, replaced by the dry rattle of the walnut and the first fall leaves whispering in the roof gutters. Judith is supposedly resting until Brendan goes home.

Judith thinks she can *not* go back to the hospital tonight. But evenings are so hard for Eric. Dinner is over by then, and long hours face him with nothing to do before he can try to settle down and sleep. He cannot read. He does not watch television. He can not get out of bed without help. His visitors are gone. He is depressed and scared. And tomorrow he will be in the operating room, his chest opened, a machine running his heart.

She is the one who made the decision. She has taken over her old role without thinking. Just stepped in being mother, wife, the center of the family. Eric's lingering mental slips worry her. Has she done the right thing?

Judith checks her voice mail: there are a number of messages from university colleagues and friends asking for an update. She does not have the energy to return the calls.

She goes through the mail, recollecting the afternoon she found the note from Natalie. But she can't worry about that now.

There is a card from Zelda and a cheery painting from Phoebe.

Judith tries her father's number. He should be aware of the situation even if he doesn't seem to care about his family. He married within a year after her mother died, and he has never gotten the names of her children straight; he calls them Donald and Billy. She leaves him a message about Eric, and writes a note to his condo in St. Petersburg.

Judith looks at her watch. It's seven, so Moira ought to be home. Judith taps in her number.

"Hello, this is Moira Shaw."

"Have I actually got a real person?" Judith asks. Moira sounds so metallic. She could be the machine.

"It's me," Moira says, "who's this?"

"Judith."

"Oh Judy! I haven't heard from you forever. What's going on?"

"Eric is undergoing heart surgery tomorrow—"

"Jesus God," Moira says. "I had my gall bladder out and *that* was rough. Walter of course was no help and Zelda was her usual obnoxious self."

Judith hears an alcoholic slur in her sister's voice.

"So, are you OK now?"

"Oh yeah. It was last year. But horribly painful. So how is he?"

"He's still recuperating from the knee. Pretty weak."

"Jesus. Excuse me a minute. I have another call coming in."

Judith finds herself on hold.

In a minute or two Moira is back on the line. She seems to have forgotten what Judith has told her.

"Have you heard from the old man?" she says.

"Not recently. How is he?"

"Still using a cane from the stroke, but he gets around. Serves that slutty thing he married right."

Judith doesn't know whether to laugh or cry. She never does at her father's doings or her sister's ongoing drama.

"Zelda is driving me crazy," Moira says. "She's only twelve and looks like the kid in *Taxi Driver*. Acts like a little hooker too. Dances around here shaking her booty for George."

"Who's George?"

"You remember him. I'm living in sin with my ex-husband."

"Moira, you sound—"

"Drunk? A little. Just a teensy bit. Sweetie, I have to go. When are you coming back? Zelda has always liked you. Better than me. She says she wishes you were her mother."

"I'm sure David and William do too."

"I'm glad you have your sense of humor. No fun here. Gotta go."

When Judith puts the phone back in its charger, she sits for a while, depleted. Moira and their mother's problems were always bigger than hers, always blotting her out.

Tea? Coffee? Chocolate. She must have chocolate.

She starts a search. She has devoured the good dark stuff Betsy sent over. She and Eric were always hiding sweets from each other; it was one of the most ridiculous things they did. She giggles. It was the only way Judith could reserve a snack for herself; Eric ate everything in sight, even if it was something he didn't like. He stashed his cache away so Judith wouldn't know how many calories he was taking in. They would each go on searches like the drunk in *The Lost Weekend*.

Judith thinks there is bound to be something in a drawer or buried in the freezer. She looks in a cabinet under a kitchen counter. No luck. She roots around among the hoary boxes and containers in the freezer. Nothing.

She finally locates a half box of Milk Duds in the library table drawer. They've turned almost white with age, but she eats them anyway. They hurt her teeth. She laughs thinking of the stupid things she and Eric have done, the things they have argued about. She hated the way he would pitch a whole handful of peanuts into his mouth at once and that he never closed a cabinet door, a drawer, or the dishwasher, so when he left the kitchen, it was a booby trap of panels to trip over or bash your head on. He ate bananas as though they had a bone in them.

He was a clown and a hero.

She remembers them rafting on the New River in West Virginia, the two of them freezing in their wet suits. He supported her going back to school. He was a good lover, and sexiest of all, he trusted her. When she told him of her therapist's scorn over her naiveté about their finances, he put the house and half their assets in her name.

"I don't need that," she said. Neither of them was very interested in the mysteries of money.

She only wanted to share his inner ledger, where he was more miserly.

When she has showered, brushed her hair, and is dressed to return to the hospital, she notices the red light on the phone is blinking. She retrieves the message.

"It's Moira. You can handle this. You're a tough little mama."

Judith smiles. She likes the description. She takes a deep breath and goes to the car and drives to the hospital.

She trudges through the halls and returns to her husband's room. Eric looks small and gray. He seems frightened.

She tidies the room and sits beside his bed. They are sealed in this airtight room, the light from the parking lot throwing a sickly light across the white sheets, soundless except for the occasional rattle of a passing cart. He is in no condition to face a surgeon's knife. So fragile. His flesh stretched on his bones. His heart will be stopped again. He is the color of ashes.

She can not live without him.

Part 5

SCALPEL

40

The Howards

Judith, Betsy and John, David and William sit in the waiting area of the surgical unit, a large room filled with anxious families. They watch the monitors mounted on the walls, like the arrival-departure boards at airports. They have been given a numerical code for Eric's name. In an hour a stylized image of a gurney tells them their patient has arrived in the operating room; later a scalpel indicates that he is undergoing surgery.

They imagine the operating room, the way it looks in movies, white coats, monitors, the gaping incision, the knife. They jiggle their feet, chew gum, hold hands, get up for water, all feeling the same hope and fear.

Part 6

OPEN HEARTS

41

David

They look like angels: ten tiny girls in pink and white puffed-sleeve dresses, playing their Wee Bonnie harps. Their glitter-covered tiaras sparkle like halos. Their teacher, a middle-aged woman with frizzy hair and granny glasses, directs from below the stage in the auditorium at Phoebe's school. The girls are playing Brahms' "Lullaby," as David enters late. He looks around for Lydia, spies her in the front row. His mother is not with her. He takes a fold-down seat near the back as quietly as possible.

He searches the stage, the identical costumes, and singles out Phoebe. She is definitely the cutest. So pretty and poised. As the tune comes to an end, the girls rise and curtsy.

A young person hands David a program. He has missed the first half of the recital. But he just could not get there. He lost the case that went to court the day before his father's surgery, and now the firm will appeal. He has been at his office making plans.

The little harpists begin the second half of the program: "Twinkle Little Star" and the theme from "Aladdin." David's eyes are again fixed on his daughter. He is amazed to see her plucking the strings so skillfully. He imagines her picking up the quarter-sized instrument and flying around the stage.

When the concert is over, he claps until the last person stops.

He goes down to the front of the auditorium. Lydia is busy talking to another mother and then she disappears backstage to pick up Phoebe's instrument. David goes out in the hall. He locates Phoebe among a group of giggling little harpists, surrounded by what he calls the "parental paparazzi." Flashes from digital cameras light the girls like stars. Moms and dads are presenting their daughters bouquets of roses in clear plastic cones. Oh my God, David thinks, I never thought to order flowers! But Phoebe holds out a bouquet to show him.

"Thanks Daddy, these are so beautiful!"

He takes the card from her hand: "Love from Momma and Poppa."

Lydia of course. And he's in the soup again.

"You were great, honey," he says. "All of you. Wow!"

He kisses Phoebe.

There is a table of cupcakes, bagels, brownies, grapes and orange slices, muffins studded with colored M&Ms. The kids are attacking the buffet. Treats follow everything Phoebe does; she gets a school trip to Chuck E. Cheese for learning her nine tables, pizza after every soccer game, a spread of goodies at school events. When he was a kid, food did not go with every event. No wonder we're all fat, David thinks.

He finds Lydia and tells her he will see her at home.

"Fine."

He can tell he is in trouble for being late and not knowing about the flowers.

On the drive home, David wonders what became of his mother. She was very anxious to hear Phoebe play. He talked to her on the phone this morning. She had brought his father the *New York Times* and was reading to him.

Yesterday when the recovery room symbol appeared next to his father's code name, the family exchanged high fives: he must be OK. The family went to the cafeteria and ate a late lunch. Several hours later a nurse approached them and invited them to the ICU to see their patient. He came through the surgery fine, she said.

David's father was propped in bed in a large sunny room. He was thinner and paler than ever. There were tears in his eyes and his chin wobbled with relief at being alive. The surgical nurse greeted the family.

"We were lucky and did not have to use the heart-lung machine after all," she said. She recited instructions for care and told them what to expect. Mr. Howard would be in the ICU for a few days, then back to the cardiac unit. She sounded confident and capable.

She placed a red heart-shaped pillow, about the size of a baby, on her patient's lap and told him to press it to his chest to cough.

Everyone smiled tentatively, and kissed David's father carefully. He looked so fragile. There was a long incision on his chest. He looked translucent, like William's old anatomical toy.

Everyone except David's mother made quick exits so as not to tire him.

When he gets home from Phoebe's recital, David takes Lenny for a run in the woods. He worries about his mother. Why wasn't she at the recital? He calls the hospital but gets no information. Lydia and Phoebe aren't back yet. He leaves a message on Lydia's cell phone, and drives to the hospital.

He expects the sunny scene of the day before, but the atmosphere in his father's ICU room is dim and surreal. David's mother is standing by his father's bed, while his father cranes his neck, his hands fluttering about almost like dance movements. His mother turns to David, her eyes dull with worry.

217

David rushes to his father's bedside. He grasps a waving, weaving hand.

"He's like a fish out of water," his mother says, "he can't breathe."

"God," David says. "How long has this been going on?"

"On and off. They keep telling me he's all right. Just needs to cough."

She offers the red heart-shaped pillow, but his father waves it away.

"Maybe some water," David says. He pours a cup and holds the straw to his father's lips.

His mother summons the nurse. The one the family liked from the day before is off duty. This one repeats her assurances that the patient is OK.

"He is *not* OK," David's mother says. She goes to the wall phone and contacts the doctor, who apparently says that his father was wheezing after his first surgery.

"He wasn't wheezing after the knee surgery, and he's not just wheezing, he's shaking and gasping for air."

David doesn't hear what the doctor replies, but his mother says, "We need to see what's going on. There's something wrong."

His father continues the eerie clawing of the air with his hands.

When she hangs up, she says, "They said call later if he's worse."

David's father calms down a little but still seems to be grasping for something, trying to swim in the air.

David's mother plops herself down in the big chair next to the bed.

"How did the recital go?" she asks.

"Great. I can't believe how good Phoebe is."

David's mother checks her watch again. Goes into the hall and calls the doctor again. When she comes back, she says, "They're going to send an x-ray machine in and have a look."

They wait. And wait.

David's mother paces to the door and back, looks down the hall, rubs his father's shoulders.

Finally, several technicians pushing a huge machine come in and take x-rays of his father's chest. The nurse says they have put in a call for a "lung man."

"Go home, David," his mother says. "This may take all night. I'll call if anything comes up."

David's father has been given a sedative, and dozes restlessly. His chest purrs like an idling engine.

"You should go home," David says to his mother.

She thinks a minute.

"I am home," she says.

David hugs her, holds on a moment.

"You need some sleep."

The nurse comes in.

"You should go home, Mrs. Howard," she says. "But be careful, this is a dangerous neighborhood."

"Let me drive you," David says.

"We've even had people attacked *inside* this place. People get in and sleep here," the nurse says.

David's mother curls up in the big chair and pulls her coat over her feet.

"No way am I leaving here tonight," she says.

David kisses her goodbye and heads for home. He thinks she is the strongest person he has ever known.

42

Judith

It is still dark when a Dr. Ritch, appears. He is tall, dressed in a preppy T-shirt, slacks and loafers. He looks like a Republican. Judith likes him: he has a calm reassuring voice and unlike the other doctors, he sits down when he talks. He looks Eric over, listens to his breathing.

William slips into the room behind him.

"Lungs are full of fluid," Dr. Ritch says. He calls for equipment, a pump and other mysterious things. He sits Eric up, and tells Judith and William to look away if they want to. Judith keeps her eyes on her husband's back. Looking pale, William slowly follows her lead. The doctor inserts a large needle and tube in Eric's back and drains a reddish-purple liquid into a gallon container. It keeps flowing until the bottle is filled.

"Gross," William says. "Looks like a vat of Cold Duck."

"About fifteen pounds of fluid." Dr. Ritch says. He detaches the tube from Eric's back. "No wonder he had trouble breathing." He sits with Judith and William for a while and then promises to see them the next day.

The nurse comes in and gives Eric a shot. He quiets down, stops wheezing and grasping thin air. Judith sits back in the big chair. Breathes more easily herself.

"Hear you guys had a bad day," William says.

They sit quietly for a while, half dozing in the room, now lit only by a small lamp and the light from the hall.

William looks tired to Judith. His ponytail needs washing. His glasses are slipping down his nose. He seems nervous. Could he be back on drugs? She could not bear that.

He hands Judith a slip of paper. "Pome," he says. Judith reads,

> What is our culture?
> We come out of our mother
> Readers of books
> Beneath is no soil
> Linoleum, cement
> Words our inheritance

Judith smiles. Her William. Funny, gifted, joyful. She notices his fingernails are chewed below the quick.

When they caught him on drugs, they were like that.

The cold day they went to him in the hospital must stay buried, dangerous as icebergs.

She studies William's face. Eric's near death has brought them all together, closer than they have been for years when things seemed to be going pretty well for everyone.

Is William safe now? If he were settled, in a job, married, in school . . . .

Doing a little of this and a little of that is like a path with too many ways on which to wander off.

She can not bear any harm coming to William. In some ways he is her favorite: the maverick, the wild one. Does she want to see him a brief-case carrying conformist? She doesn't. But she wants him safe.

But what does it matter what she wants? William is himself and no one else. From babyhood he has been different from David and the other Howards. He hears a different drummer, a far off beat that will lead him to something good—or keep him dancing in place.

Judith takes William's hand.

"I like your poem," she says. "And I like you."

43

David

Here it comes, David thinks.

"You missed half of Phoebe's concert."

"It was lovely, I saw a lot of it. Phoebe didn't seem unhappy."

"You were utterly awful at her birthday party. I did all the work. All you had to do was come and set up the piñata."

"I hate piñatas. They ought to be on the endangered list."

Lydia doesn't laugh. This is probably one of the bigger problems David has with his wife: she has little sense of humor. For him and William and his parents even a dumb joke beats fighting.

Lydia takes him on a tour of the bathroom renovations.

"Look at this door: it's a quarter of an inch off."

David wishes he could see the horror of it, but he just can't. His mind is on the appeal of his case. His heart is at the hospital. His father is thin and weak and is back where he started, unable to walk. The left leg has a long incision where the surgeon removed the vein substituting for the clogged artery in the heart. His chest is swollen, red and scarred. His right knee is still ugly, like an overripe fruit about to burst, and his feet are puffy with fluid.

"David, are you listening? I may have to sue this contractor. He doesn't show up for days at a time."

"I told you not to start on that business."

He sounds nasty even to himself. The work has begun; there is no point in bringing up the original decision.

"I had to come home yesterday to let the dog out again. You said you would be responsible for him. But I've been doing all the work."

"I'm sorry, Lydia. But you should understand I'm under the gun. The case, my Dad."

"That dog pooped in the house on our best Oriental. I did my best to clean it up, but there's a horrible stain."

Lydia insists that he take a look at the rug. He feels as though he's being dragged by the collar.

David agrees the stain is bad and the rug needs to be sent to the cleaner.

"Don't look at me like that," he says. "I didn't do it."

"Maybe *you* could call the cleaner. I have a job too."

"This won't be forever. Just be a little more patient."

"I've been patient, I think."

"You have. You've been a saint."

She looks at him closely as though to see if he's being sarcastic.

"We should get rid of that dog," she says. "We never should have gotten him in the first place. He poops like an elephant."

David is tempted to tell her about his trip to the emergency room. Maybe he could wring an iota of compassion from her. Is all this about his negligence and preoccupation?

"David."

"Yes?"

"Could you take him out now, before we take Phoebe to see Eric?"

"Sure."

David takes Lenny for a run in the woods.

"We better shape up, bro," David says. "We're in, well—deep shit."

Lydia never makes sense to him. She was reluctant to take on a pet, claiming they were too busy, but has talked for years about having another child. She even got pregnant once, but had a miscarriage. David wanted a kid too. But Lydia seemed to think it was only she who was disappointed.

She wouldn't talk to him about it. Lydia has shared very little of her inner life, something David has been brought up to believe everyone has in abundance. The Howards, even occasionally his father, tell their dreams at breakfast. Lydia said of herself, "You get what you see. I'm just not deep and full of angst like the Howards."

"Are we full of angst?"

"You're full of shit." Just when he thought she had no sense of humor, she would pull off a zinger. David laughed. Lydia walked away.

David drives over to the hospital. Lydia and Phoebe will meet him there. David's father has been moved to a room on the cardiac unit after five days of setbacks and scares in the ICU. David goes into the new room. His father is fussing with his gown. Brendon is sitting on the couch working on his quilt, his usual vegan meal nearby on a tray. His father beckons David to his side.

"What is it, Dad?" David says.

"Tell Brendan to give me his scissors."

Brendan shakes his head.

"A scissors? What for?" David asks.

"So I can cut myself out of this gown."

Oh Christ, David thinks. The Mad Hatter is back.

David decides to take a practical, common sense approach.

"We can't do that," he says, "the gown belongs to the hospital. It isn't ours."

"They only cost about three dollars," his father says.

David looks out the window. Damn, damn, damn. He gets a fresh breath.

"Let me help you into your chair," he says. "Phoebe is coming over and wants to play her harp for you." As he arranges his father for company, he asks Brendan if he has been talking crazy again.

"He has more trouble when Mrs. Howard isn't here," Brendan says.

Lydia and Phoebe arrive, and Phoebe plays her harp for her grandfather. The moment has a quiet magic: the man listening intently, a proud smile on his face, the child playing Brahms' *Lullaby*.

When Phoebe has gone through her repertoire, she bows and everyone claps. She puts her arms around her grandfather. He smiles.

She is so healthy, and he so frail. He looks tired.

"We'll get going," David says. "I'll be back tomorrow."

In the hall, Lydia looks aghast; she says, "Phew." She examines the bump on David's forehead like his mother used to examine cuts and scrapes. "Are you sure that bump on your head was from a door?"

"Yes. I expected it to open automatically."

David is tempted to tell her about the ER. The sympathy feels good. But decides to quit while he's ahead.

"I'm sorry I've been so mean," Lydia says. "About the house and all. I couldn't quite picture what was going on over here."

David and Lydia go their separate ways. She is off to her appointments and errands. He heads for East Side Square with Phoebe where they like to sit on a bench and watch people go by. It is almost her only down time. They eat ice cream cones. He can not decide how she looks cuter, with her fine hair loose like she wears it today, or in little pony tails on the sides of her head.

"How's that ice cream?" David asks her.

"Good."

"Should we take some home to Momma?"

"I don't think so. She's dieting."

Dieting? She is already so thin David sometimes worries about her. She would look in the mirror, a perfect size eight, and say, "God, I'm such a blob."

Nothing he said could ever change her mind.

Girls, David thinks: say what you will, women are not like men. And Phoebe, like Lydia, is all female. She has been allowed to play with any toy she wants (so as not to force her into gender oriented interests) and she often chooses Legos and building blocks over dolls, but when it comes to appearance, she takes almost as long to get ready to go out with him as Lydia; she will not leave the house without her purse, a necklace and bracelet.

The day is pretty; David notices the fountain is catching the iris from the sunlight, the trees on the square are orange and red, and some of the flowers are still blooming. A woman with a small dog sits across from them, and Phoebe goes over and pats him. They watch a crowd of birds peck away at a spilled bag of popcorn. People come and go, cutting across the square to the shoe store, boutiques, and the library.

Phoebe nods at a woman walking past them. "That woman has a fake Gucci," she says.

"What?"

"That woman there: she has a fake Gucci handbag."

David looks at a woman carrying a purse with stylized G's on it.

Phoebe explains the difference between the fake and the real.

Phoebe is seven years old. Is his daughter turning into a little snob?

David doesn't know what to say.

A shadow passes over the scene for him; his heart thuds. His father's request for the scissors was so bizarre. Life itself has become bizarre. America is bizarre: invading a country that had never attacked us: turning from a healthy, sane world leader into a fat, greedy, doped up bully. Violence everywhere: even beneath the quiet, orderly, everyday movements on this square. A month ago the water in the fountain's basin turned red when a local boy washed a bloody baseball bat in it. He had just killed his brother.

Car after car, one bigger than the other, goes by, each with their yellow ribbons: "Support the Troops." Support hell, David thinks: we use them and throw them away. Nobody really seems to care about the American soldiers and Iraqis dying, as long as they have their luxuries and plenty of gas.

The media has gone to sleep. Only that little known senator from Illinois voted against the war, and Robert Byrd, the ancient orator, and once KKK member, few others.

This is a shitty world he's handing his daughter. How can people stand thousands being slaughtered? The suffering is unimaginable. And it's going on every day, all over the world. Profiteers licking their chops over the blood. Washing their hands of it—in it.

"What's wrong, Daddy?" Phoebe says.

"Nothing," he says.

Phoebe pulls his head to her and kisses him. She leaves a smear of sticky ice cream on his lips. He licks it off, tasting it: strawberry.

44

Betsy

Betsy has put fresh flowers in the guest room for Adrian. It will be nice to have some life in the house. It has seemed especially empty since Eric became ill. Everything is ready. Ora, the helper who has replaced Effie—a quick moving woman from the Kentucky hills—has cleaned the apartment and Betsy has filled the fridge with fruit and diet coke. John tried to get her to buy some pints of Graeter's ice cream, the celebrated local treat, but Betsy can not bring herself to feed her overweight daughter ice cream.

"For Heaven's sake, Betsy," John said. "She's a grown woman and isn't going to change her habits."

Betsy doesn't give in. While John is on his way to the airport to pick up Adrian, she checks her watch every fifteen minutes or so. His reflexes are not as good as they once were and the other drivers go so fast. She worries about the plane crashing, the trucks on the expressway.

Adrian would scoff at her: "And maybe a giant Goonie Bird will come crashing out of the bushes."

Betsy is relieved when she hears the elevator coming, and goes to the hall to greet her daughter. God. What is she wearing? A

229

loose top and baggy drawstring pants; she looks like a sack tied in the middle. And her hair: it's like a rat's nest.

Betsy embraces Adrian, who gives her a hearty kiss in return.

"Did you have a good flight?" Betsy says.

"Great."

Adrian and John carry her bags into the guest room, Betsy following. Adrian plops one big suitcase onto Betsy's antique game table and parks her computer gear on the window seat, crushing the drapery. Betsy pictures the water rings she will leave on the nightstand.

"Do you want to rest, or go right over to the hospital to see Eric?" Betsy says.

"Let's go," Adrian says. "I can crash later. Just let me have a drink." She goes to the fridge and gulps down a can of coke. She notices Ginger in her bed under the window.

"Oh my God." She turns to John. "Is Ginger still alive?"

"Of course," John says. He sounds a little miffed.

He gathers up his keys, wallet and brief case, and takes off for the office.

When they enter Eric's room at the hospital, Betsy can see Adrian is shocked by Eric's appearance. He has been very weak, too weak to resume his therapy. It takes two people to get him to the bathroom. A hematoma has developed on his neck: purple and red and protruding like a rubber ball; his lungs are still crowded by fluid, making his breathing raspy and harsh. Sitting in his chair he looks like an old man in a nursing home.

"Hey Bro!" Adrian says. She goes directly to Eric, sits by his side, and takes his hand.

"Whassup'?"

Eric looks puzzled for a moment, apparently trying to place her.

"Oh, Addie," he says. He pats her hand.

Betsy moves about the room, restoring urinals, cups, books, pads, glasses, tissues, the red heart pillow (she hates the thing and Eric never uses it regardless of orders), the phone and call button to where Eric can reach them.

She looks at the blackboard to see who will be on duty tonight.

Lakesia comes in the open door preceded by her wide broom. Betsy introduces her to Adrian. Eric and his sister have still not said much to each other, just sit silently holding hands.

"So how 'bout them Reds?" Adrian says.

Eric smiles. He is obviously feeling bad.

Lakesia finishes her tour of the room and leaves. She's a nice young woman—Judith and the boys seem very fond of her—but sometimes she makes Betsy uneasy: she pictures Lakesia cleaning the room with no one in it.

In the car on the way home, Adrian says, "My God."

"He's having a bad day," Betsy says.

"I gather he's had a lot of bad days. What he's been through! And what you and Daddy and Judith and the kids have been through!"

"It's hard."

"The Howard understatement."

When they get home, John is waiting in the kitchen. He has three pints of ice cream on the counter.

"Um," Adrian says.

"Double chocolate, coconut, or peppermint?" John asks.

"Little of each," Adrian says.

She and John eat good-sized portions of ice cream and scrape the sides of the dishes.

Betsy does not partake, nor object.

She studies Adrian. She wonders where she got these children of hers. Eric bright, conscientious, intellectual; Adrian so casual

231

and free-spirited. She had dreamed of a daughter with whom she could share her love of art, one she could buy all the lovely dresses that her own mother spurned, wanting everything "practical"— even better: cheap. She had pictured a sylph-like girl who might study ballet or music; instead she got a sturdy tomboy who couldn't care less about beautiful things. Or things at all. Betsy's idol was Jackie Kennedy. Who was Adrian's?

Adrian and Eric both had turned away from her and John's ambitious generation; they were materialistic, "elitist." But their generation had been taught to be leaders, to be the elite. Adrian and Eric dismiss all hierarchy, privilege, status. They are so totally liberal, so relentlessly egalitarian.

John turns on the television in the den; the sound of a football game blares out. Adrian joins her father on the couch, and they are soon cheering and discussing the game while Betsy washes their dishes and spoons.

"She prefers John to me," Betsy thinks. But of course, he always let her do exactly as she pleased. Could she have sensed Betsy's rejection?

She hears Adrian roar her approval of a play, and John, usually so quiet, yelling along with her.

At the commercial Adrian comes into the kitchen and opens two cans of beer.

"We got any pretzels?" she asks.

"In the cabinet by the fridge."

Her children eat everything out of bags, and drink from cans and bottles. Nothing elegant for them. Just like her hearty German relatives. Even Lydia and David eat off plastic and drink out of aluminum, in a house almost as big as the castle.

But how good it is to hear her daughter's big laugh filling the house.

45

David

William has decided to show a movie, to cheer everyone up. David thinks it's the dumbest idea he's ever heard, but William busily roots through the shelf of VHS tapes and DVDs in the social area down the hall from his father's room. He makes plans to set up a little theater.

"What have you come up with?" David asks him.

"*Dodgeball*. It's hilarious."

"That's totally stupid," David says. "Dad will hate the thing. So will everyone else."

"It's funny," William insists.

"It's brainless."

Adrian arrives and agrees with William.

David notices her outfit: jeans and work shoes and a T-shirt she is bursting out of that says "Twin Peaks." She would stand out in this get-up, even among the hastily dressed and largely overweight denizens of the hospital.

David and Adrian go into the waiting room while David's father is being bathed and having his bedding changed, and William goes to the social area, to arrange it for the evening's get together.

"Boy, when I walked in here and saw bro at first, I thought we could all kiss him goodbye," Adrian says. "He looks a little better today. Maybe he's up for some entertainment."

"I just think William's taste is not too great. He belongs to the 'It's so bad it's good' school."

"Eric enjoys a little slapstick."

David feels a new interest in his aunt. He has never really spent any time with her without the whole family being there, usually at parties, weddings, and funerals.

"You and Dad were close as kids, weren't you?" he says.

"Pretty close. I'm just glad I was older so I didn't have to live up to his example. He was so brilliant."

"He's a hard act to follow."

"He was hell on wheels, I can tell you. Mother let him do anything he wanted. He was definitely her favorite."

"That must have been hard."

"Hard is agreeing on a movie."

"I gather you and Betsy didn't get along too well when you were a kid."

"She's an *aesthete*."

"You make it sound criminal."

"Well, she's made Daddy's life miserable with all that fussy nit-picking, that ridiculous castle."

"We thought she was a real queen when we were little."

"She is."

David tries to judge how bitter Adrian's words are, how much she has absorbed her feeling of being second best. He has never before pictured his father and aunt as children.

"Mom lives in a dream world," Adrian says. "She thought no one knew about her little fling with that opera singer."

"*Betsy* had an affair?"

"Of course, everybody knew about it—"

234

"I didn't."

"I'm not sure you were born at the time."

David can't put these things together; people are not adding up. But whatever made him think they do?

"The sparks literally flew between them and no one was supposed to notice. It was so embarrassing for poor Daddy."

"What did my Dad do?"

"Ignore it like he does everything; anyway he was probably away at school."

"Who was this man?"

"That Italian opera singer, Gino somebody. He was the biggest skirt-chaser who ever hit town."

"I picture opera singers as big fat guys, like Pavarotti."

"Oh no. Gino was great looking. They had some great looking dudes then. Still do."

"No kidding."

"Haven't you ever been to an opera?"

"I hate opera."

"We were dragged to every last one. I can't say I totally blame Mom. So she was a little ahead of her time. Girls just wanna have fun."

What a peculiar family, David thinks. He's just getting to know them. And only now because of his father's heart. Adrian's story completely throws off his picture of his grandmother. To him she was always proper and predictable. He slides the new image beneath the old, the way the eye doctor superimposes lenses to get a focus. He still can't read the chart.

That evening when David returns to the hospital, he goes to his father's room where he and William help their father into a wheelchair. They push him through the hall to the social room, a large linoleumed space with several TV sets, folding chairs propped against the walls, and a library of tapes and DVDs on shelves. William has everything set up for the show: chairs arranged around the largest TV, popcorn in plastic bowls, soft drinks chilled and ready to serve. The rest of the family, David's mother, Adrian, Betsy and John, follow. When they are seated, William turns on the TV, starts the movie and serves the snacks.

Adrian and William chortle at every bit of slapstick and every bodily fluid joke, as Ben Stiller and Vince Vaughan compete in a vicious dodge ball competition. The colors and characters are garish and violent. It is soon clear from the fidgeting and lack of laughter that no one else is enjoying the movie.

David is becoming anxious. The room is cold and his mother fusses over his father—is he too cold? He looks chilled but waves her away. She runs back to the room and returns with a blanket which she keeps adjusting around his dad's shoulders. He looks grumpy and uncomfortable. David worries that his butt must hurt from the seat of the wheelchair which is harder than the chair and bed in his room; with his weight loss his bones must be digging into the leather. He is restless, but won't give up. David's grandparents look puzzled. John squirms in his seat, adjusting and readjusting the beaded pad he brought for his back. Betsy asks unanswerable questions, like which team are we for? No one eats any popcorn; his mother grabs the bowl away from his father because of the salt. Anyway, it's stale (William got it from the shelf in the kitchenette). David keeps trying to encourage his father to go back to his room and his grandparents to go on home if they want to, but everyone sits through the whole god-damned stupid mess.

As soon as the credits roll, Betsy and John get up to leave. They politely thank William and David. His mother kisses both of them, and pushes his father back to his room in his wheelchair.

Adrian helps David and William neaten up.

"It was a cute idea," Adrian says. "And the show was a riot!" She laughs and eats the remainder of a bowl of popcorn.

"Don't tell," she says. "Mother always told me the worst thing in the world you could possibly be is short and fat."

"Worse than tall and stupid, or being a murderer?" William says.

"It's a wonder I'm not bulimic."

David is still steamed. "I could shoot you for subjecting Dad and the grandparents to that stupid show," he says to William.

"*Dodgeball* is very very funny."

"It sucks. And you suck, you maniac."

"They could have left."

"They're too polite."

All three begin to laugh helplessly.

"It was kind of funny," David says.

"I told you so," William says.

"Not the movie, numbnuts. The family trying so hard to enjoy it."

When David gets home, he undresses hastily and falls into bed next to Lydia.

"How did it go?" she asks.

David describes the evening.

"I told you your brother was crazy," she says.

46

William

William goes to a poetry slam at the Bookshelf. The bar is packed with people from the neighborhood and the university shouting out their verses and knocking back beers. William skips the alcohol, a no-no for him. With Jimmy and Hattie and Angie cheering him on, he reads the poem he wrote for his mother. Then "Death Cat." He gets wild applause. But then they all do.

One of the contestants yells, "Dude, you rock!"

Jimmy shouts, "Your poems are so cool I came all over myself."

When the excitement fades, William grabs a a booth and listens to Hattie and her group practice. They sound good. Hattie beckons him over and points to the piano, and he sits in for a song or two. If only he could be the artist that she is.

"Hey don't stop," she calls. "You're good."

Yeah, yeah, he thinks. He can do well at most anything he tries. But he has not found the key to his talent. He's nearing thirty. Still at the gate.

The Howards are all so bright, so successful. He sometimes feels like the only bulb on a string of Christmas lights that doesn't go on. He wants more than being one of a string; he wants preeminence, respect; to be the one they all defer to. The world at his feet, famous enough to not want attention.

He might start with a book: himself on the cover, made real like Pinocchio. *Pinocchio,* one of his favorite movies; not only are the scenes at sea the most lovely animation ever—like the Japanese print of *The Great Waves* his mother hung on the porch wall—but the theme, the boy who is made of wood and must become worthy of being real.

He will be posing thoughtfully in his photo, wearing an author-type sweater, trees or books in the background. No—the Bookshelf Coffee Shop. He will graciously thank a whole page of people; his parents, his friends who helped by reading and commenting on his manuscript, maybe his agent, yes, of course his agent, and his editor.

They, the family, think he is not ambitious, but he is perhaps the most ambitious of all. He doesn't want to be rich in order to have things. He just wants to have money so he can be poor with a clear conscience. As someone said to Picasso, "You want to be a millionaire and live under a bridge." Exactly.

Probably his book to screenplay scenario is old-fashioned. A graphic book or just an idea he has the nerve to sell would be more like it.

His writing has been the usual thinly disguised autobiographical stuff. He was better when he was on coke, wilder and less inhibited. He needs to be crazier, looser. He is clever, trained by the repartee of his parents. He knows their common sense makes sense, their moderation, their civil ways, their politeness and liberality. But he senses beneath, a deeper world he can't reach. He writes a new poem. He rather likes it. Or maybe it's crap. He starts to ball it up and pitch it, then puts it in his pocket.

He heads over to the hospital. William's father has alarmed everyone with toes that turned purple. Could be gout. But in general, he's improving. He has not said anything loony for days. With his father growing stronger, William has no excuse not to get his act together.

47

Judith

Chahna has one glass eye. She is a small Indian woman wearing a smock with an all-over pattern of purple and pink teddy bears.

Judith likes her immediately. They are in rehab now, their eighth move. They feel promoted.

Chahna helps Eric sit on the side of the bed.

"We're going to learn to dress ourselves today," she announces.

Eric looks unsure and Judith and Brendan start toward him.

"We can do it," Chahna says.

"How can we help?" Brendan says.

"Do not hover about."

"And shut up?" Judith asks.

"That t'would help."

Judith and Brendan retreat to the couch.

Chahna shows Eric how to pull on his knit pants. He is clumsy and slow, like the kids when they were first learning to dress themselves. She hands him a long shoe horn to wedge his feet into his new canvas sneakers. She watches carefully as he stands without using his hands; he has to make several tries. Chahna wraps a canvas belt around his waist and slowly leads him out of the room.

She comes every day for several weeks and takes Eric to the activities room where he might walk holding on to parallel bars, bounce a ball or try to play checkers. He is kept busy all day with Occupational and Physical Therapy. He runs into several acquaintances doing the same activities. The hospital is like a city within a city. Familiar faces among the staff, the doctors, the other patients.

In his room, Eric is on the leg machine, and Judith and Brendan supervise bed exercise.

Eric is still thin, has a long way to go for complete recovery, but he is so much better. The rehab director talks of going home.

He will survive.

Then what?

He had asked for Judith, and she has come and helped him through bad days and bad nights. They have had some amazing moments in spite of the anxiety they have all gone through: their scotch party with just them and their sons, even the night of *Dodgeball*. She and William and David had to laugh about it when Brendan asked how it went: everyone being so polite, and everyone's butt hurting and the rancid popcorn.

During all the frightening, painful days, they had hardly dared to believe Eric could come this far.

After Chahna has brought Eric back to his room from a workout, a man and woman appear at the doorway.

"May we come in?" the man says.

Before Judith can ascertain their business, the couple is standing before Eric, dancing up and down excitedly. They are both rather short and plump, wearing bright purple and red T-shirts that say "Mended Hearts."

"We're the Johnsons, Vic and Viv," the man says. "We hear you'll be going home soon. We just wanted to pop in and let you know you will be feeling fine in no time!"

241

"We've both had heart surgery and we're back playing tennis and walking two miles a day!"

"We feel great!"

"We have six new arteries all together," Viv says.

They are cheerful and colorful as cartoon characters.

Vic gives a short lecture on their organization, a support group for bypass survivors, and predicts a successful recuperation: "When you go home, you might feel depressed and tired. You might lose interest in sex for awhile, but in six months or so, with exercise and a heart-smart diet, you'll feel great, and ready for anything!"

"Can we answer any questions for you?" Viv asks.

Eric looks puzzled.

"Hang in there, friend!" Vic says. He and Viv look as though they are going to sing.

"Thank you," Eric says. He waves them away.

Judith escorts the couple to the door. They prance off like a dance team.

"Christ," Judith says when they are out of earshot. "Do you think the surgeon snipped out their good sense while he was in there?"

Eric laughs. Judith is so glad to hear that sound.

"They're brain-washed."

"I had a visit from the hospital chaplain too," Eric says.

"They always kick you when you're down."

Vic and Viv reappear at the doorway.

"We almost forgot. We have a Mended Hearts T-shirt for you."

They hand Eric a shirt with a stitched together heart on it, and dance away.

"I guess it's official," Judith says. "You're going to live."

"Do I want to?"

Natalie comes into the room and spoils the moment.

"What's so funny?" she says.

Eric holds up his T-shirt.

"Let me see that."

She grabs the shirt and slides it on and vamps.

"So *cute!*" she says.

That week the director of rehab says Eric can go home. Judith calls the family with the good news. She and Phoebe get together and make big "WELCOME HOME" signs in red, yellow and blue. They draw flowers and blue skies with fluffy clouds, butterflies and hearts. Betsy stocks Judith's fridge with Eric's favorite foods, and brings over bouquets of flowers.

Part 7

PROUD FLESH

48

Betsy

Betsy puts her hand on Eric's chest. His gown is soaked. It's not perspiration, but something thick and sticky. What now? She calls the nurse. This time it is Yolanda, an African woman with great dark eyes. She pulls the bandage away from Eric's incision. His chest is leaking a mix of blood and what looks like pus. A strange thing seems to be growing out of the cut.

"I'll get the doctor on call," Yolanda says.

"What is wrong?" Betsy asks.

"Looks like his incision may be infected."

Betsy is frantic. What will this mean?

Yolanda cleans the opening, a slit with something that seems to want to come out, like the first emerging flesh of a baby. She prepares a clean dry bandage and applies it to the incision. In about half an hour, the doctor on call arrives. He is young, slim, a stranger. Where is Dr. Sanders, or Hale, or Graham, someone familiar?

"Dr. Minot," the young man says. He opens Eric's bandage and examines the wound.

"Proud flesh," he says.

"Keep it bandaged and dry," he instructs Yolanda.

As though they will see her again today—or the next—Betsy thinks. Will he inform their regular doctors? Or will he just write in that record book with Eric's name on it, the one in the hall, that is thicker than a phone book.

"This is not necessarily infected," Dr. Minot says.

When he has gone, Betsy asks Yolanda, "Did he say *proud* flesh? Like p-r-o-u-d?"

"Yes, the growth. It's extra tissue that sometimes appears where the flesh has been cut."

Eric has been unusually passive throughout this incident. Betsy wants to scream. In spite of his progress, he is still so thin; his legs are swollen, his arms purple from shots. Now his incision is gaping and this thing is growing there.

Over the next several days she and Judith keep watch over Eric. Dr. Graham comes in and examines the chest and says it looks good.

"But the nurse just changed his bandage a minute ago. It was soaked!" the women yell in unison.

"We'll order him an antibiotic," the doctor says.

When that doesn't work, a tube is inserted into the incision, which drains into a plastic bag.

When Betsy leaves the day the drainage bag is set up, she is exhausted. She misses Adrian. Her visit meant a messy kitchen and extra work and an overflowing recycle bin, but she is so cheerful. Betsy drives toward home, but as though someone else is steering, she turns right instead of left out of the hospital and finds herself driving down a strange street, not knowing quite where she is heading. She keeps going, turning here and there. At too many points she passes streets where friends have lived—and died.

She drives toward Fountain Square at the center of town. So many landmarks are gone: beautiful St. Henry's church, the Samuel Hannaford Work House that looked like one of Mad

King Ludwig's castles. The department stores have decamped to the malls out on the expressways, in soul-less stretches where no one walks. There is only a Saks and a Macy's downtown, both usually empty, and Procter and Gamble's huge towers like Gestapo Headquarters with its thousands of tiny windows.

So much of the old and distinguished is covered over with new buildings, like the grand Albee movie theater where she daydreamed of romance, the Gibson Hotel, where she and John had their wedding reception: all down under the ground, the past beneath the present.

Betsy finds herself heading toward the market where she worked at her family's cheese stall.

She parks as close as she can to the market square and walks to the long hall in the center. It is closed. Of course. It's a weekday. There is only one outdoor stall open, selling spotted bananas and sweet-smelling, rotten-ripe pineapples. No vendor. The square is empty. Empty as a dream space.

Betsy tries the door of the hall, though she knows it won't open, peers through the barred windows as though she might see her mother and father and uncles, their aprons stiff with cheese, their voices shrilly repeating customers' orders. She imagines what used to be: the chopping and grinding, the ching of the cash registers, the butchers yelling at each other, all the racket and din of the place. The voices of her family.

Betsy pounds her fists on the door. Let me in. She would be safe in there. In the past. Maybe if she were back there things would happen differently. The worst could not happen; children dying before their mothers and fathers. But they are all hostages to time.

She is so tired. So disappointed.

Betsy leans her head on the wooden door. Listens to the sounds around her. Birds. Men's voices. She must get out of this neighborhood. The streets on the four sides of the market are deserted except for several groups of young black men at the corners, wearing over-sized T-shirts and baggy pants. They huddle together and talk, glancing at her furtively, threateningly.

She doesn't belong here. Not any more. Everything here has changed. It's a different world.

She walks quickly toward her car. She holds her purse tight to her side, and looks straight ahead, trying to be invisible. But there are men on each corner, in front of her and behind her. She has come too far to avoid them.

She is overly warm. Her heels click and echo on the sun-bright cement. One of the men is coming her way. The square is like a surrealist painting: empty except for the two figures, herself and the one man, moving toward each other, the buildings casting long shadows on the sidewalks.

Why has she come here? She must be mad. The man coming toward her is almost upon her.

"Betsy!"

Is she hearing things? William steps into her path from a store-front doorway.

Betsy jumps at the sight of him.

"William!"

The man coming her way, passes them. "How you all doin' today?" he says.

"OK," William says. "How 'bout you?"

"Very fine. Have a blessed day." The man moves on by.

"Betsy, what are you doing here?" William says.

"I'm not sure."

"Are you OK? You look rocky."

"I guess I am."

"C'mon with me. We'll go to the Coffee Shop and get some iced tea."

Betsy lets her grandson lead the way. The streets they walk through are littered; boarded up store fronts side by side with open shops. When they get to the dimness of the Bookshelf she is very glad to sit down in one of the wooden booths. The other customers in the bar greet William and he introduces her to two women named Velma and Ariel, and a musician named Hattie who is strumming a guitar.

William goes to the bar and returns with two glasses of iced tea. Betsy uses both hands to pick up her glass.

With the cool drink she feels better, more herself. Less a crazy old lady.

"You OK?" William says.

"Fine."

They drink quietly for a moment.

Do you really live in this neighborhood?" she says.

"Upstairs."

"Do you like it?"

"It's OK."

"I had a friend who was mugged nearby. He died."

Betsy has a store of tales about friends who have died in bizarre ways: one who jumped from the city's tallest building, one on Pan Am 103.

William laughs. "I'm super careful," he says.

Jimmy comes to the table to see if they want refills or anything to eat.

William introduces him to Betsy and says, "How's business today?"

Although only two tables are filled, Jimmy says, "Been flying about like a mad thing!"

He shakes his bar rag and takes off to get the tea pitcher.

"Were those men at the market dangerous?" Betsy asks William.

"They could be. You shouldn't be down here alone. Where is your car?"

Betsy isn't sure.

"Why do they call that thing your father has 'proud flesh'?" she asks.

"I was wondering, too. It's so gross. Like something from *The Invasion of the Body Snatchers*."

"They say it's not too serious. But they say that about everything."

"I know."

Betsy's hands are still shaking.

She has been working so hard to keep her nerve. Walking the high wire over age and death with her balancing pole and parasol.

Betsy takes her cell phone out of her purse. Calls John. He has actually remembered to turn his on.

"Come get me," she says. "I need you to rescue me."

"Where are you?" he asks.

"Where we met."

She closes the phone and turns to her grandson.

"Walk me back over to the market," she says.

The two of them go back the few blocks to the market hall. Betsy looks through the window into the dark interior with its deserted stalls and shadows, her grandson behind her.

"Look, William," she says. "Do you see a young girl in there?"

He peers through the murky glass into the dark.

"She is talking to a tall soldier in uniform."

William narrows his eyes. "Yes," he says. "Yes, I see her."

49

David

Google says "Proud Flesh" is swelling (like swelling with pride). Protruding from his father's chest, the growth looks alive.

The infected incision (if it is infected—it has been cultured twice)—makes David's father too weak to keep up with his physical therapy. He is depressed. The doctors' words are confusing: Dr. Ritch (lungs) says he's over medicated again which could make anyone feel rotten; Dr. Sanders (heart) says he is fine; Dr. Graham (surgeon) says the fever is breaking (what fever?); the patient is dehydrated, then bloated with fluids that could enter the blood stream and flood the cells. Brendan tells him his father could drown in his own fluids.

They conscientiously pull on the elastic stockings Dr. Mittendorf has prescribed, though Dr. Hale says they are useless. David wishes for just one day when nothing goes wrong or his father is not subjected to some painful procedure. The tests and transfusions, the needles and leg machine exercises are supposedly helping him, but they seem like torture. He gets more C scans, platelets, frozen plasma.

Sitting in a small alcove where David has brought his father for yet another sonogram, David tries to work on a brief. In the margin he writes: WAITING WAITING WAITING.

It is sad to see his father looking like an old man again. His model. A fine teacher with a wall full of awards. David remembers him working night after night over his students' blue books. He so earnestly wanted the students to gain the perspective of history. Sometimes he would burst out laughing. He would tear his hair at their grammar and worry about their religiosity. "They won't spell out the word God, they write in 'G-dash-D,' but all this piousness doesn't stop them from cheating, lying and plagiarizing." He combatted *Cliff's Notes* for years, and then essays sold on the Internet. "They'll take their opinions from any place in the world but their own minds."

His view of the university has darkened. It's into real estate, buying up the surrounding neighborhood and creating student dormitories luxurious as Florida time shares, with swimming pools and work-out rooms, and mini-malls with the most popular clothing stores and bars.

"It's turned into a theme park," he says. "You come for 'the college experience,' and a seal of approval, a ticket to the job market. The idea that education is intrinsically valuable is so— out— To my students Viet Nam is like the Civil War, so long in the past, dusty old history. But the past is always there, working away, crumbling under our feet."

David's father looks at his wrist as if to find out the time. It is freezing in the area where they wait for attention. "That young woman who had never heard of Buchenwald—so typical. No wonder people go jumping into new wars when they don't know anything about the old ones. Education is just a commodity. We wanted to work for peace and justice. Our students want to be hedge fund managers."

A doctor greets David and his father: a tall African American woman with corn rows, a regal bearing. She introduces herself as Michelle Johnson, Effie's daughter—Effie who worked for Betsy for so many years. David's father compliments her, clearly glad of her being a doctor. She's impressive, and David feels guilty for the way they all thought of Effie as a sort of comic character because of her naiveté and her double negatives. She must have been damned smart to to get her daughter through med school on a domestic worker's wages.

"Thank you again for the help you gave me with college," Michelle says to David's father. "I wouldn't be here without you." She steps back into the room with the machines and gives orders to the technicians.

"I never knew about this," David says. But then what does he know about any of the family? "You helped finance her education?"

"I'd forgotten. I didn't recognize her. I guess she's one of the reasons I keep on going."

"I remember her as a little girl, waiting for Effie to get off work."

"Oh yes."

David feels happy that Michelle has made his father smile. He looks like his old self. But when they return to his room, he looks tired and old again.

David is tired too. They were supposed to be home by now.

When David's mother arrives for the evening shift they cling together. She looks worn out. They are like marathon dancers from the thirties, dancing and dancing, trying to stay on their feet, beyond the point of exhaustion.

At home, David and Phoebe walk Lenny and then have dinner of peanut butter sandwiches. Lydia has an evening meeting. David is rather glad. He and Lydia, whose love once seemed inexhaustible, now seem to be shaking the few last drops out of a nearly empty bottle.

He will never be the lawyer he aspired to be. Never be the man his father is. But then he and David's mother lived so simply, not piling up debt like he and Lydia are. How did they get so far behind?

David guides Phoebe through her bedtime routine and then they make popcorn and watch *The Wizard of Oz*. They both fall asleep.

David awakens to pictures on TV of a woman offering an enormous breast to a naked man, who grabs her nipple in his mouth. Several others join them in an orgy of writhing flesh. "Sex Alley" seems to be the name of the show, on the same cable channel as the movie. More stuff he doesn't want Phoebe exposed to. How long has she been asleep? Has she been watching this? David searches among the couch cushions for the remote. Looks up at the program. Watches a moment.

He is getting turned on.

Jesus, he thinks. Ugh. He disgusts himself. People are so low. But maybe human. He locates the remote and turns the TV off. He detests those morons who watch sex shows so they won't have to have real relations with a real woman.

He wishes he could remember when Phoebe fell asleep. Was it before or after the Munchkins?

50

Judith

The phone in Eric's room rings. Natalie. Is this a good time to come over? Dr. Graham has told Judith he will be in soon to remove the growth in Eric's incision.

Judith dreads this procedure. Will it be painful? It sounds horrible. The incision looks so fragile.

Judith thinks. The removal will probably be messy and frightening.

She has noticed Natalie's squeamishness at mess and blood.

"Yes," she says. "Come on over. I'm here by myself."

After she has hung up, she thinks of calling Natalie back. That was a spiteful thing to do. But the hell with Natalie. Maybe this will scare her away, like pitching a stone at a thieving blue jay.

Eric awakens and Judith puts in reach the things he constantly needs: water, cups, tissues, breathing gadget, urinal, heart pillow.

He is hungry so Judith goes to the kitchenette next door and whips up some ice cream and milk with an egg blended in. She prepares a plastic pan of water so Eric can wash up and comb his hair. No matter, with the reversal and depression, he looks like a sick man cleaned up for a hospital visit.

When Natalie arrives she gives Eric a kiss on his cheek and presents him with another milk shake from Wendy's.

"He just drank a milk shake," Judith says.

"Gotta fatten you up," Natalie says to Eric, and guides the straw of her offering into his mouth.

Eric takes a valiant sip and pushes the cup aside.

"I only have about an hour till I have to get back and pick up MacKenzie from rhythm class," Natalie says.

They hear a quick rap on the door and Dr. Graham and his assistant come in. The assistant, Sheri, checks the drainage bag and takes Eric's temperature.

Dr. Graham says, "Ready to get rid of that pesky growth?"

"I'm not going anywhere," Eric says.

Dr. Graham leans over his patient and listens to his heart.

He arranges his scalpel and tongs on a sterile tray and Sheri places it on a table. He asks Eric to unbutton his shirt. The chest is red and torn looking, marked by the long jagged incision and that *thing* growing out of the center. Judith can barely look.

Dr. Graham anesthetizes the area around Eric's incision, and Sheri sterilizes it. The doctor slices the node out as though carving a juicy morsel of roast beef. He plunks it into a pan, a bloody hunk of flesh.

Judith watches Natalie. She looks like she might throw up.

Sheri cleans the blood from around the wound, and replaces the bandage over it.

"Keep it dry," she says.

Dr. Graham looks at his watch, opens his cell phone. Before the two leave, he says, "You'll be going home soon. The bandage on that incision will have to be medicated and changed every four hours."

With that he and his ever-present acolyte are gone.

Judith notices that Natalie is quite pale. She seems to weave on her feet, about to faint.

"Oh my God." Judith eases Natalie onto the extra bed next to Eric's, and presses the call button.

"What's going on?" Eric says. He lies back and closes his eyes, exhausted.

Enter William and Angie. They see Natalie stretched out cold, Judith standing over her.

"Have you killed her?" William asks.

"She passed out," Judith says.

Angie places a pillow under Natalie's feet, and looks into her eyes. When Natalie stirs, she says, "Breathe deep." She props Natalie up and takes her pulse.

"Take a minute," she says. "You'll be OK."

She helps Natalie sit on the side of the bed and tells William to get her a glass of water.

"OK?" Angie says.

She helps Natalie to her feet and says to Judith and William, "She'll be fine now."

Natalie rubs her eyes, as though waking from sleep. She gives them all an evil look, kisses Eric firmly on the mouth and slams out of the room.

Judith and the others sit quietly, while Eric dozes.

"I did a wicked thing," Judith says.

"Can't be too bad." William goes to the bedside tray, picks up the abandoned milk shake and finishes it.

"I told her to come on over for the fun and games."

"Of course," William says.

The nurse on call arrives, and William says, "He rolled over on his call button."

Judith sits in a chair and breathes deeply. She is grateful for Angie's help. And William's collusion. She worries about Natalie telling Eric she is jealous and spiteful, which she is.

259

51

William

William speaks at Tim's funeral. The neighborhood people crowd into the tiny church where Reverend Allen preaches. It's nothing like the funerals in the movies where everyone is dressed in black and it's raining. The sun is bright, the sky blue; people are dressed in jeans, stenciled T-shirts and hoodies, whatever they have that is clean.

Tim is laid out in a modest casket. People took up a collection for a new suit from Smitty's. He is waxy, pink-cheeked, like a saint in a cathedral, his dreadlocks neatly arranged. His needle punctures and scars and recent wounds are covered. William thinks of their visit to Gloria and shudders at how Tim might have looked when he died.

William speaks of Tim's dedication to the work they did together, the many trips to schools and churches. Rev Al prays. Angie, Jimmy, Hattie, Velma, Ariel, Mel, all the regulars from the Bookshelf, the nuns and priests from St. Vincent De Paul, the owners of the fish fry and chess players from the park, little Millicent and the kids from the steel drum band, the director at Peaslee: everyone is here. The group sings *Amazing Grace*. After the ceremony, the kids from the Lookout dart back and forth to the casket and snatch cookies from the table of food the neighbors have brought. How many funerals have they been to now, how many crime scenes witnessed?

Tim was found in the early hours of the morning the day before, shot in the head. The newspaper printed a story about Tim's good works. He'd been robbed. So tragic. A saint shot down. But everyone in the neighborhood soon knows what has happened: the familiar yellow tape surrounds the hotel Veronica, a notorious crack house.

The word gets around that Tim's body was full of cocaine, that he had been killed by dealers after their money.

William thought he knew the man. He thinks back to Tim and their last gig at the church, Tim's rough language.

He always made it strong, but . . . . Was he on something then?

Hypocrite, liar! At the same time William knows how hard Tim tried to get clean.

He goes to see Rev Al. The old man is dressed in his usual outfit from the Free Store, plaid polyester slacks, white belt and re-heeled loafers. He holds his Bible in his white, big-veined hands. Two women are at the kitchen table printing anti-war signs.

"Hi, William," Rev says. "Paula, do we have any tea?"

One of the women pours a cup of herb tea and places it on the nicked-up end table next to William. He warms his hands on it.

"The police have picked up a young black man. Seventeen years old. He will spend his young manhood in jail," Rev says.

"And Tim?" William says.

"He did some good work. He did his best."

William sits quietly with Rev Al. The man has an aura. William wonders why his friends travel to India and other exotic places to find their holy men, when Rev is right here among them.

"We must get these guns out of the hands of children," Rev says. "And dope off the streets."

"But how? Nothing works."

"Keep trying, William. Keep trying."

Rev is so frail. He has a bad limp; is now using a cane. When he goes, who will there be?

William walks back to his apartment. He passes a man braced against a building. He knows him, a Viet Nam veteran. William hands him some bills. He should just buy him a sandwich; he'll go straight to the deli and buy beer with the cash. When he turns the corner to his apartment building, he sees David ringing his bell. Dad! His heart speeds up. He rushes toward his brother. David turns, his face tense.

"What's happened? Is it Dad?"

"No. No. Relax."

William holds his sides. Takes a deep breath.

"It's Lydia and me. We're not doing so good."

William is not surprised. He has seen the tension between David and Lydia.

"I'm not a good person to share your pain with today," William says. "You've read about Tim in the paper, I guess."

"He sounded saintly, like a martyr."

"He was full of cocaine. A dealer shot him."

"Oh."

William unlocks the outer door of the building and he and David climb the stairs.

"I'm sorry," David says.

"Yeah."

William's room is hot and stuffy. Jimmy has not yet fixed the air conditioner. William turns on a fan. It blows this way and that and scoots around facing the wall. William turns it off.

"Let's go sit in the park," he says.

They walk the few blocks and find a concrete picnic table under a tree.

David admires the townhouses Angie and William had noticed the day they ate Popsicles at this same table.

"Yeah, pretty soon this whole area will be dolled up and the people who live here priced out," William says.

"The city can't let these buildings rot and collapse," David says.

This makes William mad. David is so detached, and doesn't mind starting up old arguments when William himself has a grief bigger than his and Lydia's yuppie yapping.

"Why are buildings more important than people?" William snaps.

"This is a mercantile world, William."

Now he's lecturing, like I'm a dope, William thinks. He says to David, "You know the price of everything and the value of nothing."

"And you know the value of everything and the price of nothing."

William doesn't reply. The hell with David.

Then he thinks of his father. Turning on each other is so predictable. His father once reprimanded them when they were kids and fighting, for not acting like brothers, then thought a minute and said, "Oh well, the archetypal brothers are Cain and Abel, aren't they?"

"I don't have any answers for what's happening around here," David says. "But the status quo isn't good. These black kids seem to be killing each other—and themselves."

"We want them to—like we want the Middle Eastern countries to annihilate each other . . . . Your friends the developers and the city do nothing to save the schools— They don't want the black kids educated. Where would they get the cheap labor to flip hamburgers and clean toilets?"

David looks around at the groups of eight and ten young black men in droopy pants and hooded sweatshirts—

"But these kids are not going to work for them," William says. "They can make money on drugs, or just hang out."

"This is a hell of a world," David says.

William and David sit quietly for a moment.

"Did you see any of this coming with Tim?" David asks.

William pauses. "I never seem to see anything coming."

As William and his brother try to find some way to sew up the rift between them, people pass by and stop. Dale, a black woman who washes dishes at Ollie's Trolley, says, "He'll be missed, no matter what." An actor who had a part in a Hollywood movie and now does community theater gives William a hug, and Bennydril, a druggie with gold front teeth and a chest full of gold chains says, "Shit, man. Breaks." Leonard, a Harvard Law grad, who lives in a small house on Thirteenth, filled with books and the sound of his daughters playing flute and piano, just nods sadly at William and walks on.

This *is* a community, William thinks. He doesn't envy David, who, in avoiding the poor, and living in cleaner air and neater streets, every day must creep along in a line of cars also escaping to the suburbs, which are, as Forester said of London, spreading like a stain over the countryside. He must drive past strings of ugly malls, a plastic Jesus a hundred feet high.

William is sorry he blew off David before. His brother is in pain and has come to him for commiseration.

"Let's go get drunk," David says.

"I can't drink," William says.

"Oh right."

But a beer sounds good.

"One won't hurt," he says. He knows he's wrong.

They go to the bar opposite the park, a small dark place with a few Formica tables and a neon beer sign over the shelves of bottles.

They sit on stools at the bar.

"We're a walking cliché," David says. "Lydia's working too hard to make partner. I have a lot of complicated cases going on—"

"So what are you going to do?"

David shrugs.

"What about Phoebe?"

"She's beginning to catch on."

"That's not good."

"If it weren't for her . . . ."

"Don't you love Lydia?"

"Well sure. But it's a complicated thing."

"Everybody says it's not supposed to be."

"Well, it is after you're married."

William nurses his beer, and David orders a second with a shot. They devour a dish of stale pretzels.

"I've been obsessed with Dad and business. I admit all that," David says. "I was late to Phoebe's recital, I was grouchy at her birthday party. I'm practically impotent now because Lydia's spread a ring of anger around our bed."

"Wow."

"We're members of the debtor class, living in hand to mouth luxury."

"Jesus. I didn't know it was this bad."

"We are pushed to the limit, but she talks about having another kid. I'd like for Phoebe to have a little brother or sister too. But something's gotta give."

William finishes his beer and starts another. The bartender offers him a shot, and he doesn't resist. Two men from the alcoholic drop-in center across the street weave their way out the door.

"Women," William says. "Angie wants to have a baby, too, but she won't get married."

"Do you want to marry her?"

"Well, I would—I mean—I don't know."

"We're just studs anymore. Men. Irrelevant studs to give them kids."

"Mom and Dad weren't like that. They were friends."

"And look at them."

"They might still get back together."

"Women have their girlfriends now."

"They run in packs."

"Husbands are passé."

David orders more beer and more shots. The alcohol goes through William like a spreading fire. Both he and David are beginning to slur their words.

"Lydia says we Howards are full of angst," David says.

"We are."

"And shit."

"That too."

"But back to your friend Tim," David says. "I am terribly terribly sorry."

"Me too."

"You're never tempted to go that way again, are you?"

"Who me?" William lies. "Do I look like a dick, addick I mean?"

With that, he laughs. He has drunk two bottles of beer and— how much booze? He puts his head down on the bar. Too many props are being pulled out from under him. His father set back. His mother worn out, his grandmother wandering around Over the Rhine. Now the brother he leaned on leaning on him. Tim dead, who would have said no to the drinking. But look what he went and did.

52

William

As William approaches his father's room for a visit, he meets Lydia and Phoebe in the hall. He lifts Phoebe into the air.

"Phoeble!"

"No, you're feeble!"

"Natalie's there," Lydia says.

William puts Phoebe down, and continues towards his father's room.

"And baby makes three," he says.

Lydia holds him by the sleeve.

"She's not so bad. She seems very concerned for Eric."

"It's not that she's bad . . . ."

"She's not your Mom."

William kisses Phoebe and Lydia, who wave goodbye, and knocks on his father's door.

"Come!"

Natalie is sitting by his father, holding his hand. She is wearing her tank top that shows her tattooed heart. She jumps up and gives William a hug, which he accepts reluctantly.

"How's the old man today?" he says, then wishes to bite his tongue. For "old man."

"Good," Natalie says.

His father does not look good.

He seems sheepish having William and Natalie together, an awkward threesome. Each looks around for the other to start a conversation.

"Have you any movie recommendations for me?" Natalie asks William.

"I'm hanging up my critical bona fides. My last choice was not too successful."

"What was that?"

"*Dodgeball.*"

Natalie and his father respond in a chorus.

"Hilarious"—Natalie.

"Junk"—his father.

William and his father laugh. Natalie looks confused.

More than ever William is convinced this is not the woman for his father. He and his mother always thought the same things were funny.

Maybe *he* should ask her for a date. Hah.

Olga, on duty again, comes in and approaches the bed.

"Need to empty that drainage bag," she says.

Natalie looks panicky. She reaches for her purse and pulls her sweater around her shoulders.

"I guess I better get going."

William's father does not respond. His eyes are following Olga's work.

"I'll join you," William says to Natalie. They both kiss his father, wave, and leave the room.

In the hall, Natalie says to William, "I love the way you and your father tease each other. You have a wonderful father."

"Yes."

"I wish I had a father like him."

"You do," William thinks. "You do."

William and Natalie walk down the hall together. William presses the down button on the elevator.

"Where's your car?" Natalie says. "In back or down under?"

"I'm heading for the bus stop."

"Oh."

They are quiet in the elevator, like their fellow passengers. Then Natalie says, "I'll give you a lift. You live downtown, don't you?"

"Main."

"No problem. I go right near there."

William follows Natalie to the outdoor parking lot. They walk down a few aisles. It's always crowded. She pulls her remote out of her purse and—beep beep—the lights flash on a red van.

"You navigate," Natalie says.

William does so, and in ten minutes or so, Natalie pulls up in front of the Bookshelf Coffee Shop.

"Many thanks," William says. "It would have taken me a lot longer on the bus."

"Bookshelf Coffee Shop," Natalie reads. "You live in there?"

"Almost," William says. "I live upstairs."

"I could use a coffee."

William hesitates. But maybe he's curious.

"Come on in. I owe you for the ride."

What in hell is he doing, he thinks.

Natalie hesitates, then says, "Can I park here?"

"Absolutely."

The two walk into the Coffee Shop. Jimmy is standing at the bar and gives Natalie a long inquisitive look. William responds with a "fuck you" smirk.

He guides Natalie to a booth and says, "What'll it be?"

"I think actually—a beer."

"Garçon!" William calls to Jimmy, "Two cold Buds. And be quick about it."

The ones he had with David hadn't done any harm.

Jimmy brings the beer, giving William a sour look.

William extends his bottle to Natalie to click. "Cheers!"

"So you live upstairs?" Natalie says.

"It's modest, but it has a certain *je ne sais quoi.*"

William thinks, it's about the size of Natalie's car.

"I've been wanting to know you and David better," Natalie says. "But about the time that might happen, Eric got sick."

"No time like the present." What is he saying?

Both bottles are empty, so William raises two fingers to attract Jimmy, who is leaning on the bar as far over as he can in order to hear William and Natalie's conversation. He'll be ratting to Angie and the regulars in no time.

"I don't usually drink like this," Natalie says. "But I am so tired."

"We all are."

"Do you think your father will recover all the way?"

William shrugs.

"I've been planning a trip to Nassau—I really want to go— hoping your father would be well."

Natalie looks petulant, like a little girl whose birthday party has been rained out.

William thinks of the beach scenes she has pinned to his father's wall.

"This latest thing seems so horrible."

Natalie looks as though she is about to slide under the table.

"Want something to eat?" William says.

"No, but I could use a smoke. Uh, you know . . . . My stomach's been jumping around like crazy ever since Eric's heart attack. And with running back and forth to the hospital and . . . ."

"I could blow a stick, myself." His words are a little slurred.

"Do you think your father will ever be really well—I mean—the same?"

"It'll take time."

William feels tired. He wants to lie down.

"He's such a brilliant man."

"Yeah."

William stares at the heart tattoo on Natalie's right breast. He has a strong urge to reach out and touch it. It seems to be beating.

"Know what?" Natalie says. "Do you really have any—I sort of gave it up, but . . . ."

Do I look like a drug dealer? William thinks. Well yes, I guess I do—hanging around the mother lode in Over the Rhine. Living like I do. Does she know my background?

"Can't light up in here. Don't want the cops down on Jimmy. Anyway my ditch weed is upstairs."

"I'm just so damned wasted."

Natalie is needy, William thinks. Weedy needy.

"I cordially invite you to my humble abode."

William and Natalie make their way out of the booth clumsily.

"Put the booze on by tab," William calls to Jimmy, who snaps back, "Friends don't let friends—"

"Yeah, yeah. Later."

William's room, he notices with embarrassment, is messier even than usual. There is no place to sit except on the bed that almost fills the main space off the kitchenette. Natalie sits on it and stares at the stacks of books and records piled everywhere. She leans back, seductive.

"Now let me think, where did I hide my stash?" William mumbles. He rummages in his bathroom closet and bureau drawers for the marijuana he had hidden away for a rainy day. He had forsworn all drugs, but hey—you never know. He's been proud of the fact that he hasn't gone on this search while his father has been sick. Of course, he's still sick, but the alcohol he just drank has turned his brain to mush. What the fuck did he do with his stash?

At last he finds it inside a shoe, one of a pair his mother bought him and that he has never worn. The stuff is in a baggie pushed down into the toe. William pulls it out and joins Natalie on the bed. He wraps the pot in a skin and offers it to her. She takes a long drag and passes it back. She lies back on the bed; her little false heart glowing red.

William takes a hit and lies down beside her. The alcohol and the pot make him collapse like a discarded marionette.

She reaches for the cigarette. He passes it over, then takes another toke himself. They exchange puffs until the pot is gone. He strokes Natalie's heart tattoo and her breast slips out of her shirt and into his hand. She doesn't pull away.

He rolls over on her, and nuzzles her neck. Her hair is loosened and snakes around his hand when he touches it. They move their lips toward one another. Her eyes are glassy as a doll's. Big. Big. Closer. Closer. What has his father seen in this girl?

She is pretty. Very pretty. Their legs are entwined. William has an erection. He slips off his sweat pants. Natalie slides her thong aside.

Natalie guides his penis between her legs. He's inside. Warm. Wet. His brain seems to go blank as they move rhythmically. He comes like a thirteen year old. She seems to be doing the same.

Natalie caresses William's cheek with her hand, runs her fingers over his lips. William opens his mouth to suck her finger, when something in her touch alarms him. Her hands smell of something familiar, medicinal. William recognizes the odor: the soap they use at the hospital, a germicide.

What in the hell am I doing? he thinks. He pulls away. This is insane! Awful! Really awful! Some kind of sick Oedipal thing!

He jumps off the bed. Pulls up his pants.

"You gotta get out of here!" he says. "This is crazy."

"You're right," Natalie murmurs. She rolls over and looks as though she might fall asleep.

"I'll get coffee," William says.

He dashes down to the Bookshelf and grabs the coffee pot off the burner behind the bar. Jimmy gives him another dirty look.

When he gets back upstairs, he says, "Are you OK? Are you awake?"

"Oh yeah," Natalie murmurs. "I'm fine, I just need to throw up."

She rushes into the bathroom and William can hear the sound of painful heaving and the toilet flushing. When she returns from the bathroom, William pours her coffee and finds some bread and cheese in his fridge. They drink and eat in a kind of haze.

"Don't tell anyone about this," Natalie says.

"Are you kidding?"

When they both feel sober enough to think straight, William insists on driving Natalie home in her car. They say little on the way.

"I have never done anything like this before," Natalie says.

"Me neither. I'm sorry."

After he parks Natalie's car and sees her to her door, he takes the bus home after all. He thinks everyone on the bus is looking at him, seeing into his cruddy soul. What possessed him to do such a thing? Competing with his father? Sick, sick, sick. He could tear out his eyes.

It's late when he returns the coffee pot to Jimmy, who pours him a cup and leads him into a booth and brings him a bagel. He should never have drunk that first beer with David. He could end up like Tim. But the worst part is the guilt. To touch a woman who belongs to his father! Was he punishing them? Was he curious? What did his father see in Natalie? Closed bedroom doors were always so tempting.

He's a kid standing in a hallway, hearing sounds from his parents' bedroom.

Bennydril comes in and slides into the seat opposite William, and looks into his eyes. He bares his gold teeth.

"Too much Wacky Tobaccy, eh Will?" he says. "Got any extra?"

53

Judith

Eric's chest refuses to heal. Dr. Graham says keep the bandage dry. Dr. Sanders says keep it wet. Dr. Graham's assistant suspects a stitch irritating the wound and goes at it with a razor blade. It is declared ready to clear up, and the director of rehab says to make plans for going home.

Judith and Betsy's helper Ora prepare the house. They locate linens for the rented hospital bed, install a raised toilet seat in the bathroom and a safety bar and chair in the shower stall.

"I think we're ready now, don't you?" Judith says. "Brendan will be here and they are sending therapists to treat Eric's wound and work his leg. I'll be making plans to go back to DC . . . ."

She has talked to her dean but they have nothing for her after the semester is over, and someone has been hired to fill in for her until then. So she will have to find a new place. Judith has spent little time thinking about the future; the present had been moving too fast.

Eric's incision continues weeping. Like an inconsolable widow. Dr. Graham says there may be an infection on the wire holding Eric's ribs in place, and he might have to reopen the incision.

All the plans and hopes for a welcome home are stalled. This would be Eric's third surgery in forty some days. Fear spreads through the family like a virus.

The doctors treat the infection and once again declare Eric ready to go home. Chahna makes Eric practice using the walker on his own and getting into a car (turn walker so back is to passenger seat, lower butt onto seat, swing feet in last).

Judith checks out the preparations she and Ora have made at the house. This place has had so many lives: an empty stage set waiting for actors, a magic place, a warm family home, a trap.

Maybe it will be sold . . . .

She walks around the familiar rooms, and into the garden. She is amazed at what she has acquired here, the many skills and tools and *things* she has used: microwave and muffin tins, coffee pot, Cuisinart, broiler, wok, cleansers, scrubbers, soaps and mops, dust pans, shovels, swiffer; clippers, leaf blower, dust buster, wood cleaner, paint brushes, turpentine, toilet plunger . . . .

Eric had a much smaller array of tools: a computer, the TV remote, pens, note books, a brief case, BlackBerry, typewriter, tennis racket, car keys, sky maps.

Judith had more arms than Shiva. More heads than Hydra.

She goes back into the living room: so many books. She has heard somewhere that books should be packed away when selling a house. She could never do that. "Miscreants" James Joyce called them. And that's what they are, trouble-makers, raising questions. Important questions.

If her beloved books are crowded out by computers and cell phones and email and the electronics to come, will the Howards become obsolete along with them? She and Eric considered Betsy and John dinosaurs, now maybe they are fading into the past as well . . . . peace makers, polite people, book readers.

Judith picks up a copy of *Pride and Prejudice* and holds it to her nose. The odor of paper and rosin wafts forth along with the spirit of the story and people of the page, the lives within.

What will the house bring? It's an ailing old place, always with some ache or pain: a leaky bathroom roof, a crack in the wall, termites. But it's the only real home she has ever had. The place where she has lived most of her life. Filled with memories. The death of her mother. William. Her friendships and her work, her love-making and quarrels with Eric, the thousands of meals, summer evenings with her lovely boys running about the garden in nothing but shorts, collecting fireflies.

Judith goes back to the hospital and runs into Natalie at the door of Eric's room. She looks flustered, her eyes big and glittery.

"I want to talk to you," she says.

Judith shrugs and follows Natalie to the waiting room.

Rifling impatiently through the many compartments in her purse, Natalie digs out a bill, and slides it into the coffee machine. Judith lets her grapple with the broken vendor.

"Shit," Natalie says. She turns to Judith. "Nothing ever works in this god-damned place."

"Tell me about it."

"I want to know if you are going to make things hard for me and Eric. . . . "

"What are you talking about?"

"Oh, hanging on when you aren't wanted."

"This conversation is over," Judith says.

"Don't think I don't know you set me up the day I passed out."

Judith turns away.

"Are you arriving or leaving?" Judith says. "I'm on my way to check on my husband."

"I'm arriving, and I'm not a virus you can cure."

"No?"

"No. I know what the Howard men like . . . ."

"Men?"

"William and I had a smoke together, and one thing led to another . . . ."

"I don't believe you."

"No? The stash was in a new sneaker and he lives in the shittiest room I ever saw."

William! Oh no—

"You—my son!"

Judith swings and slaps Natalie hard.

"You bitch!"

Judith is horrified as she sees pink emerge on Natalie's cheek. Natalie staggers and bumps into the coffee machine, which for the first time releases coffee onto the grill and onto her six hundred dollar shoes.

"I'm going to tell Eric about this," Natalie says.

"No you won't," Judith says.

Natalie stalks out of the room, shaking coffee off her shoes.

Judith sits down, ashamed and worried. Natalie's story about William has details that she could only know if she had been in his room. It means her son falling back into drugs. The thought that he had sex with Natalie disgusts her. It's so sordid. She will not believe that part of Natalie's story. But the smoking . . . unbearable . . . to repeat that cold leaden day they brought William home from the hospital.

The next time she and William are together, she says, "Natalie and I had a childish run-in at the hospital."

She watches her son try to compose his face into a facsimile of innocence.

She tells him what Natalie said about them smoking pot together.

"She's lying," William says.

The conversation is so painful, Judith wants to go no further. Of course he is lying. He's done it before. But she is not in the business of humiliating her sons.

"She likes to provoke me," Judith says. "But you did promise me, and above all, yourself . . . ."

"I know."

"You *are* getting a new counselor?"

"Yes. Honest to God, I threw my stuff away and Rev Allen is putting me in touch with someone good."

"I beg you to take care."

"I will."

He has said this before.

"William," Judith says. "I can not stand any more strain . . . ."

54

William

He and Phoebe dig out the signs welcoming his father home. They prop these in the front hall, then go outside and tie balloons to the walnut tree. Everything is ready. Everyone feels happy as they picture the festive homecoming.

Later in the morning William and his mother drive to the hospital. His father is outside the door of his room, in a wheel chair. His possessions are loaded on a cart, with Brendan standing alongside it. William and his mother both look into the room. The beds are made and the trays and shelves are shiny clean, ominously awaiting the next patient. Lakesia sweeps the floor with her wide broom.

It takes a long time to get the discharge paper-work finished, and they are all impatient. Finally, they move through the unit, saying goodbye to the nurses and aides. William's mother hugs Chahna and Pam, vowing she will never ever forget them. They smile and return the hugs. The Howards take the long walk through the halls to the front door. ONE LAST TIME. They hope. William is glad to be saying goodbye to the pastels, the elevators, the cheerful plants. As they pass by the large photo of

Dr. Sanders beaming down at the them, William gives a wave, and his mother says, "I think Lakesia's photo should be up there."

William laughs and his father looks puzzled.

On the drive home, William's father is quiet, absorbed in himself and does not look out the window at the sights he has not seen for so long. Brendan points out familiar things.

"There's the university. You'll be back there soon."

At the house, Phoebe runs out to meet her grandfather, and William helps him out of the front seat of the car and onto his walker. He looks awfully gray and weak. He gives Phoebe a pat on the head and lets Brendan and William help him up the one step into the hall.

He glances at the "Welcome Home" signs and keeps moving toward the den. The family follows. Isn't he happy to be home, to see their greetings? Brendan helps him fold his walker and ease onto the rented bed.

Betsy and John and Judith crowd into the room.

"It's been a pretty exciting morning for Mr. Howard," Brendan says. "Packing up, signing out. We waited pretty long to get checked out. The nurses and aides all wanted to say goodbye."

William feels the general let-down.

His mother points out the pitcher of ice water by the bed.

"What would you like for lunch?" Betsy asks.

"Nothing much," William's father says. He looks confused and impatient.

"I'll fix some sandwiches," Betsy says.

"Do you want some water?" That is William's mother.

"Grampy, did you like my signs?" Phoebe asks.

"Where are my car keys and wallet?" he says.

They are in a plastic bag the hospital has sent home with him, along with toothpaste, soaps, powder, lotions, bottles of Tylenol, and bandages, gauze, tape, and salve for the still oozing chest.

Brendan sets about arranging these things in the bathroom. He hands William's father his red heart-shaped pillow, which his father tosses back at him.

"I hate that damn thing!" he says.

William watches his mother. She looks disappointed; they all do.

Gray days follow. William goes to the house most every evening when Brendan leaves, so his mother can go to bed early. She has been exhausted and sleep deprived. His father wakes before Brendan gets there in the morning at eight, and insists on getting up to shave and shower, something that he shouldn't do alone—so his mother is up at five or six.

The routine now includes a visiting nurse every morning to dress his father's chest wound, physical therapists to work the leg and see that the patient walks around the house. All the rugs are rolled up so he has a clear path. He rather quickly graduates from the walker to a cane. After many return trips to the surgeon's office, the chest gapes less, but it still refuses to completely heal.

When the therapists have fulfilled their allotted hours, they disappear.

William's mother begins driving his father to the hospital every day, where he practices balance and has the leg worked; he exercises on the bicycles and treadmill in the orthopedic department, always with a heart monitor around his neck, and frequently checked for blood pressure. "I can drive myself," he says every day, no matter how many times his mother asks him to postpone.

Finally she says, "Stop harping about driving! You're making me crazy." She appeals to William. The picture of someone driving a car—someone who has been totally helpless and too weak to walk across a room—is frightening; William urges his father to wait just a little longer.

"I want to go to the office and see what's going on," his father insists.

"OK, Mom and I will take you."

They put him off as long as they can. He does not look strong enough to face the problems that will fall on his shoulders once he returns to work. But as he progresses, they make an appointment to go to the university.

On the scheduled afternoon, William meets his parents at the house. His Dad looks good: he's dressed in normal clothes for the first time in months: casual slacks, an open collared shirt, sport jacket and loafers (he hated the sweats and velcroed sneakers—not him). They drive to campus and his father looks about, reacquainting himself with the landscape, the buildings. The campus is undergoing changes, and they have to walk through several new buildings to get to the old gray stucco tower where history is housed. William opens the big doors and they take an elevator to the third floor with its gray walls and concrete floor. William is very apprehensive about this trip; he can tell his mother is too, but his father plows confidently ahead in the familiar halls. The door to his office has been unlocked by Jerry Romano, and William's father goes right in. He sits down in his leather swivel chair behind his desk and looks around. A beatific smile spreads over his face. He examines the objects on his desk, pushes back in his chair contentedly. Still smiling.

Jerry and several other members of the history department come to the door and say hello.

"Welcome back," Jerry says. He comes in and shakes William's father's hand and pats him on the back. The others follow. He nods at William's mother, who is soon crowded to the corner of the small office.

William looks at his mother. He can see what she is thinking and feeling. Is the history department his father's real family?

"When will you be back for good?" several people ask.

"Soon as I can—next week maybe. They're making me exercise three days a week and I have to do all sorts of stupid stuff. Watch my diet . . . ."

"Of course." "My father had a bypass." "You look great." Etc. etc.

William sees hurt in his mother's eyes, and he feels dismissed too; their wild nights are forgotten, their concern and constant fear blown off.

He says to his mother, "He's so much better now than when he got out of the hospital. Naturally he's happy to be back at work."

"Home," she says.

55

Judith

Everyone she loves is sitting around Betsy's table: the members of the family along with Angie, Brendan, and Jerry and Theresa Romano. The dining room is bright with bouquets of orange lilies and yellow roses. The sky over the river is pure blue with great fluffy white clouds bumping each other about like healthy spring lambs. John gives a toast with a dry Cabernet: "to Eric's return to health!"

They all clink glasses. Eric is going to live and be well. The doctors instructed him to avoid salt, butter, excess sugar and alcohol, shell fish, ham, fatty steaks—on and on—in short, anything that makes eating more than mechanical fuel for the body. Eric pays little attention to the dietitian's booklets and post-op instructions, but Betsy does. She serves a salad *nicoise* with a very light olive oil and lemon dressing.

Still, as the meal progresses, Judith watches Eric anxiously. She can not drop the habit. When she sees him ask for more wine and a pat of butter, she starts to object. After weeks and weeks of being in charge of his well-being, feeding him, wiping spilled food from his chin, cleaning him up like a baby, letting go is like taking a child to school for the first time. She can't let go. Of concern. Of *Control.*

"You are looking so *good*," Jerry says to Eric. "I can hardly believe that you've been in hospital all this time."

"How is the knee?" Angie asks.

"Fine," Eric says. As he always does.

He does look good, Judith thinks. It's hardly believable that he was the babbling paranoid in the hospital, the spindly invalid whose legs would not hold him up to cross the room.

"So you are a miracle of modern medicine," Jerry says. "And I guess, your own strong will . . . ."

Everyone looks expectantly at Eric. He does not glance at Judith.

"I guess that's about it," he says. "I had good doctors."

An almost audible gasp goes around the table.

Judith feels as though she has been stabbed. Fury gushes out of her astonished heart. She was with him in the hospital forty days and forty nights, enough time for Noah's flood.

A deadly moment passes.

"I think maybe Mom had something to do with your recovery," William says. His voice, Judith can tell, is strained. He can not say more. Angie squeezes his hand.

"Hear, hear," John says.

Eric does not say anything. Judith is humiliated. And angry.

"I don't remember much about the whole deal," Eric says to Jerry. "I've sort of blotted it all out I guess."

Judith thinks, that's probably good. For him. But she violently objects to being blotted out along with the painful procedures and bed pans.

Eric and Jerry talk about Eric's returning to work. Eric is driving now, and he decides to start in a few days. A light load. Just office stuff until the new term begins and he can let go the teaching assistants who have been covering for him.

"It'll be great to have you back," Jerry says. "Place is kind of dull without you."

"What are *your* plans now?" Lydia asks Judith. "Now that your patient has cured himself?"

Judith is grateful for the support.

"I'll be returning to DC soon," she says. To what, she is unsure.

"How is your father?" John asks Judith.

"He remarried you know. He's mad about the woman," Judith says. "He told my sister she's wearing him out sexually."

She's talking too much.

"How old is he?" Lydia asks.

"Nearly eighty."

Betsy and John exchange a glance.

"I'm going to stay with my sister for a while in D.C.," Judith says. "She needs help with her daughter."

"Oh, I want you *here*," Phoebe says.

Another dead silence. All look to Eric. Will he say something?

He takes a sip of wine.

"You can come and visit me, and I'll visit you," Judith says to Phoebe. "You'll love Washington."

Plans are made for the afternoon. Judith, Eric, and Brendan will go back to the house. William and Angie will stay to help with the dishes. Kisses all around.

At the house, Eric goes straight to the den and lies down. In spite of his advances he does not have his full strength back, and won't, he has been advised, for about a year.

Judith calls Moira and says she will be with her soon.

She deserves a word of praise, acknowledgement of how she pitched in to help Eric recover. But she cannot afford resentment at Eric's dismissiveness or gnawing over the bones of old offenses. She is proud of how she let the past and even the betrayal with Natalie go and helped Eric. She knows she has done the most work and is impressed with her own strength. It has been like a job, and now she is unemployed.

56

Betsy

Betsy saw how Eric's lack of praise wounded Judith at her luncheon. She feels guilty about her. They have used her. She calls Judith, makes sure Eric is not home, and asks to come over.

"Sure," Judith says.

When Betsy arrives at the house, she looks Judith over. She is pale and thin.

"May I make a pot of tea?" Betsy says. "You look exhausted and I feel that way. Like I'll never not be tired again."

Judith follows as Betsy leads the way to the kitchen.

"This place could never be the same without you," Betsy says.

She puts a tea kettle on an electric burner and two tea bags in a pot, an old cracked Deruta pottery one.

"You always loved that pattern."

"Wedding present from you and John."

The inside is stained brown.

Judith lays out cups and a plate of cookies.

"I wish we could have been closer over the years," Betsy says.

"You had your own life. That's good."

"You've done a wonderful job with the boys."

288

"Thank you."

What Betsy has to say is so hard.

"Hate electric stoves," she says. "They're so slow and then they get too hot and won't cool down."

"We talked about changing to gas for—twenty-five years?"

Betsy takes the screaming kettle off the stove and pours the tea and she and Judith sit at the table. They pass the sugar back and forth, neither taking any. Betsy stirs her sugarless tea, selects a cookie.

"Um. From Virginia's?"

"Yeah."

Judith also takes a cookie. They chew quietly.

Suddenly Betsy blurts out, "Judith, don't go. Eric loves you. I know he does. I know how you feel. I do. I felt like smacking him the other day at lunch. To not say anything about your help, after all you've done for him. I'm sure you were angry."

Betsy would like to take Judith in her arms. She never dreamed the snippy girl Eric first brought home would become the woman Judith is now. She regrets her acceptance of Natalie.

"Please. Don't go."

"Betsy," Judith says. "Eric has not asked me to stay."

"But I'm sure he wants you to."

"What about—her?"

"Natalie? She's just the male ego at work. We all make mistakes." (A flash bulb goes off: Gino in New York).

Betsy puts her hand on the teapot's belly as though soothing a child's stomach ache.

"You did leave, and maybe it was a blow to his pride—or he needed to prove . . . but I'm not defending him. It was stupid, hurtful. She won't last. You should have seen her face when she saw Eric's chest and that terrible stuff . . . ."

I did, Judith thinks.

"John says she's a light weight."

"Dear John."

"He thinks the world of you."

"Same here." Judith sips her tea, so she won't have to say more.

"Eric needs you, Judith."

"He did. But he's fine now. He's back where he wants to be, with his colleagues and his work."

"Is there nothing I can say or he can say?"

Judith shakes her head.

"Don't you love him?" Betsy asks.

"I don't know. I suppose I must . . . ."

"I know you're terribly angry. I would be. He should have gotten down on his knees and thanked you."

Judith smiles.

"I better get back to my packing. We'll see each other soon, Betsy. You go to Washington often for the museums, don't you? And I'll be visiting here to see Phoebe and the boys. D.C. isn't far."

Betsy feels dismissed. She stands and Judith gets up too. They kiss and hold each other for a moment.

"You're a wonderful girl," Betsy says. "Like my own daughter." She feels Judith tremble.

"If he asked you not to leave, would you consider it?" she says.

"He won't."

Betsy rummages in her purse for her keys as she goes to her car. On the front path she notices that the walnut tree is completely bare, like a telephone pole with arms, so ugly. She steps on one of the shells. This place has been a home for four people. A good home.

On the way to her and John's aerie, Betsy tries to pull herself together. She was afraid she was going to fail in her mission. Judith is just as proud as Eric. He should make his own apologies, his own case. Why do women have to do all the emotional work in the family?

At home, Betsy calls Eric's office.

"Could you drop by on your way home later?" she says. "Dad wants to talk to you—about something or other—"

"What?"

"I don't know. Your health insurance plan I think he said."

"It's fine."

"Well, I don't know. You know Dad—"

"OK, what time?"

"Five good?"

"Fine."

Betsy has picked a time she is sure John will not be home. She wants to talk to Eric, but is sure he won't come if she asks. A summons from his father will have more pull.

When did I become so devious? Betsy thinks. Maybe I've always been that way—telling the kids they were eating Hungarian steak when I served meat loaf because they swore they hated meat loaf. Interfering in Eric's life would be far more unpalatable than a little ground beef with tomato sauce.

When Eric shows up, he sits down with Betsy in the den overlooking the river. He looks good, maybe a little pale and thin. Some time outdoors will help.

The hawks are gliding gracefully past the big windows.

"Where's Dad?" he asks.

"He'll be along soon." Betsy looks at her watch. John should still be in his meeting.

"Let me get you a beer," she says. "Or a little wine?"

"A cold beer would be good."

Betsy goes to the kitchen and pours a glass of beer for Eric and wine for herself. Why do beer drinkers always say "a cold beer"?—no one ever drinks it warm, do they?

Oh bother, why does her mind stray onto silly things? She needs to concentrate, say things right.

Betsy doesn't want to press too hard. She goes back into the den and serves Eric his beer, and sits on the couch opposite him. She holds her glass by the stem and twirls her wine.

"Did they do that at Keysey's Cheese?" Eric says.

Betsy stops. Is she so pretentious? She guesses she is. And way too fussy. She was a little relieved when Eric said he would be going to his own home to recuperate. She can hardly admit to herself that the picture of blood or urine stains on her white carpeting entered her mind.

"How is Judith getting to the airport tomorrow?" Betsy asks.

"Lydia's taking her."

"Judith did so much for you while you were ill."

"So I gather. I don't remember much about the whole thing."

"I guess not."

Betsy doesn't touch her wine.

She and John had always vowed not to interfere in their children's lives.

"Judith came back home the minute you asked for her—wore herself out fighting your battles for you—and you need someone in your corner at a hospital, believe me."

Eric looks as though he wishes he hadn't come at Betsy's call.

"I wish she hadn't done all that. I feel bad."

"She slept most nights on that hard old pull-out bed."

"God. You say I asked her to come back?"

"The minute you regained consciousness. You were totally out of it for several days after your heart failed."

"Jesus."

Betsy lets up a little. She can see how painful it is for Eric to recall the days of his illness. "You two belong together."

Betsy can't think of anything more to say. Eric looks tired.

"Would you like another beer?" she says.

"Sure. Don't bother with a glass. I can drink it out of the can."

Betsy takes his glass, and in the kitchen relents on serving a can. Maybe it's time she let up a little.

"Got a note from Adrian today," Betsy says when she returns to the living room. "She's taking a bunch of murderers or something into the Rockies. Your *sister*."

"She's safe. They can't go anywhere without her."

"I guess not."

They watch the big birds through the window, swooping and gliding.

"God, I thought one of those was a small plane at first," Eric says.

"So did I when we first saw them."

"I should get going. Brendan hates it when I'm late for dinner. We're like a little gay couple."

"Darling Brendan." Betsy is sure she will never forget him. But when they left the hospital for the last time, she was sure she would always keep Olga and Lakesia and Alice in her heart, and all the others who shared their most intimate moments and knew her son's body inside and out, with no defenses, no pretenses—but they are beginning to fade like the images on Polaroid film.

"I will let Brendan go soon. He needs more hours and he's in demand."

"Life goes by awfully fast," Betsy says.

"I feel like Rip Van Winkle. I remember going to the hospital for my knee—it was early fall, wasn't it? And I look up and suddenly the trees have lost most of their leaves."

"It's been a trip and a half as William would say."

Betsy hears the elevator door open. Her time is up. John comes into the room.

"Eric," he says with pleasure and surprise.

"You're late," Betsy says.

293

"I said five-forty-five; it's five—well, forty-eight." And when was John ever late?

"You need to get our drinks fixed and then come sit down," Betsy says.

"Oh yeah. Can I take my jacket off first? And I have to feed Ginger." He grumbles but goes to the kitchen.

Betsy makes it fast.

"Eric, you should go to Judith and ask her to stay. Otherwise you'll lose her."

"I can't do that."

"Why not?"

"I just can't."

Eric looks lost as he had in the hospital. He's been putting on a good show, but Betsy can see he's still weak.

"If she goes . . . ."

"Give me a break," Eric says. "I lost a chunk of my life."

Betsy wonders about Natalie. Is she still around?

John comes back with two martinis, looks at Betsy's wine glass inquisitively and sits down.

"What a nice surprise," he says to Eric.

"Mom said you wanted to talk to me about something."

John taps his head. "I did?" He looks to Betsy.

"Don't ask me."

"The old synapses aren't what they used to be," John says.

The three move on to the election, their dismay at more years of war and corruption.

As they talk, Eric seems to Betsy to be testing his father's alertness. When he seems satisfied, he scowls at his mother.

"You're incorrigible," he says.

The three have a longish cocktail hour; then Eric rises and kisses both parents, goes to the elevator and presses the button; he waves from inside the cab and the doors close on him.

57

Judith

Judith pokes her head into Eric's study. He is at his desk, mounds of paper piled on it, Mehitabel sitting on them in her most imperious Egyptian pose. Eric's computer screen is bright, the cursor impatiently blinking. Judith says, "I'm taking off. Just wanted to say goodbye."

Eric gets up from his desk. They stand apart, haggard and worn out, like boxers on their last legs.

Will he ask her not to leave? Say Natalie is over. Say "well done, Judith." "I love you."

Eric shakes the papers in his hand. "These pages seem as though they were written by someone else."

Judith thinks, *He has a brilliant mind and is tongue tied.*

"That'll clear up once you get going," she says. "You always say that after a hiatus."

"Good point."

Eric comes forward and kisses Judith on the cheek.

"Will you be all right, Judy?"

"Sure."

"You have access to the joint account and you can get cash on your credit cards."

"I know."

"Don't worry about money."

"I won't."

He's so magnanimous, Judith thinks. So generous. Fuck him.

Her cab is in the driveway and she runs for it.

Part 8

SCAR TISSUE

58

David

"We have to get out of this monster," David says. He and Lydia are in their cavernous kitchen, standing across the island from one another.

He waves a sheaf of papers at her.

"We spent over two hundred thousand dollars last year. Our credit cards are maxed out."

"We're both on the way to making partner."

"That doesn't guarantee big bucks. If the firm does well, fine. One guy I know got less money on becoming a partner."

"I'm not moving."

"We should get something smaller, something closer in. Gas prices are going up. We should get rid of that gas guzzler you're driving."

"I need the size, I told you—"

"Not that much."

"You completely ignore your home for weeks and weeks and then come popping back in and take over the books—which *I* have been keeping, and don't like the way I'm running things in your absence."

"I didn't choose for my father to nearly die. Is this the last payment on your remodeling and decorating?"

David shows Lydia a page of the check book.

"Let's see."

They study their records together.

"I can't read your figures," David says. "They don't seem to add up."

"And I can't read your little anal writing."

"Well, forget it. I'll figure it out. I have to go cut the grass and trim the hedges."

"Since when?"

"Since our expenditures exceeded our income."

"David, you have never done a lick of yard work in your life."

"Sure I have. Who do you think puts the chemicals in the pool and skims the leaves out?"

David has to change his life. The last frightening weeks have made that clear. He stomps out of the kitchen, followed by Lenny.

The dog looks on inquisitively as David takes the electric shears to the long lines of privet leading to the pool. They have grown out of shape. David lops off the tops of the bushes, giving them a butch hair cut.

He hears a door slam and Lydia comes marching toward him with her features twisted and her eyes blazing.

"Stop," she yells. "Lopping the tops off like that will just make the hedges wider and thicker at the top and more spindly at the bottom. Let the yard man do that."

"I am the yard man. I let Jeff go. We can't afford him."

"Oh God, have you lost your mind? Really, from the window you look like a demented old man."

"Maybe I am."

"Turn off those clippers!"

"What?" David screams. "Don't talk while I'm working. I can't hear you."

"Turn those stupid clippers off. This is ridiculous."

David stops his work, but does not turn off the clippers.

"Gardeners cost money, Lydia."

"For God's sake, you're becoming obsessed."

"Someone has to. Now get out of my way so I can finish this so I can cut the grass and sweep the patio."

Sweat is running into David's eyes, stinging and blinding him.

"David," Lydia says, "let's talk."

David turns back to his work.

"Can't. Too much to do."

"David, stop acting like a maniac. We are not on the verge of starvation."

"Lydia, pick up the clippings—you can help—"

"David, I am talking about your mental health!" She pulls the plug of his clippers.

"God Damn it, Lydia!"

David grabs for the cord. Lydia pulls away, whipping herself across her bare legs with the cord. She turns to slap at it, and slaps David in the face, hard.

"Do that again, and I'll forget . . . ."

Lydia slaps him again, deliberately this time.

David picks up one of the clipped branches and shakes it at her.

"How dare you?" she says.

"How dare *you*?"

They lunge at each other and fall into the ivy, wrestling, pulling each other's hair. Itchy clippings press into their backs.

Lydia's top catches on a rose bush and as she tries to pull it away, catches the back of her hand on a thorn. David's knee sinks into a mole tunnel.

"Those god-damned moles!" he yells. "My knee!"

Lydia frees herself from the rose bush and picks the thorn from her hand.

"This must look great to the neighbors," Lydia says.

David lies still, like a child pretending to be dead.

Lydia pokes him. "Things have to change."

"That's my line," David says.

Lydia sucks on her hand. A cool breeze wafts over them while they nurse their wounds.

"Please," David says, sitting up, "let's get out of here and move back to the city."

"The city is too dangerous."

"It's not. My whole family lives there. They've never had any trouble—even William."

"You are so snobbish. So judgmental."

"I just hate this place. It's so phony and overdone. We could build something—something with solar heat and— Let's get out of here."

"I tell you what," Lydia says. "I'll go with you—"

David's hopes rise.

"—to Antigua—you need a break—and if you still feel the same when we get back, we'll talk about it."

David thinks over her proposition. Maybe she has a point. He needs to take a breather. He *has* been acting like a maniac. But they do need to save money.

"I think you've got post-traumatic stress or something," Lydia says. "Between overwork and your father."

Lenny, who has been hiding under the patio table, comes over and sits between the two combatants, like a marriage counselor. David pats him.

"Your father is all right now."

"This has nothing to do with my father."

"He's got William, and Betsy and John, and his department team."

Lydia gives Lenny a pat.

The dog licks her face, and the two combatants look at themselves lying in the grass and begin to laugh.

When David Googles Antigua for hotel rates—which are even higher than he thought—he realizes he is piling up more debt. He has previously felt secure about spending. His family was behind him; John gave the impression of having plenty of money. David tries to guess what his estate might be. Some will come his way when—Oh God, what is he thinking? What has he become? Eying the throne and the loot that goes with it. It's—like something out of Shakespeare! Henry the Fifth: Prince Hal trying on the crown!

59

Judith

The afternoon light is fading when Judith gets into her cab in DC. Her driver is dark brown, from a middle-eastern country. His English is minimal and he does not seem to know where Adams-Morgan is. Judith pulls the city map and a flashlight out of her purse, proud of how organized she is, and shows where her sister's apartment is located

"How long have you been in the states?" Judith asks.

"Two mawnths, madam."

No wonder he hasn't mastered the city.

Judith sits forward tensely as they drive the parkway by the Potomac, deepening blue, dotted by white boats. Along the shore are the Iwo Jima sculpture, the memorial to Lady Bird Johnson. At the end of the bridge to the city they pass the gigantic gold figure of Boadicea, the female warrior. The driver turns into Rock Creek Park and drives through the last spinning leaves, past runners along the canal banks. Judith keeps a sharp eye on the map to make sure they don't get lost.

They come out of the park onto Connecticut and then over the viaduct to Adams Morgan, streets lined by Armenian, African, Greek, Italian restaurants, boutiques, apartment buildings: a busy, funky area. Judith leads the driver to the San Remo. She pays him, tips him generously (a fellow immigrant), and enters the lobby (marble pillars, potted plants). The receptionist, an elderly black man behind a tall built-in desk, says hello and calls Moira's apartment. Judith lugs her two suitcases into the elevator, and walks down what seems like an endless hall, her heels echoing on the marble floors and walls. Her cases are heavy and her hair is in her eyes and she is hot, and when she sees Moira standing in her open doorway, she drops her suitcases, throws herself at her sister and cries.

"Jesus," Moira says. She drags Judith's luggage into her front hall and pulls Judith down the long narrow passageway to her living room.

Judith can't stop crying.

"What on earth is the matter?"

Judith can not talk. She just keeps crying.

"You need a drink."

"No. I—"

"Sit down," Moira says. Judith sits on the edge of a chair.

"Did you have a bad flight?"

Judith shakes her head.

"You didn't get lost?"

"No."

"These cab drivers are so new and they never train them."

Judith's whole body is shaking. This is so unexpected. So sudden. She gasps trying to get control, but the tears keep coming.

"You gotta stop this," Moira says. "You're scaring me." She holds her ears. "Would you like to lie down?"

"No."

"Post traumatic stress," Moira says. "Judy, get a grip!"

Judith keeps crying, loud jagged sobs. "This isn't like you. I'm going to have a drink," Moira says.

She goes to the kitchenette and returns with two glasses of red wine.

"Full of healthful antioxidants," she says. "Here." She places a glass of wine on an end table next to Judith.

Judith sweeps it off the table and it crashes onto the floor in pieces.

Moira jumps up, stares at Judith for a minute, then runs to the kitchen. Judith stares at the broken glass and the wine spreading like blood on the wood floor. Moira returns with cloths and a broom, and wipes the floor and sweeps up the glass.

"You're mad as hell, aren't you?"

"Why does everyone treat me like I'm—inhuman?"

"Because you're so perfect. And you take a punch better than anybody I know. Nobody could go through what you have and stay on their feet."

Judith wipes tears and snot on the back of her hand. It smells salty and musty. Moira rummages about and brings out a box of tissues.

"Hey, you have to buck up, Judy. I can't handle this."

Judith shakes and cries harder.

"Do you want something to eat?" Moira says.

"No."

Moira paces frantically. "I'm gonna have to call a doctor, Judith. Shall I call my therapist?"

"No. No. Just let me be. I'm sorry."

"Go to bed then. You're exhausted." Moira tries to pull Judith from her chair. "C'mon."

Judith pushes her away. She shakes her hands off.

"This way." Moira pulls Judith to her feet, with Judith trying to escape from her grip; they push and shove like little girls. Finally Moira tires Judith out and drags her toward the hall and Judith follows, with glassy eyes. Moira leads her into a small bedroom off the long hallway.

"Where's George?" Judith asks.

"Split. Said he wanted to have *fun*."

"Oh."

"Zelda will be home soon. She's at a friend's house. Take that bed by the wall."

Judith collapses onto the bed Moira points to, still crying. She closes her eyes. They hurt. She senses Moira at the door watching her.

"You're the last person I ever expected this from," Moira says.

Judith hears her close the door and walk away.

New waves of anguish wash over Judith. She can not get her breath. She might need a doctor. A paper bag. She gasps for air.

She relives the moment at Betsy's luncheon when Eric said nothing about her help. His big smile reserved for his homecoming at the university. Natalie.

"I hate him," she whispers into the now damp pillow.

She is furious at him for getting sick. For all he has put them through. For loving stupid cigarettes more than her—she blames the heart on the smoking—the doctors confirmed this—Dr. Ritch said so. How many times had she tried to get him to stop? To watch his diet? She should have left long ago. Why didn't he get his heart tested when he first showed signs of fatigue? Instead trying to prove himself with Natalie. How easily she had been replaced. How little she meant!

New anger flares. Judith clenches her fists and grits her teeth. Tosses on the bed until she is dizzy.

Her whole chest aches. Her shoulders too. Moira taps at the door.

"OK in there?"

"No. Please. I'm so humiliated."

"Don't you want some dinner? I'm fixing some soup."

"No thank you."

"Then get some sleep. I'm going to bed myself."

Judith begins to wind down. She is so exhausted. She pulls the bedspread over her legs. A small travel clock on the end table says nine-thirty. How had so much time passed? After tossing awhile, she falls asleep.

In the middle of the night, she awakens, gets up, gropes her way to a small bathroom connected to the bedroom, pees, and looks at her face in the mirror over the sink. Her eyes are swollen and her face blotched. She looks to herself like a prize fighter after a beating. She is so embarrassed, she, the good daughter, the rational one. The sister who stayed in school, who didn't sleep around or do hard drugs. Her only hard drug was marriage.

She looks around the room: stuffed animals everywhere, a poster of Justin Timberlake, jewelry dripping out of drawers and hung on lamps, books scattered across a small desk, a computer, clothes and shoes on the chairs and floor. Zelda is asleep in the other bed.

60

William

William sits at his usual stool in the Bookshelf Coffee Shop and Bar. Jimmy is leaning his arms on the bar, with his chin in his hands. He and Mel the baker are discussing the relative merits of zombies and vampires. Hattie is strumming her guitar in the nook where she'll play in the evening.

"The band wants to take the act to New York," Hattie says. "But I'd have to get my teeth fixed and learn good English."

"Bummer," Jimmy says, overhearing. "Nothing wrong with your teeth or your verbiage."

"You get your emotions across better than me," William says.

"Better than I," Velma corrects him.

"Oh, you too," he cracks.

Velma, who has logged the shots of the Over the Rhine riots she and Ariel have filmed, sits at a booth across from the bar with her partner. A stack of papers is piled between them, application forms from the Arts Council to fund a documentary of their footage.

Velma tears at her hair. "Description of project; budget to the penny; what theories do we use; proof of diversity; are we unique? Why is it art?"

"These fucking things: you have to dot every 'i' and cross every 't'—how do we know exactly what we'll do? It's like we're already done."

"Is police brutality gonna fly? They shot this kid in the *back* that started the riots."

"We should go out to Hollywood and get jobs in the movies."

"You're a terrific camera man," Jimmy says to Velma.

"What about you, William? You finally gonna get started on that novel?" Hattie says.

"I'm thinkin' on it. Yeah."

He goes over to the piano and plunks out a few bars of *Tangerine Man.*

"Soon as Jimmy tells his mother he's gay."

"We're like the characters in that play, *The Iceman Cometh,*" Ariel says. "Remember that? People sitting around a bar all day talking about what they're gonna do, but they never go anywhere cause that character Hinky or Honky or Whatever comes in and shits all over their dreams."

"They were drunks," Velma says.

"Some of us smoke pot," Jimmy says.

He gives William a look of disapproval.

This conversation depresses William. It's too—true. He hasn't done anything to change his life. He is out of excuses. The everyday summer sessions with the Lookout kids are over. His father needed him in the hospital. His mother—even David.

His last chore, driving his father to the hospital for a checkup, was done in a small suite outfitted with the usual medical stuff, and filled with patients waiting to see Dr. Graham and the ubiquitous Sheri, like pilgrims at a shrine.

When he went back to collect his father's hat, all the paraphernalia had been gathered up and the medical team had decamped. The room was empty, like a setup for a sting.

The whole season of sickness and near death has the same theatrical quality. Now the family is back outside the theater in the light of day, blinking in the bright sun.

What is he doing with his life? By the time his father was thirty, he was a history professor, aiming at department head, a published scholar, the father of two kids.

William got an ego boost from the poetry slam, and even from the kid running off his poems at Kinko's who said he loved William's work: "It's so *intense.*" William thinks, *How pathetic is that?*

Even David is seeing some daylight. A postcard from Antigua William taped on his wall shows beautiful blue water and an ancient sugar mill. It says David and Lydia are having a great time: biking, walking the beach, snuggling in terry cloth robes provided by their hotel.

William could go talk to Rev Al, but he is not interested in religion now. He doesn't know what he is looking for.

Absolution? That is hard coming. What kind of degenerate would do what he did with Natalie? He is terrified Natalie might have told his father. No, surely she wouldn't. Though she told his mother. She might claim William made a pass at her.

He feels guilty toward Angie. He wants to confess, but hangs back. He is tempted to finish off the pot in his sneaker, but the thought makes him sick. He must get a new sponsor and go back to zero consumption. Maybe he will tell David about Natalie. Would David put him down as a dumbbell? The idiot brother? But who else is there? He decides to trust David. Luckily he's in Antigua, so William can renege.

61

Judith

The bright morning sun hurts Judith's swollen eyes. She locates her suitcases that have been placed inside the door, realizes where she is. She hears Moira and Zelda talking in the kitchen. She waits until they stop and she hears the front door close, the apartment become quiet. Then she tries to stand. Everything aches.

She goes back to bed and sleeps. Later, she gets up. She digs her cosmetics kit out of her suitcase, finds her toothbrush and comb. She washes her face, brushes her teeth and tries to make her hair look like a sane person's. She puts on her bathrobe and goes out of the room to the kitchenette. The wall clock says two thirty. Where did the hours go? There is coffee in the coffee machine and a box of bagels open on the counter with a note propped against it: "Had to go to work. Be back around six-ish. Here's my cell number in case. M."

Judith pours herself a cup of coffee. It tastes burnt. She puts her head in her hands.

She dodges back into the bathroom and looks over the damage. Horrible. Puffy eyes. Hair like a bag lady's. She tries to patch up her face with makeup.

The apartment rings with regret.

She must get out of it. Get air.

She dresses hastily and walks the several blocks to Columbia Road. People everywhere, busily shopping: a cacophony of languages, the growl of cars, the weary wheeze of buses. Her head spins with confusion, panic. She needs to sit down. She climbs onto a bus, having no idea where it is going or the fare. The driver won't make change. He waits impatiently as she digs coins from her purse. She falls into a seat, studies the other passengers. They look purposeful, in control.

The bus goes down Connecticut Avenue with its blocks of shops. She gets off near Dupont Circle, sees a bus going to Georgetown. She takes it, then gets off when she sees a familiar entrance to the towpath along the Potomac. She walks to the river, past the backs of apartment buildings and businesses, the broad river on her left. She is so tired. As though trudging through meaningless places in a dream.

She stops at a stretch of huge rocks and rapids. She stands and stares at the furious water caught among the giant slabs of rock, beating the passive worn stone. The water splashes high. She feels the danger. The lure of the water.

She scares herself. She sits on a rock ledge and puts her head in her hands. She is lost. A small girl. Her mother has dropped her in the yard of a stranger's house instead of Judith's friend's, where she was invited to play. No one was home and Judith sat on the front steps. It was a big place with dark trees casting shadows on the strange lawn. Judith's dress was damp with angry tears. Finally the mail man came along and took her to the right place, like lost mail.

Judith moves, and walks over to the shops, trudges up and down the narrow streets.

At rush hour Judith goes back to her sister's apartment. She lies down on the bed in the room she shares with Zelda.

She hears light footsteps in the hall.

Zelda comes into the room. "Aunt Judy!"

Her spaghetti strap top and tight mini do seem to advertise her shape as Moira had complained.

"Mom said you were coming to visit," Zelda says. "I'm glad you're here. I always did like you."

She pitches her fleece on the floor.

"Hear you went bat shit last night," she says.

"Oh God."

Zelda appraises Judith's face, then leaves her to herself. Judith sleeps again. When she awakens, the sky outside the window is gray. She hears the refrigerator open, the television go on. Some sort of noisy game show.

Judith patches herself together again, hopes she looks better and goes to the living room. Moira is flopped in a chair holding the elastic band of her slacks away from her waist.

"Ugh," she says. "I see why they call them tights."

Judith apologizes for herself.

Moira rubs her stomach.

"Whew the Metro was crowded," she says. "Can I trust you with a glass of wine?"

Judith begins to weep.

"God, don't start that again," Moira says.

She gets a bottle and glasses. "Maybe it better be white this time."

"Oh, I hope I—"

"Joke, kiddo." Moira calls to Zelda who is snacking in the kitchen. "Bring your aunt and me some of that cheese."

They kill most of a bottle of wine, eat some lunch meat out of a paper wrapper, and then Moira turns on the news.

"That Bush is a horse's ass, isn't he?" she says.

Judith heads for the bedroom. She is so tired she can not talk. She has no idea what she will do the next day. Or any of the days after that.

62

William

He makes a date to meet David at the Bookshelf. David looks tanned and relaxed. This time William sticks to coffee. David follows suit when William tells him he should never have had the beer and shots they drank the day of Tim's funeral. After much un-William-like small talk that leaves David looking puzzled, William stutters out a version of his rendezvous with Natalie.

"Shee-it," David says. "You gotta be kidding."

"Would I kid about something that disgusting?"

"I guess not."

"Am I a pervert?"

"Probably."

"Thanks."

"Should I tell Angie?' William asks.

David doesn't hesitate.

"No."

William and David drink their coffee quietly for a moment.

"Now that Tim's gone, are you getting a new sponsor?" David asks.

"Yes. And I pitched the sneaker."

"We've all done some crazy things since Dad got sick. But your getting it on with Natalie—wow, you might need some therapy or something."

"I suppose."

David downs his coffee. He signals Jimmy for the check and pats William's hand.

"So how was she?" he says.

William takes a long walk. The blocks around the Bookshelf are looking especially seedy. The bushes and weeds of a nearby vacant lot have lost their leaves and he can see the layers of litter hidden beneath. A new homeless person has taken over Gloria's spot opposite Music Hall. A black man passes him, walking a small dog dyed pink.

What's next for him?

There is advice everywhere: spray-painted on walls, carved on public buildings (official graffiti). It is on car bumpers: "Support the Troops," "End the War," the fish symbol hyping Christianity and the one saying "Darwin." The wayside pulpit of the Lutheran church says, "Join up with Jesus." Yard signs say "Vote for the School Levy;" anti-abortion posters say "Support Life" along side scary pictures of fetuses. Advice is on jewelry: the cross, the star of David, the Wiccans' scarab, Indian totems. It is on T-shirts: "Be Kind," on tattoos. It is written in the sky and on blimps, on race car jackets and baseball stands and designer labels: buy this, buy that. It is in toilet stalls: "Call this Number," and William's personal favorite in the Bookshelf Coffee Shop men's room, "Bite a cow in the Ass."

We are a nation of preachers, he thinks.

William opens a mint that has been riding around in his pocket; there is advice even inside the candy wrapper: "Take a risk today."

He walks up Sycamore Hill. The old wooden houses on Schiller and Goethe are being torn down to make way for condos. Half a house stands gaping, rooms open to the world; wallpaper, once probably lovingly chosen by a family, hangs loose from the walls. People lived in these rooms and now are gone. He pictures his own family in their house with the side torn off, like a doll house, the tiny figures inside living their lives.

We have peeked into each others' lives, he thinks. Because of a worn away knee joint and a faulty heart. We each know snippets and bits about the others, none of them the same. So his mother Judith, and his father's wife Judith—his Betsy and David's Betsy—are not the same; nor do any of them see more than glimpses of him. Luckily.

William walks out past the hospital and toward his parents' home and Betsy and John's old castle. The sounds of cars and construction, motors and hammers ring from hill to hill. Where does he fit in?

Near the movie theater and the shops of his childhood, he smells the sweet Indian spices. The trees on the main avenue are almost bare, their red and yellow leaves piling up around their roots. He passes his family's street and walks on to his grandparents' castle. There the old babe still stands, surrounded by more recent houses. One of the colonials has been torn down and a David-type McMansion is being built in its place. There is a hideous fountain in front of the castle: lions spouting colored water. The driveway is flanked by giant pillars and guarded by a gate with what must be the initials of the new owners in the wrought iron.

William looks in the windows and decides nobody is home. Nobody is ever home today. The porches and swings are empty— where is everybody—at work? Watching TV? On computers?

He sneaks into Betsy's old garden. Sodden brown leaves cover the pool. It looks desolate.

William sits on the bench where, years ago, he sat resenting his family: they were too fortunate, smug, on their little island of privilege. Now he sees the fragility of it. He feels like one of those polar bears you see on the news, losing their icy plateau, struggling to regain solid ground. Falling into the water and becoming, some day, extinct.

The air is full of voices: Do This. Do That. You freak!

William considers David's advice to go to a shrink. But he decides to go with the candy wrapper: "take a risk."

Maybe he'll join the army.

63

Judith

Dress. Breakfast. Say good morning to the man at the front desk. Ride a bus. Walk. Sit on the porch of the San Remo. Days like that go by.

She isn't the woman she was before the days in the hospital. It took a lot to crack her, but she is split open. The old pain of her mother's words creep in, like the symptoms of polio long after the disease is gone. Maybe she was damaged goods from the beginning.

The daily fights between Moira and Zelda are painful. Judith gets the impression that Moira thinks Zelda helped drive her live-in ex-husband away.

Moira drinks more than she can handle (she downs about a bottle of red wine a day, telling herself wine doesn't count as real alcohol). She looks worn.

She and Zelda never complain about Judith, but there just isn't room for three in the apartment. Zelda finds Judith going over rentals in the *Post*.

"Oh don't leave," Zelda says. "It's so neat there's somebody home once in awhile."

"Your mother has to work."

"I know. If only she didn't hate me."

"She doesn't hate you."

"She thinks I came onto her moldy ex-husband."

Judith is struck by Zelda's sexual sophistication. She's just five years older than Phoebe.

"He came on to me."

"He didn't—?"

"He never got the nerve to touch me. Mom would do a tap dance on his balls. But he'd 'accidentally' open the bath room door if he thought I was in the shower. One day I turned it on, and hid in the hall, and there he was peeking in. He was really creeping me out."

Zelda goes over to her computer and brings up You Tube pictures of her and her friends, at school, at a party, shopping.

"Do you think I should get a tattoo?" Zelda says.

Natalie's tiny red heart pops into Judith's mind. "No."

Judith sees the two of them reflected in the glass. Zelda looks like Phoebe might in five years.

She must get a job and an apartment of her own. She can't sponge off Moira forever. Judith takes money from her and Eric's joint checking account to pay her share of the food and rent at Moira's and to put a deposit on an apartment. She looks at places for rent. They are dreary, small and expensive. She studies the newspapers and *The Chronicle of Higher Education* for job openings. She sends out resumés and applies at various schools. All she gets from her job applications are polite form letters. She writes to more places. One is in Pakistan.

64

Betsy

Betsy looks in the mirror. She is sure she has aged about ten years since Eric became ill. She considers a face lift. Maybe a wig. Her hair is so thin she can see her pink scalp through it.

These worries are postponed, when she finds she must have cataracts removed from both eyes. Apprehension fills her at the thought of re-entering a hospital. But she can't avoid it.

Everything turns out fine. The only drawback is that now, with two improved eyes, she can see her wrinkles more clearly than ever.

She feels betrayed by her body. But why? All people grow old, but her friend Myra does not look this old. She has better skin— and probably has had a real face lift.

Maybe it's worry that makes her feel so down. Eric is well. He walks to the campus every day and exercises on the machines at the hospital. But he's not happy. She can tell. He looks like the kid who couldn't learn to skip. If only things were as easy as when one's children were—children. Kiss and make it well . . . .

They haven't heard much from Judith: a letter or two, emails to David and William, post cards to Phoebe. She says only that she is job hunting, and that the weather is this or that.

Time heals all things, Betsy thinks. That was her mother's mantra. But does it? Every time she is with her friend Joan, eighty-three, the woman tells the story of when she was ten years old and her little brother got a bright red car with pedals for Christmas, while she got an ugly nightgown. Time doesn't seem to be the great healer it's cracked up to be; she thinks, *we lie in our caskets grasping our resentments and regrets in our stiff hands, like a rosary or a Bible.*

Betsy herself still resents her mother's dismissal of her little woes: "It'll all be the same in a hundred years." Betsy believes in action, in making things go her way if she can figure out how to do it. She should try to let go of her own regrets, and to accept things she can't control.

Oh bull crap. Thanksgiving is on its way. Christmas things are in the stores. Judith has had a cooling off period. Maybe she can lure her back, and take another whack at getting her and Eric together if she works up a big feast for the family. Judith has been at every Thanksgiving get together for some thirty years.

She and John were thinking of not doing much this year. They tire more easily and take more naps, and if the truth be known, Betsy has always hated Thanksgiving: she finds turkey bland and dry, the mess horrendous. She can't think of a single Thanksgiving dish she actually likes (she is a Julia Childe fan). But she has a wonderful ceramic turkey for a centerpiece and decides to use the best china though it has to be washed by hand. Ora will help.

She writes to Judith: can she come out for the holiday? Bring her sister and niece.

Betsy is very disappointed when Judith calls and thanks her for the invitation, but claims she's not quite in a position to come out: she is looking for a job, is still learning Washington, helping her sister . . . She has so many excuses, Betsy does not believe any of them. Why does the girl have to be so stubborn? No one is perfect and Eric has been terribly sick. John didn't dump *her* for her fling. Even Betsy's old grandfather had a woman outside his marriage once; Betsy remembers her grandmother crying on the bus downtown.

Betsy wonders if Eric would want her to invite Natalie to lunch, but to her relief finds she is going out of town to be with her parents.

The weather on Thanksgiving is dreary. David and Lydia are obviously tense. Eric brings over a frozen pumpkin pie that Natalie brought him. It has a kind of icy fuzz over the filling. Betsy doesn't know what to do with it. After lunch, the men retreat to the den to watch football, and Lydia takes Phoebe to see *The Wiz*. Betsy stares at Natalie's pie. It is still sitting on the kitchen counter. She pitches it in the garbage.

Later that afternoon, she stares at the gray water of the river.

"I'm so disappointed that Judith didn't come out for Thanksgiving," she says to John.

"Betsy," he says, "when will you admit—everything can't be fixed."

"All the king's horses and all the king's men . . . . Is that it?"

"Pretty much."

"I hate 'Humpty Dumpty'."

Betsy thinks, there's always Christmas.

65

Judith

She begins going to the local Unitarian church. She likes the sound of the black preacher's voice, and the moment of silence. She lights a candle for William. How is he doing? She can not help him. He will have to do it on his own. She lights a candle for Eric and one for her mother.

She haunts the museums, stares at the Bonnards, the glimpses of old gardens through doorways.

Judith continues to search for a job, and to pace the city to fight off depression.

She walks the length of the mall with its sand-colored paths and rows of trees, endless memorials to the war dead: people crying at the Viet Nam wall.

She is desperate about work. She cannot find anything.

Trudging back to Moira's, on Columbia Road one afternoon, she sees a sign in a grocery store window advertising a job opening for a check-out clerk. She has a Ph.D. She's a published scholar. But she goes into the store and asks for the manager. The place smells of over-ripe apples and Lysol. She could never take a job like this in Cincinnati, not with her background and Eric's image to keep up at the university.

Anyway, she is turned down. She can't speak Spanish.

At dinner, Judith is quiet.

"You're really down," Moira says.

Judith tells her about the grocery store.

"That's ridiculous," Moira says. "You're a gifted teacher . . . ."

From the windows there is a pleasant view of the tree tops and streets of Adams Morgan. The building is a few blocks from the zoo, so they can walk there. A nice layout, Judith thinks. Moira, the "bad" sister has done better than she, the "good" one.

After dinner the two sit in the living room. Moira tells Zelda to turn on the TV in her own room. She sits with her ubiquitous bottle of red wine beside her.

She says, "Something will turn up. When you were a kid, Judy, I pushed you around pretty good. But you never backed down."

"You used to wake me up in the middle of the night and say there was no me. That I didn't exist."

"Shut up."

"You did."

"You were the golden child."

The two talk over their lives for the first time since Judith's breakdown, maybe just the first time. Judith tells Moira about their mother abandoning her at that strange house, her repeated story of Judith being an unwanted surprise.

"That's awful," Moira says. "I guess I came along when she and the old man still cared about each other."

Yes, Judith thinks, Moira was her favorite. In spite of their fights. In fact, it seems their mother got a kick out of Moira's drinking and wild driving and too many boys.

While she was just a rebuke with her independence and ambition.

"You got over Mom's meanness," Moira says.

"I'm afraid I haven't . . . ."

"And mine. After all I was jealous. You were such a complacent little bookworm, while I was skipping school and messing myself up."

"I kind of admired you."

"Yes, you missed the central experience of our generation: rehab and being kicked around by a really sadistic, chauvinistic male."

"You had the guts to get out of your marriage . . . ."

"The first one. And the stupidity to do it again."

"You got yourself educated for a real job."

"After our divorce, I had to. And there was no question of leaving. I would have scrubbed *floors.*"

Moira puts her feet under her legs on the couch and pours herself and Judith wine.

"So why did you leave your old man after you gave up your job to take care of him?" she asks.

Judith hesitates. She has seldom trusted anyone with her problems. She sips her wine, now, though, and tells Moira about Natalie. That is the easiest story.

"One affair in thirty years!" Moira says. "That's some kind of record."

"I didn't cheat."

"No?"

"No."

"But you were here in D.C., leaving him alone. So he fucked up."

"No. He fucked down."

Moira laughs. "So she was a bimbo."

"Worse. She—seduced—William." This is the hardest thing to say. Judith's throat aches.

"Seduced! Will is a hot stud puppy, sweetheart. He was trying out the merchandise." Moira laughs again. "How did you find out about William and her little get together?"

"She told me, and I believed her. I knew she wasn't lying." Judith tells Moira about smacking Natalie.

"Way to go," Moira says. She reaches out for a high five.

Judith slaps her palm against her sister's. She *is* rather glad she slapped Natalie.

Still, what would her sons think? And Brendan? And Betsy? Jane Austen?

At the American Museum Judith sits in a small cafe in the ornate high-ceilinged hall just beyond the huge outbursts of color of the Abstract Expressionists. She holds a paper cup of tea in her hands. She and Eric were once here together. They sat at one of the small tables and drank tea and ate biscotti. Then they went up the nearby stairs to where the conservators worked in glassed-in rooms. They watched through the windows as the men and women in white doctors' coats patched the holes in canvasses, cleaned ages of grime off paintings, and stitched together torn works of art.

She is lonely as the room she is in: it is vast, full of echoes. She realizes she has always been lonely, without a mentor, a guide, a teacher. Only Eric.

If he had apologized, Judith thinks. Dropped Natalie and asked forgiveness. They might even have laughed over the whole episode. Eventually.

If he had recognized. Sure, the doctors saved his life. But they hadn't wiped his behind. She is the one who nipped at the hospital's heels, fought his battles . . . If he could just say, "Well done, Judith."

She misses him so terribly.

One sunny day, as she often does, she takes a bus to Georgetown and walks along the water, then through the streets, the ginkgoes turning them into gold corridors. She goes into the mall, takes a table at a restaurant, drinks the water the waiter brings her, then leaves before he comes to take her order. She browses through the stores, looks at clothes she might once have bought. She stares into the window of a leather goods shop: a soft chime is set off as she enters. She runs her fingers over a smooth beautifully crafted purse; the smell of fine leather has a strangely euphoric effect on her.

She refuses the clerk's offer of assistance, moves on to the next shop, Outdoor Wear. There is a cotton jacket in the window that looks as though it would fit Eric. It is khaki, unlined, light weight. The kind of thing he would wear. She goes into the store and examines the price tag and feels the material.

She buys the jacket.

66

Betsy

Every year since they moved to the condo, Betsy and John debate about whether to put up a Christmas tree. They had spectacular Scotch Pines at the castle, but now have given away most of ornaments they had lovingly collected: the gaudy expensive ones, the inherited antiques, opalescence now showing through sharp bits of peeling glass. John always argues in favor of tradition. Betsy opposes the mess.

As the holiday nears, Betsy feels especially reluctant to go through the motions. Maybe she'll break down and buy an artificial tree, something she has always hated: no fresh smell, no feeling of tradition with the little stiff limbs and unnatural green. She thinks about this and whether to dig out all the beautiful china and silver she always set the table with on Christmas Eve.

Her thoughts are interrupted by Eric, who lets himself in the back way to the apartment.

She is so glad to see him, and vows to stay out of his business, but it is only after minutes of conversation about the university and the news, that she blurts out, "Have you talked to Judith?"

"Not what you mean."

"You're going to lose her."

Eric sighs in exasperation. "Do you never stop?"

"My tongue is bloody from biting it."

Eric looks resigned.

"Mom, hadn't I already lost Judith? Remember she was the one who left me. She was so frustrated. She needed her work, her independence."

"Shouldn't she see someone?"

"Like who?"

"A therapist."

"She had one. But she had too many losses at once. Her mother, her college. She needed something . . . . We were joined at the hip for too many years."

Betsy thinks if only Judith had come to her. She would have told her how much they all loved her, how much she had meant to them.

"Judith was just a kid when we got together," Eric says.

Betsy lets up for a moment. But she has to keep trying; the family is falling apart.

"Where do you and Natalie stand?" Betsy asks.

Eric looks surprised, hesitates as though deciding whether or not to answer Betsy's question. Finally he says, "It seems she's ditched me."

"I could say I'm sorry."

"Don't worry. It's strange," he says. "Like how I've given up smoking. I just don't have any interest—I guess I was using her somehow."

"You were lonely and hurt . . . ."

"Maybe we could change the subject."

They talk about Adrian and the latest outrages by Bush and company. But after awhile, Eric surprises Betsy by returning to their conversation about Natalie.

"I suppose Natalie was my mid-life crisis. What a stupid cliché. I think I owe the girl an apology. She was too young for me. She's more William's speed."

Eric sighs and looked sheepish. "Anyway, I wouldn't be much good to any woman right now."

Betsy feels her son's embarrassment. She lets up for awhile but can't resist capitalizing on the moment.

"Tell Judith you want her to come home," she says.

"I couldn't do that."

"Why not?"

"I've already taken too much from her. I wore her out and put her in danger."

"In danger?"

"I remember so little. But I remember the nurse saying the hospital and the neighborhood were dangerous. If Judith wants to come back, she will. She knows she is wanted here."

"But women have to be told."

"If she comes back she will have to do it her own way."

"What if she doesn't"?

"We'll see . . . ."

"You are a carbon copy of your father!" Betsy says.

"I could do worse."

Betsy welcomes *these* words. Her son's near death was the worst thing she had ever experienced, but it seemed to bring Eric and John closer. They had crossed some sort of boundary that ran between them.

She includes this good development along with the news about Natalie in her Christmas invitation to Judith. She also uses Phoebe as bait. Phoebe misses her terribly, and it's important that they not lose track of one another.

She orders a tree, the biggest that will fit in the living room, drags the boxes of what ornaments are left, and invites John to help her trim. She puts Christmas carols on the CD player and joins John reminiscing about the origins of various Santas and angels.

Her Christmas Cactus blooms.

Adrian arrives.

She is wearing, Betsy notes, her usual rumpled skirt, boots, and a T-shirt with a slogan too suggestive for someone with such large breasts (Rumsfeld sucks). She slings her back pack on a fragile antique table and goes straight to the kitchen to rummage in the cabinets. But Betsy has vowed to be less fussy. Is she too old to change?

Adrian takes in Betsy's decorations. "Wow. You went all out. Mistletoe, holly, poinsettias, the tree. Everything looks great, Mom."

"Do you think so?"

"Absolutely."

"We have a lot to celebrate. Your brother is doing well. Working out. Walking to the university. He seems to be cured. And is closer to his father. You'll see. And guess what? Judith may come out."

"What makes you think so?"

"She hasn't said no."

"Ah so. And how are the other Howards?"

"William is William. David and Lydia: pretty tense. Of course he wants to move to the city and she likes that awful model home they live in."

"You're hardly the person to criticize a big house."

"Have you seen it?"

"Of course. It's vulgar."

"Right."

"But so what?"

"You're impossible, Adrian." But nothing can get Betsy down. She wraps and bakes and hums along with the Robert Shaw

Christmas carols. She ties a red ribbon on Ginger's bed. Her mood is catching. William and David bring over packages, including ones for their mother, and lay them beneath the tree. They look their best since their father was in the hospital. Phoebe is excited, examining every ornament on the tree and especially the ones her father made when he was her age: Styrofoam covered with glitter.

"Judith will get here," Betsy says to Adrian.

"And Natalie?"

"She's gone. Like a transplant that didn't take."

"Mom!"

"And if Judith could see how excited Phoebe is . . . ."

"And her mother-in-law," Adrian says. "Why not let things take their course, Mom? You know the butterfly effect—maybe that will make what you want happen."

"What are you talking about?"

"You know, a butterfly flutters its wings, and sets off a tornado millions of miles away."

"What about if an old lady sets up a Christmas tree?"

67

Judith

Judith receives the card from Betsy inviting her to "come home" for Christmas. Everyone is fine. Eric is amazingly well, walking to work, exercising. He and John have a new closeness. Natalie is out of the picture. The whole family will be having Christmas Eve dinner at Betsy's and then going to David and Lydia's on Christmas morning to exchange gifts. Phoebe is going to play a mouse in *The Nutcracker*.

So Natalie is over. Judith wonders what finally did the trick. She holds Betsy's note in her hand a long time, an elegant UNICEF card embossed with white peace doves.

She takes it to the bedroom she and Zelda share, intending to lay it on the end table between her and Zelda's beds. There is no room for it. Zelda seems to collect more stuff every day: toy animals, dolls, mugs full of pens that glow in the dark and pencils with feathers on them. Every surface from the shelves to the window sills to the desk is covered. Clothes bulge from the closet door like creatures trying to escape.

While Judith is considering Betsy's offer and all that it would mean, Zelda comes in the room.

"Hi, Roomie," she says. She looks over Judith's shoulder and takes the card from her.

"Oh, don't go, I want you here. We can ride around and look at the lights—they have cool ones way on top of the buildings."

"We'll see," Judith says.

"Who's Natalie?"

"No one."

Judith thinks about Betsy's announcement that "Natalie is out of the picture."

I'm supposed to be thrilled, Judith thinks. Rush to his side. No, things had to be said. Or even if they were said . . . .

Judith puts Betsy's card on the fridge and secures it with a magnet. She sees it when she gets ice or food. Peace doves.

Washington has one of its big storms. Judith walks through fast falling snow to get to the Metro. At last she has had a serious interview at a university. She had two transfers to make. While she was in her meeting, she felt her throat getting scratchy. She has probably blown the interview. Still the committee seemed impressed with her experience and many publications.

She has planned to trim a Christmas tree with Zelda, looks forward to sitting by the window with the good view, cutting out stars and decorating cookies, watching the snow gather in drifts on the sills, blanket the streets and trees. Like that moment long ago, when she was so happy . . . . in the tiny apartment in Chicago.

On the Metro she begins to cough. By the time she reaches the Woodley Park station, she feels hot. She has five blocks to walk to Moira's apartment. She tries waving down a cab she can't afford, but they whiz past, taken. There is no alternative but to walk on through the deep snow again. The plows are busy in the street, and there's the sound of lumbering trucks and the scraping of shovels. The air is so thin it's hard to breathe. Judith's feet are getting cold even in her boots. When she finally reaches the San Remo, she walks down the long hall, shivering and shaking like a condemned prisoner. At the apartment she kicks off her boots, puts the tea kettle on, and goes to her and Zelda's room to pull off her ice-crystalled socks.

When Moira comes home the kettle is screaming and Judith is lying on her bed oblivious. Moira calls the doctor, who diagnoses severe bronchitis. Judith must stay put, stay warm. Her bones ache. Her cough tears at her chest. Judith blames herself—she didn't take care, got over-stressed, maybe needed an excuse not to go to Cincinnati—but her decision about Christmas is made for her, and Zelda takes Betsy's card off the fridge.

68

Betsy

The winter seems especially cold. An acquaintance of Betsy's slips on the ice and breaks a hip. She has no family and must to go into a nursing home. So many traps set for the old. Betsy's own heart feels frozen.

After Christmas she and John go to Puerto Rico to a resort they enjoyed near Humacao, but travel is not fun like it used to be when jets were new and she and John were young—when the passengers were pampered, served tasty meals and offered blankets and pillows.

At Security, John's wallet and belt, his keys and watch, are taken from him for inspection; he is frisked and gone over with a wand because of shrapnel in his knee. He holds up his pants, while the man in front of him removes his wooden leg.

Far from home, in a strange bed, the sea groaning throughout the night, Betsy dreams she and John receive a call from somewhere; they must rush to the hospital. When they arrive there, the recorded voice at the door shouts, "Your son's heart stopped. He is dead. Ha ha ha!" They run through the halls, but can't find Eric's room.

Betsy wakens, shaking, electric shocks running through her body. She reaches for John. Half awake, he holds her tight. "Bad dream?" he murmurs. She stops shivering as he shields her with his warm body.

"Let's go home," Betsy says.

She and John are greeted at their condo by the dog sitter he hired for Ginger, and a box full of mail. Betsy dumps her suitcase in her bedroom and goes through the piles of ads, pleas for contribution, bills and postcards. Nothing from Judith.

John confers with the dog sitter.

"Did she eat?"

He pets Ginger. "Did you miss us?" he asks the dog.

Ginger licks his hand feebly.

He unpacks, vacuums his suitcase, hangs up his clothes, throws the used items in the wash, and goes to the office.

Betsy takes her time unpacking. The scene out her window is cloudy, the river a canyon of fog. The condo seems like a waiting room, an anteroom to—well, she thinks, death. The move here from the castle has made all her years before seem vain: her worries, her plans and projects, her restless activities, the things she wanted and the things she got. All those years in the castle are like a scene in a snow globe, with a living creature inside: herself running from floor to floor, planning and working, wanting and caring, all of it sealed off in the past.

She and John are moving toward the rim of their lives. She wonders how her own death will come. But she will never know. It will be like a bird smacking into a clean window.

In a few days Betsy resumes her docent work.

The vast museum where she lectures visitors, with its ornate draperies and carpets, its myriad rooms, white marble figures, and gold-framed paintings, is hushed. School trips to the museum are canceled due to the weather; only an occasional lone patron or a group of two or three women come in. Betsy eagerly grabs the visitors, pointing the way to the various galleries

The rooms are dark in this winter weather. Toward the end of her day, Betsy finds herself alone in a softly-lit portrait gallery; footsteps far away on the marble floors of the foyer are the only sound. The portraits are strange company. Betsy stares into the eyes of a Rembrandt Good-Wife, an old woman wearing a black dress, white collar and mob cap; their eyes connect over centuries. Pain, concern, experience, it is all there, shared.

The paint is faintly wrinkled; the surface marred by hairline fissures, the marks of time and wear, the forces she has worked against all her life—preserving the castle, the city's distinguished buildings, the family.

She goes home for the day, feeling low. She has failed to bring Judith home. And she wants her back for herself as well as for her son. But all her talks with Eric have accomplished nothing.

Betsy lies down on her bed and dozes, wrapped in a favorite quilt. She dreams of Eric and Judith, William and David, Adrian, Lydia and Phoebe, herself and John; they are their current ages, but living in the castle the way it was when she and John first bought it. All their lives are before them; their dreams are still intact. Their love is new. They sit at the table, eating and drinking; the glasses and china sparkling, everyone smiling and happy, laughing.

But the picture, like the painting of the old woman in the museum, is marred by tiny cracks.

That week Betsy invites Eric and William for dinner and the two come. Eric looks very well, his waistline more trim since his illness and new diet. William—not so good—fidgety.

"Have you heard from your mother?" Betsy asks him.

"We email," he says. "She seems OK. I'm going to go up and visit soon."

The conversation is about to flicker out when Eric re-ignites it.

"I'm thinking maybe we should sell the house," he says.

Everyone sits up straighter.

"I don't need all that space, and I'm sure Judith could use her share of the proceeds."

Betsy hears a door close.

On a life.

"Oh dear," she says.

"I won't do it unless she wants to—"

"Sell the house?" William says. He sounds bereft.

All of a sudden he is the guardian of the hearth, Betsy thinks, after being its biggest disruption. Our rebel who lives in one room over a bar.

"What would I do about all that stuff?" Eric asks.

Betsy is too stunned to reply.

"Could you maybe look the place over—see if there's anything I should store or that Judith might want?"

Wait a minute, Betsy thinks. This could be the way to get Judith back home.

"Have you written her about this?" Betsy asks.

"Not yet."

"Should *I*?"

"*No!*" John and Eric shout in tandem.

"Have you talked to a real estate agent?" John says.

"Not yet," Eric repeats. "It's kind of messy and dusty since Judith and Brendan left. I'm afraid—"

"Ora and I can come clean up," Betsy says.

This is just the project she needs.

As soon as Betsy has a free day, she and Ora go to the old Tudor and begin their work. They scrub floors, wash the bathroom fixtures, go through the closets.

Betsy jots down the items that should be kept if Eric and Judith actually decide to sell, which she hopes they won't: the Ukioye prints, the Indiana LOVE poster. She examines the Chinese candlesticks and the vase from Venice. Both are cracked. She checks the kitchen cabinets, and pitches useless tin pans and broken cups into a waste can.

She hears Ora call her name, and she goes to the hall where Ora had been neatening closets and mopping.

"I'm in here," Ora calls from the study. Betsy goes into the room.

Ora is poking her mop into the recesses of Eric's closet, and pulling at something stuck in the back. She drags out a dusty, plump, red cloth heart. She picks it up, makes a face, and gingerly holds it at arms length.

"What should I do with this old thing?" she says.

Part 9

HEART CHAMBERS

69

David

The glow from David and Lydia's trip to Antigua has faded. It seems as though all they have with each other is sex. Occasionally. Angry sex. Otherwise life is a constant fuss over who's going to take out the garbage, get the cars washed, do the shopping, call the plumber. David's mother did all that—and so did Lydia's—one reason she's so determined not to take on time consuming chores. David knows he is messing up Lydia's image of herself as Super Mom; the perfect loving parent, the brilliant lawyer. But her remodeling and shopping have taken on the character of addiction. Their credit cards are maxed out. He cites his grandfather who never paid a cent of interest in his life.

"I didn't marry your grandfather. Or did I? John's a nice old man. But all you Howards are so stuffy. So Cincinnati."

"It's not like I've refused to go into debt."

Their love for each other is stiffening like the newly dead. He punches the wall of the den with his fist and it makes a big hole.

"This God-damned place," he says. His parents' house had walls so thick and hard it was difficult to hang pictures. Cincinnati is a red brick and stone town, he thinks—or was. Now it's full of places like the straw house of the Three Little Pigs. You could huff and puff and blow them down.

In January David gets an email from his mother: she misses Phoebe, well all of them. Could he and Lydia and Phoebe come to Washington for a visit? She has recuperated from her bronchitis. She has an apartment of her own now, a small place, and she has a professorship at a university where she interviewed at Christmas. She has much to do to get back into teaching: projects to grade and paper work to do. She feels she can't leave DC at the moment, having just gotten a proper job, so a visit to Cincinnati is out, and anyway it would be great for Phoebe to see Washington. Wait till spring and warmer weather and then come out.

David suggests this to Lydia, but she says it would be better if just he and Phoebe go. She's on a major case involving hospitals—a big split from an alliance, with personality problems muddying the negotiations. The phrase "douche bag" has slipped through an email.

OK, a cooling off period might be good, David thinks.

In April he and Phoebe make plans for their trip. Lydia buys Phoebe a new Juicy Girl tote bag. She makes, David thinks, a big show about missing her daughter and forgoing the wonders of Washington, but he feels she is damned glad to get rid of them. At least him.

At the sight of suitcases getting packed, Lenny begins running around in circles and jumping on the furniture. Lydia insists that David send him to a kennel. No way is she going to walk the dog and clean up his messes.

"He always comes home sick from the kennel," David says. "I can get the dog walker to come over to take him out."

"Last time she didn't show up."

Lydia gets that look. David drives Lenny to the kennel. He hates the place: big dogs in cages barking and little ones yapping.

The custodian swears the animals are walked several times a day. David wonders. On the way, Lenny looks dejected. He knows exactly where he's going. When they pull up to the place, David pats Lenny on the head and assures him he'll be back soon.

"At least *you're* going to miss me," David says.

Lydia drives David and Phoebe to the airport. Phoebe clings to her mother for a moment, then walks confidently to the gate, pulling her little wheeled case and carrying her new bag. She's quite a pro. She's been to about five states and to London and Paris to visit one of Lydia's friends.

As they descend to DC, David points out the Washington monument to Phoebe. He is anxious as their cab takes them through Adams-Morgan, hoping his mother will be located in a safe, pleasant place. He is dismayed when they pull into her street where the San Remo is like a fortress among run-down single and two family houses. The front yard of her building is weedy and the gutters are rotting away from the roof. He pays the cab driver, and he and Phoebe walk up the few steps to the porch. He rings the bell with "J Howard" next to it on a slide-in card. The front door is glass paneled. Is this place safe?

Soon he hears his mother running down the steps and the door is flung open. She takes David and Phoebe in her arms.

"Oh, I'm so glad to see you. Come in. Phoebe, you've grown inches. How are you? Where's Lydia?"

"She had to work," Phoebe says. She is already developing the defenses of a child between hostile parents. "She really wanted to come."

"I'm sorry she couldn't make it—but come on in."

David's mother leads the way upstairs and into a small sparsely furnished living room.

"I'll put you in the extra bedroom," she says, "and Phoebe can take the twin in mine. She leads David into the tiniest bedroom he's ever seen. He can almost spread his arms and touch both walls. There is a small painted table, a chair and lamp table.

"How was your flight?" his mother asks.

"Fine." David is let down by seeing his mother in these rather dark and dowdy surroundings. The house he grew up in was not fancy, but it was a generous size, and his mother had her garden, and after he and William left, a room to herself where she could study and sometimes paint.

Her bedroom here is slightly larger than the one David will be using: twin beds, a desk that looks like it came from a yard sale, a pair of lamps.

When David and Phoebe are settled, David's mother sits them in the living room and offers them lemonade. They both refuse; they drank orange soda on the plane and are full of peanuts. David wants to say something reassuring, but can't.

His mother leads them to a deck that overlooks the downstairs neighbors' yard: plastic chairs and a barbecue grill on the limp grass, and a small forsythia is trying to bring a little spring to the place. On David's mother's deck there is one canvas folding chair and a metal table.

"Not much of a view, but I like to step out here to breathe. I have my coffee out here in the mornings; it's quite pleasant."

To David it looks lonely.

In the living room David sits in one of the two over-stuffed chairs and looks about: a small TV, a desk with a laptop, a bookcase (again yard sale stuff). The walls are decorated by museum reproductions and a few of his mother's drawings. A small gray cat appears from under the couch, slinks over to him and winds itself around his ankles.

David's mother picks up the cat and offers it to Phoebe, who reaches out eagerly and keeps it on her lap, petting it until it purrs.

"I love your cat," Phoebe says. "Is it a boy or a girl?"

"Girl."

"That's why she's so sweet."

David takes a playful swipe at Phoebe.

"What is her name?" Phoebe says.

"Mehitabel."

David's mother asks how they like her "little pad." She is obviously quite proud of it. But it is so bare, so minimal, David thinks.

"It's nice," he says.

"It's hard to find a convenient place in D.C.," his mother says, "so I was really glad to find this. I can walk to the Metro and stores and I'm right across the street from Moira and Zelda."

David doesn't like what he's seen of Zelda. She's too sophisticated, and besides he's jealous on Phoebe's behalf.

David's mother cooks dinner that night and serves it by candlelight in the tiny dinette off the kitchen: pasta with chicken, tossed salad and ice cream. The wine, David notes, is cheap and smells faintly like the stuff Lydia uses to clean off chipped fingernail polish.

They seem like strangers, making conversation. David's mother tells him what places might be good to visit.

David reminds her that he went to law school here, but of course there are many new buildings and memorials, and while in school he had not had a lot of time to hit the tourist spots. He asks Phoebe what she would like to see.

"Is there a GAP?" she says.

Both David and his mother laugh.

"Somewhere, but you can shop anywhere."

"I guess you're right," Phoebe says. "I'll save that for New York."

On Saturday the three of them take the sight-seeing bus to Mt. Vernon and go to President Kennedy's grave. They have tea at the East wing of the National Gallery in a small café by a fountain. In the big shop on the lower level they buy postcards for Lydia and William and David's father and John and Betsy. Phoebe picks out several for her friends. She is fascinated by the jewelry displays and David reluctantly buys her a set of Egyptian beads (like she doesn't have enough stuff). They walk up the marble stairs to the mezzanine and stare out at the Calder mobile dominating the huge space. Phoebe loves it.

That night David takes his mother, Moira, Zelda and Phoebe to a Tapas restaurant where they order small dishes of squid, shrimp, olives, mushrooms and grilled egg plant. They pass them around, everyone tasting everyone else's selections. The girls get along well. Phoebe is fascinated by Zelda's gadgets: she has an I-Pod around her neck and a BlackBerry, and she and Moira argue over her using them at dinner.

"Turn that off and put that thing away, girl friend."

"Oh shut up, *girl friend*."

Zelda reluctantly pulls her I-Pod out of her ear. She shows Phoebe how her BlackBerry works, then puts it in her bag.

"Can I get a BlackBerry?" Phoebe begs.

"Maybe later, not now," David says.

"*You* have one."

"For business," David says. "I'd kind of like you to look around at the real world."

"That *is* the real world," Phoebe says.

To these girls, David guesses it is—a society somewhere in space, with images for friends.

By the time their cab delivers them to the San Remo, Moira is fairly drunk (David noticed she ordered a second bottle of wine—at sixty dollars a pop—on his tab), and almost trips getting out of the cab. Zelda steadies her.

A kid shouldn't have to do that, David thinks.

As he and Phoebe and his mother walk across to her apartment, he whispers, "I'm afraid Moira drinks too much."

"She's been very helpful to me. She and Zelda both."

David thinks why can't she take help from her own family at home?

When Phoebe has been tucked into bed with many kisses from her grandmother, he and his mother sit in the small living room and talk. Purposefully, David gives her copies of the Christmas photos he took. The Howards have always taken a group portrait in front of Betsy and John's big fireplace at the castle. Since their move, it is taken by the small fake hearth. There they all are: David and Lydia, Phoebe, William, Betsy and John, David's father. His mother looks puzzled as she examines the picture. There is someone missing; they both notice the gap. It's her.

"How is your dad?" his mother asks.

"He's looking good."

"He went through hell. Does he talk about it?"

"Not much. Just says how embarrassing it was to haul a urinal around, or how he had to shower with three people looking on when he got home. He's playing a little tennis. He'll probably be flying soon."

"What about William?"

David studies his mother's face. How much does she know? Her expression says she knows everything. But how?

"He's on the straight and narrow. Oh, and Natalie's melted away like the Wicked Witch of the West. Maybe someone threw water on her."

"Or coffee," Judith says.

"What?"

351

David awakens on Sunday to the smell of breakfasts at home: toast and coffee. Captain Kangaroo and Mr. Green Jeans would be on the TV; he and William doing last minute home work, his father behind the newspaper. David likes the memory; we want people—he thinks, especially our parents—to stay in their assigned roles; they should never change, should have no other life.

He goes into the kitchenette where Phoebe is spreading strawberry jam on her toast while his mother pours coffee.

"I wish you could stay longer," she says.

"Me too," Phoebe says. "I love it here."

She lets Mehitabel jump into her lap and pets her.

"Maybe we could get a cat," Phoebe says. "Could we *please*, Daddy?"

"Sure, Pheeb. Do you think Lenny would be OK with it?"

"Do you want eggs or anything?" his mother says. David shakes his head, takes two pieces of toast and liberally spreads them with butter.

The sun is shining through the window, so David suggests they go down to the mall.

The paths and museums are full of sight-seers. It's a pleasant picture: the long stretch of the mall, a mix of sun and shade with the capital at one end and the Lincoln Memorial at the other. Phoebe skips ahead.

"Where's Abraham Lincoln?" she calls back. David points toward the monuments.

From this cheerful scene, you would never believe, David observes to himself, that the country is engaged in a pointless war, that coffins of dead service people are arriving daily wrapped in red white and blue like Christmas presents . . . . Of course, this has to be imagined, for the media has been prevented from putting these images on TV.

The people strolling look so hopeful, so appreciative of their beautiful capital, so interested in its history and proud of their share in it. They—we—David thinks, for he shares their love and hope—are worshiping an ideal, a past, one that, if you study history, maybe never was.

The country's ideals are so shiny, so intelligent. Yet its people have been tragically bamboozled by bellicose know-nothings, its treasure squandered in benefits for the very people who don't need more ("the haves and have mores"). The cynicism, the overt greed of this makes David feel sick. His mood darkens as he watches the people at the Viet Nam memorial, some weeping, searching for the names of their family members and buddies.

"And now we'll do it all over again," his mother says.

David and his mother and Phoebe walk past the World War Two memorial: big, garish. No one is crying. It is too long ago. Its wounds are passing into history; they are invisible, deep in the hearts of the families with lost forbears, on the blue numbers on the arms of camp victims. Also passing on.

"Grampa John was in World War Two," David tells Phoebe.

From her reaction, David is not sure his daughter has ever heard of it. If she has, it would be like the Civil War is to him: picturesque, facts in text books.

"What did Grampa John do?" Phoebe asks.

David hasn't the faintest idea. He should talk to John. Probably even his father doesn't know.

Time goes so fast. The present tramples all over the past.

Meanwhile the people visit the national shrines, hopeful, wanting to believe the country's myths. To live up to its ideals. He too.

"Daddy, are you OK?" Phoebe says.

"Oh yes."

He wishes he could take Phoebe to some safe place, away from a country turning the rest of the world against it, sending sacrificial boys and girls to fight the wars of rich old men, away from the tension at home between him and Lydia—out of a society sexualizing and exploiting little girls. He wants Phoebe to use her excellent brain, be a Madame Curie or a—God he can't think of any women who have accomplished big things, only a few politicians and movie stars. What writer? He knows of no George Eliots or George Orwells among modern women. Maybe that French woman. Real prophets.

David pats the plane tickets in his breast pocket. Checks his watch. They have plenty of time. He loves Lydia, but he does not want to go back home to the status quo. What can they do? Couples therapy? Lydia wouldn't go for it. He could propose a trial separation. But he wants Phoebe with him.

"Daddy look!" Phoebe says. She points to a small carousel set up on the mall. "Can I go on it?"

"Sure."

David buys her a ticket at a booth and escorts her onto the round platform. There are no other children riding. Phoebe goes from horse to horse. They have white or black faces, curly flowing manes, wild eyes, noble tales lifted high. Such romantic horses. Phoebe selects a white horse with a bejeweled saddle and David helps her into the stirrups.

"Hold on tight," he says. He jumps off the platform.

He and his mother sit on a bench and watch as Phoebe grips the pole and the off-key music starts. The music begins to play the tune on-key as the ride gets going. David watches closely. Phoebe smiles and waves each time she comes around into sight. He waves back.

David thinks of moving out. But he would have his daughter only on weekends, maybe not that often—be one of those Dads that cluster together at soccer games—or singles bars. He fantasizes just taking off, Phoebe and himself, disappearing. Getting on a train and heading for Canada.

The carousel music goes sour again as the ride slows down. Phoebe clings to her horse.

"Can I go again, Daddy?"

"Sure. Stay on. I'll get you a ticket."

David buys another ticket at the booth and takes it to Phoebe.

"Hold tight."

"I know."

Phoebe pats her horse as though he's alive.

"I love this horse," she says.

"You picked a good one."

The music starts up again, Phoebe waves, and around and around she goes. She's still the only kid on the ride. She looks lonely. David waves back. There is something so touching about her enjoying her ride all alone.

David hops onto the Merry-Go-Round and takes the horse next to Phoebe's.

70

David

hit. Rain. It doesn't look like good flying weather. David hates turbulence. Of course when he and Phoebe get in the air, he mustn't let on that his stomach is flopping around. He has to stay cheerful and calm so Phoebe doesn't get scared.

"Can I do anything to help pack up?" David's mother says.

"We're fine." David and Phoebe throw the last few items into their bags, and David checks his watch.

They hear the honk of a cab, and David and Phoebe gather their bags. David's mother walks them down to the front porch. They all kiss goodbye, with "love you's" all around.

"Say goodbye to Zelda and Moira for us," Phoebe says. "They are so cool."

As David and Phoebe pull away, David watches out the window at his mother waving and waving.

Who is that woman? David thinks. Do I know her? Did I ever? She's gone out of focus, like Betsy did when he heard about her affair. Would his mother turn into someone else when he left?

The flight is moderately bumpy, but you can stand anything for an hour, David thinks, and he is in no great hurry to get home.

He's obviously not going to escape with his daughter. But he feels so trapped in his lavish lifestyle. He hates the burbs. As long as they are in the McMansion he will never fulfill his dreams. Maybe he will devote more time to his pro bono work.

When David and Phoebe arrive at the Cincinnati area airport they see Lydia waiting at the gate. She is wearing a turquoise T-shirt, jeans and crocs. She is so beautiful and she looks happy to see them; of course, her glow is mostly for Phoebe. He kisses her on the cheek.

"What do you say we stop at Walt's for dinner?" Lydia says.

Walt's is David's favorite restaurant, but a place they seldom go: big portions of ribs, mashed potatoes, slaw, biscuits. They never take Phoebe there, and it has been off limits since David gained so much weight gorging at the hospital.

David and Lydia have beer with their gooey sweet ribs, and Phoebe has a smoothie. Is David wrong or does Lydia seem unusually anxious to please?

Driving over the bridge to Cincinnati, David feels a lift. He does love his home town. It's a solid place. Conservative in a good way, and conservative in a right wing way, but it's full of families that last, lifetime friendships (he still is good pals with his high school best friend). It hasn't gone in for glitz in a big way, thanks somewhat to Betsy and her ilk. It's beautiful sitting on the river. The skyline is from a fairytale, with the Church of Immaculata's spires topping Mt. Adams, the parks and green hills. He drives along the river on Columbia Parkway and out to his suburb. Once past the malls and tacky strips beyond, the pear trees are heavy with white blossoms. The woods behind his house are beginning to turn green. As he gets out of the car, Lenny almost knocks him over with a welcome home.

"You picked him up!" David says to Lydia. He leads Lenny outdoors for his run. Surprisingly, Lydia follows him with Phoebe.

The woods smell of mold from the winter's leaves tamped on the earth. Wildflowers poke up among them. Phoebe picks a bouquet of violets.

Back in the house, David takes off his jacket and slumps into a chair. Lydia asks about his mother, and he tells her his trepidations about her living conditions and how tired he thinks she looks.

"She's had a rough year. Your father's illness in a way was harder on her than him."

Lydia seems almost glad to see David. Does she have a new decorating scheme in mind?

Phoebe is tired from her trip and gets ready for bed without much reminding. When David goes to her room to kiss her goodnight, she is bathed and smells of lemony soap and looks very content to be back in her own room with her line up of stuffed animals and her familiar blue quilt with its pattern of white clouds and stars. "Good old bed," she says, and snuggles down.

Lydia sits beside her while David reads her Dr. Seuss' *Sleep Book,* for the hundredth time.

When she is quiet, and clearly asleep, Lydia and David get ready for bed. David is tired from the emotional drain of seeing his mother, and the homecoming. The line at Security had been long, and the metal detectors and electronics seemed futile and threatening.

Lydia appears from her dressing room in a sheer blue nightgown, one of David's favorites.

"I have big news," she says.

Aha, now it can be told, David thinks. She's made partner. No wonder she's been so amiable all day. She beat him to it. But he has to be glad for her. She has wanted it so badly.

"I'm pregnant," she says.

It takes David a moment to digest what she has said. He is stunned. His first reaction is relief: thank God he hadn't done anything rash. Or said any hurtful words. His second reaction is total joy! She will need him again. They will go to Lamaze again. He will carry things for her. He will get up with her at night when her body gets too bulky for comfort and she can't sleep; he will rub her feet.

"This is so great!" he says.

"Of course I'll have to fix up the bedroom next to Phoebe's. Do some redecorating." David must have changed expression, though he would give Lydia the moon at the moment.

"Kidding," she says.

"I like the bidet you put in," he says.

"I want to hold up on things. Take some time off so . . . ."

He knows she is thinking of the miscarriage.

"David, I do love you. It's just—I can't be a Howard. I'm not an intellectual. Your mother is such a giant of the earth. I'm not like her. She's so brilliant and creative."

David sweeps her into his arms and kisses her all over her face.

"I thought you looked especially beautiful."

"I haven't told Phoebe yet. I waited till we can tell her together."

They go to bed cozy and loving, and make love.

At breakfast they tell Phoebe, who jumps up and down. A real baby to play with. A sister.

"It will be a girl, won't it?" she says. "She can sleep in my room with me. I have plenty of space. I won't need a cat now, Daddy."

David kisses his two women goodbye and drives to the office. Alone, he has a brief moment of panic. A new life. More responsibility. Choices closed. He can no longer count on his parents and grandparents to hold him up. They are vanishing.

He pulls into his designated parking space in his building. Goes through the corridor to his office, says good morning to the receptionist. He puts his briefcase on his desk and checks his email. He begins work on the appeal of the case that was bugging him so when his father was in the hospital. He almost convinced himself that he hated his life, that he must make changes, become his real self, maybe leave his wife, move to the city, be more like William, helping others, become less of a consumer, less ambitious and driving—someone other than the man in the Boss suit with the briefcase full of papers. But now, he looks at himself, and thinks, "this *is* me."

He likes his routine, his work, his status, having control of his life: everything handy: his barbershop, his bank, his dry cleaner, all nearby so he can concentrate on business.

He is turning into his grandfather. Which is OK. He will be the steady center the family needs, the continuity. Phoebe and the new baby and the others will need a man like him.

Or is he just plain boring?

Whatever, he is happy.

He loves Lydia and she loves him. All their differences and quarrels will disappear now.

Won't they?

71

William

It begins with a glass of water in the Bookshelf Coffee Shop. It is late August, almost a year since William's father nearly died. Jimmy brings William a glass of ice water, sparkling, fresh, with a slice of lemon. It looks like at least a quart.

William has just seen pictures of kids in Haiti, drinking from ditches and eating grass, kids in refugee camps waiting in line to suck moisture from a drain pipe. He feels sick. He takes a sip or two of his water and pushes it away. Enough to provide a day's drinking water for a kid.

He knows now in a flash how he will take that risk he promised himself. He has found that he likes helping people. He cancels the sandwich order and calls Angie. How long would it take to get a nursing degree and where should he go to start the process? He is thinking of something like Doctors Without Borders. He can't afford a medical degree and he'd be near forty if he went after one. Nursing would be the way.

How weird is it, that his role model is a girl?

He and Angie decide to work together.

William debates whether to take out a loan to return to school—he will have to acquire some undergraduate credits before he can get into nursing. John would probably lend him the money without his having to pay interest, or give it to him. But he decides to do it on his own. He postpones telling the family about his plans. Betsy would worry that he might catch some terrible disease in a third-world country. She would know at least one person who died that way.

What about David and his father? Would they scoff at his plans, think his idea too extreme, tell him he could do plenty right here, or that he's never shown any aptitude for medical work?

He will try his idea out on David, though he can already see his expression: his little brother is climbing another tree that won't hold him, not quite as stupid as drugs, but almost as dangerous and probably unrealistic.

As though having more kids and living in a house big enough for an African village is "realistic." David is clearly ecstatic at Lydia being pregnant, while the world is vastly overpopulated. He is jogging and lifting weights and eating more protein (every time William sees a steak, he flashes on the cattle in Colorado holding pens, living in a few feet of mud and feces). David is toning up and slimming down to be the perfect Dad and the youngest partner in his firm (he's made it, and the new stationery is being printed, and he has moved to an office with a better view).

William visits his mother in D.C. She likes her new position. In fact, away from her home, she seems inordinately happy. He tells her his plans, but she doesn't appear to be as thrilled as he thought she would be. She seems suspicious. Asks if he has a new sponsor, and how is Angie.

"She's such a nice person," she says. Could she somehow know about his having sex with Natalie the day they smoked dope? David wouldn't rat on him.

William drops in on Reverend Al. As usual, Rev is surrounded by pamphlets and workers planning anti-war projects. He has gotten more crippled, and sits in the midst of the activity, directing, advising. He smiles at William.

"Sit down. Sit down. It's been awhile."

The usual tea appears at William's elbow, in a mug from Mel's bakery.

William tells him of his plans.

"How is your father?" Rev says.

"He's back at work, busy as ever. Seems to be fine. But he's pretty much alone. I can't get him to talk about how he feels, if he feels weaker or scared of a recurrence or anything."

"He has been in the valley of the shadow."

"He just isn't an emotional guy."

"All people have emotions. We just express them differently."

"He's a tough nut to crack."

"You will be here for the next several years. Dad will be OK. I think he will be proud of what you are planning to do. I certainly am."

In the valley of the shadow. Yes, that is where William's father has been.

And a new member, Mr. Death, has joined the family circle, smiling, twirling his hat. His father won't say hello. A historian, he won't look back.

But the whole bizarre and frightening time in the hospital has taught William that he must move on quickly, no more dabbling in this and daydreaming about that.

He feels elated that Rev approves of his plan, is proud of him. He will become a real person. William has told many lies in his coke phase. He backslid. Drank and smoked pot again. He fucked his father's girl friend.

William is sure of one thing: he wants no part of the commercial world. He sees society as a monstrous dark citadel and himself as "a consumer unit" running like a Kafka character from the grasp of its institutions: the church, the state, TV, the Internet, the malls, all wanting him to join the getting and spending, acquire things, a house, a car, gadgets, little baby consumers—

William accepts David's invitation to visit his new digs. As they walk down the long hallway toward David's office, it is clear his brother is the new big dog. Other lawyers pop out of their offices to meet him, and secretaries welcome the two, paying tribute to the new partner. It is impressive. In spite of his new resolves, William feels a small pang of jealousy like a hunger pang.

He oohs and aahs at the roomier, more importantly located office, the new gigantic desk.

"I haven't selected any art yet," David says, indicating the bare walls freshly painted a stylish red. David throws William a little bone. "Do you know any geniuses?"

"Only in the graffiti genre . . . ."

"Oh."

"I'm happy for you, bro," William says. "This is just what you wanted, and you've worked hard to get it."

David pushes back in his chair, studies William.

"You think it's—ordinary."

"I didn't say that."

"I can tell by your expression."

"No, really. And I guess you and Lydia are getting along better with the new kid on the way."

David almost smirks.

"*Oh* yeah."

"Phoebe will be better off with a little brother or sister," William says.

"She wants a sister. She's out of her mind she's so happy."

"And I guess Mom is pretty proud . . . ."

"I'm hoping it might bring her back."

"She has a full-time job now, and she's always needed to do her own thing."

"Well, but—"

"Betsy must be thrilled."

"She is. Dad's illness really took a lot out of her."

"And John. He's proud of your partnership, I bet. Well, the baby too."

"John's my hero."

"Not Dad?"

"Well Dad, too. But I could never be a scholar. Too many problems for too little pay."

David has never told William about the woman harassing their father. William sees him as a man in charge, a pilot, a potential university president, not a man with fears and problems. There was always too much in the present to fill in past events.

David offers William a cup of coffee and they go into the conference room and sit in cushy chairs at the long, highly polished table. A tray holding a coffee decanter, mugs and a plate of cookies is laid out for them.

They both take coffee and proceed to polish off the cookies.

"How do you think Dad looks?" William says.

"Fine."

"Will things ever be the same? He almost died. I never thought he could die."

"It was a wake up call, for sure. I'm pumping iron and working out every day. Eating right—except for those cookies. How 'bout you?"

William shrugs. He has left behind the Wonderland of the hospital they fell into through the Looking Glass. He has stepped out of it—but not into the smug world he knew before, rather into another Wonderland. The one set in the strange medium of time and riding on a ball whirling in space. A magic world beyond any fantasy. Lit by stars millions of miles away. Sustained by the incredible sun. A dangerous, beautiful, bizarre world.

"I appreciate the family more," David says. "Even you."

"Fuck, Dude."

William knows this isn't the right moment to tell David his own news. His plans might make David's cozy world seem tame. His decision, one-up-man's-ship. But he blurts out anyway, "I've-uh-got some news of my own."

What makes him pick this moment, anyway—envy? The desire to stick a needle into David's sweet dream? He is afraid something mean will show in his face.

"I'm going to school to get a nursing degree. Angie and I are planning to join Doctors without Borders, go to work in one of the countries that don't even have water for drinking, much less sanitation."

"Whoa." David takes a moment to absorb William's news. His expression is like William's earlier—not without envy.

David strokes his chin as though he has an Elder's beard.

"How are you going to pay for the schooling and all?"

"Loans."

"Do you realize how long it takes to pay them off?"

"I'm checking."

"Well, good luck."

Does he think William can't take on responsibility and stick to it? That he will find some easy way out?

"I mean that, William. Your idea is great," David says. "The world out there is a mess. It needs healers."

William says he must take off. The brothers stand and reach out for a hug, but as they touch, they grab each other by the shoulders, and begin trying to wrestle each other to the floor.

"You'll never be able to take me, little bro," David says.

"I always could. And you're getting soft."

William gets David in a half-nelson, but David breaks his hold and squeezes William around the chest. William pokes David in the belly.

Both David and William are panting as they struggle. They knock over a chair that rolls into the conference table. William goes down on his knees. David reaches for him, but William trips him and David sprawls beside him.

The door opens a crack and a woman looks into the room. Notices the crashed chair, its wheels spinning.

"Is everything all right?" she says.

"Fine," David says, smoothing back his hair.

"Great," William says.

When she leaves, they flop into chairs and laugh.

"Did she say 'take it outside, boys'? Or is Mom here?" William asks.

"I have to go to work, you retard," David says. He adjusts his tie, and this time embraces William.

The next day Katrina hits New Orleans, and on TV William and Angie see the people, mostly black, without food or dry clothes, wading in their own mess in the shelters, like cattle in holding pens, or captives in the belly of a slave ship. It is as though a giant sliding door has been opened, revealing the hidden world beneath the spin of myth and story. They see people stranded on houses floating in the uncontrollable waters. William and Angie pack up and go down to the flooded city to help out.

William thinks: it's all about water.

72

Judith

September 24, 2005. A year since Eric's heart stopped.

In her extra bedroom, Judith has set up an easel. She draws furiously, the first time in her life she has worked at drawing with such passion. With just charcoal and butcher paper she sketches her fury at the on-going war. She tapes a handle to the back of the poster she has made for the peace march, a photo of a little boy whose arms and legs have been blown off. His limbs and head are bandaged. He has the most terrible pain and sorrow in his eyes, as if he is asking the world, "Why have you done this to me?"

Judith has lettered across the top of the photo, "The Price of Oil is Too High."

She and a group of women from her university have been working all summer, helping to get permits, setting up tents, painting posters, and spreading the word about the three days of protest. There will be marches all over the world today against the Iraq war.

When one family member is threatened by death, Judith thinks, people do everything they can to save them—as the Howards have done. Then they go to war and kill a few thousand people—and then more.

Judith waits on the porch of her building until Claire, a professor in the Spanish department, pulls into the driveway. She carries a sign: "Katrina, Iraq, Abu Ghraib: What Does it Take?"

The women hug and move on to the San Remo to pick up Moira and Zelda. Zelda's sign says, "Bush, You Lying Turd!"

Claire parks as close to the mall as possible, driving around a few times to find a space.

It's a cool sunny morning and it looks as though the march will be large: the estimated crowd is a hundred thousand. Judith's group walks down the mall. A faux military cemetery is made up of hundreds of small white crosses arranged in neat lines, each one standing for a dead American. Empty coffins are wrapped in American flags, reminding the crowd that they have not been allowed to see the bodies that have come home. Music comes from the stage near the monuments.

The women join the march around the White House: all ages are there, young people, old people, parents with strollers, people in wheel chairs. Several protesters are masked as Gandhi, Martin Luther King, Jesus. A group of women carry a banner: "MILITARY FAMILIES SPEAK OUT." A large painting of a dead soldier goes by, with name and birth and death dates: he was 20 years old.

Amazingly, among the thousands on the mall, Judith runs into several more protesters from her university. They seem nice; she's looking forward to knowing them better. With women gaining power, hands have been held out to her.

Again, surprised at the odds, she sees a group of Cincinnatians, her friends Joyce and Tommie who since the beginning of the war have been keeping a vigil on a street corner with a group of women dressed in black. They are led today by Reverend Allen in a wheelchair. He holds a sign saying, "God hath made of one blood all nations of men."

"Hi Judith!" her friends from home call out.

Judith and her group follow the parade around the White House and down the length of the mall. Close to noon, when they are near the edge of the crowd, Moira and Zelda drop out.

"Lunch time," Moira says. "And I need to go on to work. I don't know what I'll tell my boss." Zelda wants to carry on, but she is pried away by Moira. "Enough is enough. I don't know what I'm doing here."

Zelda props her sign on a bench and reluctantly follows her mother.

Judith melds back into the crowd. It has grown since they started; more and more people join in the chanting "Out of Iraq," "Stop the Killing." Judith stands among those ringed around the White House. Nearby a man in a tuxedo and a woman in a black satin evening gown carry posters: "Small Government; Big Wars. Billionaires for Bush." A large banner says "Thou Shalt Not Kill."

The crowd is more mature than the ones she and Eric joined in college, peaceful except for the anarchists, who are dressed in black and shouting. She is angry too, furious: over two thousand Americans dead, thousands of Iraqis. Trillions of dollars squandered. That the country has re-elected the man who brought this on.

Judith catches sight of a familiar figure. He is standing by himself, among the crowd surrounding the White House. Oh God, she thinks, of course Eric would be here.

She is at an angle from him and observes him without his seeing her. He's wearing light slacks, no hat, a casual suit coat. He looks just like he did before his illness. No one could guess what he has been through.

Should she go over to him? There stands a man to whom she has been married since she was nineteen, to whom she is still married . . . . She knows every vein, every hair, every scar on his body. She knows his flaws, his strengths, his appetites. He was her whole life a year ago, months that seemed unending, trying to hold him back from death.

A man in a skeleton suit walks between them.

This moment can't pass as though it never was.

She should at least say hello.

She should ask him how he is feeling.

Judith turns away from Eric, and walks back toward the mall.

She passes a man on stilts, a woman draped in the American flag, as she melds into the crowd. She is out of Eric's line of vision. She sees a fellow faculty member and waves at her as though waving down a rescue vehicle. Before the woman sees her, she turns and looks back through the crowd she has put between herself and her husband. Eric is still there. To spend your life with someone you made children with, argued and fought with, to make him your whole world while he struggled for life . . . To have seen his open chest, the stuff that came from inside his heart and lungs . . . .

She walks back to Eric and taps him on the shoulder and says, "Don't I know you?"

He turns. Surprise and a smile light his face.

"Judith," he says. "I left a message on your answering machine this morning."

He shifts nervously.

"And?"

"Do you want to get rid of the house?"

Judith has to laugh. He's impossible!

"I bought you a jacket," she says.

73

Betsy

September 24: the date that changed her life, the day of David's call from the hospital. Betsy will never forget it.

"Is that water OK?" Norma says.

"A little hot," Betsy says.

Norma puts her hand under the hose and adjusts the temperature. The water turns cold. Why is it, Betsy wonders, that the water in beauty shops is always either too hot or too cold? Norma gets it to a sort of lukewarm mix and scrubs Betsy's scalp. The shampoo smells good, like apples. Betsy enjoys having her hair washed, though Norma has a rough touch. Betsy's old scalp is tender.

When the rinse is done and a damp towel is plastered on Betsy's neck, Norma leads her like an invalid to a chair. Betsy requests a dry towel and walks carefully: the chair is ringed by curls of hair like some primitive voodoo site; it has a foot rest that can trip a person; everything is a trap when you are eighty.

"How are we doing it today?" Norma asks.

"Oh, the usual."

Betsy stares into the mirror; she looks like a drowned rat.

She decides she will definitely get a wig. But she wants a good one. She'll probably have to go to New York.

"How's the family?" Norma says.

Betsy says fine. She thinks, if Eric has scars, he has concealed them. Says he doesn't remember much about the whole ordeal, just an occasional flashback of a woman with a glass eye, being asked his name and the date every day. But he has to have changed. Regardless of his John-like skill in denial.

"To have children means you will never have another moment's peace as long as you live," Betsy says to Norma.

"I hear you."

Norma has some children's drawings and photos of her daughter taped to the mirror. The child's drawing is the same flower Adrian drew as a child: a big yellow circle of petals with a dark brown center and flat green leaves.

Norma leads Betsy, now in rollers, to the dryer and Betsy retreats into her own thoughts. No sooner has Eric recovered, than Adrian is unhappy. She's in the California wilds again, where she can hear the mountain lions roar at sundown, and sometimes has seen them. Her woman friend has gone to Idaho to start a restaurant and Adrian is alone. And lonely.

Of course John didn't say a word when he read Adrian's letter.

Nor did he say a word when William came over and announced that he was going to New Orleans to help the flood victims.

"Those streets have dead bodies floating in them, and think of the diseases and germs floating around!" Betsy said to William. She told him the story of the nineteen-thirty-seven flood when the Ohio River reached all the way to the market area and destroyed her family's warehouse, and how her mother developed asthma from working in the cold water, trying to save the boxes of cheese. William just laughed. "I knew you'd have a story for me."

When he left, Betsy said to John, "Haven't we had enough worry for one year?"

"William is a grown man."

"And what about Adrian?"

"She's pretty independent."

"Nothing ever bothers you!" Betsy complained.

Sometimes she'd like to smother him with a pillow.

But what *can* she do about her daughter? She wouldn't be happy coming home. She's adventurous and tough. Strange— people are supposed to have free will, and as a parent you preach and provide examples for your children, then some gene from a long dead ancestor pops up and trumps nurture. Adrian probably got her personality from the original yeoman in Betsy's family who first milked a cow and made cheese.

It is so unlike Adrian to complain. Betsy regrets her rejection of her daughter, her favoritism toward Eric. Adrian has a good heart, and that's what matters.

Well, it's what should matter.

"Would you like a manicure?" Norma says.

Betsy looks at her nails. They need work.

She takes a seat at Norma's little table and gives Norma her right hand to dip in the bowl of warm water.

"Are you going skiing this year?" Norma asks.

Betsy sighs. "I don't want to. But my husband will probably insist."

She has not had her usual energy since Eric was ill. She has been napping more and longer, ignoring things that would at one time have pushed her into action: a dusty shelf, a grimy— She can't think of the word she wants. Oh yes, base board.

"How long have you been going to Aspen?" Norma asks.

"Since God created it."

"You've been married how long now? More years than anyone I know. My Mom divorced my dad when we kids were in grade school. What's your secret?"

Betsy shrugs.

Love. Whatever that is.

Sex. She and John have had a good run. But she is tiring of it, as she has of so many things that were once so pressing and important. John still wants it. He takes Viagra.

Money. Well, it's true: a little money smooths the rough edges, provides privacy, helps kill boredom.

She thinks, I guess we have had a good marriage in spite of our differences. We didn't want anyone else, not for long. We wanted the family to stay together. I didn't want my children to ever suffer pain or disappointment. I wanted them to be safe and happy. But they are scattered and alone. She mutters to herself, *I should have drowned them at birth like kittens.*

Norma has painted Betsy's nails a hot pink.

"OK?" she says.

Betsy holds her hands out in front of her.

"Fine."

With her hair fixed and her nails polished, Betsy feels better. She thinks back to what she has pondered. Love is the most important. In all its varied faces and disguises, its gushing heat and resigned acceptance, it is what got the family through their bad year. It is the most challenging thing of all; requiring understanding beyond your ability, sacrifices you don't want to make, patience you don't possess.

As Betsy takes off her plastic smock and retrieves her purse from Norma's sticky shelf, she remembers that she is to be a great grandmother again. David and Lydia seem happier, but they have so much on their plates: two kids soon, two careers. They seem to think the coming child will make everything dandy, but God knows babies are no cure for marital problems. Betsy knows a couple who had *three* more, and *then* divorced. And young people have the craziest ideas of baby care. Lydia is talking about actually *swaddling* the child: such antique nonsense!

Well, she mustn't give up hope for any of the young people (how Phoebe laughed when she called David that). She hopes Eric might get together with Judith in Washington and bring her home. But *she* can do no more. The future is up to the butterflies.

Betsy goes shopping.

74

Judith

*J*udith and Eric's conversation is drowned out by the chanting of the protesters—"Out of Iraq. Out of Iraq! No more war!" The two join in, and march around the White House, then along the mall. A man takes a photo of Judith's sign and she gives it to him. When the yells die down, Judith says "I think I need to sit."

She and Eric find a bench away from the main action.

"My feet." She extends her legs, slips off her shoes, and wiggles her toes.

They hear the music of Joan Baez from the stage by the monuments, faint, as though from years past. The trees cast pleasant shadows on the grass, like the ones at the old Tudor in Cincinnati.

"So do *you* want to sell the house?" Judith asks.

"Only if you want to. I thought . . . . That's not what I meant to say."

They sit quietly, listening. People walking by greet them.

"Hi, beautiful," one woman calls to Judith.

"Do you think we've accomplished anything today?" Judith asks Eric.

"We once got the country out of Viet Nam."

"Things were different then."

"We need the draft back."

Eric's jaw is clenched.

"Course we bombed the hell out of them."

This is the old Eric. Angry Eric.

"We need to do more than march."

"We wanted in but they wouldn't let us."

They talk the way they did before the year that just passed.

The shadows grow longer. The music changes.

"I probably should get a cab while I still can," Judith says.

"Where is your place again?"

"Adams Morgan."

"Oh right, David told me," Eric says. "We could share a cab. I'm at the Sheraton. I'll drop you off."

Judith and Eric walk outside the barricades around the mall, where traffic is flowing.

They are quiet in the taxi, sit on far sides of the seat, look out the windows.

Judith watches Eric's expression as they arrive at her building. He doesn't give a clue to his feelings.

"Would you like to see the jacket I bought you?" she says.

"Sure."

"I guess it's a habit, picking up something that looks like it might work out."

"Might work out": the phrase is loaded. At her door, Judith grapples with her purse and Eric digs in his pocket as each tries to pay the cab driver.

"I've got it," Judith says.

Eric puts his wallet back in his pocket. Judith leads the way and inserts the key into the front door lock. Eric gazes around at the neighboring houses and the San Remo.

Once they are in the living room, he looks over Judith's bookshelf while she puts her purse away and opens a window.

"Could I have a glass of water?" Eric asks.

"Sure."

Judith goes to the kitchenette and gets two glasses of water.

Eric swallows his water in one gulp while she sips hers.

"You seem well," Judith says.

"I am. I'm fine."

Eric looks around at Judith's room.

"It's like our first apartment in Chicago."

Judith's heart fills with the sweetness of the memory.

"Yes."

Judith can't look at him.

"The jacket," she says.

She goes to the bedroom and finds the jacket she bought. This is too crazy. She hangs it on the closet door, and returns to the living room.

"Can't find it," she says. She sits down. "I'll locate it though."

"That's OK. It was nice of you to think of it."

"It was weird."

From the open window, they hear music from a neighbor's radio.

"Habit I guess."

She takes Eric's empty glass and goes to the kitchen to refill it.

"So how goes the battle for bull goose at the university?" Judith calls.

"I turned it down."

She's surprised. Yet not surprised. "I'm rather glad for you. It isn't you."

Judith hands Eric his water.

"The money was tempting."

Of course. He could never compete with his father financially by being a department head.

"I'm going to get more active. I'm going to run for Congress."

"Whoa! Really? You don't do things by half!"

"I can't sit by with these maniacs getting us deeper and deeper into wars. I want to get into the fight."

"I need a drink," Judith says.

"I'm aiming at 2008. I need time to get my name out there."

"I'll get some wine," Judith says. Anything to get out of the room. And she needs the wine.

When she comes back to the living room, the cat comes out from under the couch, stretches lazily, winds around Eric's feet.

"What's her name?" Eric asks.

"Mehitabel."

Eric smiles. Judith serves the wine and puts the bottle on an end table.

"Can you get elected?"

"Stranger things have happened. I can win the primary. Make as much noise as possible."

"At least you're on the east side of town. What does John think?"

"He's going to raise money for me."

"Great."

"And I'm selling the plane for some dough."

Judith takes a gulp of wine.

"Mom freaked out. But she'll come around," Eric says.

"I wouldn't underestimate Betsy."

"I think she's finally given up on us."

Eric looks as though he is struggling to say something. Finally, he blurts out, "She says I was thoughtless and unkind when I came home from the hospital."

Talk about sudden shifts in the conversation, Judith thinks. "Well," she says, "you were recuperating. You were very sick."

Wasn't this what she wanted to hear? Why is she letting him off the hook? This is one of her many flaws. She can not accept sympathy, praise, or apologies. Even when her whole being is demanding them.

"I feel guilty," Eric says. He takes the wine bottle from the table and pours himself another glassful. "For a lot of things."

"We all do."

"Could we start over?" Eric says.

"From where?"

"The time we met in history class. The day you wrote that great paper."

"On Thucydides."

"Herodotus . . . ."

"No . . . ."

Oh have it your way, Judith thinks. People's memories are never exactly the same. And even after thirty plus years, she can't get behind Eric's surface—any more than one fictional character can jump into the point of view of another. Only the reader, interloper, Peeping Tom, can do that. She and Eric are separate worlds, separate states of being. She has discovered flaws, from the first days when all she could see was perfection: Eric's good looks, his intelligence, his strength, his discipline, his liberality. He had all that, but she has learned he is also self-centered, demanding, egotistical, sybaritic, somewhat pompous. Why has she been so surprised to find the traits of ordinary men in him? She has her flaws too: she is needy, emotional, supersensitive, proud, conflicted, prone to grudges and . . . .

Mehitabel jumps into Eric's lap, curls up and purrs. Judith wonders if she wants to do the same.

While she is thinking this, Eric stands and studies her book collection again.

He could never sit still for long except when working at his desk. He glances into her bedroom. "Is the rest of your apartment curbside stuff too? You were always great at finding things."

As Judith follows to steer him away, he steps into the bedroom and sees the jacket hanging on the closet door He lifts it off its hanger, puts it on and pulls it around him.

"It fits fine," he says.

"It looks good."

He lies down on her bed.

"Hey," she protests.

"You jumped into my bed," he says.

He reaches out his hand.

Judith silently joins him and he pulls the jacket over the two of them. Mehitabel follows and curls up at their feet, and purrs.

Judith feels so good being touched and touching. To feel kisses on her neck and warm arms around her. Their old passion flaring.

Eric says, "I never really—" Judith puts her fingers over his mouth.

He had disappointed her. He betrayed her. Yes. It would always be between them. The flesh never forgives. He is cracked forever, flawed.

They lie together entwined like Kokoschka's lovers.

Eric's arms around Judith are strong, the muscles rebuilt and hard. The wraith of the hospital has disappeared like a ghost.

Eric murmurs, "We do love each other."

"Well—"

He says, "I need you."

It's like a fairy tale, an opera. Magic words. A secret name spoken.

"Please come home, Judith."

She would have Eric, her sons, a new grandchild, John and Betsy. Her magical garden. But real life pushes its disapproving face into her dream. She recalls the madness of the hospital, the rotting apples in the DC supermarket, her devastation. The cracks she can fall through, widening.

"My job," Judith says.

"Don't you want to get back into the real fight, too? You could run my campaign. We'd be a great team like in the old days."

"We have so much history," Judith says.

"The good kind."

"I have a shot at tenure here. . ."

And a political wife? Being a team notwithstanding, the role is second place. Ms Supportive. She failed at that before, and had paid too high a price for this place of hers to leave it. He would need so much from her. And he had already taken so much.

But also given . . . . He has been a great teacher. He would be a great Congressman.

"Let's not talk anymore," she says.

Their bodies take charge.

75

John

"Where's Ed?"

It is after twelve; the members of John's Tuesday lunch club are ready to order, but Ed hasn't shown up yet. The ten who are present are seated around the u-shaped table in Hartzen's back parlor. No one is much under eighty and several are well over. They lose a member every year. John says the meetings are like Agatha Christie's *And Then Were None*, in which one by one, men gathering together are murdered and the group gradually shrinks.

Bin, John's old law partner, now ninety-two and more forgetful than ever, looks at the menu and says he thinks he'll try the wiener schnitzel. It's good here. Hartzen's is Hungarian. The dark room is decorated with a border of hearts at the ceiling, and a few sets of antlers on the red walls.

John sits at the head of the table, next to an ex-mayor. On the sides are two retired labor men, a one-time council member, a judge who is in a wheelchair, and an African-American member, who served on the board of elections. While they wait for Ed, they report on their ailments and those of missing friends: bad backs, broken bones, hip replacements, heart surgery.

Ed, who was a state senator, finally appears at the door looking a little out of breath and harried.

"Where have you been?" several of the men ask. Ed goes straight to Bin, who is happily pouring sugar into his iced tea.

"Binnie, you're here!" he says.

"Why yes," Bin says. "Good to see you, Ed."

"I went to your house to pick you up like we said, and you didn't answer the door."

"John picked me up."

Several of the men chuckle. Bin has struck again.

"He called me this morning for a ride," John says.

"Jesus, Binnie," Ed says. "I crawled into your house through a window. I thought you might be—well, in trouble or something. I'm lucky I didn't get arrested—or shot."

Bin looks puzzled.

Ed finds a chair and picks up a menu. He's laughing now and the others laugh at his predicament.

The waitress, Ray, comes in and poises her pencil over her order book. She's been their server for the thirty-some years the men have been meeting. She knows who likes what. She could probably take their orders in her sleep. Maybe she does.

John is fond of his friends. Together they fought the old-time bosses, their party controlled the city council for some years, sent one member to Washington. They brought a transit system to the city, elected a governor, integrated the council and the parties.

As always, the talk turns to politics. The men are worried about the future of the country, the war, the growing economic instability, the abridgment of civil rights, Katrina—the weakest, most heartless response they have ever seen to a national disaster. These last five years have been the worst anyone can recall, and most of them are World War Two vets, some survivors of the Korean War; they've been through the McCarthy witch hunts,

Viet Nam, the Nixon years. John has always been sure a kind of pendulum operates in human history—when things swing too far in one direction, they inevitably swing back. Now he wonders. It may be too late. So much damage has been done.

The food comes, and the conversation lightens. Once again, they agree, the Democrats have shot themselves in the foot, snatched defeat from the jaws of victory. If only Gore had been able to look an audience in the eye and sound as if he meant what he was saying. If Kerry had fought back. If Clinton had kept his pants zipped.

In spite of the group's depression, there is much laughter as the men finish their lunches. Though Hartzen's has fine desserts, no one orders apple pie anymore, or John's favorite, the chocolate roll with whipped cream. Bellies have grown and digestions have become less forgiving of rich food. The men shake hands and pat each other on the back as they leave the room and head for their cars.

"Christ," the ex-Congressman says. He looks at the judge negotiating the doorway in his wheelchair, several others on canes, himself on a walker. "We look like Napoleon's retreat from Moscow."

On the way home from the office that afternoon, John turns on the car radio. The deaths in Iraq have mounted, more car bombings, children killed. Relief is not getting to the flood victims in New Orleans. The higher ups in the military have weaseled out of their responsibility for the torture at Abu Ghraib—blamed "a few rotten apples" as usual—lowly enlisted personnel. In the court room, as elsewhere, no one takes responsibility for his actions. It's always, "what happened," not "what I did." This is not the country John knew as a boy and a young soldier.

He and his fellow service men came home from the war so full of hope. Now he worries about the destruction of the country, the city, the earth. But maybe a wind is blowing. Working with Eric will be good, though running in this conservative city is such a long shot. He will do his best, though his contacts who might contribute are moving toward self-preservation. There will be plenty to do in the interim until the election, but the campaign will not be all consuming for three years. His lunch group is not likely to help. Is he up for it? Will he even be alive?

Betsy says nothing ever bothers him, but of course that's not so. The strain of this year has been unrelenting. His son almost dying. He just can't express feeling the way Betsy does—the way women do. Around them he feels like a clumsy oil-slicked pelican among a flock of song birds—the way they go on about their emotions, endlessly discussing how they feel about everything. It has always been his job to stay calm and strong—first born in his family, an eagle scout, leader of his squadron in the war, head of the family as husband and father, senior partner of his firm.

Betsy is worried about Adrian. And they haven't heard from William. John resolves to write his daughter a letter when he gets home. Though writing personal letters is not his forte. He can never think of what to say.

Brendan said the Howards were the nicest family he had ever worked for. They *are* good people. They came together as a team to help Eric through his illness. They all have their faults, but that's only human. He's glad David is doing so well. Maybe now he can settle his debts. William might need help, but John hopes he will be able to pay his own way. They all probably think John can help out if they need him. But he is not as well off as people might think. He is less productive at his firm now, and he has lost a good deal in the market.

John is proud that Eric has gone to Washington to protest the war. One year since his "sudden death." He wishes he could have gone along, but that much walking might be too tiring. He might even suggest to Betsy that maybe they should not try to ski this year. His legs are beginning to go. (Why do old men's legs seem to get weak and women's don't? Betsy's legs are still youthful and strong, narrow ankles and shapely calves).

Maybe he should even consider retiring. He will have to look over his financial records. He hates the changes in his practice: the lack of good manners; the library he so loved, the long rows of solid leather books, replaced by the Internet; interoffice communication done by email. Cell phones. He has one of course: you can't not have one. But people have them glued to their ears; yesterday a man next to him at the urinal was blabbing into one of the damned things while peeing.

John turns his car radio on. Nothing but idiots ranting and spewing hate. He switches the dial to FM: music. He considers stopping at the supermarket to pick up a few things, but decides not to. Betsy is still annoyed at him for his last trip, when he brought home a gallon jar of Thousand Island Dressing. He thought she'd be pleased.

He pulls into the garage at the condo, thinks through the process of getting out of the car and into the apartment. Push the remote on the visor to close the garage door. Pull on the brake. Turn off the ignition. Where is his hat? Backseat.

He punches in the numbers on the—what is the word?—keypad— His brain is definitely developing gaps. He takes the elevator to the apartment.

As the door opens into the front hall, he calls out to Betsy so as not to startle her. No answer. For almost sixty years, almost every evening, she has been home to greet him when he comes in the door. It's after five. He looks on the hall table for a note. Nothing.

John feels a coldness in the apartment, as though something uninvited is in the rooms. There are no lamps on, and it is so quiet. The word *Mortality* forms in his mind. A big dark word. He shivers.

He looks in the bedrooms and Betsy's bathroom for her. Her footprints are on the soft white rug. He calls out to her again, but the rooms are deathly still.

Outside the window, the big birds are swooping and gliding.

John goes to the kitchen to greet Ginger. With all her ailments, she cannot come to him anymore. She is lying as usual in her little green plaid bed with the sheepskin she used to love to pull around and growl at. And woe to anyone who tried to touch it.

"Ginger?" John says.

She does not raise her head.

"Ginger?"

John goes to her. He kneels down and strokes her neck. Her eyes are closed. Her little belly, usually moving as she works at breathing, is still. He feels for the tiny pump of her heart. There's no beat.

John gently lifts his dog into his arms and smooths her long fur. He sits on the floor, his back against the kitchen island. She is growing cold. He wraps her blanket around her and rocks her like a baby. He can't help himself. He cries, great deep sobs. He cannot stop. He tries to blow his nose and blot his tears, but the tears keep coming and coming.

He goes on crying, holding the last of his dogs. Poor little Ginger.

His cell phone rings. He grabs at the pocket of his shirt, his pants, his jacket. Where is the damned thing? He locates it on the chair beside him, too late. He fiddles with the thing, retrieves the message the way Phoebe taught him. Eric.

John cries harder.

He hears the elevator open, and in a moment Betsy comes into the room. She takes in the sight of him sitting on the floor, holding Ginger. She comes over to him and puts her arm around him.

"Well," she says.

John tells her about Eric's call.

"And?"

"He saw Judith, and she wants a clean break."

Betsy takes a deep breath. Thinks a minute.

"It won't be clean," she says. "Those two will keep on dancing until death comes knocking on the door again."

"You think so?"

"Look at us."

Betsy begins to weep along with John.

The two old people sit together, crying, and rocking their little dog.

Acknowledgements

Thank You

Above all, to Sid Weil for reading the many many drafts of this novel. Probably ten.

Also to Ceil Cleveland, Stephen Birmingham, Gene Young, Barbara Allen, Judy Sharp, Margo Pierce and Joan Robinson for reading and giving excellent criticism and suggestions, making this a better book.

And to my late friend and fine historian, Dr. Jim Cebula.

Also by Dorothy Weil

In Defense of Women: Susanna Rowson (1762-1814)
Continuing Education
Nightside
The River Home
River Rats
Life, Sex and Fast Pitch Softball
A Good Woman

About the Author

Dorothy Weil grew up on river boats as the daughter of a steamboat captain. She is the author of seven books, including a comic novel bought by Disney Productions. She has worked for many years as a free lancer, publishing in periodicals throughout the country, and she has served as writer-producer with TV IMAGE, INC., a production team winning many national awards. She has a studio near her home where she paints and shows her art and photography.